Join My Cult!

JOIN MY CULT!

by
James Curcio

NEW FALCON PUBLICATIONS
TEMPE, ARIZONA, U.S.A.

International Standard Book Number: 1-56184-173-0
Library of Congress Catalog Card Number: 2003104240

First Edition 2004

This story is based on true events. Names and locations have been changed when necessary to protect the identity of the participants.

Cover art by James Curcio

The paper used in this publication meets the minimum requirements of the American National Standard for Permanence of Paper for Printed Library Materials Z39.48-1984

Address all inquiries to:
NEW FALCON PUBLICATIONS
1739 East Broadway Road #1-277
Tempe, AZ 85282 U.S.A.
(or)
320 East Charleston Blvd. #204-286
Las Vegas, NV 89104 U.S.A.

website: http://www.newfalcon.com
email: info@newfalcon.com

CREDITS

Author: James Curcio (Agent 139)

Co-Authors: Jason Stackhouse (Agent 506), Ken Schaefer (Agent 888), Sarah Dudzic, Ayun Holliday.

Cover art: agent139

Cover Photograph: Judith Curcio

Co-conspirators and editorial: Agent 506, Agent 79, Agent 444, Agent 242, Agent 156, Agent 140, Agent 036, LAAR, Agent 888, Eianorange, Pesky, Shifty, Ylang-Ylang the Helpful Bonobo & the ZenseiderZ Foundation

Special Thanks: Jason Wyse, Kate Penna, Christie Casey, Sol Amoun, Frater Gazebo & the Psion Project

The Author(s) may be contacted at **james@joinmycult.org**

TABLE OF CONTENTS

000. The Boundless Light.. 9

00. Intention Abstract: It is Learned by Walking (Gabrael's Prologue) ... 10

I. You'll Never See Him Coming 14

0. A Fleet of Shards (Alexi's Prologue) 20

Chapter 1, Grid 1: If You're Falling, Jump 22

Chapter 2, Grid 2: Mother Hive Brain Unveiled 33

Chapter 3, Grid 1: A Crush Proof Box 47

Chapter 4, Grid 1: A Visitor 62

Chapter 5, Grid 2: IT 71

Interlude I: Alexi's Dreams: The Myth of Orpheus 89

Chapter 6, Grid 1: The Lost Night.. 96

Chapter 7, Grid 1: Meredith... 117

Chapter 8, Grid 2: A GOOD Fish is a DEAD Fish (Exception: Cod)..... 123

Chapter 9, Grid 2: Save the World, Burn it Down 129

Birth Pains: (Agent 139's Introduction) 139

Interlude II: The Myth of Orpheus 146

Chapter 10, Grid 1: The Journey 152

Interlude III: The Myth of Orpheus 166

Chapter 11, Grid 2: PG. (Pig Without an 'I') 180

Chapter 12, Grid 2: The Cartesian Mystery Cook;..................... 198

Chapter 13, Grid 1: The Downward Spiral............................... 221

Chapter 14, Grid 1: Anti-Climax 230

Chapter 15, Grid 2: The Labyrinth 242

Appendix: The Mother Hive Brain Documents 273

000. THE BOUNDLESS LIGHT

"Everywhere I go, in every experience, I see life constantly on the verge of death, the intensity of it almost overflowing, overwhelming me precisely because every thing is, from the moment of its creation, so close to its own annihilation. Life exists to the extent that it stands in stubborn and harsh contrast to its own non-existence. One who is alive, truly alive, experiences Eros for life, as the tension between what we see as being through becoming is contrasted with the darkness, the hallow absence—not the light!—at the end of the process.

Through this we may see the first will-to-meaning in the struggle between the secret gravity of our end being ahead and behind us, and our constant attempt to create a beginning, an eternally present moment, right now.

It is at first apparent that everything is dying, the undoing, the nega-tion, resonates throughout everything, a Cerberus that barks in warning: 'do not enter, no one ever returns.' Yet, in passing through the gates he guards, one is immediately overwhelmed by how alive everything is, standing in contrast to the pessimistic cry that had set a pall upon the world; all living beings, screaming together 'I am!' defiantly against the coming of the dawn. Should we choose life, accept it fully as it is without doctoring, we must join in to this chorus with all of our strength, become a part of the song rather than an individual standing outside, merely listening in rapt attention.

For those who would cling to a static solution, whether it be a canon, manifesto, or the words of an orator or messiah, I would recommend they take Crowley's words to heart: 'O ye who dwell in the dark night of the soul, beware most of all the herald of the dawn!'"

— Aleonis De Gabrael

00. It is Learned by Walking (Gabrael's Prologue)

> Nothing on the face of this earth—and I do mean nothing—is half so dangerous as a children's story that happens to be real, and you and I are wandering blindfolded through a myth devised by a maniac.
> — Master Li Kao (T'ang Dynasty)

My first waking impression this morning was a hazy glance through frostbitten glass at an overturned trash can. The sound of a dog rummaging through the garbage. The gentle pattering of sleet on the roof. Doppler shift as a car turns on slick asphalt. Sentence fragments, thoughts bisected in a 3 x 3 set of windowpanes on the far wall. If you're really intent on a decent reproduction of the event, lie down and close your eyes. Imagine a chill sensation, a hazy image of a toe with overgrown toenails sticking out of the bed covers, and then a camera pan to the rusty trash can outside. Not a dramatic opening for a book, but it's all this day has given me.

None of this bodes well. My head feels like an empty shell. Qliphothic, surely. Oh yes, to be sure: the number of panes in my window has control over what the day has in store. It's still dawn, turquoise twilight, and I'm all tangled up in the sheets. What I really want to know is... where is my coffee, where are all the lithe nymphs I was promised when I joined this God-forsaken "mystical order"? They promise Love, Light, and Liberty, instead I get an empty apartment full of books and a goddamned pet spider monkey. It just goes to show, never believe what you read in books.

Get out of bed with a wince, because the hardwood floors are about four degrees warmer than ice, and hunt for a pair of socks for what seems like an hour. This is the part of being an Invisible Master that I think gets lost in the translation: getting up in the morning to a freezing small apartment in Chestnut Hill and hunting for your socks as you wonder why this morning reminds you of the Moon card and, metaphysically speaking, to menstrual blood as it was believed to be the receptive agent in the birth process. A beginning to be sure, but for what?

My mind jumps around. I haven't done morning exercises yet. You have to keep yourself invisible because otherwise they'll realize you're still a primate just like them, and the whole game's off. Jesus was wise not to cast himself down from Herod's temple at Satan's request. More's the pity.

I carefully slide open the drawer of the chest by my bed, and review the letters I've received this past week from potential new recruits. Reports from agents in the field. Updates from those in other divisions of the Order. I stop suddenly on a letter I received from one of these potentials. As I read it once, and then again, I find myself absently running my finger up and down the side of the page, relishing the texture. Alexi... Alexi... now I remember, he's the initiate that wound up in that asylum. He has promise, if he ever makes it out of the rabbit hole. I fold the letter thoughtfully and pocket it. The others I replace in the drawer.

Yes, it can get downright lonely, this life. As you go through your day, just remember there are masked ones; it may be that yonder beggar is a King. A King may choose his garments as he will; there is no certain test. But a beggar cannot hide his poverty.

My role is to act as a mirror for the higher selves of those around me. Let them project what is beautiful in them on me, and then turn the mirror around and say, "See?" Being invisible in cities is especially easy: just be an extra for the scene. Eventually you reach your destination and you can give that "special someone" the push they need. I am invisible, hidden between the lines, but always in the back of your mind now.

The positive side to being an adept is that you affect the future of the world towards evolution, not through demographics or tax cuts, but through interaction with people's internal lives. The downside is that you never really know what effect you've had. You are invisible. The causeless cause.

Every action from the smallest to the largest is directed at advancing the evolution of the species, taking whatever risks are necessary to attain that peak of pressure that results in genius or insanity. Or both. It may be that the evolution, the future of our species, depends on the fringe, the counter-evolutionaries, the possessed shamans artists and lunatics... It is towards the youth in this vein that I direct my efforts.

When I say evolution, I mean the unfolding of the potentialities contained within each of us, like a rosebud gradually opening into a flower, the potentials encoded in our DNA spirals which only the right sequence of events can unlock… Like us, each of these "locks" is unique, and so we must find equally unique keys. You too are an Agent for the self-guided evolution of the species, though you may not know it yet.

This is what you are an agent *for*, but what are we agents *of*?

I personally think of this, of Her, as our mother of birth and death. When you offer yourself up to Her, she takes you in and guides your actions. When you offer yourself to Her, and pass the gate of your death and birth, you are faced with a choice: return to the world, motivated by compassion, or remain forever in that dark womb, a shaman or lunatic.

When I turn on the evening news—something I do less and less these days—I begin to wonder if it is too late for humanity This pessimism is not really in my nature however. Even if it is a losing battle I will fight it with the tools afforded to me: the pen, the word, and my embodied messenger clothed herenow in the flesh. I took an Oath, and I will follow it to the best of my ability until death claims me. No hunchbacks out of you, soldier.

By the time I have my clothes on, I'm wondering why I just thought that. Certainly the sentiment won't find itself in anything I write. My secret is safe with me.

Twilight has given way to a rosy dawn; the last sliver of the moon, visible through three panes of glass, is now all but gone. Soon that rosy dawn will turn golden. And thankfully the dog has ceased his noisy rummaging.

Out the apartment door with my hair still wet, down the block where I wait at the same bus stop every morning. Each day I catch the 8:20 bus with the same assortment of people. This cold, icy morning in the short days of December is no exception.

As you may have guessed, I am the type of person who catches every detail, but I rarely speak except when it is required for an assignment. Subjective investment in a situation mars your capacity for keen observation. There are three people in the 8:20 crew, besides myself. A wrinkly shell of a woman wrapped in something coarse and thick—wool or burlap; a bubble-gum popping brunette who always wears sunglasses, probably going to the liberal arts college at the end of the line; and a boy in his late teens. The boy catches my attention, as he somehow manages to be even more generic than the girl: blue eyes, worn Converse sneakers, ragged dirty-blond hair. No soul anywhere to be found. The Mr. Bungle t-shirt throws a small kink in his character, but with the faded, faraway look and bloodshot eyes, the whole package strikes me as a living, breathing caricature of the late 1990's. Spending an hour in front of the mirror trying to look like you haven't looked in a mirror your whole life.

We never speak to one another, except when the boy bums a cigarette, which admittedly is rather often.

Now I'm leafing through Aaryah Copelan's annotated version of the *Sefer Yetzirah*. On the back cover it claims that the invocations therein were used by ancient rabbis to communicate telepathically and to fly. Though the image of medieval rabbis flying through space to do battle with evil-doers is a compelling one, I'm having a hard time finding the method from the text. Must be missing something. I suppose I am also to believe that yarmulkes were originally worn because they make you more aerodynamic when you fly around in your merkevah chariot. Now the bus has passed by Lenny's, the boy gets off. As he brushed passed me I noticed that his eyes were darting around in fear and confusion.

Before I get any farther, I should tell you more about my profession. When I get off this bus I am no longer head of the Philosophy department of the aforementioned "liberal arts college down the line." I become Aleonis de Gabrael. One does not act a part, one is the part. We trade one illusion for another and are our representations—don't let your reflection fool you. The magus is more powerful than any God, and the most powerful amongst the legions of the damned is Maya, lord of illusion.

As I have hinted, I am a member of a spiritual organization. Exactly which organization isn't important—we make up fronts all the time just to keep new recruits guessing. It would seem, at first, that a "spiritual organization" is a real contradiction in terms. And this is precisely why we handle things the way we do, and why I am the head of "new recruits" as a neophyte in the Order. The bus is rattling laboriously over cobblestones now, which means the next stop is mine. Time is short so I must be swift. These have all been answers to questions you don't yet have—but you will. Refer back to them when you have completed my report.

Ah, here's my stop now. See you on the other side.

I. You'll Never See Him Coming

The objective: to make you circular. Work you just enough so you can work yourself, so hallow the ground and don't put up a fight because when it comes it will come like a thief in the night.

— Aceyalone

Modality
splitting seams seems
splitting through a cracked mirror.

Baggypuddleeyes in the mirror. Seated in a white room. Acrid white, white like surgeon's gloves. Upon a stark sailor's bed, long and needleknees pulled up to the thinbelly. Old electric-chair cross over the bed.

I'm here to tell you a story. It isn't the story that you will read in the newspaper, though you can find that readily enough. At least three suspects, all ostensibly members of a shadowy terrorist organization known as the 'Mother Hive Brain,' were responsible for the destruction of a Lenny's restaurant in Devon, PA. Agent 139, Jesus, and myself. Johny, poor little mislead, clueless Johny, now locked away indefinitely in the American health-care system.

Yes, this is what you will read in the newspapers. As is regularly the case, the truth is a great deal interesting, and a great deal stranger. Bear with me, follow me through these labyrinthine hallways, and I will lead you to Her.

Passing priest of the new psychological order. Wears the white robes, follows the arcane texts. Passes out communion. They call it an SSRI, but it's all the same. "This is for your own good…"? Swallow. I will tell you quick before IT starts fuzzing, the moments get long, knottingtied to the air, painfully attaching you to the hollowness of this present moment with taut intestines. You still feel the numbness, you know? That's a reassuring companion. Keeps you through the long days and even longer nights. Only this lingering sensation of numbness, of what has come before and no longer touches you directly, keeps you breathing, keeps you glued to this fleeting nothing, to this pale life. It has been said, I may

14

be finished with the past, but my past is not finished with me. I am trapped, looking backwards. My purpose, my meaning, is only to retell my story, my past.

Thick pain in the chest brings me back. Right under the sternum. That's the thinbelly hollow spot. Like swallowing saliva, keeping awake. Spat in a glass and swallowed it afterwards. Got sick. So now it's white rooms that go on forever and priests up close.

Haven't seen Agent or Jesus since we were taken into custody.

Just swallowed back up. Didn't understand them. Don't think they meant to be understood. Jesus of the eternal return. Had to show up and turn everything upside down.

White walls are here because they caught me Working. Bombed the Hive building. The flames danced and sang about me. Something the Agent said came back to me then, a commentary, a running monologue: "Millions of souls were freed from slavery to the Great Eye, Novus Ordo Seclorum, Eye of Shiva, blaster of towers... Of course the gate-keepers brand me a 'terrorist.' It is no matter. Through the power of association the entire structure will topple in due time. This is high ritual, and the ultimate sacrifice for the survival and evolution of my species, which I love so dearly. Even my friends and teachers have disowned me. Horus, the bull of your father is avenged. We can now return to our mother, whole. The dove resides within the blasted tower, and within that destruction, that madness, we lay the seed of the purest aspect of life..."

The whole structure erupted in a final, defiant exhalation, breathing out foul, billowing columns of smoke. Its systems coughed and spluttered. The whole world was dancing and singing. We sang: Alas! With ruthless hand you have destroyed this fair edifice...it falls and decays! And then, right before the cops came, we started a chant. It just came up out of nowhere...

In the temple of the temple of the temple of the Holy
sits a woman who is waiting who is waiting for the sun
in the temple of the temple in the temple of the Holy
creeping shadows falling darkness she is waiting for the sun.

For the people of the people by the people making people
in the temple of the temple of the temple of the Holy
She is weeping for the people of the people
making people in the temple of the temple in the temple of the sun.

No one's listening are you listening? I'm not listening
no one's listening in the temple of the temple in the temple

of the Holy to her crying she is crying I am crying in the
temple in the temple of the temple of the temple of the sun.

Hearing voices crying voices wailing voices all in chorus
of the temple and the temple and the temple of the Holy
falling deeper ever deeper even deeper than the Holy
in the temple of the temple in the temple of the sun.

Meds are kicking in now. Soon the thoughts will leave me altogether.
Let me tell you now how I think, because this is my story. You have to
see it with my alien eyes. I am the gravel underneath my feet. The distance between two things; I am, essentially, a relationship. There is no
synthesis named Johny. There never was. Just a fragment.

Cold feet at the bottom of the plank the farthest thing from me. Twitch
the corpse toe left, then right. What twitches the toe? Where are the
commands sent *from*, and who tells the Commander to issue the order?
Agent would have said "the void in the relation of subject and object."

I'm that void. The Cartesian gap. Some call this relationship perception: a shackle and chain, linking this to that with invisible cords. There
will always be the subject, the object, and me, that eternal, emasculated,
passive silence, the [   ], trapped somewhere in the middle. These things
in themselves are not without me to relate to, although that relationship
chases its tail as a dog. Ah yes, I remember now, some Artaud. *All these
abysms conscious recognizes in itself; and yet, doesn't the relationship
eat itself ouroborus-like?* Yet I feel this very weight upon me with every
moment, breath, gullet swallow, DOWN/down/down/down to be devoured and excreted.

These words eat themselves. These words are hungry. They don't
relate to themselves. They are trapped in [   ]. These words fuck themselves, and think they've gained something in the morning, aside from a
sore back and throbbing head. These words have stubbed their toe, and
whine about the unfairness of it all.

For a moment I zone out of this monologue to find just a brief flash of
the present moment. My hand, seeming grey and lifeless, clutching a coffee mug emblazoned with the Lenny's logo. *Wait, I haven't bombed the
Lenny's yet!* I'm just writing my future in a daydream, getting ahead of
myself...

————◆————

It was three weeks after Alexi's release from the hospital. In fact this
was the first time he had left the comfort of his home. Now he was re-

turning to all of his old haunts, trying to rekindle the magic that he felt before his mental collapse.

One of the lights directly over his head was flickering slowly, like a strobe. He felt a moment of deep dread, déjà vu from a nightmare. This sensation was horribly disquieting to him, and he got up to change tables, motioning for his friend Ken to follow.

Making their way past the usual Lenny's patrons, waving offhandedly to some, they sat down in the opposite corner of the room, beneath a plastic potted plant dangled octopus-like from above.

They couldn't help but hear an angst mantra (if ever there was one), coming from behind them, a scratchy, desperate sound: "...ever conceived of by...monkey soups. We'll be breaking, taking, and stealing everything you motherfuckers ever dreamed up, every logo you have ever designed, even if it's bolted down. Split the spine, forward, then backwards, then straight up and through the roof. It'll be the biggest, baddest, meanest Dionysian revolt of rock'n'roll and anti-Semitic Jews that Corn Flakes have ever set their greedy little eyes on. Yes, we'll be swimming in the septic tank offices of the everyday. We'll be coughing up whole lungsfull of Kurt Cobain and Tickle-Me-Elmo dolls in malls." Ken glanced behind him. The boy rocked back and forth slowly, the hood of his blue sweatshirt pulled over his dome-like head. Glassy eyes stared fixedly at the half-empty cup of coffee before him. *Wait, I haven't bombed the Lenny's yet. I'm just writing my future in a daydream, getting ahead of myself...*

Likely another ADHD Ritalin burn-out, Ken thought. Alexi was forced to look away. He felt momentarily nauseous. Déjà vu...*again?* Or was he just remembering the remembrance?

"The revolt from the inside didn't work. I played your games, bought your albums and wore your fucking t-shirts. The only solution to a circle is a straight line, a straight beeline out, over, beyond! The Mother Hive Brain syndicate must be the line, beeline! and hit them where it counts. I...triangle!" the boy exclaimed, leaning back, his eyes bugging out. "Triangle!"

"Beep! A beep it goes!" He looked around suspiciously as he linked three paper clips together in a triangle, dipped it in nearby imitation maple syrup, and stuck it to his forehead regally, as if it were a crown. "This is where... This is how I contact them. Jam the signal! Ha..."

Banging on the table with his fist, he continued, "Their transmitter device, which transmits its insipid reality to the masses, receiving messages from the hidden brain of the system, must be removed. Devon Lenny's must be destroyed!"

Alexi looked over at Ken and, attempting to ignore the strange foreboding he was feeling, chuckled warmly. As they reached for their cigarettes simultaneously, the Lenny's industrial strength smoke remover started popping and snapping with the loud staccato of an AK-47.

Across the room, a man dropped into a low crouch, a horrible growl issuing from his throat as he ducked the bullets streaking overhead. It was the growl of a starved wolf. As the man writhed forward snake-like, Alexi could see that his face was grizzled, like the side of an old football; Manuel Noriega on a bad day. A thick shadow of stubble framed his face, and he wore a pair of camo pants and a black, stained wife-beater.

Ken stood up and offered his hand to this man, worn and hardened, he imagined, from years of painful service to his country. Blank eyes devoured him coldly from behind a pair of scratched aviator glasses. Apparently Ken didn't know who he was dealing with. This man hadn't said a *word* in any language in over ten years, and hadn't been known as anything other than "Crazy Uncle Eddie" for twice as long. (Even the "good old boys" from the LZ, now long since dead and gone, used to call him Uncle.)

Hunched by the still spinning barstool, Crazy Eddy regarded Ken through the imagined bamboo bars of his cage. Light fell sharply on his sweaty face in bands, as if through Venetian blinds. As Ken approached, Eddie saw him flanked by the countless beady, bloodthirsty eyes of spider monkeys, wearing jungle sodden combat fatigues, bearing rusty knives, sharpened sticks, and cannibalized automatic rifles.

The feral survivor in him rose to the surface. He sat up straight, eyes locked on his captor, eyes dilating. Only one sentence escaped his sandpaper lips, moving sluggishly from lack of practice; and he said it just as he'd said it then, years before when he ran off into the wild suburbs of Philadelphia, a raggedy-ass joint hanging off his lip, his old 'Nam flight jacket still hanging on his skinny shoulders, "I don't hold hands—I eat them!"

Eddie was the kind of guy you didn't fuck with just on principle. Maybe it had something to do with the crazy gleam in his pot-reddened eyes, or the way he'd swagger about the house, half-naked and covered in vomit, his .45 quietly rocking back and forth on his hip holster, that told you to keep your distance. He was larger than life. He'd get in the car at 3:00 a.m., immediately after finishing a case of beer and a liter of glistening amber rum, and yet somehow you just knew the motherfucker'd be there in the morning. Nothing could touch him, precisely be-cause everything had touched him.

He'd sit in his old creaking rocking chair, one leg kind of cocked to the side over the hand rest, his shotgun jutting from between his legs, and stare at you. Just stare at you, his mouth hanging open a little, the smell of Captain Morgan lingering in the air there around his cake hole. Johny, (his little nephew who just happened to be sitting in Lenny's at this exact moment, a paper clip triangle still plastered to his forehead—reaching into his uncle's jacket and pulling out what happens to be a live grenade), would sit around and stare back, far too terrified to get up and leave, just preparing for a host of flies or a nest of yellow jackets to come swarming in and take refuge in that warm, wet mouth of his...which Johny remembered all too well. He was a caricature of himself... (...pulled the pin and threw...)

There was no time for Ken to react. A horrible explosion rocked the building. The last thing they heard was the sound of shattering glass. Ken, in a flash, wondered how he was going to explain all of this to his mother. There was an unbearable pain, a light, and then darkness. Alexi felt like he was drowning...or trapped in a dark elevator, plunging downwards. *This is the last time I'll think, the last time I'll feel.* Blood gurgled and gushed into his throat. I never felt anyone at all. *This was the end of Western Civilization, of steam engines, of all of those people in China. No more children, or Emerson Lake and Palmer, waiting in line to pee, or chocolate syrup.* It was over. These final thoughts played themselves out in a series of spasmodic electrical pulses within his shat-tered nervous system. It was as if it had never begun at all.

0. A FLEET OF SHARDS
(ALEXI'S PROLOGUE)

Gabrael,

I'm in the hospital now, writing down the closing chapter of this story. While I do this, I look back upon the project you asked me to undertake, exploring what led me to you, but I feel that I've only provided a veneer.

You asked for a concise record of my probation and instead I give you a jigsaw puzzle of my parts which, if put in the proper order, like the permutations of the name of God in Sefer Yetzirah, will make me whole again.

I feel an overwhelming compulsion to schematize my experience. I have digested and regurgitated these events countless times. They are jumbled and rearranged, reinterpreted, and recontextualized by events running both directions in my timeline. In the process, these disparate events become me, my alpha and my omega.

We cannot understand a thing until we make it in our own image. For my own part, I can't seem to avoid putting myself in a hall of mirrors...and, it is only through our own darkened mirror that we can see each other. Those events, those mirror reflections that do not resemble us disappear. They hide, unnoticed, as a part of our shadow.

When we see our reflected opposite in that mirror, we are pulled up to its surface, maybe through a fascination with what stands on the other side, if we could only break through. So far in my experience, the result of this action, this attempt at reconciling opposites, is either frustration or assimilation. If we do manage to appear through the looking glass, we merge with our opposite there on the other side. They become us, we become them. Our union and dissolution is at first bliss, but afterwards there is nothing to be done. And, if you are like most other Americans, you are still here, alone no matter how many thighs or oceans you have parted, existing in spiritual exile from the world out there.

Thus I see this account in many ways as an attempt at valid communication, where the hall of mirrors of my ego will reflect a bigger picture, a birds-eye view. If I cannot understand, relate to and experience another as they are in themselves, without the intrusion of my perception, then perhaps we can relate through what I create.

The story you have before you is, at first, the mere appearance of the events that have transpired, and it was only when my imagination began to run wild, when the white walls of my room became a blank slate for my projections, that the real story, what you're looking for as my appointed teacher, become apparent. Even then it was clear, at least to me, only as a sidelong glance, a fleeting mirage in the corner of my eyes. Whenever I look directly at anything, it disappears. I've learned that these projections, these ocular hallucinations, playing themselves out as the external circumstances that create my life experiences, were simply references to inner truths. Not the truth, but *my* myth, *my* truth. To you, I hope, these phantasms will appear clearly. This is, as you know, why I first approached the Order.

These painful, somewhat lonely realizations have led me to yet another conclusion: I have not yet managed to turn around from this inner journey and come back into the world of events, a prophet, a warrior— a *Yes*. I spend days looking out at the world, internally and externally silent, lost somewhere in the gap between possibility and actuality, the past and the future. The moment passes me by. My soul is catatonic. What am I waiting for?

It is slow, gradual pressure that is the formula for both genius and earthquakes. Life tells us our secrets in these cracks, the way events conspire with each other in hidden grottos. This movement is at times very subtle, over a long time, like plate tectonics. If you don't have the right eyes, you might miss these patterns altogether. Although our lives do not occur in geological scales of time, it is still the gradual pressure and our minute reactions, our habits, that actually speak of our true natures. Our true will and intent is contained in potential within each of us, though in many it is buried very, very deep.

I was young at the time the story begins, still half asleep in the dream of my childhood. We were all too young, but who amongst us can predict precisely when the pot is finally going to boil over? There is a time, for some of us, when we are able to step outside the events that formed us, the environment that shaped us, and in that moment, we look back upon the sum of our experience and ask "where was I in that?" Where in the equation do you express yourself, not as a reaction but as a whole person? And, should we be unable to find ourselves in that equation, do we then become, as the sleeper awakening, indifferent to the events that composed the whole of that dream or memory? Do we turn a blind eye upon our past when we step forward?

Love is the law;
Alexi

CHAPTER I, GRID I

IF YOU'RE FALLING, JUMP

Our lives become larger, more expansive, when we include the *other* as a part of ourselves; their "meaning" (or will to meaning), is superadded to our own. This is why I think the dialectic of self and society, (oft considered a juvenile idea, a dilemma you'll grow out of, that you will acclimate yourself to, as a boy who slowly slips into a pool, first his toes, then his feet, eventually his whole body submerged), is in fact one of the most crucial issues at any stage of ones life. To agree upon a joint meaning, one of us must make a concession, inevitably, one of us must give over to the will of the other. Once, and only once, in my life I lived for another. Have I ever recovered? And the cost of keeping myself intact is complete solitude. What you may see of me is not me. Only my writing, viewed in retrospect from my death, will shed any light on what I was and what I have done.

— Aleonis De Gabrael

Ken looked as if he was about to fall. A hand rested on his shoulder—not confining or uncomfortable, but firm nonetheless. There was something about Ken, a look, a particular manner of speaking, that told you he wasn't going to let himself pass through any day unscathed. Only he knew what sin he was guilty of, what pear he had stolen in his youth, and what action could provide absolution. His secret was well-kept. Whatever it was, he let everyone know that he'd never let himself live it down.

"Steady there." Alexi looked directly into the eyes of his friend. When he was convinced that Ken was clearly not going to fall over, he let his hand slip down and rest at his side.

There was a momentary pause wherein everything slowed down and Alexi looked Ken over and reflected. *Ken wore a wide-brimmed felt hat, probably inspired by watching Stevie Ray Vaughn, and a long black trench coat. In his thick hands perched a perpetual camel wide. His instrument of choice was the baritone sax, certainly his character was best described in the low register, circular, swinging—*

Both of them were made up this way, not so much physical bodies as a collection of ideas, last night's reading or listening material taken all too literally. They wrote their own descriptions. The old writers rule-of-thumb "show, don't tell," fell on deaf ears with these two. This intentionality wasn't dishonest, it was exaggeration. Subtle self-mockery. They were in essence melodramatic, out of control method actors with a bag-full of props they could use to lay bare a nerve or generate respect—book titles, cigarettes, ideas—but no one seemed to call them on it. In fact most fell right into the game.

Ken's demeanor complimented Alexi's through negation—for all of Alexi's intellectual melancholy, Ken could always find the chink in his armor of rationalization with a slightly more laconic, morose logic, and expose the underlying emotional cause. This negation worked both ways, as the razor edge of Alexi's intellect likewise revealed the unharnessed raw anger lurking beneath the surface of Ken's exterior.

After pausing a beat, Ken nodded absently in response to Alexi's comment, then lay down on the wide futon that took up most of the floor space in his room. The air was choked with smoke, burnt tobacco and incense mixed with the heady scent of blazing candles. The door was half-open, casting a long thin beam of light on one side of Ken's face. The effect was striking: it looked to Alexi as if he were cut in half.

These were the kind of nights you can only have when you're young, when you're old enough to think you know what's going on, and yet too young to realize the danger in this kind of thinking. There was a certain scent in the air, almost like new, budding flowers, that only the young at heart can smell, even in the dead of winter; to the old, that is to say, to the dead, even in the feverish growth of spring, not a whiff of it can be found. This scent was palpable, but it was only the lure of the unknown, the chaotic beauty of each night as it unfolds. For at least two of the participants on that chill autumn night, it would soon turn out to be one of the most memorable evenings of their existence in this reality grid. Not that any of them knew anything about reality grids. Yet. Alexi got a serious look on his face as he continued with his internal monologue, setting the stage for himself. He wasn't even aware of his hands idly fumbling about nervously.

"Mind's working fast?" Ken asked in his under-spoken way. The two of them had spent so much time together that speech was unnecessary...except to provide tone, atmosphere.

Alexi nodded.

"What on?"

"Something that happened a long time ago..." Alexi was being elusive again. He shrugged nonchalantly, as if to stall any forthcoming questions.

"No mysticism, half-finished thoughts...just blurt it out," Ken said.

Alexi seemed at a loss, his hands spread wide.

"Ken, we're talking about me here. It wouldn't be any fun without my mysticism, now would it?" Alexi still got mysticism and obscuritanism mixed up from time to time. He smiled, but it wasn't all mirth—there was a touch of bitterness bruising the humor. "Would you like me to do something?" he asked at length.

Ken's only response was a curious look in Alexi's direction. "Something? Could you be any more specific?"

Ignoring the point of Ken's question, Alexi extended his hand and continued, "How long have we been waiting to get this thing started?" Ken looked at him blankly, but Alexi could tell he'd piqued his interest. "Lean back. And relax. You remember the things I've shown you lately to clear your mind?"

Ken's broad head bobbed forward slightly. He reclined even further on the futon, moving a few pillows so that he was completely comfortable.

"Every now and then I meditate on my own," he said, now lying prone on the bed.

"Well, use all you know. I have my own preparations..."

"O.K., man. I don't know what you've got cooking in there, but I'm game."

Alexi was already lost in thought.

——◆◆——

Minutes later, the air in the room grew still. It was as if it had become a breathable liquid, thick and viscous. With this thickness came a feeling of foreboding. To Ken, there was something about the room, as it was, at that very moment—the candles flickering at an even rate, the haze in the air, even the look on Alexi's face—that seemed strange, alien and disquieting. What was most unsettling was that he knew he had been here in this exact situation not once, but countless times before. He was waking from an endless sleep, and yet simultaneously pulled into an endless wake. There was something nauseating about the feeling, a disquieting vertigo. *Am I dreaming?* he wondered, suddenly feeling very vulnerable and uncertain. *It wasn't dreaming. It was waking up.* Our awareness, which he was suddenly thinking of as dreaming, rather than waking, was always one, two, three levels abstracted from anything real.

This uncertainty was about everything, too—gravity, the mechanical certainty of the seasons... Suppose, as Einstein once did, that we are all in a huge elevator accelerating upwards. We witness the effects of gravity, the effects of the seasons, and the effects of our emotions but never see into the thing itself, when it happens, where it happens.

He had been struggling with the feeling that there would be no happy ending, that all of our lives were hurtling straight for a catastrophic collision yet no one else seemed to see it. He had to pretend his eyes were closed just to avoid getting locked away. For many months now, each day grew longer and less satisfying than the one before it; it seemed like all anyone did anymore was bark orders or obey the call of their master's whips: calendar, work day, weekly schedule... He was floundering in college and couldn't shake the feeling that it was as much of a dead-end as working in the 7–11 down the block. Either way it was their box, their values that he was expected to evaluate his own actions within, neither of which resonated with what he found when he looked into himself.

Days were lost in a gray haze. The world he was being sold was even more disappointing when it wasn't on television. Fear of death was nothing to him compared to the fear of mechanization, the fear of becoming a robot dutifully serving the machine. When he slept, he would often have horrible dreams of people marching in perfect rows, half-machine men with glittering circuit boards in their heads—they were Orwellian dreams.

These dreams, which would otherwise be so easy to dismiss upon waking, were driven home with an icy terror whenever he looked closely at those around him. They also seemed to be falling lock-step into a march that held no sway over him, no matter how hard he strained his ear to listen. As he might say, something didn't *smell* right here...

Because of all this, he was more than willing to try something, anything, that would allow him to escape from the relentless stranglehold life had on him, to breathe freely again. And it was because of this honest desperation that he was willing to buy anything that was sold to him, which is what any acting guru, anyone willing to take on that role, needs to make the first incision.

"I'm ready," Ken said quietly. It was sub-vocalized and Alexi didn't appear to hear. "Am I dreaming?" he asked again, this time aloud.

Alexi put a hand on Ken's shoulder, raising the other in the air for a moment like it was a benediction. The air grew warmer. "We're all dreaming," Alexi said enigmatically, his voice certain and calm. Ken's previous beliefs kicked in for a moment, and he felt the urge to laugh. *He thinks he's fucking Jesus Christ.*

He couldn't deny, however, how comforting it felt to have someone around who knew what was going on. At the least, he certainly presented himself that way. He'd give Alexi the benefit of the doubt. They'd been friends for some time, and although his recently found mysticism was a little hard to swallow, it also presented ironically solid ground.

"The world would be a better place the moment everyone admitted they don't know anything, the moment they stop putting on a show," Alexi would say randomly, with enormous melodramatic flair after a similarly dramatic pause. The self-referential irony of the statement seemed to be lost on him. Or maybe he was aware of it, and it was all a joke. Most people didn't take it all that seriously. To do so would be to buy into a fantastical world composed not of actual rules governed by reality, but of personally established rules that affect reality. In fact, Alexi claimed that reality was a completely empty term. "A mutually created, social concept that keeps you in line," he would say, munching on a burger at Lenny's.

"...We're all dreaming and we choose, in a delayed choice reaction, what our futures will be," Alexi continued a moment later, his voice legato, his eyes unfocused. Ken snapped back into the moment. "Look back Ken, look way back to the places you go and then disregard as unreal."

Alexi's eyes suddenly focused rapidly as he held his hand a few inches from Ken's head. "Do you feel that?" The tone of his question was sharp. It reversed the direction of his previous comments, made him forget them.

There was a buzzing inside Ken's head. He didn't respond. He had the feeling that the actual makeup of his body was fluctuating somehow. The sensation felt like super-fine mist or an icy drizzle. Light static. Not able to make sense of the thought or the feeling, instead he focused on the stream of letters in his minds-eye, moving frantically, permuting into new shapes and forms, coiling in what was an unmistakable spiral. The spiral, and the letters, began much like a visualization inspired by eyelid patterns and the flickering of the candles but soon it was too distinct and peculiar to dismiss as a daydream.

He remembered having felt like this many times before, but never before had he been quite so self-conscious, so crisply aware... He was hovering somewhere between awake and asleep. Theta range. He realized that he was speaking to Alexi and had been for some time, although he couldn't be sure what he was saying. Ken's vision became blurry as the room slowly faded out of his view, giving way to a wholly internal reality.

The clock ticks its beats off regularly, measuring the rotation of its mechanical innards and the seconds, minutes, hours, days of being locked away. Her wrists are numb from the jester's cold metal restraints, her naked body aches from weeks without movement. The cell door opens, and the brilliant light pains her eyes, so used to absolute darkness. Standing there is the man at the center of the spiral. He unlocks the handcuffs and throws them to her feet. He speaks only one word, and that word is "Destiny." There is a hole in her chest, a product of the despair fashioned from her isolation. A hole that longs with an indescribable hunger, desiring a taste so bitter and so sweet that she is dragged to her feet by it. The pain which had been sublimated for so long suddenly focused in one brilliant moment, as if all her experience, all the time spent in solitude had suddenly crystallized, her hope, in opposition to the despair, revealing itself through this man. He leads her to the top of a mountain, motioning for her to sit and together they admire the view, feel the wind in their hair, the granite under their feet, and the scent of the ages.

"That is what can be. Feel the joy of just being free as one's self, not confined in the mold of any invisible master. Beware, most of all, your own self-inflicted limitations—the jester is still lurking nearby, leering like a carnival ride. He will tempt you with false happiness, deceive you with empty promises, and cast you aside in an instant. There is also the scholar, who means well, but will not let you live. He will treat the symptom, and not the problem," he says, an incredible peace in his voice and posture.

Hope shines in the sky, giving her warmth. And the jester lurks a few paces behind, waiting—

Ken was shaking. There appeared to be a purple phantom glow all about his body, like a retinal afterimage on a sunny day. A trick of the eyes, surely.

"That's enough," Alexi said, and fell back, apparently drained.

Ken reacted violently: thrashing about on the bed, mumbling, talking listlessly. Occasionally, he would stop for a moment, and then a moment later burst into hysterical belly laughter. "You live in a halfway house between insanity and absolute, complete freedom," he said, suddenly very sober.

"I don't know what you're talking about," Alexi said nonchalantly, nibbling neurotically on his shirtsleeve. The exaggerated self-confidence that he radiated a moment before was gone. He sat slightly hunched over, almost squirrel-like. Smiling in Ken's direction, he asked "How do you feel?"

"Something is...different." Ken seemed to struggle to find the right words, finally resigned, and asked, "What did you do?"

"What I was told," Alexi said, far too quiet for Ken to hear.

"You're ridiculous." He paused. "I never know with you, man. Sometimes I half expect you to—with one of your too-big, toothy grins—proclaim that you've been putting me on this whole time. But really, what did you do?"

"We all have energy around us. It is us; you cannot separate yourself from your energy. Our consciousness is electro-chemical." Alexi lit up another cigarette, and added offhandedly, "got to add to the ambiance." Alexi's speech had an off-kilter, loping stride that made Ken think of William Shatner and Leonard Nimoy simultaneously.

Ken shook his head. "Cut the crap."

"With practice, we can learn to control this energy—to do nearly anything with it. To take and give it to others, affect the eventual outcomes of things... You must understand, there is an intricate unseen... dimension...to events. Intent, concentration, will, whatever you want to call it, leads this energy, if it has a vessel fit to manifest in. You can think of it in these terms: whenever something happens, it inflects itself forwards and backwards in time, affecting the lattice of all past and future... what is it?" Alexi stopped, noticing Ken's brow wrinkling.

"Do you mean you sometimes take this energy from unknowing people?"

Alexi chuckled. "When it's necessary. Or useful," seeing Ken's look of disdain, he added, "We are all One. Taking and giving are two sides of the same coin."

Ken nodded. "It is logical."

"Machiavellian, perhaps, but logical. Anyway, I can show you how to utilize it in time," Alexi said.

"How is this energy different from energy of other sorts—physical energy?" Ken asked.

Alexi thought for a moment. "The difference is simply wavelength. A certain range of frequencies, you could say, are visible to us as color...

think about all that exists out there that we simply don't have the apparatus to perceive? On the quantum level the difference between particle and wave is purely a perceptual one. When air is vibrated we experience sound. Even so-called solid matter is dynamic. Glass is a liquid. What I'm saying is that we can generalize and say everything is energy—vibrations of a medium in various modalities. I also have an intuition that energy is consciousness. This energy is expressed in a variety of ways. It is focused in a specific way within our nervous systems, which allows it to will itself into motion... into awareness of itself. God is 'I am that I am.' Regardless all energy is conscious whether or not it relates to itself and thereby has the illusion of self-awareness."

Ken sat back for support, still trembling.

"It actually isn't all that hard to see energy all around you. It's...semi-transparent, like glass under water. Changing your belief causes different patterns of thought... different energy patterns, do you see? When I'm really tuned in everything is vivid and brilliantly alive, and I often experience sensory crossovers, like scents perceived as colors, or sounds perceived as both aural and visual... It's like one sense bubbles into the others, kind of overflows because it's so strong. The first warning I must give you: decide who you share with carefully. Taking, like giving, is a somewhat intimate process... Everything is a circle—you can't really invoke something on someone else without invoking it on yourself... The more your energy interacts with another, the more their life is bound up in your own, and vice versa, so watch it... I'm not sure why, these are just the rules. You'll get the hang of it—" Alexi coughed. "Like I said an intent is not enough on its own; the force still requires a vehicle, a form, a child of this will, in which it can manifest... You must make a vessel of yourself, for this seed to grow."

Ken nodded.

"How long have you been waiting for this to happen? For me?" Ken asked.

"I? Not long."

"Of course you."

"Not necessarily. I don't completely understand it myself—I just know that I get messages, from time to time, from elsewhere. Out of phase times or beings. I see everything as a whole, the present fragment disappears. I can't explain it all right now. But you're tired, we'll talk in the morning. Just keep one last thing in your mind, before you drift into sleep: every event affects every other event and creates a sort of ripple that in the end...changes everything. And events are manifest energy. All you have to do is ride the wave, man. Uhm...you can just tell when you're on the beam. Well, good night."

Once Ken had been situated, Alexi returned to his room. For over an hour he sat unmoving, thinking.

———◈◈———

Agent 139 looked over at Johny and smiled mischievously. They were seated in Lenny's, basking in the sickly glow of bright fluorescent bulbs. The Agent tossed a coin up in the air and slammed it down on the table suddenly, making Johny wince in surprise. "Only absolute chance is a fair leader," Agent 139 said to him. "Never forget that." Jesus gave them a discriminating look. He then looked down and checked his makeup in a pocket mirror.

———◈◈———

Alexi was standing on a beach in Atlantic City, New Jersey, his hair whipped by the violent and bitter wind that came in tremendous blasts from the sea. Because it was a winter day, the shore was otherwise completely abandoned. The sun half-hid behind a hazy patch of clouds, and offered no noticeable warmth to the beach below.

Directly beside him stood Samantha, one hand resting comfortably on the back of his arm, the other dangling listlessly at her side. They were close to the shoreline; flecks of the salty water sprayed them in the face as the waves came crashing down endlessly and tumultuously. Each stared out to the horizon, rendered speechless by the effect the passing storm was having upon the black, opaque water.

He looks expectantly—

"What do you want?" she asks with her eyes. In other words, "who do you want me to be?"

A seagull landed and cocked its head, one beady eye regarding them coldly. Knocking on a rock three times, it hopped back, partially extending its wings, calling out shrilly once and then again. This knocked Alexi out of his trance, and he stared back. "Three, and then two," he said softly, the sound of subtle concern creeping into his voice. It ruffled its feathers in what he would have described as an exasperated manner, called out four times, and took flight. Smiling briefly, he turned towards Samantha, preparing to say something—but that something never came. He froze solid as a statue, suddenly enraptured by the expression he found there.

none of the words are mine anymore
(were they ever mine?! am i a puppet?! am I real?!)
(shut up.)
the thoughts that fill my head other voices
other ideas others
Other
i am Other (others)
i am escaping

She didn't seem to notice his silent admiration. People only look truly human when they think no one is watching. Everything around her was perfectly still, as if she had been trapped within a photograph. Only the waves continued to crash, moving in regular fractal-like patterns to the hazy horizon.

In this instant, she appeared suddenly and inexplicably beautiful. To Alexi, she looked nothing like before. Except for her eyes. Her eyes appeared the same, blue and too wide somehow.

change the lipstick change the hair
who am i now? who am i now?

i am Other
(other than...?)
(shut up.)
other than nothing is something
i am anything.

He wondered if this was "the why": the universe chose to become aware of itself, had split itself into lifetimes of exile, merely to experience these moments of union, dissolution in eternity, bliss.

It had absolutely nothing to do with who they were, as it was every bit as likely that it could have been someone other than Samantha who had allowed this experience to become...theirs. Yet it had been Samantha, and was destined in this arbitrary way. This, Alexi realized after the endless moment began to pass, was the game of "us," possibly the only game worth playing—the game where the center of concern, and the center of being, is within the mutual world of co-creation. Alexi wondered if she was thinking the same thing. She was still looking out thoughtfully over the waves. He was sure she was.

they cast me in a role and i become
(change the lipstick, change the hair...)

i am not   i am not i

am not understanding you
SMILE
i am somewhere else i am
(LOOK!) i am (LOOK!) i am
stuck
(broken record. sorry. my mind stutters.)
who the fuck am i
are you
  am i are you am i are you am i
    are too am not are too am not are too
      nnnnkkkknnnnnkkkknnnnnkkkk
I AM NOT LISTENING
(shhh.)

i am so
are not (am too) are not (am too.)

it's all about rearranging rooms.

toodeepkneedeepwaistneckeyes
i am drowning /says nothing/
  i look over at Him and smile. It will be better soon.
(?!)

CHAPTER 2, GRID 2

MOTHER HIVE BRAIN UNVEILED

For only after men had tried their hand for thousands of years at merely objective philosophizing did they discover that, among the many things that make the world so puzzling and precarious, the first and foremost is that, however immeasurable and massive it may be, its existence hangs nevertheless on a single thread; and this thread is the actual consciousness in which it exists.

> — Arthur Schopenhauer,
> *The World as Will and Representation,* Vol. II

[The following is extracted from Mental Status Examination of the patient immediately prior to transfer to D Building, performed by Bernard Spitzer, M.D., Ph.D.]

Patient is a six-foot, four-inch tall Caucasian male presenting with marked agitation and disturbed affect. He attended the interview dressed indifferently (shirt buttoned unevenly, unmatched socks) and appears to have drawn zodiac signs on his exposed flesh with a felt tip pen. According to the observations of his ward staff, the period of his mood swings has drastically shortened in recent weeks, with an accompanying intensification of his depersonalizing ideations and delusions of reference. While he disagrees with the observations of the ward staff, the patient seemed somewhat pleased that I had scheduled this interview to review his treatment plan and diagnosis.

Evidence of disorientation as to self, place and time quickly surfaced in the course of our interview. "Within himself" the patient claims to possess three distinct ego-identities in "this reality grid," as well as several other distinct identities in "associated grids." (Perhaps the handwritten communications the patient has been handing the nursing staff at the medication window are addressed to identities in these "other reality grids"?) When I sought to establish with which hallucinatory ego-identity I was speaking the patient's agitation increased markedly. He reported that his agitation stems from frustration with the perceived "limitations of the me in this space-time reality grid" as well as the "limitations imposed by the quantum probability matrix or novel run upon this single thread," I noted that the patient is on a token system for behavioral reinforcement and can gain access to additional privileges or resources through good behavior, thus giving him incrementally greater control over these perceived "limitations"; the patient called me an idiot.

Seeking to expand our interview into quality-of-care issues, I then asked the patient to explain these "limitations" to the best of his ability. He seemed amused, then quickly assumed a flat affect, stating that he "feels the need to be with, in time, the same being he experiences out-of-time." He then broke down and began crying inconsolably, repeating "I miss her, I miss her."

The patient calmed remarkably quickly for the apparent severity of his emotional outburst and elaborated on his previous statements regarding "this single thread," which I take to mean the patient's actual ego-identity. He expressed a belief that emotions are the "super-glue of the universe," maintaining an individual's place in a particular "reality grid." When I sought further clarification, the patient likened emotions to "anchor points" and stated his need to "understand every thought, every emotion, every sensation," despite their originating "from Elsewhere." The patient was unable to specify where this origin could be located and became amused when I asked. He indicated to me that he found my questions specious and simple-minded, and further stated that "creatures of enhanced brain evolution are unable to communicate their non-verbal experiences to primates caged in the hallucinatory here-and-now."

It was at this point, seeking to change the subject back to quality-of-care, which I inquired of the patient as to the nature of the "being" he sought to "experience in time." He indicated that he could best express his thoughts non-verbally and requested drawing implements. Upon being handed a page from my notebook and a pen, he stabbed me between the ribs with the pen and nearly punctured the lining of my right lung. As he was dragged away by the orderlies, he explained his action in the following way: "You can consider this pen the zen 'stick of encouragement.' *Now* do you understand the nature of the Being you experience in time?"

Following this assault, and my confirmation of the patient's disintegrating mental status, I requested that he be transferred to D Building's high security ward. The initial reports from Dr. Fein have been poor, indicating the patient's withdrawal into an increasingly psychotic state. He is not yet responding positively to increased medication (Chlorpromazine 150 mg/day, Fluphenazine 15 mg/day) and has been added to the ECT candidates list pending his next Mental Status Exam. Dr. Stackhouse has given him the assignment of writing a journal about his life in the hopes that this will allow for greater insight which may allow us to pursue less intrusive therapeutic approaches.

Light filtered through the dusty pane glass windows across the room. The windows were divided into 4x4 sections by strips of stained wood. It was a long, narrow classroom, with stucco walls, off-white and covered in a lattice-work of cracks. An old, temperamental coil heater in the corner hissed as the professor, a thin, pockmark-faced man paced back and forth on the creaking floorboards. Although he was balding, his wild, curly hair, goatee and intelligent, darting eyes betrayed his relative youth as a teacher and gave him a mischievous, plotting look. In fact, he looked quite like the devil. Students shuffled in their seats. Some of them pulled out books; all of them did their best to appear studious.

The professor ceased his pacing and looked over the class with his clear, blue eyes. He took in one deep breath, held it, and then leapt into his classic rapid-fire lecture technique. "The fish is a symbol of fatherhood, of motherhood, of the perpetuation of life which generally occurs. The letter N, (Nun, N, in Hebrew means 'fish'), is one of the earliest hieroglyphs of this idea…"

K turned to J and whispered "I found a paper posted on campus today that I think you really must look over." Although he said it quietly, there was a definite urgency in his voice that caught J's attention immediately. "Have you ever heard of the Mother Hive Brain?"

J merely stared at K incredulously for a moment, his mouth slightly ajar, and then looked back to the professor.

"…In Hebrew mythology, the symbol is connected to Noah. Note also that the symbol of the fish has been chosen to represent the Redeemer. The early Christians used the symbol of the fish to represent their martyr. It is of note that the letter Nun corresponds to the astrological sign of Scorpio and to the Tarot card of Death, which is the thirteenth card, 13 being the number of steps on a gallows. A tacit mythological truth is that death always implies birth, and that the two are really not at all different, being but two phases of the same process. From the standpoint of anthropology, you can see the symbol of Osiris coming from vegetable societies, where the crops are 'slain' each year and grow anew from the earth. You may refer to the mythology of Isis, Osiris and Horus for further details, as well as some hints at what the ritual is to resurrect the slain God." The Professor chuckled lecherously, peering over at a girl third row from the back with a tight, low-cut yellow shirt and caught himself daydreaming briefly about one-on-one study time. He cleared his throat when none of the students even smiled. "Uh…take a look at the symbol for the astrological sign of cancer, or the yin-yang glyph, or… opposites are equal, you see, and… Yes, uh… Remember, Osiris is a black god… One must constantly keep in mind the bivalence of every symbol. …As for the prophet, madness is also a phase of his intoxication. Now we turn our attention to Parcival, the divine fool, who accidentally turns everything upside down…"

J looked questioningly over at K, who shrugged and then passed folded papers across the table.

M.H.B.S. transmission 1H:
Grand Lodge LUX:

Transmission to Order of the Hidden Path, Devon PA:
Script for Infomercial. Scene 1.

LERI: ALL IN BLACK, LIGHT (BUT WARM) MAKE-UP, SITTING IN FULL-LOTUS WITH A SERENE SMILE; ALWAYS LOOKS DIRECTLY AT THE CAMERA WITHOUT BLINKING.

ANNE: GENERIC INFOMERCIAL BLOND; HIGH-WAISTED, BELTED KHAKIS WITH EITHER A FLORAL OR DENIM BLOUSE TUCKED IN A LITTLE TOO TIGHT, HAIR PARTED AT THE SIDE, VERY PINK MAKE-UP, PREFERABLY BLUE-EYED.

CRAZY FINGERS (a.k.a. 139): MILITANT MAN, FATIGUES AND CAP INCLUDED, TOTING AN OBSCENELY LARGE GUN, STROKING IT OCCASIONALLY.

RAY: DARK-SKINNED (PREFERABLY) AFRICAN-AMERICAN MALE, HAIR CLOSELY CROPPED, BUT NOT BALD, DRESSED IN KHAKIS AND A SWEATER, WITH A DRESS-SHIRT COLLAR STICKING OUT FROM UNDERNEATH.

GREG: CONFUSED GEN-XER, SKATER CLOTHES AND PIERCINGS, HAIR FROSTED BLONDE, OBVIOUSLY HIGH, VERY "COOL" (PERHAPS AN OPEN SHIRT TO SHOW OFF THE CHEST.)

RACHELLE: HIPPIE-TYPE, LONG SKIRT, MOCCASINS, HEAD-BAND. LONG, BROWN HAIR AND EYES, NATURAL LOOKING MAKE-UP, OBVIOUSLY HIGH (PERHAPS GIGGLING EVERY ONCE IN A WHILE)

ROBERT: ALMOST GENERIC INFOMERCIAL GUY (SEE BELOW) BUT WITH A DIFFERENT COLOR HAIR, SLIGHTLY DISHEVELED, AND TAKING HITS OF POT THROUGHOUT THE SCENE IN RANDOM CUTS.

BILL, BOB, etc.: GENERIC INFOMERCIAL GUY; BROWN HAIR IN THAT RIDICULOUS JIM-PALMER FROM THE MONEY STORE HAIR CUT WITH NAVY OR BLACK DRESS SLACKS & MATCHING PATENT-LEATHER SHOES, BUT INCREDIBLY BRIGHT, TACKY AND CHEER-FUL SOCKS THAT ARE VISIBLE WHEN HE IS SITTING. PINK OR PUR-PLE SHORT-SLEEVED DRESS SHIRT. NOT GAY, JUST "FRIENDLY AND UNINTIMIDATING" (I.E.: I AM A NICE GUY. BUY THIS FURNITURE FROM ME AND LET ME SLEEP WITH YOUR DAUGHTER.)

BLACK OSIRIS: HAGGARD CAUCASIAN MAN IN PURPLE SILK BATHROBE, GAS MASK, AND PINK BUNNY SLIPPERS. RAPPER DEMEANOR.

(The cast is arranged around the stage in various casual poses. As each performer speaks (s)he crosses pointlessly, often to lay a hand on another performer's shoulder. Infomercial friendliness in tone.)

Leri: Try this: Every morning as soon as you wake up and each night before you go to sleep, say to yourself, simply and clearly, "I am a neuro-surgeon."

Anne: There are no roaches here. (CUT TO SHOT OF ROACHES, PREFERABLY CRAWLING AROUND ON AN ANNE-LIKE WOMAN, WHO IS SWATTING AT THEM DESPERATELY) We can plainly see.

Crazy Fingers: (CUT TO AN "ON-LOCATION" SCREEN, NYC, MAYBE WITH A "SATISFIED CUSTOMER" AT THE BOTTOM) If I were inclined towards personifying Leri, which I am at times, I would say Leri meta-programs us. How can this be? I struggled with this one for awhile, and the best explanation I can give to someone who hasn't interacted with Leri on this level yet is that while we watch this program, or read this script, certain issues are discussed, which cause the readers to think about them, and somehow in that process, through that process, the ideas insidiously work their way into the readers' reality-maps.

Anne: The beauty is that associations can be rebuilt. (CASTS A FISHING LINE) When I tell you that fish is good, you're called to won-der what has previously been associated with fish. (MAKES EXCITED FACE, REELS IN LARGE PLASTIC FISH) We could, for instance, assume that the fish is you.

Greg: Whatever, man. It doesn't matter.

Ray: (CUT TO SHOT OF HIM AS "CHIEFTAIN," TRIBAL DRUMS PLAYING IN THE BACKGROUND) It doesn't matter if you believe it. Just plant the seed.

Anne: Can't see yourself doing it?

Greg: Sure you can! I, like you, work in big and unfathomable ways. We work on different levels. Fish swim at different depths. Saying "I am a neurosurgeon" calls up vast amounts of angels and energy!

Black Osiris: (NODDING) Tryin' to get a mainline... Brother of man, son of God...

Rachelle: Soon what we want to be and who we are meet and we are one.

Robert: Go ahead. Say it. "I am a neurosurgeon."

Leri: Practice saying it when people ask you what you do. You might feel like a complete fool.

Ray: (CUT TO SHOT OF HIM AS A SLAVE-TYPE, DRESSED IN RAGS, KNAPS IF POSSIBLE, WITH A HUGE SMILE AND A SLICE OF WATERMELON) That is okay. Step forward and say it anyway.

Greg: "I am a neurosurgeon."

Rachelle: You may be a waitress in a cafe.

Greg: (DRESSED AS AHAB) You may have gills and scales.

Robert: You may work as a temporary secretary or as a delivery boy.

Anne: You will be in control of your future.

Leri: You look in the mirror at yourself. You suddenly realize that where "you" are is neither a question of "where" nor "when."

Crazy Fingers: We live in a world where what we know doesn't correspond to what we experience, and what we experience does not correspond to what we "know" others experience. I think that's part of the reason why the conspiracy theory is so popular right now—because the linear-minded monkey is prone to assume that "the truth is out there" and that someone must be pulling the strings. To be honest, I don't believe this. No person or organization is pulling the strings. That's what MHB is all about—hive mind works without any observable decision making on any level.

Rachelle: (BLANK AFFECT) A neurosurgeon re-programs.

Leri: He does it through the correlations noises, sounds, and experiences we have with each other.

Greg: ICU.

Robert: I see you?

Greg: (LAUGHING) Well yes, through the eye. It's easier to write scripts for oneself in code.

Anne: (MILDLY CONFUSED, LIKE SHE HAS LOST HER PLACE IN THE SCRIPT) …Intensive care unit?

Leri: It is easy for those who have studied the correlations between various myths and traditions; seeing the psychological correlations between certain names, numbers, and concepts, one can create and understand in Archetypal Metaphors cogent with their Personal Human System, or PHS™.

Anne: (CONFUSION MOUNTING) Is "C" for control?

Leri: (REVERENTLY) Only for the initiated.

Robert: Whatever stuck out the most to my mind, I found, was always synchronous with the internal meaning of the sign I was studying. Channeling Oprah Winfrey has never been so easy.

Leri: Yes, you see, the word of God, the logos, is *all* language. The world as we know it is imaginary…perhaps our senses but most definitely our thoughts about what any given thing "is" are subject to change when we shift our beliefs for the better…

Black Osiris: Indeed, my brother. Mummify life in concepts, walking on valence shells in this holographic fractal spiral we surf'n straight to hell…

Bill: That's very interesting, Leri. On the other hand, I'm discovering that nothing can be trusted to remain the same.

Robert: (NODDING) It's not a bad thing at all. That's taken me a long time to realize, not to cram down my own throat like some Sodom apple.

Leri: Yes. As you are now seeing, quite clearly…oftentimes, we can become pretty complacent in our beliefs. We may feel safe and comfortable, floating pleasantly downstream on a warm, sunny day. But then suddenly you found that you have been in error with respect to your interpretation of reality. You feel a terror, a fear, welling up inside you. Yet what you feel is not a fear regarding any particular object…instead what you are experiencing is a break in the tissue of temporal, spatial, causal relationships by which objects are supported, by which the subject too is supported…but is it there? Is it over here? You experience it as a void, or a God, or a spirit of some kind…

Rachelle: Yes. I am who I am. If I tell someone who I am, then I'm not her. But you know who I am by who we become.

Audience member: (SHOUTS) If you don't believe me, then you can taste me!

CUT TO COMMERCIAL

Leri: Identify yourself as a neurosurgeon. Join the Mother Hive Brain syndicate. Take that step.

Ray: (TO HIM DOING A GANGSTA RAPPER POSE, WITH A HUGE BLUNT BETWEEN HIS TEETH, DRESSED IN HEAVY HIP-HOP GARB AND TONS OF GOLD) And one day, you'll find yourself operating on another human's brain.

Greg: Do you think you'll be a neurosurgeon, then?

Rachelle: Well, I got some good news for you people.

Anne: Every adventure begins with an incision.

Leri: You already are. You are neurosurgeons.

Bill: (TO SPECIFIC AUDIENCE) You are a neurosurgeon. You are a neurosurgeon.

Ray: (CUT TO HIM DRESSED AS BLACK MUSLIM W/ BOWTIE, AND SEATED WITH HIS LEGS CROSSED. SAID IN A VERY RELAXED MANNER.) I am a neurosurgeon.

Greg: Hey, everybody, what do you do?

(AUDIENCE RESPONDS)

Rachelle: The first phases of meta-programming begin when a sentient system decides to *start* making autonomous decisions, now… Do you remember your first taste of autonomy? The first time you consciously disobeyed your careful social programming? What did you do?

(INDIVIDUAL AUDIENCE MEMBER RESPONDS)

Robert: Hey that's great.

Bill: Let's shout it, so all those wage slave losers in the bar next door hear us.

All: WE ARE NEUROSURGEONS!

Ray: (CUT TO WHITE MAN WEARING RAY'S CLOTHING AND PLAYING HIM IN BLACKFACE) Take it to the streets!

ALL: We are neurosurgeons!

Greg: Call your family tonight and give them the good news.

Rachelle: Fuck med. school—it's expensive.

Robert: (TAPPING HIS HEAD) Be a neurosurgeon up here.

Bill: I am.

Anne: We are. Together.

Greg: (DRESSED AS AHAB) Avast I say!

Ray: (CUT TO RAY DRESSED AS FIFTIES HOUSEWIFE) Oh, I don't earn a lot of money yet, but I've got a spatula and a wire whisk and I'm sure when the time comes I'll know just what to do…

Anne: We'll be having the time of our life.

Greg: One more time, so it'll seem like this play's got a real ending!

ALL: We are neurosurgeons!

This was a public service announcement brought to you by Ayun Halliday, Larry Snodgrass, and the Mothers of the Cuban Revolution, et al.

J read this a number of times before slowly putting it down on the table. The professor was still talking, making less and less sense as the setting of the sun marked the end of class. His comments seemed to be in some form of code. Between the professor and the peculiar script, he was on overload.

"That concludes my lecture for today," the professor said, reaching for his books. "Uh… I'll be testing on the mythological significance of the Fish next Tuesday. So, don't forget to…" without finishing his thought, he put on his wide-brimmed black hat and was out the door.

"Fish?" K mouthed at J.

"Have you ever heard of the Order of the Hidden Path?" J asked. The other students were quietly filing out of the room.

"No. The O.T.O., A∴A∴, Golden Dawn, Rosicrucians, Templars, the Order of Jacques De Molay…"

"But no O.H.P.? And no Mother Hive Brain?"

K shrugged. "No."

The last student left the room and turned off the light, leaving them in partial darkness.

"The 139 thing is weird too. The number has always stuck out to me though I can't say why. There's a vacation coming up—how about we take a trip to Devon?"

"Just because of this script?"

"Eh, you found me out. I was planning on going home and visiting my girlfriend anyway. Call me after Anti-Religious Philosophy."

Like every other class this semester, the teacher waits in an atmosphere of heavy brooding for all of us to arrive before beginning. He sits quietly, at the end of the table, occasionally looking up over his bifocals to inspect us. Generally, after scanning the room with his brow furrowed, he would raise an eyebrow, and then turn his attention back to his notes, building internal momentum. Then, with the same Olympic air of drama and enthusiasm, he stands up and leaps headlong into a lecture. Today's lecture is on Kierkegaard's Fear and Trembling. I would tell you what it was about but I spent most of the class writing down ideas about Feuerbach, who we just covered, and letting my subconscious listen to his lecture. The subject-predicate argument. A nice little word game on Ludwig's part, though in my opinion you're as well off disproving God with logic as you are proving him with it. Faith doesn't work in a syllogism. Ah see, here's the connection already—if you know Fear and Trembling, and the Knight of Faith, you know precisely what I mean. Good thing I don't have to do anything at all to let this sink in and rattle around. When we deal with Nietzsche next, and his philosophizing with tuning hammers, I'll probably be ruminating on Kierkegaard. It also strikes me as slightly strange—the classroom lights always remain off. For some reason, none of us ever think to turn them on.

J's dorm room was a clutter of books, half-empty soda and beer cans, and the distinctive musty scent of new music equipment and marijuana. He sat in front of the harsh glare of his monitor, mumbling to himself and puffing on a Marlboro red. The Marlboro man was not only an icon—the Marlboro man was a shepherd, a biblical shepherd, leading his followers into the cyclical, mythological world of addiction.

The phone rang.

"Hey, it's K. How was old fire-and-brimstone?"

"Same as usual. Fear and Trembling. Unbearably weighty stuff. The infinite despair at being despairing of one's finitude or whatever. What's going on?" J held the phone to his ear with his shoulder as he continued to type. He slid Das Ich into his CD player and tapped his finger on the receiver in time with the beat.

"I did some research on the name Aleonis De Gabrael. But... I don't know, man. My most reliable source says he was born in 1776 in Rouen, France. He disappeared in 1799 and was presumed dead. The Order of the Hidden Path was a mystical organization started only two years ago by some kids in the Philadelphia area. 1799? Where did you find this character? Then I see his name coming up in posted documents on mysticism and magick over the last few years, and he keeps mentioning the 'Mother Hive Brain Syndicate,' his 'teacher of *the* Ancient Mysteries' which has...this part cracked me up...'an unbroken lineage to the Secret Masters of ancient Egypt.' Who, the sister-fucking pharaohs? ...Hey will you cut out that tapping? They had one main treatise, which was registered with the Library of Congress two years ago. I couldn't find any sort of connection between the organization and Aleonis, at first." He paused dramatically. J resumed his tapping.

"I did a little more research, mainly on the Internet—so validity is a question there. Right, well, at any rate, I found a message board on joinmycult.org with some postings by people claiming to be members. ...One was apparently written by Aleonis de Gabrael. The only explanation is a short message before the post: 'for general consumption, until the publication is completed.' Well, here it is. I have to warn you though, the note really doesn't make any sense. I'll e-mail it right over. So how are you, man?"

J shrugged, staring at an empty bottle of Jose. "I'm unfortunately not especially loquacious... I didn't sleep much last night—add that to 1/3 L of tequila among other things on an empty stomach—serve chilled over ice. ...The result: a happy but generally groggy J."

He heard clicking on the other end—K was probably sending that e-mail—so he continued. "You know. The story of my life can be printed on the back of milk cartons. There's a wanted sign involved. Help wanted, please inquire within. I should consider resigning before Oprah Winfrey straddles my tongue. Listen: save yourself. Oprah's an evil, unforgiving bitch."

"...Riiiight. O.K., check your inbox monkey man."

```
From: K <seveneyes@marijuana.md>
Reply-To: <seveneyes@marijuana.md>
Date: Nov. 1, 1995 12:19:28-0700 (PDT)
To: J <agent139@astromonkey.net>
Subject: Crazy shit, dude.
```

Your first mission is an apocalyptic one—about the Prophet Priest. The Order has concluded that the Prophet is living in or around a city in the suburbs of Philadelphia known as Devon. We have reason to believe that his name is J. Roberts. Track him down and continue the cycle.

The first cycle has completed itself. This means 1997 is the year of Disappearance-Destruction. And now the year of the Fish dawns.

Gabrael, 0=11
www.Z0s.org

———◆———

J shrugged, repositioned the headset on his shoulder. "Yeah, that is mildly interesting," he said flatly. "And I'm bored senseless. Let's take a cab to the station then, hmm?"

The cab was a rusted yellow monster wearing checkered white and black war paint. Fuzzy pink dice swung freely from the rearview mirror. The interior smelled like old leather and rancid pizza.

Their driver was crowned with a regal blue sombrero, faded leather chaps the same color as his face, and a button-up plaid shirt. The chaps laced up the sides with a long, thin cord woven through tiny metal eyelets. Sliding open the window that divided the front seat from the back, he said, "My name is Mohammed. I will be your driver for the evening." K got the feeling that it would be a good idea to find another cab.

The car screeched into action, deftly maneuvering about wailing pedestrians and homicidal drivers in luxury cars with high cheekbones. The driver turned his dark eyes on K. They seemed hollow and yet somehow luminous.

"Where are you from? Certainly not New York?" K asked, trying to be conversational. He figured that sombreros weren't common fare in the city. *Shouldn't he be looking at the road in this traffic?!*

The driver paused. It may have been for the sake of theatrics; one can never tell with taxi drivers, especially in the Big Apple.

"No, my little rabbits." His voice had a thick accent which neither of the passengers could place. Middle-Eastern and Spanish? "No, I am not from around *here*." His emphasis on the last word was extreme.

At the next red light, the driver slowly turned to regard them, and then said, "I am in fact from Palestine." He continued to stare, unblinking, for many long, uncomfortable moments. J was forced to look away and chew on his thumbnail. Finally, they whipped through Times Square.

"Mohammed is my name—and I have come with a message from God."

Their rusted yellow steed neighed, puffed smoke, and pulled into a side alley. Before either passenger could complain, Mohammed produced two .357 pistols from under his seat. They were spray-painted neon pink. Around the muzzle the deep cobalt of the metal showed through.

"These," Mohammed said, puffing up his chest like a peacock, "are my peestals. Ah, my little rabbits—now," he pointed one of the guns at J, who was completely frozen in place, "say 'there is no God but God.'" Although his voice was calm and even, there was a dangerous look in his eyes. The muzzle of the gun staring at J's head like a cold, unblinking eye was enough. Their adrenaline was flowing. Should they try to run away? Try to fight? No chance, at least one of them would get it.

Blinking rapidly, J took a deep breath and held it. Time seemed to stop, but Samahdi was not yet to come. What the hell? Damning his impotent Kundalini, J said, "there is no God but God."

Mohammed spun on K, who was trying to keep himself steady by repeating, "I am the single eye perceiving itself" monotonously, mantra-like.

"Say I am the Son of God!" the man barked violently.

K, knowing his vital essence intimately, knowing that he was the vine rather than the branch, said, "I am the Son of God," beaming all the while.

Mohammed's face broke up into a mass of wrinkles—"No! Say *I* am the Son of God!"

"...You are the Son of God." In looking back, J realized that it was this encounter in particular that gave K the idea that he, too, was the Son of God.

"Very good." Mohammed nodded. "Yes, my little rabbits, you have done well in knowing this. Now I will take you to where we are going. To go to where it is that we are not at right now." J looked over at K and took a deep breath. "...to the *forbidden bridge* which spans the Abyss of Reason. You, Agent 139, shall lead the way."

J looked confused. "Agent 139? How do you know my email address?"

Mohammed looked frustrated. "Follow the goddamned script, okay? It's not like I write this shit," he said, his accent completely disappearing.

Chapter 3, Grid 1

A Crush Proof Box

...In possibility, however, everything is possible. Hence in possibility, one can go astray in all possible ways, but essentially in two: one form is the wishful, yearning form, the other is the melancholic fantastic—on the one hand Hope; on the other, fear or anguished dread. Fairy tales and legends so often relate that a knight suddenly perceived a rare bird, which he continues to run after, since at the beginning it seemed as if it were so very near—but then it flies off again, until at last night falls, and he has become separated from his companions, being unable to find his way in the wilderness where he now is. So it is with the possibility of the wish. Instead of summoning back possibility into necessity, the man pursues the possibility—and at last he cannot find his way back to himself. —In the melancholic form the opposite result is reached in the same way. The individual pursues with melancholy love a possibility of agonizing dread, which at last leads him away from himself, so that he perishes in the dread, or perishes in that in which he was in dread of perishing.

— S. Kierkegaard

The leaves of the trees turned into a blur of pastel, whipping by at a dizzying rate. This morning was a cold one, but for the pair sitting comfortably in the interior of Ken's car, the brisk autumn air was no deterrent. Ken flashed Alexi a smile as he whipped around a turn well above the supposed limit. Alexi returned the smile with a toothy grin.

"I really feel more alive, I've got to tell you," Ken said, without taking his eyes away from the winding road for a moment.

Alexi nodded, fumbling around in his pocket for a cigarette, somewhat crumpled despite the claim of a "Crush Proof Box". He pulled out a tape and put it in the deck. Whenever there wasn't something to say, whenever a few minutes needed to be killed, cut off and simply removed, a cigarette was lit.

"How so?" he asked in response to Ken's assertion, his feet tapping in time with the music. *Building and building, he thought to himself, the image keeps getting brighter, the sounds louder, more exciting...*

"I'm not completely sure if it's a good or bad thing—it sort of hurts in a way, you know?" The way Ken dragged out the last few syllables told Alexi he was deliberating over something.

He nodded again. "Living you mean? Of course." He figured he wouldn't press the point.

"More so," Ken repeated, whipping the car around another turn at an impossible speed, "colors are brighter, this cigarette feels like my first..."

Alexi chuckled. Nothing like romanticizing one's eventual, self-inflicted demise, he thought, dragging hard on his Marlboro.

"Hell, driving right now is a religious experience. I'm one with my car. Taoism at work, you know?" To prove his point, he increased the speed even more. The engine, which was purring in pleasure like a large cat, a hunting cat, now erupted into a roar.

"She's real happy with me right now," Ken said.

———◈———

A few nights later, Alexi was sitting alone in his room, hunched in front of his computer, cackling occasionally to himself. The sound of clicking keys came in sporadic bursts as he typed, and then paused to reread what he was writing.

The refresh rate of the monitor is precisely the correct frequency to induce insanity in primates, he mused, dragging hard on his cigarette. He could feel the burning deep in his lungs, but stubbornly took another drag immediately afterwards. *To hell with quantitative tests. You don't know cigarettes cause cancer unless you get it.*

```
From: <alexi@mostly.com>
Reply-To: <alexi@mostly.com>
Date: Nov. 1, 1995 9:19:32
To: <mysterylodge@aol.com>
Subject: A parable.
```

...There is a difference between knowledge and under-standing. Why is this? Knowledge must wait for some-thing...before it becomes applicable, and that which it waits for is never certain. These events are the foun-dation stones for the building which has not yet been

created—this building with my name written on every
brick, window, and speck of mortar…

He looked up when he realized the phone had been ringing and hadn't
noticed. It was Ken, asking if he could come by.

"Sure. Save me from my imprisonment," Alexi said quietly, with a
touch of sarcasm.

———◆◆◆———

Alexi sprinted to the door when he heard the bell ring, jumping over a
coffee table on the way. Ken was peeping through the window at the top
of the door.

When he opened the door, Alexi could tell that he was dressed for a
night out: a black wide-brimmed hat, trench coat, and a number of crystals about his neck.

"What do you have in mind for tonight? I've got to be back by about
11, school tomorrow, but that aside…"

Knocking the beads of rain from his hat, Ken sat down.

"Do you remember Shadows?"

Alexi nodded. "We went there once or twice early last summer, yeah."

"They have something on Wednesday nights, and I got free tickets
from a kid at West Chester."

With a grin, Alexi asked, "You mean you actually go to college?"

"Sometimes," Ken said, heading towards the door.

3:9 [Lounge of Shadows: Tables and chairs, mirrors across the room,
surveillance cameras above, industrial and goth music. Camera follows
them down the stairs to the club. Cut to a cheap VCR flashing
"RECORD" with black-and-white footage from one of the surveillance
cameras above. Zoom in on Ken and Alexi seated across from one
another at a table]

Ken: I've had this feeling lately—

Alexi: (cutting him off) Like something is happening and we're just
little pawns? Like this is only the beginning? (Ken looks over at Alexi.
Alexi is staring at himself in a mirror across the way, fixing his sunglasses.)

Ken: (smiles) Yeah, something like that. I've been on edge lately.
(pause, looking at Alexi, who is still looking at himself in mirror.) Are
you being narcissistic again?

Alexi: (shrugs) I'm listening. Recently, I've had a really hard time with something myself. But you go first.

Ken: (stares blankly into the air) I didn't have any purpose. I was floating in apathy. I guess I still am. But something is picking up. Someone in the background, writing and editing this script. (Ken pauses as several newcomers walk past their table and into the next room.) It's more difficult, I've been noticing that within the last few days I've been able to feel what other people are feeling... I can't go into crowds anymore...

Alexi: (nods) I've been having spells where I slip into third-person.

Ken: (bends over and opens his backpack) Third-person?

Alexi: Yeah. Basically it's like I'm watching myself from the outside...dissociation? It usually happens when I'm under a great deal of stress, or when my mind and body are completely at odds. It has to do with my director/actor trip, I think. From a bird's eye view, there is full awareness of what is occurring, but I'm unable to do anything about it. (pause) Some part of me wants to fail so badly...

Ken: (fumbles around in his backpack, places tube of black eyeliner on the table and pulls out a battered notebook with labels on the cover and papers jutting from the edges) It's funny you should mention that...

Ken: (A barely decipherable Sisters of Mercy song plays in the background. Ken opens his notebook to one of the pages and begins to read.) Take me away and make me someone else. Just let me get away from what I am for a little while. Just for once, let me get away from the deck of cards fate has dealt me. Let me slip slowly away until I'm someone else... Someone who outwardly matches who I am—female. Take me, strap me down, and cut away the bad with manic precision until only the good is left. And you have the realness in your belly, the soft tissue so vulnerable to the cold blade of my knife, yielding before it parts way and lets the blade in, spilling your guts to the floor, letting loose a coil of living pipe... (Ken continues, cut to Alexi dragging on cigarette.) Wondering where all the joy in life went. She is blindfolded, unable to scream, unable to speak...

Alexi: (looks over at Ken.) It makes me wonder why every new level apprehended is paradoxically another cage to escape for the sake of the next; each "advance" is met with higher demands, lower rewards, and stronger cage bars. Bizarre, bright blue alloys and snake-like dancing girls. (He shrugs with a chuckle.) I don't know, Ken. It seems you think your personality has fractured. Why?

Ken: The writing is metaphorical, but when you get down to it, those fragments are all just a piece of your self. They're more distinguished then a mood.

Alexi: (takes off sunglasses, glances at his twin reflection in the lenses, and places them on the table) I ask because I've theorized the same thing. I mean the fracture, of course. I find myself wondering why it would happen...whether it's a natural process... (after a dramatic pause, begins speaking to a third person who's not there in one of the empty chairs): Masks that people wear for everyone else. A problem arises when the mask becomes too natural; the person can't differentiate between "self" and "it" any longer. If I experience something, doesn't that make it real? Picture an onion, sliced in half... (Alexi chops downward with the edge of his hand. His hand stops just short of a wine glass seated on the table. There is a loud noise, a clear, crystalline note, and the glass explodes all over the table. Ken and Alexi sit, blinking at each other for a moment, before Alexi continues as if nothing ever happened.) Uhm... The layers build up on top of themselves, there's no "core," no "absolute." My persona has not only split, it's growing an awareness, a decision-making capacity, of its own. There isn't one persona, one self, that rules. The act is out of control.

Ken: (nodding and smiling subtly.) I think we can do what we want, unbound boy. It's such a trivial thing to say that there are no absolutes, though. Self contradiction? Is that phrase absolute? Everything I think I know is untrue, and probably not even useful to the task at hand... I am. I can be reasonably sure of that. Everything else? A madman's dream? Objective reality? Ovaltine? (pause) If you can follow the no-arrow thread that runs between my words and think the non-thought that can be the only true thought, I'll give you a cookie-dough dispensing phallus. (He stands abruptly and gestures towards himself.) Follow me.

Alexi: (follows curiously.)

Ken: (leading him to the coat room.) You remember how silly I used to always be, and how overtly masculine?

Alexi: (nods)

Ken: That person walking around, claiming he was me? I really don't know who he was. He was wearing this flesh, but he wasn't me. He wasn't... I don't know how to put this. That thing I wrote wasn't just a sophomoric metaphor. (somberly) As time goes on, I become more and more convinced that my true self is female.

Alexi: (long pause) You have three.

Ken: (looking confused.) Talk about a non-sequitur.

Alexi: (continuing) You have what you consider your "real self," that happens somehow to be female. Pure, childlike. I won't ask what a "real self" is, or what specifies one self as true and one as false—that isn't a thing you can really pin down with words. ...There's a part of you that tries to overcompensate and smoke-screen the issue of your gender, and then you have this dignified part that seems distinctly male.

(Cut to Agent 139 talking to Johny: ...always three. Even Plato recognized that.)

Ken: (nodding) I knew this. I have names for them, in fact. In order: Meredith, The Jester, and The Analyst. The last one is my most classic defense. Cold, hard, intellectual, and purely mechanical. Like clockwork.

Alexi: Even your facial expression tells it off. It can be pretty distinct. (Puts on sunglasses again.) It's called shape-shifting. I swear Ken, we've both got to appear fucking insane, when compared with the emphasized world-view. Imagine trying to explain this to one of the suits upstairs. ...borderline schizoid, histrionic, delusions of grandeur, all of the common labels. Either way, once a classification has been made, then that's the explanation for our behavior. It destroys the worth of what we have to say so that they can continue to believe in a world that corresponds to their beliefs...feeling secure in that belief. Throw away all classifications except when they're needed to convey a point.

Ken: Exactly. (slightly sarcastic) And hey, being delusional makes life more interesting.

Alexi: (pause) When we go to places like this, the whole night is filled with an expectation; you're waiting for something to happen, and yet it never seems to fully materialize. You dance, talk, wait—and yet that "it" never comes. You chase after it with hope, at the same time resenting that force which thrusts you into that pursuit in the first place. The source of that drive seems to be inside, and so it appears there is no one to blame except yourself, and maybe... (pause) that "it," that unspeakable thing that we chase day and night, tirelessly, is a genuine experience of unfettered self. And it spirals... (trails off)

Ken: (nods slowly, frowning slightly.) We are driven, and the only thing I think that can drive a man so far into things he has no business meddling in is the urge, the need to fill that unquenchable pain and void. It needs to be filled, but nothing does the job.

(B-Roll: People milling about outside the club.)

Alexi: (standing up) Let's meet the crowd. More on this later.

Ken: (after him) You weren't surprised by what I've said, hmm?

Alexi: (over his shoulder) Little surprises me.

———◆———

Aptly enough, the club was barely lit; what light there was came from purple and pink bands of glowing glass tubing running along the floor—that, and rapidly flashing strobes. Columns of cigarette smoke were revealed by the swiveling lights while thin tendrils of it reached languidly down to the floor below.

The two of them danced for about half an hour, amidst a crowd of pale skinned men and women clad in velvet and leather. Finally they took a cigarette break in one of the plush alcoves that lined the room. A blond teenager in a faded Mr. Bungle T-shirt tore past them, merely a blur in their peripheral vision, shrieking "I've got Godot in my pants! I've godot Godot in my pants!"

"There's something else I wanted to talk to you about," Ken said, rolling his eyes at the youngster as he disappeared rapidly into the convulsing crowd.

Alexi was looking intently across the room, desperately trying to catch the face of a man, sitting on a bench across the way. He had been feeling an unearthly tug from that corner of the room all night, and was almost certain it was coming from him. All he could discern at this distance was long hair, pulled back in a ponytail, a baggy white shirt—Victorian, almost what he fancied Byron or Shelley would have worn.

"Hm?" Alexi asked, trying to brush his now unruly and sweaty hair from his face. "Continue."

"There's this hole right here," Ken said, pointing to his chest, "and it needs to be filled." Sympathy? Alexi regarded him closely now.

"Metaphorically speaking. Loneliness?"

"Sort of. Let me put it bluntly—I need a girlfriend. You have Samantha, I don't." His hand waved over his chest for a few moments. "It goes deeper then that, of course, I just don't know how to verbalize..." His face showed smoldering agony for a brief moment. Slowly, his hand dropped to his side, and the look disappeared, replaced by his usual cold and yet good-natured visage. He watched a girl on the dance floor while he spoke. He'd been watching her all night. She had long red hair, eyes that were constantly roving around, taking in her environment, and she also had—Ken imagined—incredibly soft, painted lips. Like every girl he watched, he knew he'd never talk to her, and loathed himself for feeling the way he did. It shouldn't be an issue.

He looked Alexi straight in the eye. "I need a person to listen to me and to listen to, a person to love and be loved by, a person to share myself with. But everywhere I turn I see nothing but emptiness, cheapness, and a little buzz hiding behind a crispy candy shell. Are we all incapable of looking beyond what superficially re-enforces our own insecurities? These people don't want love."

"Ken, you don't go looking for love. Let me tell you something right now: for as long as you look, you'll be rewarded with nothing. When you finally give up, you will find what you're looking for. We always get what we ask for."

"Always a pessimist," Ken put out his cigarette and stood up.

"Maybe I am, but that wasn't a pessimistic statement. It just may take a while," Alexi glanced across the table into the group of people gyrating underneath the countless strobes and black lights. "We look but we don't touch."

Ken wrinkled his brow. "That's crude."

Alexi laughed. "That's not at all what I mean. We don't put our money where our mouths are... We are still trapped in our minds...but not for long... Philosophy is not written by those living life. And yet here I am: a philosopher, analyzing action. Ready for another bout with the dance floor, are we?" he asked, getting up.

———◆———

About twenty minutes later, Alexi was sitting by the bar, gulping down his third glass of water in a row. He suddenly felt a pull to his left side, a sort of indescribable tingling, and before he realized it, he was looking directly at the man he had been staring at earlier. The first thing Alexi noticed was how bright his blue eyes looked, almost luminous. He was sitting with his arms crossed, although it somehow made him no less approachable, looking at the people on the dance floor, his lips curling into a slight smile.

———◆———

The man tilted his head politely. "I'm Aleonis de Gabrael."

"Alexi," he said, putting out his hand. The man shook it with a powerful grip. His hands were slender but masculine. "Have we met before?" he asked, trying to search his memory. Something familiar about this man, both like looking in the mirror and seeing a long lost friend...

"Not as we now are. You look like you want to talk, but I have business to attend to," he said, a tone of finality in his voice. "I'll be talking to you soon."

"I thought I'd met you before," Alexi said, thinking he had put two and two together.

"We talk all the time," the man said, disappearing into the crowd and dismissing any thought Alexi had that this was an acquaintance he had somehow forgotten. "All the time."

A little shaken, Alexi grabbed another glass of water.

⟫•◈•⟪

When it neared eleven, both of them charged into Ken's Maxima, sweaty and grinning wildly.

During the ride home, it turned out that Ken had seen that man, Aleonis De Gabrael, himself. "Yeah, I've seen him before," he said. "I was walking down College Avenue, when I was staying up at Penn State, and I caught sight of this guy. He was about 6´, reddish hair in a ponytail that hung to the small of his back, cruelly beautiful, but that's a minor observation. He was standing in the middle of a group of sloppy drunks, his hand planted on the forehead of one of the sloppers. The drunk was slowly buckling, about halfway to the ground, when he asked, 'Is this the sign of the cross?' To which our auburn-haired friend replied, 'No, 'tis only a marking.' At that, ponytail swerved off to one side of the street, and then ran, noiselessly, across the street. Something about this guy really hit me. The actual feeling was so mixed: dread, joy, empathy, a kind of animal lust that I've never felt before...and more... I thought, he's one of us... So I took off across the street...fast as my rubbery legs could carry me. When I got within tailing range, I hung back and followed. He was walking quickly up behind other guys... They parted, without looking back, without a word, and led him into the middle of this formation. After about thirty seconds of silence, they started talking in an amiable manner. They were approaching a semicircle bench, made of stone, when I got the idea to talk to them. I started to speed up my pace, just as they turned into the bench, military style. They all stood up on the bench at once—all on the same foot—spun, and turned to face me. Now, there was something in their stare that was just...unexplainable. I couldn't talk to them... Something in my head wouldn't give even as I dug my fingernails into my palms. And so I walked on in silence for five miles back to the place I was staying."

When he was finished telling his story, they were back at Alexi's apartment. He hopped out of the car and went around the back.

"I keep telling you—go around the front. I don't want to run you over. And...and be careful. I've got a weird feeling."

"As always," Alexi said, bounding up the hill.

M.H.B.S. transmission: Addendum to Script 3(8):

Leri: (NODS EXCITEDLY) Everything is just a frequency. A waveform.

Bill: Crack whores never have any teeth. It's a conspiracy against us "decent folk."

Anne: (THOUGHTFULLY) Like ripples on water...

Black Osiris: Bagua circles on clamshells...somewhere in Costa Rica butterflies flap their wings and 10,000 babies cry like the eyelash flutter of tinsel ailerons painted crimson red dye, tingling turquoise ergot rye—crash this ailment that has us in a nosedive, Masonic skull'n crossbones conspiracy...

Robert: I have this problem that there are thousands of rooms in my head, but I can't utilize them simultaneously. I have to actually leave the house and climb back in through an outside window if I want to get into another room. And one gets tired of being a shattered mirror, after a while.

Leri: But they're all just different vibrations of the same medium. Once you really learn how to be the neurosurgeon that you are.

Robert: Yes, I am a neurosurgeon.

Leri: By the way, most of what got me into deep waters was thinking about synchronicity and the tendency of people with like frequencies to merge. Union is annihilation.

Robert: (TURNS TO FACE CAMERA WITH LERI, BOTH STARE, UNBLINKING.) Now we are ready for theory.

Black Osiris: Thaaat's right... Learn 'em some a that Brother Octopus styles.

Crazy Fingers: (BRANDISHING KNIFE MENACINGLY) Only when people block out information do they find it boring.

Robert: (STANDING UP AND WRITING ON CHALKBOARD)

Belief model
|
Emotional commitment to stimulus
|
Sense experience.

Leri: The belief model is synthesized through comparison with past experience. You can think of this as "reality-testing." There is verification of the belief model through sense experience, and sense experience through the belief model we keep in our internal hologram. That way, we can keep a certain amount of validity within the system. Emotion seems to act as the binding glue between the two. The whole system I generally refer to as a "world-view." Most people have just a few realities available to them because of an incredibly rigid emphasis on "stable" personality requiring one personality paradigm that correlates to a certain series of sense phenomena; anything outside the range of those potential experiences is rendered impossible through that disbelief.

Anne: That's how Mother Hive Brain Agents work.

Leri: It all goes back to my thinking about holograms and morphogenics. But I want to avoid technical terms for a while. I guess another angle is that we're the fractured pieces of the same mirror. So in one way, you are only experiencing yourself through another at all times, but you're also piecing together what was divided and continues its existence through union. So I guess, like everything else in the universe, it's just an ink blot test, and your decision to make it one thing or another gives it it's existence as such, and gives you the responsibility of the outcome as "creator."

Greg: (LOOKING AT LERI) As I remember you pointing out to me once, on the one hand we are the ones who determine the nature of reality in how we go about reacting to it, there is a Nature external to us that predisposed us to look at the world in a certain way in the first place. Which is action, and which reaction? Are they simultaneous? Are they even separate? This is a problem that quite obviously stems from a linear (Copernican) waking world view which doesn't coincide with our dreamtime non-linear existence.

Leri: Our existence is both not either separately.

Crazy Fingers: Are we talking about states of time or causality? Thinking in terms of "before" and "after" implies thinking in terms of a first cause. I think that the idea of holographic reality helps shed at least some light on the issue.

Rachelle: It's tortoises all the way down, maaaan…

Leri: Quantum Causality. It all ties together inevitably. There is an "implicate enfolded order" which exists in an unmanifested state and is the foundation upon which all manifest reality rests. This is a thought integral not only to modern physics but also to religious and metaphysical thinking for more than 4000 years. Parts are seen to be in immediate connection, in which their dynamic relationships depend in an irreducible way in the state of the whole system… Thus, one is led to a new notion of unbroken wholeness which denies the classical idea of analyzability of the world into separate and independent existing parts. As I'm sure you've realized, Western psychology attempts to break consciousness down into separate pieces and analyze functioning through those dissociated parts. You can't reverse engineer a human from its constituent parts. Similarly you can't reverse engineer a person from the events that have created them. Consciousness is holistic, and emergent.

Rachelle: Mmm. So all of this inevitably leads into the idea of people coming together?

Black Osiris: Now you talkin'!

Leri: People on the same wavelength naturally attract to one another and have a feeling of "being at oneness" with each other, not to mention the urge to create something that they cannot yet put their fingers on.

Black Osiris: I'm on the wavelength bro… People think I'm talking code…

Anne: Aren't you?

Black Osiris: Naw man, I'm jut sittin' atop this wheel of fate, spinnin' it 'round, picking up speed 'n feel, the underground prophet of this new millennium…

RANDOM "YES MAN" IN STARTER JACKET, ADIDAS, LOTS OF GOLD CHAINS, WALKS BEHIND HIM, STANDS WITH ARMS CROSSED.

Random Yes Man: Yeeeeah, thazrigh—Black Osiris pushin' daisies...gyroscope lucifugin' babies.

OTHER ACTORS SHIFT UNCOMFORTABLY

Black Osiris: My digestive tract is solar powered, burning marine layer off ya eyes... Conscious level: preaching freedom of the mind while they pollute this shit... Say see but I say hear here—I just got no flow... Undertow in this bitter ocean bottom... Lips made of rubber, heart elastic, verbals drastic—open your eyes.

Random Yes Man: Word. Open your eyes, cross pollinate.

Robert: Indeed, indeed... This is something I've been doing a lot of thinking about as well. But about holograms, a hologram is something where every piece is an exact representation of the whole and will reconstruct the entire image on any scale. The brain's deep structure, for instance, is holographic. It structures all of our senses holographically from a single energy frequency, and distributes it throughout the system. Now to understand this, you really have to understand how Fourier Transforms work—

Rachelle: (CUTTING ROBERT OFF) I'm pretty sure that we are naturally drawn towards people with complementary frequencies. "I'm on your wavelength, man" isn't just a random phrase.

Anne: I'm looking for a natural, necessary interaction. Things happen because they have to. IT couldn't have been any other way. I wonder about this all the time. Being who I was at the time, would I have done anything in my life differently?

Leri: (GRINNING) I suppose that either you experience it or you don't. I know that, for myself, I have to make myself forget things so that they can occur naturally. Like this conversation we're having now... Every time I do a "ritual," to avoid "lust of result," I have to remove the memory of precisely what I did, distance myself from whatever it was that I did, and get on with living until the results show themselves. Of course, every intentional act is a "ritual" act, so there's something interesting here. If misinterpreted, one might be prone to say that there's something pathological here.

Robert: Our brains are naturally programmed to do it.

Anne: Is that what I've seen called "the psychic censor" in a lot of psychological literature?

Leri: Why, yes it is Anne. The amount of input we could get, for instance, from just sitting in a room full of people is so much that we have to filter out the flood until it's a steady stream of drops. Selective memory. What we filter out is based on our disposition.

Greg: I know you've tripped face before, so you know what it's like when some of this filter gets turned off. Psychotic breaks also seem to result, at least in part, from an underachieving filter. Of course, it is probably a result rather than a cause, and sometimes we intentionally try to turn off those filters so we can break through to the "other side." To see underwater, you have to open your eyes.

Crazy Fingers: Goggles help, too.

Anne: How can I understand all of this in terms of my own life?

Leri: As I know that you are reading this, that all of the symbols are conveying their meanings to you on many different levels, I see that all of this information will be absorbed in a naturally conducive manner.

Anne: So people will automatically and selectively work it into their scripts without necessary, active decision-making on the conscious level?

Leri: So long as it is processed fully, yes.

Crazy Fingers: Knowing something seems only possible in systems defined by their own axioms, like mathematics... If I were to change my belief map, I'd be thinking in other terms, having different experiences, and validating different experiences as "true." Every belief system is valid on its own grounds. It's incredibly limiting to only have one.

Robert: Contradiction isn't a sign of error, it's a sign of "truth," or it comes as close to our experience of it as possible.

Rachelle: What about people who stick stubbornly to just one way of interpreting the world?

1970's STOCK FOOTAGE OF LION EATING A GAZELLE ACCOMPANIED BY UPTEMPO (180+ BPM) POLKA

Rachelle: All colors and all possibilities. The universe chaotically tosses things into and out of form. All we have to do is play.

Black Osiris: (ADJUSTING GAS MASK) Yeaaah... Now I'm show'n the depths of my subconscious ocean... Trombone Dictaphone, this is beyond definition. Propagandizing mushroom clouds, atoms dance seven shrouds...electrons hop orbital paths... Shivashakti these electric clouds… My scalpel come at you from every angle… Even Apophis can't handle this—clicking holocaust in a shutter visual…focus.

Robert: We are neurosurgeons.

Chapter 4, Grid 1

A Visitor

Around every would-be hero arises a tragedy, and out of every tragedy
—a death, the death of that hero, as he chases the ideal that his heart
and eyes have allowed him to taste for but a moment.
                                                    — Aleonis De Gabrael

The warmth of the apartment was a shock to Alexi's system. After rubbing his cold hands together, he let out a grunt and headed to his room.

He collapsed in bed without bothering to turn off the red light. Womb-like. Something immediately caught his notice—an intense feeling, like at the club. It was stronger, and left him slightly nauseous. *No, not the same presence.* A warmth at the base of his skull, a vague uneasiness.

This brought back memories that he couldn't quite place—lying in bed as a child, looking up at the canopy of threads he had woven into an intricate web around him, and many years later going back in the woods behind the apartment, staring out over the water flickering like candle-light, opening up his mind... Back in the room now but the voices were still there with him. Whispering voices all around him, like chattering rats in the walls. He shivered, and tears spontaneously sprang to his eyes. *A billion years, a billion years. We have waited in the spiral, a billion years we have watched...*

He bolted upright in his bed and looked around. Nothing. Then, almost out of nowhere, this peculiar feeling became a distinct warning. Instinctively, he spun to face the wall to his right.

It rippled and bent like elastic. A vaguely human form was trying to force its way through this barrier, and although he couldn't see any eyes, he could feel it regarding him intently. Tenaciously. It had a horrible facsimile of a human face, with long, hollow eye sockets and a stretched jaw.

Alexi fell back in terror, but forced himself to regain his wits. He was having a vision of hundreds of them, all ascending and descending a giant, glowing double helix, phosphorescent DNA staircase. Near the top, he could see seven beings, unusually bright, shimmering in every color of the visible spectrum. The very top was out of his line of sight, blocked by the seven. *Focus.* Eyes, come on now... Unmoving, the form simply stood there, watching.

Alexi got a hold of himself and began chanting, attempting to center himself and banish it. It gave no resistance, and was gone in a matter of minutes. Shaking from a wave of exhaustion and fear, Alexi collapsed onto his futon.

A moment later, he grabbed the phone and dialed Ken's number. After explaining what happened, he continued. "I think I should probably tell you about some other things—this is escalating faster then I thought it would. Philosophical quandaries are one thing..."

Alexi paused. "Gabrael... Now I remember... I suddenly remember having a conversation with him...though maybe it was a dream? A day-dream? I... can't seem to place it. But I remember..." Alexi trailed off, his eyes unfocused, as he went back, and down, into this recalled memory.

He was seated across from this man, sipping casually on wine from a wide-lipped goblet, the sounds of a chittering monkey emanating from an adjacent room.

The man leaned forward suddenly, his intense gaze pulling Alexi in further. "It's time to get straight with you. This peculiar text you have before you is the result of my studies on the culture and mind states of young adults in and around the innocuous suburbs of Philadelphia in the early 21st century. I am helping to promote...divergent genes, you could say. Viral memetics."

Alexi searched through his pockets for his cigarettes but found none. Gabrael continued.

"I enter these places as no anthropologist would—to bring you the flavor and texture, rather than the facts."

"Are we talking about some book you've written, or are we talking about right now?" Alexi asked.

"There's a difference?" Gabrael shrugged. "It is the wave-front crashing of the present that contains the only empirical truth, indeed the only ontological truth, valid *only* in the context it arises in. Each of us have an agenda which shapes our behavior and the world we live in as much as we are shaped by it. Every action and character is metaphorical of another on both smaller and larger scales. In our alchemical marriage in the present, as we interact, we help each other grow... find our traits merging as we serve as each other's teachers, facilitators, friends, and lovers."

Alexi nodded slowly. "I think I follow..."

"Our story is a mythological pantheon. ...Some book I've written, Alexi... this is *your* story. You will send me your first draft from a mental hospital." Alexi's mouth dropped open, his eyes raised in confusion, but Gabrael continued as if he didn't notice.

"...Certainly it would surprise most people that these events occurred. But you and I both know these mysteries occur all the time in the frantic copulations of the seemingly everyday so long as our perceptual focus is internal, gazing into the world of psychic experience and dream, rather than external. Events lose their chronological order... instead we find them transpiring in the order of recalled memories. Our memories are stored as associations and so, as we recall them, we recall associated events which may have occurred either before or after that event. You will continue to experience these events in a dream-like fugue."

Gabrael paused long enough to let this sink in, and pour himself another glass. "Want some?"

Alexi blinked a few times. "N-no. Thanks."

"Very well." Gabrael leaned back. "Perhaps all of this explanation isn't necessary if you understand the *Leitmotiv* in the mythic rather than musical sense. As Joseph Campbell summarizes in his Masks of God IV, speaking of Joyce, Mann, and indeed all the creators of myth... let me see here..." He glanced around the table, quickly producing an earmarked book which he miraculously opened to the right page.

"...throughout, mythological themes echo and appear, re-echo and reappear, in such a way as to suggest that in our lives today, largely unrecognized yet present, the archetypes of mythic revelation are manifest and operative still... Chance occurrences scattered through a lifetime, when viewed reflected in a mythic form, come together and show an order in depth that is the order of man everlasting; and to effect such ideated epiphanies, where to the unassisted eye only disconnected fragments would appear, both Joyce and Mann have employed the rhetorical device of the *Leitmotiv*, the recurrent verbal constellation, to bring together apparently unrelated, widely separated occurrences, persons, settings, and appearances."

He closed the book slowly, again looking up with those luminous blue eyes. "I think that sums it up quite nicely, don't you? While we may speak numerous times about something—let's say fish, for instance—on the one hand we are, of course, talking about fish in different contexts. But, in another sense, we are talking about the same thing: we are, in fact, relating the other circumstances surrounding that "fish" with each other. We are weaving the chaos of our lives into meaningful patterns. There now, do you see?"

Alexi nodded. "I think I changed my mind about the wine, could I have some?"

Gabrael nodded.

As Alexi reached across the table, his hand accidentally bumped into Gabrael's glass, which tumbled end over end, seemingly in slow motion, before crashing to the ground.

He started. *On the phone. I'm on the phone with Ken. None of that happened.*

There was a long pause on both ends.

⎯⎯⎯⎯⎯⎯⎯⎯⎯⎯⎯

"Has anything like this...manifestation...happened to you before?" Ken finally asked.

Manifestation? Oh, the gumby-meets-the-grim-reaper thing that was coming through my wall. Of course. "Well, yes." Alexi rolled over on the bed, and ended up tangling himself in the phone wire.

"We had a seance, a few years ago—" he started.

"We?" Ken asked.

"Yeah, me and a few girls. No one you know, but..." Alexi trailed off for a moment. "Well, I'll skip the long explanation; one of the girls got thrown into a closet. It sounds silly, but it was actually quite amazing to watch. I think I was probably too frightened at the time to fully appreciate it, you know?"

"Get on with the story, man," Ken said.

"Yeah, well. I'm still worked up at what just happened, so bear with me. And let me get another smoke, all right? After what just happened, I more than need one."

"Of course. I'd never get in the way of a man and his free will."

After setting the ash tray within reach of the phone, Alexi continued. "She just floated up about two feet off the ground, and then was thrown, quite violently, into my closet." The first drag made him lightheaded. He ignored it and had another.

"Whoa. Go back a little bit. You're giving me the effect and not the cause."

"Well, we had been planning for a few days on doing some sort of conjuration. I did all of the reading involved, or everything I thought I needed. Various books on ritual and sigil magick, the *Necronomicon* —"

Ken let out a snort that promptly turned into a full laugh.

"I've always been somewhat skeptical about the validity of the book, to say the least," Alexi caught himself breaking into a smile. "And they just had to drag Crowley into it somehow. But you can conduct an effective ritual with an eggplant and a copy of Winnie the Poo. What counts is congruence, regarding your intention and within the structure of the ceremony itself, and...will. To build 'the *Necronomicon*' all it takes is some cursory Sumerian mythology, an understanding of basic Occult science, any moron who's read Agrippa and Crowley and understood even one tenth of the content can construct a moderately convincing—and working—ritual. It is as valid as any medieval grimoire that you will easily find. It contains an initiatory process not unlike what I've found reading about Merkevah mysticism, or Crowley's 30 keys of the Aethyr... I suppose I forgot one of the first lessons one should remember: never call up something you cannot put down. That's applicable in psychology as well as magick."

"I just love how off topic you can get sometimes," Ken muttered.

"I'm even worse than usual, right now. That's understandable, given the recent circumstances..."

"Oh Jesus. Before you go on, I need to tell you what I found tonight on the way home," Ken said abruptly. "For some reason when you said 'circumstance' it reminded me. ...Not like that makes any sense. Not like anything makes any sense. Okay, so get this. I'm just off Egypt Road, right, when I suddenly see something loom up out of the mist. I slam on the brakes, and have to compensate a little to keep from flying off the road or hitting it. I pull up short enough, and there standing in the beams of my headlights, surrounded in mist like a prop from a horror movie, is a wooden cage. I immediately leapt out of my car, and put it in my back seat."

Alexi laughed. Ken was the only person he knew who would stash a wooden cage he'd just found in the middle of the road in his back seat.

"...When I got home, about fifteen minutes ago, I brought it up to my room. Now, understand, this cage is a good four feet tall. It was fun trying to sneak it by my mother's room. Inside it was a figure, wrapped in burlap, hanging from a noose. At first I was really terrified I'd find a once living... I don't know, something in there. Animal, baby, who knows? But it was just newspaper. Written on the top of the cage, in red paint, were the words, 'we give this—a sacrificial flower.' Fucking weird, right?"

"Truly bizarre. And I want to see it soon, but let me finish. We did everything we had to, I guess, because it worked. Well, at least in the most basic sense. One of the girls started mumbling at first. She wasn't making very much sense, pointing at the corner of the room and just...whimpering. So I looked over, half-afraid of what I was going to find. Part of me might have been excited too, I can't deny that some of my motivation had been to, well...just to see if it worked. I was young. At first glance, I didn't see anything. So I looked closer and thought I saw some sort of man-shaped shadow, which didn't appear to be cast by any of us. It was moving about, and we were all moderately still—except for the girl in the corner, of course. All of the electrical lights in the room went out...all that we had were a few candles. It was then that the girl got thrown into the closet, like I told you, and so I started tearing around my bookshelves, trying to find something to dispel it with."

"Well?" Ken prompted.

"I didn't have any of the required components for a full banishing, nor did I have the concentration, so I did the only thing I could do—I bound it."

"You bound it? I'm not into this shit, or haven't been for very long, so could you tell me the specifics?"

"Basically, it was weakened, and locked into my room—"

"The room you have right now?" Ken interrupted.

"No. We moved. For a long time it was so weak I could barely tell that it was there, watching me. But as time wore on, I would wake countless times in the night. Often, I would see something, but I usually just closed my eyes and went back to sleep—disbelief can work wonders, you know. When I brought friends over, many of them would mention that something 'wasn't quite right about it.' Then, whatever it was started showing itself more often..."

"And you think it got out?" Ken asked.

"I really don't know. Impatience is one of my shortcomings. I just wanted something, anything, to happen at that ceremony. You learn from your mistakes, right? Well, the same was true with my binding ceremony. I didn't know what I was doing, hell I don't know what I'm doing... I still don't completely believe half the things I've seen now with my own eyes. So I have reason to believe that it wasn't bound for long. I suppose something caught its interest... I can't help but think that it's linked to Gabrael..."

"Shit," Alexi heard Ken take a long drag on his cigarette—a crackling sound following by an unusually loud, slippery inhalation of breath. "So what you're telling me is that it just popped in to say 'hi' tonight? A kindly hello?"

"Something like that. I can't ascertain any sort of meaning or intention beyond making itself known to me. I don't know how I can express the feeling I have about this whole situation, it's beyond words... My life is becoming a metaphor for itself, and I feel as if there is this created norm—shall I say, a created, wholly fabricated reality. That's the cultural reality that people are pulled into out of necessity, you know, work, pay for the kids, and simply exist. Watch some TV, go to Disneyland, maybe buy a few stuffed dinosaurs, always nod your head with your eyes closed. Somehow, that program hasn't worked on us—we slipped through the cracks—and so long as we can avoid it taking hold of us, and so long as we can trust one another enough to hold a worldview apart from that one, there is no limitation, except those we bring with us. This isn't about us, really. How many others are feeling this, feeling alone, orphaned and without a real family or community, without real life connections... maybe some of them aren't even able to articulate what they're feeling... but if we can find each other, and band together..."

"The only organization that really works is a disorganization," Ken said, as if it were obvious. "Anything done well is done automatically. Like playing an instrument. You practice and you practice in private, play your bad notes. When you get up there and shine... well you've seen Charlie Parker. You think that son of a bitch even knew how to put one foot before the other, as high as he was? But no one could play like Bird back then. And it wasn't the heroin that made him play like that, either."

A glazed look in his eye, Alexi nodded his head. "Fingers of an unseen hand."

⎯⎯◆◆⎯⎯

M.H.B.S. transmission: Addendum to script 2C:

Crazy Fingers: We both accept that although we might design the future for ourselves, we do not "know" it. Expectation forces a limitation.

Greg: Yes, however, ignoring the question because we don't have an answer can prove to be dangerous. Answers exist to spawn more questions. Hey, what connotation does the color deep blue have?

Leri: A dark tunnel, or...a desert, with a light to follow.

Robert: A northernmost star. North is always the direction of the future, of the unknown. It is what we're pushing towards right now.

Crazy Fingers: The path of Gimel leads across that desert; the high priestess, the virgin. Her color (on the king scale) is blue, her number is 3. 139. Of course 139 is our number for the path of the Bacchante, perhaps seeking absolution in the annihilation of opposites? The conflict, and thus the darkness or confusion, is the product of a contradictory energy: daleth, the wife, 4. Which all goes back to a series of experiments I began in March. These are all different vibrations within the same domain, different shades: light blue, dark blue. There are also correlations with the color green, (number 7), that I have yet to investigate, (beyond 3+4.)

Robert: What in God's name are you talking about you deranged fuck?

Leri: Everything is a metaphor.

Anne: I thought everything is a frequency?

Leri: Even frequencies are metaphors.

Anne: Lately I have been having a hard time understanding people when they are speaking to me. I usually just have to nod my head and pretend. I think it's these hypnotic drugs Leri has been feeding me.

Leri: (LOOKING AT ANNE WITH A LECHEROUS SMILE.) Sex can be a functional sacrifice for nearly any number, although the rite is different dependent on the quality of the number.

(CAMERA PANS TO LEFT, FOCUSING ON BLACK OSIRIS AND CRAZY FINGERS.)

Black Osiris: (MUMBLING, LISTENING TO WALKMAN) …People think I'm talkin code… Tryin' to get a mainline to illuminatory consciousness… Revelations had in this. (TURNS OFF WALKMAN, TURNS TO CRAZY FINGERS.) Yo dog, the other night, I'm dialed up on the m'fuckin morphone, sailin' down the Nile…

Crazy Fingers: (ASIDE, ALSO MUMBLED) The Secret Chiefs cooked you up a shot?

Black Osiris: Yeah she got me high waiting on hold, face shifting n' seeing poppyred Tarots pulled… She was all, "sorry there is no Ankh-F-Na-Khonsu at that address… Are you looking for the Priest-Prophet of Infinite Space Haar-Poor-Krat?"

Random Yes Man: Damn... what did you say to the bitch then?

(CAMERA PANS BACK TO CENTER)

Anne: I am a blue wounded little sparrow, wanting to be a spiritually aware, purple sparrow. (CUT TO DISNEY'S SNOW-WHITE SCENE WHERE SHE'S SITTING IN THE FOREST SINGING WITH THE BIRDS.)

Greg: I am the square that desires to be a circle by means of pi.

Leri: I am the superior alien. (CUT OF LERI IN THRONE, WITH HUGE LIGHT COMING FROM BEHIND HIM, DRESSED ALL IN WHITE, ON CLOUD, MASTURBATING SERENELY.)

ALL: Yet we are already neurosurgeons, and may be where we Will.

(They chuckle and then freeze. Hold the freeze as the audience grows uncomfortable and then call curtain.)

CHAPTER 5, GRID 2

IT

The deeper I dig, the more I find what I already knew but somehow forgot.
— Aleonis De Gabrael

Listen: In 1947, Aliens landed and retroactively fabricated a reality and culture known as "Japan" in the world's consciousness. The Americans bombed "Japan," but were unsuccessful in destroying the (evil) Mother Hive Brain.

Mother Hive Brain moved quickly, acting through inconspicuous agents: Japanese beetles. They are the earth's primary inhabitant, according to a recent study of utmost precision, with a ratio of 4:1 (weight) and something like 10,000:1 (overall population.)

So, these (evil) little beetles spread across the earth, destroying rose bushes, and wreaking havoc. (NOTE: It was a group of well-armed Japanese beetles that shot Kennedy, instigated the Vietnam war, and controlled Ronald Reagan via remote control.) At least, this is my current theory.

— Mugwump Jizm, senior editor

IT was an average evening in the decidedly average suburbs outside of Philadelphia. IT was an engineered blandness, a well-constructed picket fence, a Ford Aerostar, an overwhelming urge to purchase bigger and better goods, a primate wonder-land, all mind-controlled by the aliens through remote controlled Japanese beetles. (But we'll get to that in a moment.) IT was a half-empty box of Milk Duds, a litter-stained bus stop, and a boy named Johny. IT was Johny, a blonde haired, rather confused-looking boy in his late teens.

IT was the many-as-one and the one-as-many. IT sat down at the bus stop and waited. IT wore an unspectacular pair of Converse shoes, worn thin along the bottom, faded jeans, and a Mr. Bungle t-shirt.

People, primarily garbed in garish stretch pants, ran to and from the large structure, rarely looking away from their frantic scurrying. Johny put his hands in his pockets and looked down at the dirty sidewalk.

Always the same crew waiting in this particular junction of the concrete jig-saw: this old, crazy lady, a cute girl that took art classes down in the city, and a queer, silent guy that always looked at Johny with an even, piercing gaze. Sometimes Johny felt the urge to speak to him, find out what his deal was, but mostly the tall silent dude just creeped him out.

Johny glanced over the shoulder of tall silent dude nevertheless and started skimming the newspaper he held before him.

Youths Destroy Local Video Store

King of Prussia, Pa – March 5

Shattered glass and chaos greeted the patrons of Rockbuster Video at 2121 Gulph Rd in King of Prussia Pa as two unidentified suspects ran wild through their midst. Local law enforcement officials have been working in conjunction with the FBI on this case. The FBI has yet to make a public statement about the incident but there is reason to believe that this may be tied to other terrorist activities that have been occurring in the greater Philadelphia area. There have been reports of similar activities, ranging from arson to kidnapping, throughout the East Coast in recent months.

Nevertheless, Chief Fergeson, the acting deputy of the King of Prussia Police Department, had the following to say, "...there is no reason to believe that there is any connection between these events and other events which may or may not be happening. Rumors to the contrary are clearly hearsay."

The victims of this most recent attack were all unusually sympathetic with their attackers. "It all happened so quickly," says General Manager Patricia Hillman, 41. "I was just about to charge someone for not rewinding their video, when I hear the sound of an engine revving outside the building. Just then I saw the car come crashing through the window. Videos were flying everywhere. It was like a scene from a movie. I was shocked. And in the midst of it I remember thinking to myself... we are going to have to re-shelve all of those movies..."

Patricia was not alone. On Thursday, this usually quiet video store was disturbed by a reckless driver and his accomplice. Witnesses say a burgundy Dodge Aries crashed through the front of the store two nights ago, around 7:20 p.m. "There were shards of glass and videos everywhere!" says Jeremy Jenkins, 18. "It was so awesome. They just crashed through the front window, got out and returned their videos. I wasn't even gonna charge them the late fee, but the long-haired guy in the robes insisted."

The two suspects rented a video game console, and even paid late fees, after doing thousands of dollars worth of damage Thursday night. Witnesses say that both were red-eyed and smelled strongly of marijuana. "I was scared at first, but then the Jesus guy handed me a joint and told me all was forgiven. He even paid his late fee on Victor Victoria. I found myself liking him somehow, as if he had stepped out of one of the movies here. It was totally cool." The joint was later confiscated by the police as evidence.

According to witnesses, both suspects were polite and respectful, and paid for everything they rented. "It was real odd," says Patricia. "Initially I was angry and terrified. But the short haired guy took me aside and explained it all to me. He said something about how everything everywhere was a myth, and the window of the store had as little to do with the actual reality of a video store as a chess piece has to do with the game of chess."

Later, according to the police reports, the two youths exited the store unopposed. Clarence Jenkins, 45 and a loyal customer to the Upper Merion Rockbuster said, "They was just walkin' out that there door. I stopped and asked the long-hair if he was going to leave the car there... and he laughed at me. Then he tossed the keys to me and told me the car was mine. I didn't understand at first, until I saw the bobbing-head elvis on my dashboard. I guess I was just too shocked to recognize my own car. I still dunno how the bastards got my keys."

Despite his efforts, the pair of suspects exited the establishment and left in an early 90s Nissan Maxima. Any citizens who think they know the location or identities of these individuals should immediately contact the Times-Herald anonymous tipline at 555-INFO.

———◆———

A colony of ants scrambled about his feet, carrying little bits of a discarded, half smashed Twinkie back to their nest. He lit up a cigarette less than a minute before the belching behemoth, otherwise known as a "Septa Bus", lumbered to a halt in front of him. Long ago he discovered that the best way to call this peculiar animal was to light a smoke.

———◆———

The plastic, steel and rubber doors slammed shut. There was a deep, throaty hissing, like a snake—amidst the confusion, Johny looked up the short flight of stairs, black and ribbed for traction. The bus was filled with people, strangely back-lit pig-pen alcoves, the thin and yet cloying smell of fear. The interior of the bus was claustrophobic and cage-like. He nervously glanced at the driver, who seemed thoroughly uninterested.

"Hurry up," he said. His voice was slow and distorted, muffled and far away.

Johny nodded and fumbled for some coins in his pocket. The driver motioned towards a metallic face near the front console. The face chattered and made hungry slurping sounds. He could feel the people behind him growing irritated. Blinking and shaking his head, he crammed the coins into the hungry face. It gobbled noisily, swishing them around in its mouth, thick with corrosive acid—Johny was sure—and swallowed them.

He shuffled toward the back of the bus as it began to move. He caught a snippet of conversation as he passed "...we should start a band called 'isolation booth.' ...yeah, all the musicians can be locked in a padded room and kept on a steady thorazine and morphine drip..."

The bus started with a low rumble, pitching him back two aisles. He found himself half sitting, half lying on a pair of hard orange seats. As he sat up he felt the gooey suction of a piece of recently chewed bubblegum peeling off one of his hands.

A most nautical man, sitting directly across from him, stood up and turned to regard his two companions, muttering something that sounded like a question. The roar of the bus drowned it out. This man was short, contemptuously hunched over. He wore an old navy blue military uniform of some sort. Johny was also surprised to note that he had a worm eaten peg leg. "Call me fish-meal," he muttered, a hazy, squinting eye fixed most peculiarly upon Johny. Then, turning hard to stern to face one of his compatriots, (who happened to be dressed like Santa Claus), he asked "some thyme, Robert?"

"I'm sorry, I don't have a dime," said the slightly red-faced, middle-aged man in the Santa outfit with apparent disinterest. His eyes were unblinking, staring out the enormous tinted windows at Johny's back.

"Avast! I would borrow a portent of thy thyme, O seeker of bio-electric and intrauterine arcana! Your legume kidneys have round afoul, sir! O muddy understanding and loveless heart, you. You… You…" He gesticulated wildly, paused, and then continued. "…And impaired hearing into the bargain! I said I would borrow thy thyme, not thy time nor thy dime, thou prier into vaginal mystery with the tawdry telescope of mechanistic philosophy! I DEMAND YOUR CERVICAL ATTENTION! Avast, I say!"

Santa seemed absolutely baffled, even slightly offended. "You know I wrote some of that. If I don't wind up suing you for plagiarism my publisher surely will." He looked over at Johny, winked, and gave a loud, jovial belly laugh. Time seemed to grind to a halt. Johny prayed silently that this man would stop looking at him with those piercing eyes.

The third, sitting quietly up to this point, ran a finger across his thick, salt and pepper mustache. "Time, thyme, dime. God damnit gentlemen, we have a Movement to start." He pulled out what Johny imagined to be a map of some sort and gestured at it. "See, riiiiight, over here: there is a front which is already engaged, slowly being beaten back by a lack of morale. This is of little concern to me, as it's not a highly tactical point…"

The red-faced man shrugged. "It's of concern to me, mustachioed pompster. I've got a great deal invested in those boys, and apparently Gabrael's intrusion wasn't enough." The man gestured at tall silent guy, who merely nodded very slowly before his head sunk again behind the back of a book.

The Sefer Yetzirah, by Aaryah Copelan? Gibberish. These men were all in league with each other. Some sort of horrible plot. Johny's eyes started roving back and forth rapidly, panic driving a hot blush to his cheeks. "…And please don't kidnap him this time! God knows what he wrote that off as—he probably thought he had been whisked away by spirits or conveyed some deep mystical secret by angels. That's how Islam started, you know. And now look at all the trouble that's caused."

The man with the mustache growled. "There are two rules you've forgotten: never kidnap someone you intend to befriend, and never, ever, conduct a land war in Russia. You know better than to fuck with a Russian..." He did look remarkably like Stalin.

Tall silent guy looked up from behind his book to quietly mutter "Or China."

Johny was utterly baffled—and enthralled. This was even better than MTV.

"What does 'friend' ever mean to you?" Robert asked, also under his breath.

"Comrade," Mr. Mustache had been hunting through his pockets for something, and finally produced a lollipop, which he promptly unwrapped and shoved into his mouth, sucking furiously.

"That's precisely the problem. We're talking about people here, not Ideas. Not regimes. Has Mohammed been sent to make the pickup for the converts?"

Still somehow standing on his one good leg, the "Captain" spun around towards Johny and pointed with a gnarled, accusatory finger. "O God, look down and see this squint-eyed man, blinded by his own rules of office! They are three times enslaved who cage themselves, most deaf of all who cringe and hide behind that tyrant majesty—appointment book, plans for the week, schedule to follow, love to provide!"

Johny stared ahead blankly, hoping that if he ignored him he would go away.

Meanwhile, Stalin continued his conversation with old red-face. "Yes, he has been sent. We have three positions. I am all for forgetting the first minor front like I said...no matter how much that makes your weak heart cringe, Robert." He gestured again at the map, this time with his glistening lollipop.

The naval officer spun back around, and screamed "And I, who will to hunt the whale!" It didn't seem to be directed at anyone in particular, and he was summarily ignored.

"The greatest concern is the 'front' of friendship, which is nothing now but a front, for far too many," red-faced-Robert said, gravely nodding at Stalin. "We have to continually remind ourselves why we do what we do. Let's not systematize the chaos. We'll lose the reality war without even putting up a fight, that way. And if your enemy is war itself, the only way to fight is by changing the world one person at a time."

The "Captain" continued, undaunted. "Avast, ye soulless and unmeta-physical lubber! Think not I yet seek still the white-skinned 'whale'? Tis worse: on horror's scrolls accumulate fresh fears and deeds that call in doubt God's truth. I say that thou hast need of doctoring, for all thy pride hastes thee to sodden ruin. I have need for a mortician, or a fine French maid. Thou thinkst thou knowst but thou knowst not, O wretch!"

Johny could not hold himself back any longer. "What's Mother Hive Brain?"

The cabin seemed to fall silent, except for the far away humming of the diesel engine. Red-face regarded him with bright eyes. "Do you realize that you're stuck in a novel?"

Johny was unaware of this fact.

The bus came to a sudden stop in traffic and Ahab came crashing to the ground. From his position on the floor, free of the accent he had been mangling, Johny thought he heard him say "Our agents will contact you when you're ready." With that, he stood up, handed Johny a single piece of paper, and the three of them got off the bus after it had ground again to a halt. The paper looked somewhat worn, and the type was that of an old typewriter.

The Mother Hive Brain Syndicate
Grand Lodge
Document LVX

"If you're falling…jump!"

These are the basic precepts of this anti-Mother Hive Brain syndicate. Any resemblance, correlation, or synchronicity between this agency and the "Mother Hive Brain" or the subversive agent known as "Robert Anton Wilson" is purely coincidental. We operate within the proper penal and moral codes of EVERY society and frown very much upon all bad things. (If you're a Federal Agent looking into us because of that whole "bomb incident" in '96 all we can is that we were far too busy organizing all of our meth labs to possibly be involved.)

MISSION STATEMENT:

The MHBS is a brotherhood of emancipation. All Agents will do what is in their power to free rather than enslave others, (Agents and otherwise.) To be free, one must seek to be responsible to themselves, and thus aware, of all of their actions. They will strive to bring their subconscious intentions, motivations, and actions into the light of conscious awareness. Always struggle to exceed. Seek the stretch, but do not push it into pain.

We acquire information and supply it to those who want to know. We do not confirm or deny the truth of any of the information which we provide. However, we do hereby state that all of our missions, if followed to completion, will indeed lead to "increased evolution" and the "potential of heightened consciousness frequency" as defined by Agent 777 in a hash-induced stupor.

Agents are responsible for missions as well as recruits, but have access to all information related to those missions upon request.

AGENT RESPONSIBILITIES:

1. Agents will seek to awaken others in all manners, covert or otherwise, using methods such as pranking (reality tunnel manipulation), consensual drug induced psychonaut travel, tantra, etc. We define "awakening" as the state in which one has been cut off from ossified ego and belief models to the extent that they are capable of making choices *now,* for the sake of pleasure and the benefit of the species. The two are not mutually exclusive. The goal seems simple: *think for yourself.* The deeper in you get, the more difficult this "simple" thing becomes.

2. Agents will perform activities on a regular basis that will aid in their own self development: yoga, tai chi, martial arts, art forms, or other ritual practices may be chosen as their primary method, though of course experimentation can only lead to new and necessary experiences for advancement.

3. Agents will keep a record of their work although it may be presented as fiction or be the focus of their art form, (i.e., musical compositions, etc.)

4. Agents that do not supply recruits in a reasonable amount of time or refuse to follow through on any

assignments will be terminated in whatever way we deem necessary.

5. Be a doctor of teeth. As it is written— "My teeth, although not purely scientific, (being primarily apocalyptic), are functional as canines, molars, and small lunar excursion modules. I investigate foreign territories with my teeth, and make them just like me."

Information that the Agency considers "Confidential" must not be conveyed in any form without the consent of the Agency.

QUESTION EVERYTHING.

AGENCY RESPONSIBILITIES:

1. There is NO Agency. Thus, the Agency has no legal liability in relation to the actions of Agents, because, we repeat, *there is no Agency.*

2. The Agency is required to fulfill requests for information from all active Agents. If an Agent desires, for instance, a contact that is learned in Celtic Rune Magic or how to clean an M-16, the Agency will find said contact within a reasonable amount of time. This may be done through whatever methods the Agency deems appropriate, which may include telepathic or synchronistic communications. You must make yourself a fit vessel for these communications, or you may miss or misinterpret them.

3. Agents may feel free to resign at any time, except during a sensitive mission, in which case they may resign at the completion of the mission.

"It is learned by walking."

DO YOU AGREE? (Y/N)

The bus continued on as Johny became lost in thought. Blocked memories from his childhood, now bubbling to the surface…

Johny was seven and standing in his backyard, his plump belly sticking out under a short green shirt. His parents didn't usually let him out, but he often managed to sneak away when dad was at work and mom was drunk.

The sun beat down on his bare back, warm and stinging. It was then, while looking at the rose bushes in his back yard, that IT suddenly came to him. He was intently studying the Japanese beetles scurrying about the roses lining the cracked picket fence, when he realized that they weren't alive at all.

He picked one of them up. The light danced off its iridescent back while its legs continued to move. There was a definite pattern in the tiny shell—what looked like the letters "M" "H" "B." He ripped the thing's antennae out, and it suddenly ceased moving, just like his remote control car when he tore the receiving antennae from its hood. There was no twitching of pain, no attempt to escape. It simply ceased moving and fell limp.

The car had been a present for his fifth birthday. He got a good beating for "spoiling it." Even more so when he told them that the car had said "mother hive brain" in an effeminate, un-car-like voice, which naturally frightened the boy. It frightened his father even more. Especially when Johny cocked his head to the side and repeated over and over in a monotone drone:

motherhivebrainmotherhivebrainmotherhivebrainmotherhivebrain
motherhivebrainmotherhivebrainmotherhivebrainmotherhivebrain

He had been locked in the closet for three weeks, his parents slipping food and water in once a day. Ultimately, he had lived in a closet all of his life.

The bus pulled to a hissing stop in front of a large, glowing sign. The dazzling neon distraction read "Lenny's." Realizing a cultural Mecca when he saw one, Johny stepped off. A number of teenagers were milling around outside the double glass doors. Their skin appeared ashen. It could have been the bright fluorescent lights…or a complete lack of proper nutrition. He wondered if these were also Agents, but then reminded himself that although all MHB agents pose as malnourished teenagers, not all teenagers are MHB agents. Or at least he assumed, seeing as …

His twenty-second attention span was exceeded by this train of thought. Johny looked down at his watch. The harsh reality of time was inevitable; the mechanisms that drove the clock simultaneously ran the world, through association. A chicken was an egg's way of reproducing itself. The messenger of Saturn affixed to his emaciated wrist grimly reported that the time was four-twenty p.m. Batteries dead, he assumed. It couldn't be much past ten.

Irritated subconsciously at the universe's lack of respect for the dead battery in his watch, he walked toward the not-at-all welcoming entrance to the Devon Lenny's. As Johny approached, he realized that the loitering patrons were downright corpse-like: sallow skin, purple bags under their squinty eyes, (or was that makeup?), multiple body piercings, sagging posture. They gave him a peremptory head-nod as he walked by.

By the payphone, there loitered another youth in dreadlocks. He was wearing a pair of oversized denim coveralls that a walrus could have gotten lost in. Out of the corner of his eye, Johny saw what appeared to be eels, writhing stickily in the space between the slimy denim and the man's flesh.

"Hey kid, do you—." he started, lifting his hand up to his mouth in the approved 'smokin-a-joint' position. His voice was deep, and cracked on every consonant.

"Y-yeah," Johnny confessed. "I party…"

"I got the L.B.J., man."

"Y-y-eah?" Johnny inquired. Johnny didn't exactly know what "the L.B.J." was. He was pretty sure he had heard about it being the latest big drug craze since sniffing glue.

"You know it," the eel man said, his eyes widening. "Twenty bucks a dose for the Transcendent Union of All Drugs."

All doubt in Johny's mind vanished once he heard those capital letters. This guy knows his shit, Johny thought. As he handed over the Jackson, our comrade-in-eels opened his mouth and withdrew what looked to be a slender paper cylinder in a garish purple bag. He handed the parcel to Johny.

"God is an eel, kid. Remember that," the eel man said matter-of-factly, sticking his hands in his pockets and rocking back on his heels.

Johny nodded, and walked through the door and on into Lenny's.

Normally, he would have stopped and stood in front of the counter, trying to look as calm and in control as possible. Today, he made no attempt to hide the sweat rolling from his brow or the eagerness in his eyes. He didn't stop until he was in the men's room stall where he then unbuttoned his pants and sat down.

The toilet seat was cool and slightly damp to Johny's naked, nervous buttocks. He fished around in his pants pockets until he had produced the

L.B.J. (or T.U.O.A.D. as it is known to DEA agents who still refer to joints as "marijuana cigarettes"), and a lighter. Expectation and happy anxiety flooded his mind as his fingers opened the bag and removed this preciously engineered chemical marvel. When he got a good look at it, though, he was thoroughly disappointed. To him, it looked like the battered old joint he found in his "crazy" Uncle Eddie's flight jacket from Vietnam.

He and Uncle Edward Crowley sat on the porch one day and smoked it down to the end. Johny, who was only six at the time, had found the next two hours of the day rather confusing. He then ate, and went to sleep for a while. Uncle Eddie was rambling something fierce about "Those damn V.C.! Motherfucking A∴A∴! I'll hunt the bloody Templar to the end of the earth, fucking goat-headed turn coats!" when he ran off into the wilderness of suburbia, never to be seen again. Johny thought he saw him riding around on a lawnmower in the backyard at four in the morning, but when he ran out, shirtless and out of breath, he just found a path of cleanly cut grass, leading off into the forest. He had tried to pursue, but—

He looked down, alarmed at the burning joint in his mouth. One minute he was holding it... He looked at his watch. It was still four-twenty. How the fuck did it get so late? He must have been in here for hours!

"Aw hell!" Johny mused. He took a deep drag...

...held it...

...and exhaled about a thousand years later. The entire bathroom swirled around him at a delirious right angle to the first three dimensions. He took another drag, and another. The cherry on the end of this...this...spaceship...glowed long and true and the smoke went deep and bubbled up through his spinal cord, through his brain, past his mind, and deep into the hollow bowl where his soul would have been.

Presently, half of the joint was gone, and the bathroom swirled on triumphant as the Steely Dan tune on the bathroom speakers took on more depth and texture than one would expect out of a bunch of ex-Bard students. It flowed through delicate sonic channels, it lingered on the quivering petals of flowers, it leapt and it spun and flew and danced and...

...and made honey? Steely Dan was gone. The joint was gone. Johny was inebriated. Okay, so he was fucked. Hard. By giants. And goats and horses and Moses. Something, buzzing furiously now, and crawling... Eyes. Come on now. Johny struggled to open his eyes for a moment before realizing that they were already open, and he was simply ignoring the fact that the bathroom was now entirely overrun by bees. Not just bees, but wasps and hornets and yellow jackets and cicada-killers crawled on the walls, floor ceiling... In short, every surface made available to them by their six legs and two wings.

A surface that included Johnny.

A deep, comforting voice inside Johnny told him, slowly and with unimaginable depth of feeling, to be still and to remain calm. He would not be hurt if he moved as slowly as he could. All over him swarmed the fierce six-legged host. He felt the slight, tickling breeze of their buzzing wings all over his face. Their combined sound was so overpowering, so unsettling...and he wanted so badly to jump and flap his arms and run. To this, the voice replied that his certain death would be prolonged and extremely painful. Johny felt quite sure that he could trust it.

"I don't understand the bees," whispered Johny to no one in particular. His lips felt like Jell-O.

"The bees? You want to know about the bees?!"

That voice was real, now. It had come from the combined sound of the insects buzzing their wings, a symphony of exoskeleton and movement. Crude digital sounds. The voice continued to speak, growing higher in pitch. It took on a piteous, squeaking tone. It grew hips and blonde hair. It got famous, then fat—and no one could rationally explain why. Sally Struthers appeared to Johnny about a half-second before Johnny realized that he was standing up. It took him a few more seconds to realize that he was not covered in insects. The joy he felt at this realization refreshed and invigorated him more than any antibacterial soap. This abundance of pleasant feelings so enraptured him that it took a full ten seconds to realize that he was in a hospital.

Children cried everywhere. He was pretty sure he was in Ethiopia, or some other African country. Flies blanketed starving children, their horrible gaunt bodies baking in the Sahara sun. Sally's lips began to quiver, and not long after, she broke into tortured sobs. Her eye makeup ran and smeared and tainted her briny tears the most delicate electric blue. A moment later, she restrained herself, and went down on her chubby knees.

"The insects, Johny!" she screeched. "All the insects, Johny! So many of them..." Sally Struthers' head melted away, along with her body, Johny's body, the hospital, and quite possibly the rest of the world. Her voice continued: "The insects are more than anything you could ever dream. They hold the essence of everyone who has ever been, and is now no more. You could say, Johny, that they were psychic. You'd be dead wrong, but I cannot put it into terms you would easily understand. They are all separate and identical parts of the same entity. That entity is the Mother Hive Brain. MHB is the spoke that holds the wheel, rolling out of its own center. It determines where that wheel is going. It is the love of a kind experienced by the dancing hydrogen atoms in the very heart of the sun, the blissful infant suckling at its mother's breast. Think about it this way: ants have hive mind. Yes, even ants, which you oft ignore in contrast to the mighty worker bee," her voice was becoming lower now, possibly even male, growing disjointed under the weight of conflicting Brooklyn and Australian accents. "A colony of ants on the move, on the make with the freak-freak from one nest to another exhibits the soft, supple, Kafkaesque underbelly of emergent control of the masses. As gigantic, uncontrollable hordes of ants break camp and head west, traveling en masse in large Conestoga wagons driven by miniature oxen, hauling eggs, larva, pupae and the crown jewels along with their families, other ants of the same colony, patriotic workers that believe in the ideal of the common man are hauling the trove east again just as fast, while still other workers, the intelligence officers, we may assume, who perhaps acknowledge conflicting messages, are running one direction and back again completely empty-handed with brief-cases under their arms. Still elsewhere, some ants plot the assassination of Abraham Lincoln. Just a typical day at the office. Yes. Yet, the ant colony moves. Yes, the ants control it all. Without any visible or detectable decision-making at a higher level, it chooses a new nest site, mysteriously signals workers to begin building, and governs itself, all with an invisible hand, the invisible hand of the One Hive Mind. OHM. An Agent will contact you soon."

And there was nothing more.

Johny came to on the toilet, a throbbing pain deep in his temples. He still clutched the stump of a joint in his hand. It had gone out only about halfway through, so he carefully placed it in the bag. That Nine Inch Nails love song, Closer, was playing over the in-store speakers. This fact was easier to handle than the insects. Did that happen to me?

<hr />

Somewhere, in a galaxy far, far away, Agent 139, Agent 506, and Jesus were all seated in the interior of a cream '91 Nissan Maxima, swiftly on their way to Lenny's.

"Dreams last night...first one starting out in this authoritarian school. I'm involved in a game, looking for someone around all of this computer equipment. Macintosh, midi, overcast. Fades into a post apocalyptic city. I'm sitting at a restaurant, flickering lights overhead. There's an explosion, fragments of rocks, metal everywhere. I scream a name, 'Alexi,' I think, and then...just the pain. Lying in darkness, not sure if I'm alive or dead, wetness running down my face, sticky in my mouth. Darkness, and I'm walking now, a survivor of whatever wiped everything out, a tower belching smoke and fire on the horizon, a Prophet, mighty in Work and Word, looking around this burnt out city...visiting the society that is now nothing except dirt and ash, having pity upon them in their spiritual death, their Wake-less dream...it used to be the city of my dreams, but something destroyed it. Used to be people, real humans, that lived in this terrain... I'm not sure how I knew this...but they'd all long since gone away. Not with a bang, with a whimper. Rows of uniform buildings like teeth. But the explosion just finished it all off. I see myself lying prone at my own feet, whimpering. A broken, bloody shell. Begging for the seconds to disappear, fade into the light beyond darkness in eternity. I share the light of my eyes with his blindness. This is the secret of grace, I realize. I, Jesus, the son, am reborn to myself. I am Osiris and Horus, begotten by the word, living in my former death. But the dream doesn't end here, I keep walking. Factory here and very tense—the machines are still running, sparking. Factory workers are on the periphery—never really quite visible, but eyeing me—and then it goes to this party, lots of combat, lots of fireworks. I build some sort of explosive device for a woman's approval, but Mary gets pissed. It alternated with a Quake style movie that I'm also a part of. The woman is suddenly playing a dimple-chinned Mike Douglas character... She has the best gun—interfaceable with her computer through little sensor boxes and Windows 95. Cars are involved, and my brother, Patrochlos? Greek. Telemachos and Patrochlos? Anyway, he discovers that I've been driving his car—sunnier, newer dreamscape for this, the party flashes back, with alternate suburban house 'scapes. Then I'm back in the Quake movie, a tough, well-armed girl being eaten alive by a monster that has a looped digestive system. I keep thinking I'm going to get out as I watch my skin blister and waste away. Somehow it ate my eyes but I could still see; a filmy membrane sucked them right out of their sockets. This creature produces valium in its digestive system. So here I am, a malnourished warrior girl being slowly dissolved." Jesus looked over to see Agent 139's reaction. "I wish we could be each other for a day."

Agent 506 grunted his agreement from the back seat.

"What were you thinking about?" Jesus asked him a moment later.

"Well, if you really must know. I was thinking... A biologist with a history of tooth decay invents a symbiotic microbe which lives in the human mouth and feeds by cleaning our teeth. It secreted calcium, which is poisonous to it, controlling its growth and preventing it from eating the teeth themselves. So this guy, he wants to spread the thing to the world, but it'd never fly, FDA and human squeamishness and all, so he becomes a party animal. He throws wild parties at the lab, kisses female grad students, whores, babies. He backwashes in sodas left on tables. He bums drags off cigarettes. He grants humanity eternally clean and healthy teeth but dies of a terrible cocktail of STDs."

Another beat. "Wait isn't that kind of what Mother Hive Brain is? I mean... mimetically... An evolutionary virus..." Agent 139 asked.

"Damnit man, can't just one thing... just one thing... be taken purely literally? Just for what it is?" Agent 506 threw his cigarette out the window with a sharp flick of his wrist and then looked dead-ahead.

Jesus guffawed so hard he almost drove into a blue civic in the other lane.

"This conversation is over," Agent 506 said, icily.

——◆——

M.H.B.S. transmission 12Y:

Leri: Once we can program, we ask ourselves: where are we going? Where do we want to be?

Rachelle: It works better than one would imagine. Better than ones imagination could imagine.

Anne: My recent experiences are a testament to that. When we don't know what we want, we wind up willing all sorts of contradictory realities and events into existence. One's life is a direct manifestation of one's being.

Leri: Reverse "life" and "being" and the sentence remains true.

Rachelle: "Spirituality" is right here, right now, not something to be held in contrast to physicality.

Bill: Beware falling objects, subliminal references, et cetera.

Anne: A neurosurgeon must wear a helmet on these premises!

INSERT REALLY BAD FAKE LAUGHTER THAT GOES ON FOR THREE SECONDS LONGER THAN IS COMFORTABLE. SOMEONE ADDS A KNEE SLAP, SOMEONE ELSE WIPES A TEAR.

SLIGHT CHUCKLE. THROAT CLEARING BY ONE OF THE MEN

Robert: (STANDS UP WITH A LOOK OF HORROR. STUMBLES TOWARDS CAMERA.) In the Middle Ages, most people believed tomatoes were poisonous. I tend to agree with them. I'll tell you something else. I worry about you, Leri. He has too many thoughts in his head. Quite frankly, I think that it's the bitter harvest of a seed planted by malignant forces conspiring to appropriate "minds" as receptive as his. Yes. Leri is acting as a conduit for these sinister, other-worldly beings. (TAKE HIT FROM PIPE.) No one of sound mind and body would vomit forth such lengthy, garbled crapola. Through much contemplation and numerous acts of sexual communion with my hand, I have discovered the identity of these nefarious bad guys. The leaders of their horde have assumed a "human" form so "that" their filthy excrement might be more easily massaged into the squishy brains of their victims. And they're all Jews. All of them. The end. Goodnight.

Anne: (IGNORING ROBERT'S OUTBURST) But haven't you been noticing blue a great deal? I see it everywhere.

RACHELLE WINKS

Rachelle: (Singing) Eye sea? Blue sea. You like me see blue sea. Oh the humanity!

Robert: (STAGGERS BACK TO CHAIR, PUTS HEAD IN HANDS AND BREATHES HEAVILY.)

Leri: We live in a world where what we know doesn't correspond to what we experience, and what we experience does not correspond to what we "know" others experience. I think that's part of the reason why the conspiracy theory is so popular right now—because the linear-minded monkey is prone to assume that "the truth is out there" and that someone must be pulling the strings. To be honest, I don't believe this. No person or organization is pulling the strings. That's what MHB is all about; hive mind works without any observable decision-making on any level.

Black Osiris: Time to start spreading us a little pollen, ain' that right boys 'n girls?

Anne: Pollen?

Leri: That's how we look at spreading memes.

Crazy Fingers: Viral marketing.

Anne: Memes?

Black Osiris: Bees help big flowers make little flowers, Anne. A meme's a... thought-language pattern, a contagious one.

Leri: (READING FROM DICTIONARY) "A unit of cultural information, such as a cultural practice or idea, that is transmitted verbally or by repeated action from one mind to another."

Anne: Like... "mother hive brain," or "I am America's favorite soft drink," or "I am the monkey flower, pollinate me," or "I am a neurosurgeon," or...

Black Osiris: So like I was saying about d' bees...

Leri: (CUTTING HIM OFF) They have no vested interest in the spreading of pollen. It's just an accident that flowers capitalize on. It allows them to reproduce.

Black Osiris: Yeah, yeah! Gettin' wu wei with that shit. If I'm really doing things right, I'm doin' them effortless.

Crazy Fingers: I was watching Muhammed Ali box today. He looked almost careless to an untrained eye. But he tore Holyfield apart, or more accurately, pecked at him until he made himself fall apart.

Leri: That's why Bruce Lee was so impressed with him.

Black Osiris: So ya see, If I'm operatin' effortless, dialed up the morphone see, then I'm really spreadin' pollen.

Rachelle: There's a saying in the Hopi tradition... when you're acting effortlessly like that, you're "on the pollen path."

Leri: In fact I don't think our message would make sense without recognizing that. We spread the Word without knowing what it is. We are the fingers of an invisible hand.

Rachelle: (AFTER TAKING A HIT FROM JOINT) Joy above me, joy beneath me, joy behind me, joy above... I'm on the pollen path!

INTERLUDE I

ALEXI'S DREAMS: THE MYTH OF ORPHEUS

Orpheus awoke in a flash of feverish images and stale sweat. Immediately leaping out of bed, he looked around wildly. The image of two women coming to him, naked and glowing blue in the light of the moon, was still carved upon his inner senses. Remembering anything else was a little like trying to catch the elusive snipe. Always a step ahead of you, always the perfect prey because it isn't really there. Desert mirages. He stretched out to his full height and took in his surroundings for the first time this morning.

It wasn't until this moment that he realized that sunlight was streaming in through the dirty glass of his chamber window, casting dazzling globules of light from the foot of the bed to the far end of the room. For a moment he was stricken. Pulling the blinds back fiercely, he stuck his head out the window and looked up towards the sky. Blinding light cascaded down upon him, and he fell back, shielding his eyes. Curiosity overtook him and he looked out once again. A grin grew across his face, and he felt as if he could float, as if he were floating, as the balls of light around him danced in an ordered symphony of descent and ascent amidst the void of endless space.

This giddiness crystallized into a daring idea. He gathered his clothes, and without the meticulous care usually attended to his routine and appearance, he was out the front door of the mansion. A voice, dry and hollow, warned him of his folly, but he paid no heed. He would find no rest, and no peace, until he knew who he was and explored what lay beyond the safety of the walls he had erected. Considering the energy raised within him by his perfect, non-possessive lust for those girls in his dream, he flew down the marble steps that descended into the garden.

For many hours he walked through the winding passages of the labyrinth. Crumbling statues of familiar, forgotten faces peered out at him from recessed alcoves. The tall, pristine walls of pruned bushes grew unkempt and wild, and jasmine was in the air. The statues lay in chunks at his feet, and often he would nearly trip over an arm or a head. There was something free about this chaos, something summer.

As if by some unseen magic the seasons were turning before his eyes. Dead leaves lay in clumps at his feet, and now the smell was of rot and decay rather than jasmine or honeysuckle. The air remained almost uncomfortably warm as the sun beat down from above stronger than ever. It almost seemed malicious to him now, especially as it cast clawed shadows from the skeletal bushes and vines, trapping him in a cage of light.

As he continued on he became certain that the very light that had led him in his ecstatic flight was malicious and bent upon devouring him.

Occasionally pathetic brambles would reach weakly for the sustenance of the sky, but they found none here. This was the desert. Sand covered everything that sat still, and with a little time, it could devour anything. The sun roared, and now more terrified than anything else, Orpheus scurried on, stumbling and tripping, into its heart.

The desert seemed endless. He made his way forward, following a set of footprints that lead him over what seemed like an endless procession of dunes. He shaded his eyes from the baleful lion in the sky.

On the horizon, he saw a black speck. As the speck grew, revealing itself as a lone rider on horseback, the sun veritably fell from the sky. He wondered if he merely saw a mirage, but quickly knew that it could not be. A long, ragged gray cloak whipped behind the rider in the sand whirlwind of his progress, and now Orpheus could see that most of his body was wrapped in faded strips of cloth, perhaps once a bright vermilion but now the color of dry blood. Behind the rider, an army of giant spiders marched, the setting sun reflecting off their shiny black exoskeletons and spindly barbed legs.

The rider pulled up short while his host retreated behind him and formed a perfect circle. His face was still concealed by the shadows of his hood and the brilliant red stain of the sun on the horizon.

There was a long moment of silence as Orpheus stared up at the still form. Out of the corner of his eye, he saw a giant beetle grab the sun and drag it below the line of the horizon.

Slowly, the rider pulled back its hood with a three-fingered, wrapped hand. Its face was ancient, a mass of skin flaps and crisscrossed wrinkles and scars. A series of wires and tubes ran from its neck around the back, disappearing in the now flattened cowl. The eyes that regarded him were coal black, yet full of a severity and strength that Orpheus had never before witnessed. When it spoke it did so slowly and with a deep baritone that sounded like the passage of millions of years upon a rock face.

"The consequences for your actions," it said, "will be most dire and severe."

Orpheus stood resolute, even though he didn't truly understand what his "actions" were.

"There is no return from the lands that you will pass on to," he continued. "There is no redemption from your fate. Your destiny is as precise and exact as the work of my host." He motioned to the mass of arachnids behind him, standing still as stone. This was the voice Orpheus had heard in the garden, the voice that had tried to turn him about. "...or the tick-tock of a clock. Will you hear my council?"

Orpheus nodded slowly, at a loss.

"Turn about. Return to your home. Take not one more step into this dread territory, for you will learn things here that will make it impossible to return."

"You cannot leave through the door you entered," Orpheus said quickly and rhetorically. Speaking tore at the battered lining of his sore throat, and his voice was hoarse and more ragged even than the fell rider's cloak.

"So it is. Know that I am Choronzon, the lurker at the threshold and guide of stray sheep."

"Will you let me pass?" Orpheus asked.

"I will." The specter grinned secretly. "But I will always come behind you, for I am also the whisperer of doubts, Choronzon the coffin-worm, and the end that comes all too quickly."

Orpheus walked on, past Choronzon and his host of spiders. Soon the desert had swallowed them up; he glanced over his shoulder shortly afterwards to find no sign of their passage. One foot after the next, that was the only sign of progress, and the only result was a gradual decent into unconsciousness. Blackness overtook him, and the sands covered his body.

<hr>

In the chaotic dreams or fever-visions that followed, he saw himself as a faceless man nailed to a cross. He had a yawning black void for a head, spiraling forward, backward, every which way into eternity.

Below him, the cross sank into thick, matted hair that revealed itself as the head of a great goat with gravestones for horns. The goat stank of copulation and rape, the most bestial orgies of sperm and blood that our heritage stands upon.

Above him a three-headed dog gnawed hungrily at his extremities, his left arm, his head, his right arm. The past, the present, the future. Above the dog stood a labyrinth that sank back beyond the field of his vision, and atop this labyrinth stood the statue of a man, bearing the perfect Renaissance proportions, with a crown perched atop his head. And as the dream unfolded itself, the statue spoke seeming nonsense: *I are father and son still woman, who Came in by the gates of time protected by ABRAXAS wrongly called Cerberus who carries himself as OsirisHorus the bull of his own father. I am pulled by sun and moon and in them both in the morning— We were designated as a man— We are lined up on the cross of the shub shubby the TUB tubby Niggaruth. We the heart beating in the play of Bacchus and to Bacchus rejoicing, the lionhead returned again by Mrs. devoured, in order to insert the head into its correct place.*

He awoke from the dream to a burning sensation. Eyes slowly opening, he saw the rough surface of asphalt beneath him, black agony against the raw flesh of his face. With a moan, he sat up and took in his surroundings.

A long road stretched in both directions, slick from a recent rainfall. The twisted branches of trees threatened to overtake and consume it. Upon closer inspection, he could see that the road was in ill repair, the yellow traffic lines were faded almost beyond recognition and the edges were cracked and crumbling.

Through the silhouette canopy of trees he could see a violet sky. The smell of earth and rotting leaves reminded him of autumn. Something about this place was familiar, unsettlingly so. Like a memory shoved deep into the far recesses of the mind, it comes back to haunt in dreams and when the walls cave down… Or when you leave them.

Orpheus started walking down the road. Houses jutted out of the mass of trees and brambles, all abandoned, a mess of rotting boards, shattered windows and scuttling rats. The silence that hung over this place was liquid and contagious, a foul liquor that clung to everything it touched. Still he walked on.

To his left, he could see the trees thinning out into a wide field. Turning to it, he was relieved to feel the moist soil underfoot. Then, further off in the field, he saw a twisted metal form, bright yellow in some places and rust red in others.

The bus stood like a fossilized dinosaur in a museum. The windows were cracked and broken, the paint worn thin, the tires slashed and empty; all of this was reflected in the wide field that this artifact had finally come to rest in, a sea of dead reeds, the color of bleached bone, swaying in the crisp autumn wind.

He slowly trudged closer to the vehicle, cautiously and full of trepidation, as one might approach a corpse or other hidden horror. From this distance he saw the number 13, faded but still clearly apparent, on its side. There came a glimmer of recognition, but what it foretold he couldn't tell. That number seemed to grow larger and larger, or he was being drawn into it, and he stopped, dropping down to his knees, his mouth slack. The reeds continued to ripple, and in the distance three black birds circled around lazily. Even when the wind began to howl and the sky blackened there came no reaction from Orpheus. Eyes dead, mouth open, he sat in the field as it began to rain.

Huge sheets of it poured over him as he stared at that number, and he could hear sounds. Young voices forming a chorus in their disharmony. What to adults sounds like children playing to the children sounds ominous and terrifying. Some are predators and others are prey.

He could feel the lunch box held tight to his chest, hiding his unease at the paunch underneath. Tension balled there. Staring up the mud-encrusted stairs of the bus, past his grey, playdough hand clutching the box, sat a hunched form.

"Come on kid." The words held an air of exasperation. Here it was, this bus, this very bus that carted him off to Fairview elementary. Anxiety embodied. The slate smell of flatulence and Freetos. There was a blood red grin carved deep into the stern, slack flesh of the driver's face.

"Don't just stand there, get on the bus. You have to get on the bus. It's the law." The voice seemed to issue from the gash across his face, but there was no movement.

The door opened mournfully. The storm screamed all around him, purple and furious. He walked inside, clutching a lunch box that wasn't there.

As he approached the seat, trying to smile but feeling it sit awkwardly on his face, he was struck along his lower legs and ankles, and he immediately tasted blood when his head hit the floor. Laughter echoed all around him.

Peering up over the edge of the torn vinyl seat cover, he saw two cold brown eyes leering down at him. The eyes, he knew, belonged to Dave, a predator. His nose stung as the syrupy red humiliation began trickling down his face and pooling on the floor. The side of the seat was a plateau face, the top was barely visible, and above them, those leering eyes at the top, calculating its prey's next move.

"What's wrong, legs don't work?" he heard from the top of that cliff face. It echoed for minutes in his head. He curled into a ball and pretended he wasn't there, which brought on another raucous peal of laughter. His breath leapt from his lungs when Dave's foot kicked him in the side. Hard. "Speak to me when I talk to you." He'd probably heard that the morning before from his father, wielding a belt and smelling like liquor, Orpheus thought.

Orpheus looked up and saw a face both twisted and horrible. The eyes were like a gecko's, looking constantly in all directions, always searching hungrily for prey. It had a short muzzle, like a cat, but its tongue was long and lolled out, hanging limply over razor sharp teeth. Thick white drool ran in long strands and rivulets to the floor as it spoke.

"What's wrong, faggot?" it asked, its foul breath making him cough, one of its eyes staring in his direction. A ragged claw came down softly beside him, a thinly veiled threat.

All around him came a falsetto response, "Yeah faggot? Faggot?"

"You tripped me," Orpheus said, trying to hide the shaking in his voice. He started to get to his feet and wipe the dirt from his clothing. "Asshole."

"What did you say?" Dave asked, apparently quite insulted. Orpheus could see the heads of other beings peer over the edges of the seats at him, each bestial and alien in a different otherworldly fashion, each making a clicking, insect-like sound of anticipation for spilled blood and the humiliation of the weak, small and unfit. The tempo was slowly increasing. He felt Dave grab for him, but he was quicker. Rolling to the side, he used his momentum to spring to his feet and make a mad dash for Her seat.

The clicking grew to a painful volume; Dave hissed in pursuit. He was running with all of his might towards those two blue eyes. Dave's breath blared like terrible trumpet blasts behind him.

She was too frightened to come to his aid, but he knew from experience that for some reason they would stop if he could get to Her.

The bus fell silent. He could see Her smiling at him, then nothing. Orpheus found himself sitting in the back of an abandoned bus, pulled up into a fetal position, choked with tears, as a storm outside quickly blew past.

"Who am I?" he asked aloud. The storm rumbled in the distance, almost in answer.

Chapter 6, Grid i

The Lost Night

I will not serve that in which I no longer believe… Whether it call itself my home, my fatherland or my church; and I will try to express myself in some mode of life or as freely as I can and as wholly as I can, using for my defense the only arms I allow myself to use: silence, exile, and cunning.

— James Joyce

"What do you want?" she asks aloud. In other words, "Who do you want me to be?" And she compromises. It wasn't what he was asking, but it was what she heard, what she knew. It was, then, what he was asking.

Alexi hung up the phone tersely. He had been talking to Samantha—plans were lined up for the night, though his enthusiasm had waned. *Frustration was blinding him, and although he could rationalize the source, he realized that all perception was fragmentary, all emotional responses biased, over-acted gesticulations in a mirror. She never listens, his mind was thinking—but part of him stood back, watched it run through these frenzied patterns. Like a dog jumping through hoops, the mind is apt to run through pre-programmed patterns following an emotional trigger. Trigger, response, trigger, response. Like clockwork. He was setting himself up for a big fall. But why, why? I want this so badly why can't I get inside the pattern and make it stop…?*

Stop dictating to yourself! STOP STOP STOP! He threw a crumpled piece of paper into the trash can across the room, and sat down to prepare himself for the long night ahead. He proceeded to scribe runes on his arm, copying from a notebook held open with his other hand.

There was a confident knock at the door, which meant that it was probably Ken.

"Come," he said, preoccupied with the scribbled symbols.

"Hey man. Is Jason showing soon?" Ken asked.

"He should be. I'm figuring we'll talk for a few hours, get momentum going, then we'll go for a walk in the woods." He looked up from his book and faced Ken, attempting to conjure any remaining luminosity in his eyes, but his voice remained hollow. "Do you remember the feeling you got last time you were there?"

"Well, yes. Kind of a calling from somewhere deeper in...may I?" Ken asked, pointing towards Alexi's computer. His bulletin board system was now a meeting place for over three hundred callers in the area.

"Sure. I also think that we should introduce Jason to the inner circle, if you know what I mean."

"Perfectly," Ken said, clicking away at the computer, cigarette in one hand.

Alexi turned his attention back to his arm while Ken grumbled about the inefficiency of PCs in comparison to Macintosh computers. Slowly Alexi's methodical drawing deteriorated into a dragging scrawl, his face hard and blank.

Ken stopped typing and turned around in his chair, noting that his friend's facial expression had changed dramatically. He spoke slowly, as if he was searching for the proper words. "Now, you and I both know that sometimes one gets an instinctive urge to do something..." Alexi nodded, stroking his goatee absentmindedly. "This was the case for me last night... I did my yoga and vessel care, and started drawing runes upon myself—and I'm not much into skin art... I lit a candle and began my preliminaries... Relaxation, shutting off one sensory input after another, and so on. I let the patterns on the insides of my eyelids kind of lull me... And I felt very, very light, as if I was hovering above my body... I don't remember falling asleep, but I assume that was what happened eventually... I just slipped into dreaming without being asleep, and awareness never left... I awoke this morning to a sound, like dripping water... And when I looked around, the candle was still burning. It left a big mess. Beside my bed was a poem, not written in my hand though I can't imagine who else would have written it... ...*in the temple of the temple of the temple of the holy...* I'll have to show it to you later. Any further description would simply not work at this point, but what I experienced was so beautiful... It truly felt as if a lifetime passed between closing my eyes last night and opening them this morning, wondering why the hell the ceiling was leaking until I saw the flame of the candle, and only upon seeing the flame did the memories of this whole other...existence? Hit me... I woke up a completely different person. I must also say that I was really bummed in a vague, otherworldly kind of way when I started... Well, I'm still reeling with the implications... I'm not even sure that it was what they call 'astral travel,' but it was something," Ken said, staring at the wall now as if back in the trance.

"We'll talk about this in more detail later, I have a feeling that they're going to be here soon, so I'm going to head out for greetings," Alexi said, pulling on his trench coat and blowing on his long painted nails.

The moment he opened the door, he saw two other teenagers fast approaching on the walkway. The boy was slightly stockier and shorter than he. A green, slightly ragged trench coat, glittering with Russian military pins was pulled up at the collar. His face was somehow familiar, although he'd never seen it before. Behind him, a girl struggled to keep up. It seemed that she wanted to remain nondescript, wearing baggy, poorly matched clothes, though her pale skin, bright red hair and blue eyes remained striking. Through the cloud of their breath, Alexi noticed tiny crystals of ice falling from the sky—neither hail nor snow.

"Jason, I presume. Well met. You look like a crazed communist, if I do say so myself."

Jason broke into a goofy smile, his dark brown hair, curling over his left eye.

"Yes, it is nice to finally meet you. Call me Chairman Mao." Almost as an afterthought, he added, "Oh, this is Renee," motioning towards the redhead beside him. She nodded enthusiastically. Alexi would have considered it a cheerful motion, if not for the slightly crazed look in her eyes.

———◆———

They headed toward Samantha's house, just a few miles down the road. The cabin of the car was plush and comfortable, if slightly dirty. Ashes clung to everything, and the windows were yellowed with nicotine. There was a distinctive scent hanging in the air, neither pleasant nor unpleasant, that triggered an unusual nostalgia. Outside, the last rays of the sun were falling out of the sky, as the now hard-driving sleet heralded the first days of winter.

Ken turned on the radio as they tore out of the driveway.

"...in other news, Barbara Dempsey, a waitress at the Devon Lenny's was brutally stabbed to death today. The murderer is still at large. And now, a word from our sponsor..."

He absently flicked the seek button. There was a drizzle of static, then a calm voice began speaking, "The essences and entities of our ancestors, the spiritual fossil fuels, have been either evaporated or obstructed by the machinations of mankind. Radio waves, cellular signals, and even global satellite positionings (as some form of invisible yet detectable, technologically concocted ley lines) have all but chased away the supernal magics of A.T.W.A. except in those places where poverty is so damaging to the populous and industry so scarce that the ancient spirits are allowed to congregate." *Essences of our ancestors? Spiritual fossil fuels?* Alexi's mind reeled for a second. At first blush this was nonsense, but something in it resonated with him. He thought of the shadow he had seen in his room, of the figures on the helix. *Why were these beings trying to contact him?*

"We find the most potent emissions of natural magic emanating from those lands which retain some vestige of virginity: Haiti, Afrika, Tibet, the Amazon, Samoa, Easter Island, The Yukon, Siberia, and certainly the list continues. But these lands are at risk as the wrecking ball of capitalism swings against the infrastructure of direct communion with the fertile earth. It is not A.T.W.A. hirself who shall cast vengeance upon the likes of man and his tyrannies, but instead the ancestral monoliths whose anger has been awakened from digging too deep in the soil and diving too deep into the oceans: the Elder Gods, the Loa, the heterogeneous entities of Diasporic consciousness, the Djinn, and the countless and untranslatable spirits whose names mankind once recalled and whose eminence mankind once respected. It is unfortunate that these gorgons of ages past are growing intolerant of man. They cannot be appeased or placated with anything other than voluntary human sacrifice. They require the suffering of your children. They will have your blood as you have drained theirs without any reverence whatsoever…"

Glancing over at Alexi with a smirk, Ken flicked the dial again. A deep, throaty voice burst from the car speakers, "God Warned Us This Day Would Come!" it proclaimed.

"This should be fabulous," Alexi said, turning up the volume dial.

"The Bible predicted that an end-times Beast 666 Universal Human Control System would be used to control and enslave humanity: 'That no man might buy or sell, save he that had the mark, or the name of the beast, or the number of his name' (Revelation 13:17). Thus, we knew it was coming. Now, finally, it's here, just as was prophesied!" The voice continued, building to a fever pitch, a crescendo of bible-thumping-good times which spoke volumes of family picnics and Roman Catholic Crusades, holier-than-thou ideologies and hot dogs.

"What the fuck kind of radio stations are these?" Jason asked from the back.

"The last one was college radio," Alexi said over his shoulder.

"Project L.U.C.I.D. is being implemented at the direction of the Inner-Circleof the MotherHiveBrain." It said these last words unusually fast. Ken and Alexi both shot each other questioning glances, and then shrugged simultaneously. "Using the global Internet, the system has been developed and is being installed by international corporations, working jointly with United Nations consultants and U.S. intelligence and laws enforcement personnel. This project has been underway for nearly a decade and will hit full scale in the year 2003. Project L.U.C.I.D. is Satan's diabolical, end-times system of total and absolute human control. It will put mankind under direct subjection to the Antichrist and his jack-booted, Gestapo-thug, official-clothing-wearing-product-buying-sex-crazed-storm-troopers! Every government on Earth will willingly coop-erate to oppress its citizens. There will be nowhere to hide!"

"This guy just might be onto something," Jason said, only half jok-ingly. Alexi was forced to half agree.

———◆———

There were three buildings on the property—the house, where Samantha's family lived, the carriage house, which would later be used for many of the get-togethers, and a crumbling old barn behind it. A path led from the house up to a wide field on a hill. Beyond the field was a forest, choked with brambles that clawed trees with bony hands.

You could feel the age in everything. It showed itself in how all the pieces fit together, in how the wood smelled, in every creaking board and rattling window. Each building retained an imprint of the people who made them. The entire property had this quality, a haunted ache that whispered the distant loss of a forgotten past through the trees Alexi was reminded momentarily of his dreams the night before, but then realized he couldn't recall specifically what the contents of the dream had been. He remembered the girls, of course...something about a bus? And reptiles?

It was the forest that caught Jason's attention immediately. "What's over there? It feels odd."

Ken looked at Alexi knowingly. "Yeah, we've noticed the same thing."

The group headed into the main house, after appeasing the giant mas-tiffs pacing outside with pats. (Renee made a point to steer clear of the massive dogs, commenting to no one in particular, "I love cats, but large dogs bother me...")

The kitchen was in its perpetual a state of organized chaos; a seemingly endless procession of heavy-set boys would scamper through the swinging door at the back of the room, framed by old stone walls, or the mastiff's would lumber about, yelping and making a commotion. Dawn, Samantha's mother, was often in the kitchen; both organizing the constant disarray and taunting it to new levels of entropy; cursing and thriving off the disarray.

Alexi introduced the group to Samantha, who gave a nod. She gazed wide-eyed at each in turn, with cat-like ambivalence and aloof silence. She was standing with most of her weight on her left foot, thrust far behind. Her usual defensive posture.

Dawn entered with one of the dogs right at her heels, and immediately engaged Alexi in conversation.

"You're running a little ragged," she said bluntly. Her observations were almost always right on target.

He sat down on a stool, and motioned for the rest of the group to follow Samantha downstairs. "I'll come down soon," he said, when Ken seemed hesitant. Satisfied with that, he exited.

Alexi turned back towards Dawn. His posture was more slumped now, his head hanging heavily toward the ground. Her inquisitive eyes searched his. The knowledge that she could generally see through all of his histrionics and postures didn't make him uncomfortable, in fact, it put him at ease. At the same time, it made him more likely to posture in an even more absurd manner then he would normally. He knew she enjoyed a good act.

"I'm just a little...anxious. That's all. I often get stressed out trying to keep the energy up. People don't realize the levels of pressure I put myself through to make everything run smoothly, to mediate between the people, not to mention the amount of time involved in preparation."

She nodded, satisfied, and gave him a maternal pat. "I figured as much. Well, I noticed that you've been toying around with our piano some—it's nice, it hasn't seen much playing in such a long time. Why don't you go play and relax?"

"I'm not much good," Alexi said, trying not to sound dejected. Whenever he caught himself using that tone of voice, it usually made him feel guilty, which made him all the more irritated. *I'm not much good,* he mocked himself in his head. *You sound like a bratty four-year old.*

"The technique might be rough, but the ideas in your head manage to get out one way or another. Really, you're too stressed. Play a bit. The guys might get a little annoyed at the delay, but they'll have to deal with it."

He nodded, absently twirling his finger around a lock of hair.

"You really are out of it. Go in there and play some."

——◆◆——

The group came up from the basement to listen, and gave a round of applause when he was finished. The sound of the last note died slowly in the large wood room, reverberating for what seemed like minutes after the key was struck.

Samantha walked over to his side and sat down, looking into his eyes silently. He stared back; it seemed he remembered them from somewhere, long ago—or somewhere, far ahead. Just then, Andy appeared from the kitchen, waving towards the congregation around the piano.

Alexi sighed and nodded, "I suppose we should begin."

——◆◆——

After a few mesmerizing hours of talking in flickering firelight, Alexi stood up quite suddenly. The fire had died low, occasionally letting out a sizzling crackle. The air had the oppressive but pleasant scent of roasting wood and incense. The wind wailed outside, stronger than ever.

"It's time for a walk. For most of us…" he said, pointing towards Samantha, who had fallen asleep on the sofa. Once she was asleep, little less than an earthquake could wake her.

"Well, first… Jason, come to the car with Alexi and I. There's something we'd both like you to experience," Ken said. He was sitting in a corner, half-shrouded in the smoky shadows.

——◆◆——

The three headed out the back door into the parking lot and into the Maxima, now frosted in a half inch of snow and sleet.

"In," Ken said to Jason, gruffly.

Jason sat in the back seat, with Alexi beside him and Ken in the front.

"Close your eyes and calm yourself," Alexi said to him. On cue, Nine Inch Nails began blaring on the stereo, thanks to Ken.

Both of them lay their hands on Jason's head and concentrated. Time passed. Except for an occasional muscle twitch on Jason's part, everything was still. When he started moving about erratically, Alexi backed off.

"Wow," Jason said, wide-eyed. "I…"

"We'll talk about it later," Alexi said, chuckling. He lit up a cigarette and handed it to Jason.

"No," he said quietly. "Renee doesn't let me smoke. Well, that's not quite true. I'm not smoking for her sake, though. The asthma and—"

Alexi shrugged and handed it to Ken, who was still glaring at Jason.

"Doesn't let you…?" he started.

"Let it drop for now," Alexi said, trying not to laugh at Ken's slight overreaction. "We can talk about free will later."

Ken smirked in return, nodding. "Polluting the masses! Corrupting the children!" he shouted, of course referring to himself.

Jason looked through the windows of the car longingly.

"We do need to head out there soon—preferably without Renee. I don't think she's really ready for what you guys have to offer. What did you do to me? I feel different. Like…" he stammered for a moment, and then let out a reptilian shriek. "Like that."

Ken shot him a questioning glance. He shrugged nonchalantly. "Let me get my Russian trench coat out of your trunk. And my goggles."

"Just in case you need to see under water, eh?" Alexi said, smirking.

Jason nodded, smiling. "You never know."

"You're a weird one," Ken said, eyeing Jason solemnly. His comment wasn't deprecating in any way.

⪦⬥⪧

Alexi pitched more wood on the fire. The red embers hissed and popped hungrily. After putting on his jacket, he motioned for the group to follow him.

Renee looked up from the book that she was glancing through.

"Hey, Jason. Where are we going?" she asked.

"I dunno." He looked uncomfortable. "Could I talk to you in the other room for a moment, please?"

Alexi shot him a questioning glance, but he led Renee into the other room without a word. Ken merely tugged on his boot, ignoring the whole situation.

"I'd like to go too, y'know?" Andy said. "I've felt pretty left out tonight. All of this mystical…stuff." He ran his thick fingers through his hair quickly, nervously.

Alexi nodded, "You can come, although I'm not promising anything."

Jason returned to the room. Renee followed, looking no one in the eye. She flung herself into a chair without saying a word.

"She's not coming," Jason said, matter-of-factly.

"I noticed," Ken said under his breath, opening the door and heading into the storm.

Renee looked around the room, her gaze defiantly finishing with Jason. Unflinchingly, she said "Yes. I am."

"I told you…they said the place we're going is somewhere down a long slope—" Jason started.

She stood up and put on her jacket slowly, deliberately, without looking at him.

Alexi looked over at Jason as he lit his cigarette. "I think that settles it. There's no reason to leave anyone out. When you start that, you begin resentment, and who knows what can come out of that negativity in the end. Everyone determines their own level of involvement."

Jason's shoulders slumped. His facade of control had abruptly collapsed. Merely nodding, he headed out silently behind Ken.

—————◆—————

The five of them headed swiftly up the hill behind the Carriage house to the field. The grass was long dead, withered brown husks clinging to the frozen earth. The path, merely a gravel and mud indentation, wound up a slight hill, flanked on both sides by ominous, hunched trees. Alexi stopped abruptly as the path slowly gave way to a large field, turning towards Jason in a quick, fluid movement.

"Where would you have us go?" he asked, barely audible over the wind and creaking of the trees that encircled them.

"I figured you were taking us somewhere…"

Alexi nodded, "I may be. But I'm asking you a question. Feel it out."

Jason closed his eyes for a few long moments. Andy looked impatient, and stuffed his cold hands into his jacket. Time passed slowly as the wind beat mercilessly, yet Alexi stood motionless, watching Jason's every movement. Andy let out a loud sigh.

A tree branch nearby cracked and split from the tree, falling to the ground. Jason opened his eyes and pointed to the far corner.

"I'd say…go in that direction. It feels, I don't know. The air is thicker there. If there's a path, follow it down and to the left."

Alexi smiled, looking over at Ken.

"Interesting," Ken said, his lips so numb from the cold that the words felt funny as they left them. He was doing his damnedest to light a cigarette in the howling wind and sleet.

"I think you're right, J.B. Lead the way," Alexi said. Then, still staring intently at him, he mouthed "panther," almost as if he was saying it to himself. Nodding, he continued on.

"J.B.?" Jason asked, now behind him.

Still nodding, Alexi said "Jason Benson" over his shoulder, although he wasn't sure if it got lost in the chaos around him.

He winced. "Just call me Jason, ok?"

As they slowly made their way across the field in the miserable conditions, Jason tapped Alexi on the shoulder.

"You mentioned a panther? What did you mean?"

"I was just talking to myself."

Jason had a far-away look on his face—his mind was elsewhere, although only for a moment. When he came out of his trance, his eyes were a little more lively, his movements possibly more refined.

"Right...we'll work on focusing that more sometime. It's inside all of us—I mean, an animal...what's the word I'm looking for? Archetype, I suppose. There's a saying that 'you don't choose the animal, it chooses you.' You'll just know." He paused. "The totem is an anachronism from a distant time, and although it can bring you closer to your center, it can also further fragment your ego. It can be an ally, or a beast. If the animal gets out of control—look out." Alexi smiled, all of his teeth glinting from the otherworldly bluish glow reflected off the snow.

"My totem is the bear, if you haven't already figured it out," Ken added, flatly. "Right now, my focus is on another issue. It gets in the way of totem work. I keep having these dreams...this dream, actually. It's re-occurring...bizarre. It's simultaneously surreal and more real then my waking state."

"I like cats," Renee piped in. Alexi quickly nodded at her. No one else seemed to notice.

Ken gazed up at the stars in the sky, his vision of the field completely dropping away as the night swallowed him. "I don't know if I can really say it in words..." His voice had a monotone quality to it, as if he was talking to himself. "I think Alexi knows. Don't ask me how, he just... Well, I don't want to puff up his ego any more..."

Alexi flashed a warm smile.

"For a long time, I was this social thing," he started. "I like to refer to him as the Jester, because he's all false mirth and empty promises. And if this group doesn't work out, that's what's going to happen to me again. All overcompensation. I lived many years of my life inside of that shell, and I didn't even see it. But I started thinking about my childhood. I am, by nature, female." His voice grew soft at this proclamation, as it always did. "It's really confusing, because I am not attracted to males, so if I was to become female, I would be lesbian." He sighed and then continued. Alexi caught something in that sigh, as if it was slightly forced. Was the last statement untrue? Or was it something else? "That's not even quite right, the female part of me is almost like another person inside me, striving to get out. In that way, it's like having your own girlfriend, although it's far from narcissism. That's Alexi's department, right man? Well, anyway, my father's death intensified this problem, although it didn't create it. So, to the dream bit: I've had this re-occurring dream that I am a female named Meredith, in the future. A friend of mine, a friend much like Alexi in many ways, actually, convinces me to get the procedure done. What he doesn't tell me is that the procedure involves the incursion of machinery into my body and mind. Shining metal bits, tubes, wires—I am turned into a cyborg. One of the implants forces me to be in complete servitude to this man who is my master, a different guy than the one who talked me into it in the first place... The rest of the dream involves me doing menial and sexual favors for this guy, with absolutely no control."

"Sounds like marriage," Renee said, quietly.

Jason raised his eyebrows. "Interesting," was all he had to say.

"I'm Orpheus in my dreams," Alexi said, half muttering. No one asked, so he didn't explain.

By now, the lights from the carriage house were completely out of sight, blocked by the lifeless trees. The Spartan wind had already numbed all of their faces and chilled their fingers.

Alexi sped up and went to the front of the group, his eyes tearing slightly from the frigid air. Ken was lost in thought...

———◆———

In the darkest and quietest of forests, I sit and wait for the fates. But they never come. I sit and wait for salvation. It too never comes. I stare up through the canopy of the trees, stare up at the bright stars, untarnished by the lights of civilization. A few deer graze nearby, next to a clear brook running through tangled vegetation.

She misses blue flowers braided into blond hair by less-than-cunning fingers between the buildings they had momentarily escaped. I am dancing in the grass in the golden, golden sun where they were beautiful singing voices they embraced and she knew she knew she was going away, but she held on anyway, she held on selfishly to the sweet air and song and voice that would be lost forever soon.

> *beautiful beautiful beautiful girls*
> *danced under the moon and sang*
> *to each other*
> *played pretending played pretending all the while*
> *that they weren't in love*
> *that they weren't complete*
> *the outsiders Other jealous and intrigued...*

I miss blue. I concentrate inward and begin to shine with a soft glow. Reality bends, warps, twists away. The dry fragrant air becomes damp and musty. The forest floor dissolves to yield to smooth concrete, and the lights hurt my eyes. There she sits, just waking up from perhaps a perfect world, back to the harsh reality of the ticking clock, and the Jester slowly making his way down the corridor. His mind is blank, as it usually is, although the thought of control excites him, perversely. He tries for a second to hold back a smile, but his lips part and he is grinning like a fool, his heavy boots echoing on the hard floor. She knows he is getting closer, his footsteps growing nearer, sharper, a businesslike, crisp sound. His heavy, slow breathing is barely audible, yet it is all she can hear aside from her own tortured sobs.

"Over there," Alexi said, brushing some of his hair from his eyes. Ken was knocked out of his reverie. He pointed to a path about fifty meters off that led into the forest, on a steep downward incline. The path was clear of debris, although the thorns and brambles had grown long. They now fell in tangled, spiny clumps across the way ahead.

Ken lengthened his strides to catch up with Alexi. "Why am I stuck with an exterior that is so out of phase with who I am?"

"A rhetorical question, I assume?" He didn't slow his rapid pace.

"Yes, but it is the source of my anger—a lot of it. There's really little I can do to rectify this to my satisfaction. Just for the chance, Alexi, I feel that I'd give up a lot. If I had been born female, I might never have been so full of fear, shame, anger, and self-loathing. When you drew that picture in my journal the other day, the picture of me as I could have been, you did a better job than anyone could have. And here you are, human."

Alexi stopped on his heel and turned. "As are you. Think about it." He emphasized those last three words. Ken looked at him, one eyebrow cocked, an expression that asked "What's your point?" Alexi shrugged and continued walking. "I do my best. Was it better that I drew it or no? The iniquity is only more apparent. Come, clear your mind of that as much as you can for tonight. We cannot turn our backs on our problems, but we may be well advised to avoid warfare on every front."

"You should listen to your own advice, my friend," Ken said. Alexi cocked his head, acknowledging the comment as valid. "Oh, one last thing. A reiteration, really: pivotal to everything, this must work out. You said you'd be pissed if it failed, and then seemed to reconsider... I'd be gone in a flash of false mirth and empty promises. And hurt, deep down."

"That's a heavy load for one man, Ken."

"It's not really up to just you, so don't feel that I'm pressuring you. I know that's not what you need."

"Much of it is on my back regardless. There is a subtext to everything we do... that we are gathering people, preparing for something. We don't even know what *it* is ourselves but we feel it so strongly that there is no doubt. But think – where is this going? How will it work? We all have a very clear picture of how we *don't* fit into the present culture. We all know that the status quo of suburban white-bread America is incapable of supporting anything but robots and people who take advantage of robots. And we all know that we may only have a few generations left to decide as a species if we're going to make the conscious decision to evolve as a people, as tribes, or if we are going to remain separated, estranged by hate, and strip the planet of life. But I see only two ways of changing any calcified system: either blowing it up or changing it from the inside, a brick at a time, using the same mechanics they do. Beating them at their own game, as they say. Violence begets violence, right... that's not an ecological option. And I don't think any of us are willing to play 'their' game—what do we really expect to happen?" He paused. "Maybe we shouldn't focus on the 'them' so much, but instead look at the 'us,' and continue to grow so that we can spread our message far and wide, even if it is so simple as 'you really can be whoever you want to be and do whatever you want to do.' If, and it's a big 'if,' we can learn to work together... The only thing I know is that I will never give up."

Ken had no response.

Alexi looked back at Andy, and realized he was thoroughly miserable. "What's eating at you?"

"The wind. What the hell are we doing?"

"You'll see. Don't worry too much about the cold—once we're in the protection of the trees, you'll barely notice it. Anyway, I imagined you'd want to be involved in this little expedition. That's right, isn't it?"

That shut him up. In fact, mentioning the protection of the woods seemed to speed him up a great deal, and soon they were out of the open field, and the harsh bite of the air. The path was really just a giant mud-slide devoid of vegetation, possibly an experiment in land erosion. The incline of the path was even steeper than had been apparent at a distance, and most of the group began down timidly, especially Renee, who was quickly losing her breath. Alexi, however, growled and charged headlong down the hill, leaping from one side to the other to slow his decent over the small chasms and gullies that riddled the way to the bottom.

Ken pointed at Alexi, now far ahead, with his lit cigarette and said to Jason, "he's enthusiastic at the most random times."

When they reached the bottom, Ken and Alexi waited for the rest of the group to catch up. They stared through the naked, skeletal trees at the night sky, brilliantly lit by the near-full silver moon, temporarily mesmerized. Though they could still hear the wind bearing down on the trees above in giant blasts, it was eerily calm, still and silent except for the light rustling of falling snow and the sharp crunching footfalls of their companions. The two of them stood at the bottom of the valley, at their feet lay a fallen tree that reached all the way to the other side of a whispering stream. The path stretched in either direction, parallel to his stream which ran the full length of the dale.

Once they were together here in this silent valley, they found themselves standing in a ring beside the path. Their hands met, in unison now, arms linked. They slowly began turning counterclockwise. The movement was slow, steady, and became quickly hypnotic. Alexi wasn't sure what had prompted the action, and could tell from the looks on all of their solemn, curious, and frightened faces that no one else knew, either. A sliver of fear ran up his back, like frigid liquid dripping in reverse, and Alexi tried to pull back but found that he could not. Somehow the hypnotic swaying of the trees, the flakes of snow falling in slow motion, drifting to the ground around him in a halo of moonlight, compelled him to take the next step, and the next...

Again, without any prompting, the group unlocked their hands, and began moving in concentric circles, some clockwise, some counterclockwise. Now Alexi felt very confident, strong, and incredibly old. He had the feeling that he was an emissary of some kind for these woods, that they would teach him, care for him, and train him to complete their mission. What mission? And who are *they?*

Sharp claps rang out in the still air. Alexi had ceased circling, and was now clapping loudly in a specific pattern. Three, then four, then two, then seven. Again, and again. The others ceased their circling now and turned inwards towards him, offering a monotone chant to the claps, EEEOOOOOOOOOOOOOOIAAAUUUUUUUU, rising up together like smoke through the clustered trees.

As suddenly as it started, they ceased, blinking. And they remained paralyzed in this confusion for many minutes.

Ken turned towards Andy, who was now standing somewhat awkwardly along the side of the path. "Can you do a little searching for us now?" Andy raised a playfully skeptical eyebrow. He had no idea what Ken was talking about. "Close your eyes, follow your instincts, and feel around."

Andy puckered his lips for a moment, and blew on his chilled hands. Deliberately, he closed his eyes, and then, in a burst of movement, began stomping directly into the woods on the other side, in the direction of the stream.

After he was out of earshot, Ken laughed and looked at Alexi. "I think he's going towards where the pull is strongest, but...I never thought he'd completely ignore the path."

There came a splash from the woods. Andy had found an obstacle— the stream. Dejectedly, he sloshed back to the group.

"I was sure that was the right way," he said, trying to shake the frigid water from his boots and lower legs.

"I think it was," Alexi said, "but you could have followed the path. Come on."

They all headed north on the path, awed by the crystal clear view of the moon, despite the beads of ice that were still falling all the way down to them from unseen clouds above. Soon, the last murmurings of conversation stopped. The sound of their footfalls echoed endlessly, broken only by an unsettling rustling that came frequently from the deep woods to either side of the path. Though the ground only sloped down gently at this point, it felt as if they were descending deep, very deep, into the earth.

"This forest always exudes a certain air—you always feel like you're being, I don't know...observed. Do you feel it?"

Andy nodded. "Now that you mention it, yes." There was a slightly sarcastic undertone to his voice. Alexi simply wrote it off as his irritation at being outside in the cold with pants and shoes that were certainly soaked through to his skin.

"I wouldn't call it an evil feeling, just...hollow somehow. There is, I think, a source of this. Ken and I came this way a little while ago, but stopped before getting to any obvious nexus. Tonight, we'll try to find it. It seemed as if we were drawn to it, and have been ever since setting foot on this property."

Renee was wheezing.

"Are you alright?" Alexi asked, concern creeping into his voice.

Renee waved it off, and coughed before she could give a verbal reply.

There was a large tree lying across the path, blocking their way. It was when Alexi leapt atop the slimy log, that he first saw what had been calling to them. He stopped short, almost sliding off of the slippery surface, and turned around toward the group. "You've got to take a look at this..." he said, springing over the fallen trunk.

A number of buildings sat in the middle of the woods, as if they had been picked up out of a bygone era and left, giant trees sprouting all around their frames. The main structure was about one hundred feet long, possibly fifty feet wide. Its size and apparent age were what first caught Alexi's attention—it certainly hadn't seen use in at least fifty years. The roof in the front of the building was collapsing, and the whole of it was coated in mildew and moss. All of the windows were barred with old, rusted iron rails, leaving crimson stains where they were joined with the concrete of the walls. The stream ran alongside this building, and across from it was an old spring house. In front of the main building was a rusted incinerator, surrounded by piles of charred metal and tires.

Jason stopped in his tracks. His eyes were half closed. "This is it, isn't it? The source." There was an eerie edge to his voice.

Nodding, Ken took a few steps away from the main structure. "I've had dreams here. There's something watching us from the inside."

Andy glared at Ken quickly. "Will you stop recommending things like that to me?"

With his eyes still half-closed, Jason turned towards Andy stiffly. The motion was puppet-like and more than slightly unnerving. "No," he said, incredibly slowly. "He's right."

Andy bit his lip, and then nodded slowly. "Ooookay." He paused, then continued. "Sure he is, now. That's what I'm talking about. It's like things are suggested and then when people agree on them together—"

Alexi cut him off. "—They feed off of that reality, which is of course co-created... You get it."

Andy looked over at him blankly for a moment, and then he smiled. "It's common sense."

"Perhaps," Alexi cocked his head slightly. "But most people are unable to realize the implications beyond the words." Andy looked perplexed, so he continued. "I mention that it is warm. Suddenly, you are more likely to not only agree with me, but to single the warmth out of your experience."

Andy chuckled. "You're assuming that everyone will always agree with you."

Ken was watching this conversation, but his thoughts were veiled behind a stoic mask.

Alexi smiled grimly. "No. I assume that everyone will agree, or at least filter their experience relative to, 'the group.' Of course it's not always true, that's where congruence comes in."

Jason shook his head, not convinced. "That's not all there is to it, man."

Ken finally spoke, though it was unclear whose comment he was commenting on. "Do you think?"

This comment gave them all pause a moment, before Alexi finally concluded the conversation. "Even Judas fits into the formula, Ken. Conflict polarizes us further, sharpens our fuzzy convictions. We contribute our vote in consensual reality, even by not voting. A society needs its outcasts to retain its identity."

⊰•⊱

The group fanned out for further investigation. All of them were wide-eyed, stumbling about in a haze. Alexi could feel the hair on the back of his neck rising, and it was all he could do to keep from crouching and letting out a defensive growl. The sense of dread was shared by all; it was as if the buildings themselves were an agent of unfinished business, of old, crumbling dreams, of an ancient people whose myth had long since been forgotten, which threw this mourning into the azure twilight of the pre-dawn sky.

Ken called out when he had found the foundation of another building long since burnt to the ground, and everyone ran over to him.

"I was just noticing…this could have been a road." He motioned around him. "See how the trees are all cleared out or very young in a straight line all the way to the left, and then, to the right. I would guess," he said, looking at the trees directly, "that these new trees are no older than twenty years."

"Why do you think these woods are so angry, Ken?" Alexi asked suddenly.

Ken turned around, the cold leaving a scowl on his face. "The McMansions are fast approaching...and these were once used as sacred lands, don't you remember Dawn talking about that?"

Alexi nodded, "Yeah but— ...did you hear that?"

There was a scuffling sound somewhere in the darkness. They all froze in place. A form, long and low to the ground, darker than the night, rushed past them. It moved too fast to register anything beyond a blur.

Alexi scanned the moonlit tangle around him. He heard another crash, and the popping of dry leaves. Looking in the direction of the noise, he saw Jason clumsily trudging past the building toward a circular grove of trees that stood behind it, on the far side.

"Hey Jason, what a—" His question fell flat in his throat. There, in the middle of the grove stood a hazy blue form. It looked like moonlight collected on shimmering water—and if it hadn't been arranged in the form of an upright human, he would have assumed that's what it was. Still, it could have been a trick of the eyes, but something in his gut told him otherwise. He felt both nauseous and inextricably pulled towards it.

Jason continued forward, now gliding through the underbrush like a spectre himself. Alexi froze, watching transfixed as he crossed the periphery of the trees. The woods fell silent as Jason stood there. Suddenly the tugging sensation in Alexi's stomach stopped and Jason fell, seemingly unconscious, into the underbrush.

His senses returning to him, Alexi called out to the others and rushed to where Jason had fallen. As he approached he heard the unmistakable sounds of retching. There, in the circle of trees, Alexi found him, writhing and vomiting amidst their tangled roots.

Leaning over, he put his hand on Jason's shoulder firmly, and rolled him over so he could look into his eyes. Already the bout of sickness was passing, and Jason looked back at him with a perplexed look.

"What just happened? It felt like I was vomiting up glass," he finally managed to say, his voice scratchy.

Alexi bit his lip. "I honestly have no idea. You're alright now though right? Can you walk?"

Jason slowly got to his feet, feeling a little bashful about all the concerned stares that followed his every move. "Guys, it's ok. I'm alright."

Alexi suddenly chuckled. "Hey Andy, how would you explain this?"

Andy smirked. "Shut up. Just shut up."

They backed up to the fallen tree that marked the entrance into this section of the woods. "I suggest we do investigation on the inside tomorrow, in the light of day. Whatever that thing was…seems to have left. But I don't think we should be hanging around any longer," Alexi said.

"Agreed," Ken said, tersely.

They all hurried back to the house.

Over the course of the next few days, we all returned to that place a number of times. The inside was filled with old automobile parts, corroded machines, and a car straight out of the 1920s. Ken had come to the conclusion that it was what he called a hack-shop. I couldn't shake the feeling that there was some sort of connection between this, and Gabrael, the vision…there was something tenuous about all of my experience, like all of the existence present to my eyes was a set, paper-thin, that I could cut through with the knife of my perceptions… As if… As if I could pierce right through and drive past the movie set, right on past and onto the next stage. And this tenuous spiders thread, the link between these different realities, was the direct cause of the mysteries that had suddenly entered my life without any explanation, the people, the feelings, and even what I was seeing seemed suddenly perfectly scripted, order formed slowly from the puzzle pieces presented by my youth, and yet this order was absolute chaos, and what I had called meaning was meaningless.

You see, throughout my life I had been struggling with two tablets of values. On the one hand, I had the virtues and values that were natural and intrinsic. All of them were qualities which could not be moderated, doled out, or restricted by a governing body. Creativity, love, lust, trust, friendship. Joy shared and losses endured together. These things do not have weight, you can't touch them, and oftentimes, we are hard pressed to even define them.

On the other I was presented with this pied piper of brand names, dollar signs, rules and regulations, social responsibility and respectability. These are quantitative, and are values which can be commodified. This myth held no sway over me, yet throughout my birth into adulthood I watched those around me, hypnotized and enraptured by this melody.

Was it merely adolescent of me to watch them stroll aimlessly through routine lives of "shoulds" and "shouldn'ts" and raise my voice with discordant notes? Was it schizophrenic of me to recognize that the trained patterns that these people elicited, when well bred with this quantitative tablet of virtues, was of benefit not to them, not to their communities, but instead to the disembodied organizations that ruled the world?

Of course, I can't analyse my intuitions from another, unbiased perspective. Intuition is possibly the most personal and inexplicable of our senses. True or not, these questions were as natural to me as breathing, painting, or making love.

Though I cannot deny that the cultural song I was born into still speaks to some, it was never a tune I could play along with. However, unlike many who attempt to march along, beating off-kilter, I recognized my strengths for what they were. I trusted what my heart valued more than what I was told to value, and I strolled off into the woods, heedless of the pack.

Yet I was finding, to my amazement, that I was not alone in these woods, or in my need to find a myth with real, personal value. Alone all of my life, estranged from any sense of greater community or real value, I was overjoyed by this. But I really had no idea how to proceed with it, or how to broadcast this message to all of these wanderers, winding their own paths to a center, an end which is still unknown to us all.

What we are looking at here is an apocalypse. Spiritual, cultural apocalypse is much more subtle than mushroom clouds, fallout, and radiation burns. People can deny it. No statistics can prove it. The only evidence we have is a feeling of profound loss, and hope for a future that does not reduce the qualitative values of life to quantities and for companions to share these stories with so that they can have value, and pass on to our children in the next world.

Reflecting back on this, I believe many in my generation have been so called. Not because we merely want to be important, but because we know that we are coming down to the wire.

Ahhh... Now we are back to that veiled center of the labyrinth... Called for what? To do what? And by whom?

<hr>

M.H.B.S. transmission: Out-takes 7L:

Leri: Once we can program, we ask ourselves: where are we going? Where do we want to be?

Greg: One must be a whole, undivided being. A divided state can never stand.

Rachelle: Whooooah. (Pause a beat.) "Spirituality" is right here, right now, not something to be held in contrast to physicality. What you are thinking about right now plays into what you will be living tomorrow.

CHAPTER 7, GRID 1

MEREDITH

Who is the third that walks always beside you?
When I count there are only you and I together
But when I look ahead up the white road
There is always another one walking beside you
Gliding wrapped in a brown mantle
I do not know whether a man or woman
But who is that
On the other side of you?

— T.S. Eliot

A sleek black car pulled into the parking lot, hubcaps bending the ruddy sky in their mirror polished surfaces. The rumbling of the engine and the sound of its passage, the grinding of tires on gravel, the low purr of the engine, seemed to awaken me from a daydream of another reality, another existence. The memories faded quickly while staring at my image in the mirrored hubcaps. My ruined mind knew, with deep and overpowering certainty, that this was the decision point. This very moment was the fulcrum of my future, and there was certainly no time to daydream. I stood up, grabbed my bag, and approached. The wind had recently picked up. Something in the background writing and editing this script. The cold caused the exposed flesh of my upper chest and arms to raise in gooseflesh. Shivering unconsciously, I stared deep into my own eyes for a few seconds, still caught in my own reflection. For a moment, I almost fell in love with those eyes. A stray tear rolled, or maybe it was a raindrop. There was a sort of shame that came along, directly after I realized what I was doing, a feeling like being caught masturbating. It was more than I could take, and I looked away...stifled that love right then and there.

The window rolled down, revealing a stark interior, and a man I might have once known. The clouds thickened, and he glanced up and to the right before meeting my eyes. The movement of clouds was impossibly fast, like time-lapse photography. Smell of ozone in the air.

"Time to go Meredith," he said. Time paused, as if to take a breath, and then resumed. A lump had formed in my throat, and a thousand doubts crept in and began to stew. I made my way slowly around the front of the car, more sounds of grinding gravel under the hard soles of my shoes, until I stood at the passenger door. The engine continued its deep throbbing rhythm as the first few swollen drops of rain fell from the rusting sky. I reached out for the door handle, amazed at how small and utterly powerless my hand looked against this stranger's machine. Frail. I was sweating now, and starting to shake, but I had an odd resolve in my defeat, that last unremovable self-dignity. I stepped into the car.

Once inside, I stared dully out the window at the scene rushing by. We seemed to be getting deeper the city, away from the McMansion homes, Paxil stores and feverish gaiety of the suburbs. The sun, perhaps also having given up, stole away, captured by a thick gray cloud. Endless blocks of factory rolled past the windows, and I realized that his hand had been resting on my thigh the whole time. He smiled, but there was no warmth in that smile. You could tell he could kill and keep smiling like that, baring his uniform white teeth almost aggressively, possessively. He had a coffin face, not natural in any sense, predatory but not like an animal. An animal cannot have ill intent. It kills and hunts according to its nature. My resolve snapped and I felt revolted at the touch of his cold flesh. Something else was there, just beyond my reach, that frightened me.

The car pulled up to a gate in the road. The stranger rolled his window down and spoke into a box. The gate rose and the car crept in, past the barbed wire and mesh fence yellow with paint, streaked rust red in the rain. His hand was resting lightly on my crotch, again a purely possessive gesture, and I felt cold all over, and nothing else.

He stopped his car in front of a stairway leading to a door, and at that point I knew, beyond any doubt, that I was supposed to get out. His hand returned to the steering wheel as I slipped out of the car. Not once did he look at me. I shut the door and hugged myself against the cold as I walked to the staircase. As I drew closer, I noticed that the entire structure floated about a foot from the ground, making the stairway, in essence, a gangplank. I took my time with the steps, thirteen of them, trying to think of any way to take back my decision. My hand felt the steel of the doorknob before I realized what I was doing. Turning it quickly, almost in frustration, I stepped inside. All of my perception seemed a procession of flashing, still slides. One vivid freeze-frame jumped into the next.

I was in a waiting room. It had a drop ceiling, fluorescent lights, and beige carpeting. I sat on a chrome chair, and started to relax, telling myself that it was all some big misunderstanding. I let my thoughts drift to nowhere in particular, running my fingers up and down my cheek, looking through the curtain of my hair at the inner door. Waiting. I didn't have long to wait. It burst open and I fell out of my daydream, the electric pulse of shock running the full length of my body.

Four stout men in black suits were upon me, took a limb each, and carried me off down the corridor, screaming. The reaction was automatic and involuntary. Thrashing and kicking and squirming as much as possible, I was unable to break their firm grip. We entered a larger room, and I felt cold steel underneath me. I was undressed and strapped to a form fitting, unbearably frigid steel table in a trice. My screams broke into sobbing, hoarse moans. The webbed nylon straps that held my limbs in place were also too much for me to escape, and so I lay still. There was not a thing I could do, and realizing that, the rest of my mind broke. The flashing images, my direct experience, became a shambles-I heard the hoarse moans of sex, the bite of a whip, a waiter walking up to me in a restaurant. Are you being served? Yes, I've already ordered, thank you. He's looking down at my breasts, and I feel ashamed. Or is it a sort of muted flattery? Riding on horse back as a child, the leaves of the trees whipping by so quickly, my hair in braids. I feel so alive, I was thinking. I've just got to tell you. But there was something else there too, I was running away. Wanting to feel closeness, long Sunday mornings bathing in the sunlight with the windows open, spring air blowing the curtains about, the object of my affection curled up beside me, an unsettling tumultuousness-but it's all fading away now, growing dimmer and more uniform. Trying to cling to those fading images, not wanting to be left all alone. The images were gone, replaced by a purely physical sensation, working in subtle, almost liquid waves and crests. I was turned on; there was a damp heat in my groin, steadily growing up into my abdomen. This was revolting somehow, horrifying. It took me a few seconds to gather the willpower to look around. A man was approaching, his eyes replaced by precise mechanical lenses. The rings around them spun on their own as he walked closer. Machines came up out of the floor to my sides and at my feet. From the ceiling, a semicircle of surgical instruments rapidly descended. I looked at the surgeon again, and I could sense nothing behind those lenses. Nothing human. They focused and refocused as he manipulated equipment out of my sight. Sweat rolled off of my head at a ridiculous rate even though the room was cold. There was a sharp jab as he injected me. My nipples tightened and, strangely, I could smell myself in the antiseptic air. My mind was racing, still screaming even though my voice had given out minutes ago. The surgeon put his hand on my fore-head, pushed my head back, and began to push a lubricated plastic tube down my esophagus. Although I felt the pressure from this, I did not feel any pain. He lifted a scalpel and began to cut... I lost my vision...and most of my mind. I heard saws, felt a gut wrenching pressure, and then an odd stillness. Before I passed out, I felt all of my ribs crack neatly at the spine, courtesy of a rib-spreader.

I came to in a chair. Two of the dark suited men were flanking me. In front of me, there was a desk, and the back of a high wing-back chair. I assumed it was an office. In the corner of this office, there was a full-length mirror and two windows. Outside, I could see that it was night. There were no stars.

"Meredith," spoke a familiar voice from behind that chair. I snapped to look in that direction, even before I was sure I heard anything. There was a tingling in my temples. What was left of my mind seemed to work now in well organized, simple reactive patterns. It was more efficient, I realized.

"Yes...master?" I heard myself ask.

"I want you to go look in the mirror. Take a good long look at your-self." I felt afraid, although the sensation was distant and translucent. I started to open my mouth to plead with him, and there was a pressure on my temples, a great roaring screaming cacophony in my head. I rose, and walked to the mirror as the noise and pressure lessened. In the mir-ror I saw the same eyes staring at me that I had seen in the stranger's car window. Metal covered my head, except for the face, ears, neck and arms. A ponytail stuck out from the top. The only other untouched sur-faces were the palms of my hands, the soles of my feet, and an area that included my breasts, crotch and buttocks. I wanted to cry, to scream and kick and thrash and a thousand other things, but the pressure and the noise came back. All I saw my reflection do was smile and pose sugges-tively.

"Meredith?"

"Yes, master?" I said, still looking into the mirror, batting my eye-lashes.

"What do you want?"

"Whatever pleases you. I will be whatever you want me to be. I will degrade myself to pleasure you."

Still looking into the mirror, I had a hard time remembering what it was I saw in those eyes. They were empty, and I existed only to be filled. The sweet, grinding noise closed in once more, and I knew something had ended.

———◆◆◆———

Samantha and Alexi were sitting in the low grass at the top of her field. The two of them sat, looking at each other and at the colors shooting across the horizon, as the mastiffs ran wild around the field. The sun was just beginning to dip lazily beneath the tree line, bruising them a deep purple, silhouetted starkly against the vivid sky which was itself slowly giving way to black. There was an energy in the chill air, pained but enjoying the almost brutal beauty of it all. It was a defiant sort of power.

"To think that all of this will be for nothing because of our blindness. We all see everything, and…yes, because of that, nothing." The sarcasm in his voice was undeniable. The thought was cold and pure, like an ice-cold bath that invigorates, but the words rang hollow and false. "We look ourselves in the mirror each day, and throughout that day, all we see is reflections of our selves, never past them. Never through that mirror image. And when we get involved with people, how much of them are we really seeing—how much of it is really just projection? Is our contact real, or are we bound to lose our self in the process of identifying with our horribly tenuous *perception* of self? …I mean, I feel all this love for you. It's overwhelming. But is it really you that I love? I can't tell what is genuine anymore."

"Don't worry," Samantha said, not making eye contact, "there are some things that can't change. Think about what it feels like in my arms. You make everything so hard for yourself."

Alexi smiled bitterly; Samantha was fidgeting absently with her sleeve, staring ahead blankly. His act had a strong hint of the contrived, and yet there was sincerity in his eyes. He believed it, at any rate. "The way of the world is change," he said, "it is the only absolute we can expect to experience. Change thinly veiling nothing, like crepe paper." He paused for a long moment, and then turned to look at her deliberately, his voice lower and quieter now, grating hard at times and yet at others, full of softness. "I spent… I know not how long walking about as if I were in a fog. Let's just say that I was not yet born, and the very innards of my subconscious were still being carved away by days of unrecalled experience. And then, almost as an accident it seems, I saw you and exploded out of those subterranean passages, running headlong into sunlight. I was blinded by it. My eyes met those, your eyes, and in meeting themselves outside, turned inwards upon themselves, upon me, and recalled my past and future as if it were all a dream, occurring in the flash of an eye. This is what happened, Samantha. I saw myself for the first time, and giddy from the experience, charged headlong into all of this new territory without a consideration of repercussion, and without the realization of my potential folly. My youth is betrayed in this action, as is my heart, for I have done something which speaks from my center, or rather, I have allowed myself to Hope for such a thing to be. Now, watching the orchestration of my design, after it has played the first few notes, and those most hesitantly, I see it fall out of tune, and I cannot help feeling absolute despair. I see nothing ahead that gives my heart any pleasure. I have read ahead in the script, Samantha. It isn't going to *work* this time, Samantha. This has to fail so that it can succeed, for others, in the future… This is a tragedy. And all tragedies end in death."

"Alexi…" there was a definite pleading in her eyes; a request to stop his hurting so that she could stop hers. "We will stay." She finally looked up at him. "Why is this so important? Why can't you just… I don't know, relax? Don't you see the sun…" Her voice trailed off, and she stared intently at the pattern of the threads in the blanket they lay upon, as if they were suddenly of great interest to her.

"No," Alexi said, a bit too harshly. He realized it a moment later. "Look, it's alright. I worry too much. That's all." There was little conviction in his words. By his intonation, he said the exact opposite.

/and sometimes the cold is unbearable/

As the sun sank beneath the trees and all the colors dimmed into utter blackness, the energy slowly changed. It was no longer bitter-sweet. The admiration for beauty was gone, as it fell through defiance and into resignation. There is a certain moment, when autumn turns to winter, and it isn't a moment you can mark on a calendar, or put a number or even your finger on. There's just a particular transition that happens, maybe it is the last breath of what was new, what has become old, that escapes at this moment. This intangible change was mirrored perfectly by Alexi's facial expression. He let out a long sigh and stood up. It was night.

CHAPTER 8, GRID 2

A GOOD FISH IS A DEAD FISH
(EXCEPTION: COD)

When we crucify a man…he should confounded well stay crucified.
— Robert A. Wilson

"What would you like to drink?" Barbara half-slurred. Johny knew that this primate was called "Barbara," and that she was "pleased to serve him," courtesy of a small plastic badge, adhesive, and the remarkable invention we call language. Contrarily, the fact that she was a greasy, tranquilized, exploited serving wench shrink-wrapped in synthetic fabric was rather apparent to him as his eyes did the best they could to avoid caressing her heaving form.

Johny suggested, "Coffee?"

"We're all out of coffee. Can I get you something else?" she asked. Johny could see that she copped some sort of masturbatory thrill from informing customers that their lofty consumer goals could never be sated.

"M…Mister Pibb?" he half-squeaked. Her eyes lit up as she heard Johny say the word "Pibb".

"Never heard of it," our serving-wench grunted. Johny was looking at the Mr. Pibb logo on the menu now, staring holes in it. He was busy imagining the logo erupting into flame when, to his surprise, it did.

"I'll just have a coke, then," said our humble Johny. Barbara nodded, and loafed off to the kitchen. Not wanting to waste the opportunity, Johny pulled a cigarette from his pack, lit it from the still-flaming menu, and sat back to smoke it. This was his first chance to observe the denizens of the smoking section on this busy evening.

In the booth immediately next to him sat three boys in their early teens. One of them, a round smiling youth in a Rage Against the Machine

T-shirt, was busy defending an important issue to his two black-clad associates.

"This is the only t-shirt I own that isn't black!," he argued. "All my pants are black, all my underwear is black, all of my lipstick is black. Hell! Even these fishnet stockings I'm wearing on my arms are black!" A fine example of the gothic underbelly, Johny thought.

His friends seemed to be losing interest quickly, as were our eyes-and-ears manifested in the plebeian form of Johny. He looked over just in time to see Jesus Christ walk by in a floral skirt and a see-through sweater, followed by another long-hair carrying a home-built sitar, wearing green goggles and a surplus Army trench coat. Jesus was wearing a navy blue T-shirt under the sweater that read "Death to all Fishes." Johny had a hard time believing that either of these two had ever done any time in what his Marine-Uncle liked to call "The Service". They were "funny," as he'd say: "not funny ha-ha but funny queer." Behind these two strode an auburn haired man wearing mirrored Ponch shades, a black wife-beater with the word TOOL emblazoned on the front, camo pants, and combat boots. All three of them reeked of marijuana.

"Can I get you something to eat, sir?" growled an underpaid Barbara. Johny snapped out of his daydream. Something in her eyes suggested that she had either asked Johny that particular question one time too many, or she was rabid and fading fast. He could swear that there was frothy spittle flecking her chapped lips.

Johny quickly replied with, "A Super Bird, please?" By the set of her eyebrows, Johny was convinced that some dearly loved relative of hers had just died—and that it was somehow his fault. She stared at him for just a moment longer before she harrumphed back from whence she came.

━━▶◆◀━━

There was a loud metallic clatter when one of waitresses walked into the cook. Jay, the mystery cook, looked over at Barbara. She scowled at him. He shrugged nonchalantly and tried to put his puffy white hat back on straight. As she walked away, he thought he noticed a tiny antennae poking out of the back of her dress, but his conscious mind quickly wrote it off. His brain, like all brains, was programmed to establish its set of rules, (the catch word was "reality"), based upon the present, established norm. The truth was, Jay simply hadn't snapped yet. All mystics have had psychotic breakdowns, although not all psychotics are mystics.

He tried to ignore the elevator music, pumping vigorously out of the round metal speakers in the smoke stained ceiling. He began slicing up a Super Bird while his subconscious listened attentively to the subliminal alien transmissions.

Jesus slowly devoured his bacon, lettuce and tomato sandwich, licking his fingers clean of mayonnaise and glistening pig grease. There was a distant, crazed look in his eyes. He was seated on a toilet in a small bathroom. The plastic plants in the corner added a merry, joyous feeling to the room, like a slightly out-of-key Christmas carol played on a tin flute.

Finishing the last bite of the sandwich, Jesus stood up and crammed his fingers deep into his throat. A giant stream of vomit poured into the toilet violently. It sounded like a waterfall. Little Niagara.

He staggered up to a mirror hanging over the sink, staring long and hard into his own eyes, as he smeared bright red lipstick onto his lips and chin, inspected his long arching eyebrows, and then chuckled, although it seemed forced and nervous.

In a sudden explosion of anger, he slammed his fist into the mirror, shattering it and splattering blood across the shards.

"Fat bitch!" he screamed, feeling much better.

As Johny sat waiting for his food, a man in a wheelchair rolled over to his table. There was the strong smell of onions as he slouched to one side. Though the costume was different, Johny thought he looked a lot like the sailor he had seen on the bus earlier.

He turned and regarded the kid in the Rage Against the Machine T-shirt, mumbling something Johny couldn't completely make out. "A thundercloud from below... I am the God who created this farce." His eyes darted from side to side as he spoke, and although his frame was thin and wiry, he spoke with a profound presence. Even the waitress, oblivious to everything short of an atomic blast or a perceived slight, paused and looked his way.

He turned back to Johny. "O my friend, who has lost his way within himself—contorted and wrenched by the invisible hands of Fate—how is it that you have ascended to such heights, without ever stopping to look around you? Why do you leap from stone to stone...and never look down? Like the beginning of Beethoven's 5th it knocks, pounds. It berates. It screams. And still, you do not hear it!"

Johny looked down at his scrawny legs. "Who are you?"

The man continued undaunted. Johny assumed that his question had been rhetorical. "For the height to which you aspire is also the depth to which you sink; as the tendril branches of the Tree of Knowledge stretch up to the clouds, the roots too sink deeper and deeper into earth and sediment, sucking up hosts of answerless questions and filth from top to bottom. The timbre of each melancholy note resonates with the ache of your Hope, your tallest branches stretching further still to be above, while the weight of your mass drags you further into the mud. And, as your branches begin to reach those clouds, you are hurled into a convulsive terror, a loneliness without end, a delirious fever named Unattainable Hope, Infinite Possibility... In the innermost, most subterranean recesses of your Self, I can hear you screaming 'how is it that no one can hear me, from up here? Why do they not understand? And now...now I do not even understand myself... I am the day after yesterday, and I refuse myself. I turn away from my unattainable future, I cringe from the memories of my past—they will not let me go on. And I grow more and more unbalanced as actuality pushes me on further without a choice. My longing for a companion is so unbearable that I soil it with the filth from my roots; my need for communion is so great that I cannot dare open my mouth; my hate for my friends is so great...because of my love...'

"Must you turn yourself away—from yourself—and cast Hope to your opposite? Would you be any happier a 'no' rather than a 'yes'? You still long for freedom, my friend, and that longing is your cage. You do not even realize what you are missing, or what it is that you are longing for, but something in you calls out to be aware. You have become parched in the desert of apathy, and thirst for the Bacchic springs forever out of your reach. And while your highest aspects thirst for freedom, so too your basest roots thrust outwards and strangle the hopes—"

At this point a red-headed girl built like a sparrow wandered into the smoking area. She had that mild-mannered heroin-chic that was all the rage, the paradoxical combination of unnaturally red cheeks—carefully applied pigment to simulate the sex flush—contrasting skin that was almost slate gray-blue. Her eyes were glazed over, and yet the way they moved from side to side across the room, scanning every detail, suggested that if she wasn't intelligent, she was at least cunning. It was a hungry look, like a wolf that had gone far too many days without a good meal, and was now desperate enough to consider human flesh a suitable entree. The man paused in the middle of his monologue and asked Johny if he knew her.

Of course, Johny realized that aliens only take redheads, because the aliens are actually Japanese. The Japanese like redheads. Wisely keeping his opinions to himself, he merely nodded. "Yeah." It was certain that, if she hadn't been abducted yet, she was soon to be.

The man in the wife beater leaned over. He had apparently been listening in on the conversation. "I used to date her," he said, pulling his shades up for a moment to reveal bloodshot eyes. As if anyone in a ten mile radius hadn't at least slept with her.

Jesus, suddenly recognizing the bird woman, became livid and leapt from his seat beside his militant pot-head friends. Simultaneously, Wiry-wheelchair-man spun his chair around like a motorcycle driver, leaning into the screeching turn, following Jesus, who shot over to her table, ejaculating a long monologue which reeked of sarcasm even more than Frederick's onions.

"I want you. Not because I know who I am or who you are, or what it means when people say stuff, or why there are three pieces of bread in a club sandwich, or what animal bacon really comes from, or for what reason I feel the urge to strangle myself at least four times a day. But people tell me that I should want someone. So I guess they're right. Or, even if I don't guess they're right, they'll probably sneak into my head late at night and make me do their bidding anyway. I find myself, sweating feverishly, my eyes half open—they never seem to fully close—wondering about pigs. And if, under your skin and jewelry, there is a fresh club sand-which lurking, waiting. It makes me hungry, and so I start to think about Ben and Jerry's ice cream. But anyway. I think about meat on a hook a lot too. Sort of hanging there, maybe still twitching a little bit." He paused for a moment to nonchalantly stick one of his fingers into a nearby ketchup bottle, wiggled it around a moment, withdrew it with a slurping spurt of scarlet and licked his fingers clean. Everyone at the table watched him silently, incredulously.

"Mmm... The pits of Abaddon." He licked his lips. "Sex makes me feel better about myself. A club sandwich! God damn. I'm getting excited just thinking about three pieces of white—or even wheat—bread. Contained within those alluring and yes, mysterious, layers of white bread is fried pig flesh, a mystical revelation clothed in the obscuritanism of toast! All I really care about is the pig flesh. Sweating pig flesh. Supple pig flesh that I can show off to my friends, or consume and excrete. Smooth pig flesh at first. Cut open by the butchers knives, the living organism laid bare to its primal core. And wham! A luscious club sandwich. Just like that. This is just between you and me, of course."

Chapter 9, Grid 2

Save the World, Burn it Down.

Where equality and fraternity lie, there can be no liberty.
— Robert A. Wilson

...But first an important note. After World War II (the sequel to the smash hit "War to end all Wars"), many people produced offspring. Space, style, and the writer's own fractured attention span prevent a detailed analysis, but for a variety of reasons all of these folks needed a place to live. Did I mention that the economy was booming, and there was such a thing as trust in leadership? That there was an American dream that many thought would amount to more than a stain on the sheets in the morning? Thus the mighty bastion of mediocrity was established, spat out into the world, and eventually dried, crusted over, and needed to be eliminated. This phenomenon, this really-not-all-that-revolutionary-revolution (though important to our semi-linear thread, a scrap of plot), was called the suburbs. These bleak and warring nation-states served but one purpose, transparent to all but the keenest, trained, red-eyed observer. That purpose (which led to the death of John F. Kennedy), was simple: to distribute drugs to children. This, my horrified friends, was a secret even to the government. It was devised, operated, organized and funded by the Vatican.
— Mugwump Jizm, senior editor

After Jesus' sermon against pork, the group fell silent. Johny was surprised when the girl simply smiled enigmatically when Jesus finished. Producing an unusually long cigarette from her purse, she nodded slowly. "What's your name?" She took a long drag and exhaled slowly, letting the smoke curl around her thin lips.

Wiry-wheelchair-man blinked slowly. "Frederick."

Jesus merely shrugged. "Drink from my mouth and you shall be as I am, and I shall be you."

"That's nice, dear," she said in a sultry voice that was barely a whisper. It came off like a slap in the face without one consonant of audible sarcasm.

The man with the shades turned towards Frederick, and then back to the girl.

"Show the man some respect, Pig," he said slowly, privately wishing he wasn't so damned attracted to her. *God damn brainstem. Down boy, down. And learn some taste while you're at it.* "By the way, Freddie, my name is Agent 139." His speech was mildly slurred, and his lips moved irregularly when he spoke, as if he was either trying to overcome a speech impediment or chew a particularly resilient piece of gristle.

The girl smiled too innocently. "If you don't respect yourself..." She trailed off and shrugged mildly.

Frederick laughed unexpectedly. "The brotherhood of man has long been involved in the act of sodomy and incest! The pollutants and degenerates of a society are the society, they're it's result, the reaction and backlash from our own nature upon the system which we attempt to force upon it. I know your type 'dear,' and it's just another example of wasted bacon. You could be so much more."

"How many of you are on drugs?" Johny was forced to ask.

Everyone in the smoking section raised their hands.

"Oh."

Jesus suddenly spoke up. "There's a sucker born every minute."

Johny looked his way, expecting an explanation, but none was forthcoming.

<hr/>

At the same time, in another reality-grid, Gabrael leaned closer to Alexi and nodded. "This has been one of my premises in my recent work, and I've done a great deal of fact and fiction reversal—writing the fact as fiction and vice versa. I think it's telling of our culture's current mindset that "myth" has been relegated to the position of "untruth." I don't think most people have a clear grasp of the concept of a metaphor, or more importantly, how it is that ones life is a metaphor relating to itself, that all experience is strictly metaphorical, that individual existence is a poem constructed in the language of ones internal dialogue, the interpretation of perception. The dialogue and the reality are not only related, they are absolutely dependent upon each other. I've had this feeling lately that the very act of creating this metaphor manipulates reality to fit along with it. For all I know, there really are a bunch lunatics running around Devon as we speak, to whom the phrase 'I am the monkey flower' has a great deal of meaning..."

⇒•⇐

Agent 139 suddenly rose. "I am the monkey flower!" he proclaimed. The waitress grunted and began ambling his way, prepared to tell him to sit in his seat and be a good patron. The Agent gave her such a withering stare that she stopped in mid-stride. "Hear me out!" he screamed. Even the suits in non-smoking stopped, their forks dangling in their suddenly limp hands.

"Fuck it all. Thirty million years of evolution for 'Singled Out,' the Spice Girls, and sublimated brutality. Thirty million years and Eminem is the most forward thinking artist on the air? Come on and come off it, you fucking disappoint me. You're letting your religious iconography be populated by the likes of DMX and Pepsi Cola? I'll have another hit off the joint and continue to be mindfucked by the boys on the major networks. I mean, I am, after all, nothing more than a product of this...rightright? That my consciousness is not congruent with the agreed upon world view—that is a fluke, a minor mishap, an inconvenience at my expense? A country based on the rights of the many at the expense of the one—who ever thought that the many consists of the one?—and we expect to have individuality? Individuality is itself a trap, a sham. What does this strip-mall of insecurity, this plethora of sensory over-stimulation lack? To use the terminology of our late syphilitic friend, a will to power, a will to meaning."

At this Frederick looked confused. "Late?" he asked. The Agent did not pause, however. He had a far away, highly ecstatic look in his eyes. The tone of his voice had changed, it was now deep and powerful. Johny could see that he was brandishing a curved hunting dagger behind his back.

"Why do you call yourself 139?" Johny asked suddenly, completely spoiling the mood.

Agent 139 looked over his shoulder at him. "Top of mind aware-ness... branding and marketing... haven't you been listening?"

Then, back to the larger audience, he continued his sermon, "Meaning is not contained within the world as it is. Nor is hope, evil, or justice. It is a human, cultural and subjective reality cast upon a blank set. When a group of people accept the same movie, the general consensus creates 'reality.' We could choose anything. Anything at all. This is what we chose? Come on people! It was the intention of religion, then country, now business, to create a world-map to be cast upon the stage, so that large scale transaction, and communal living, may take place. A sacrifice of the individual for the sake of the many. They sold it, you bought it. But don't you see? You too can be a fisher of men!"

"...What happened when this happened? The 'shamans' of all ages determined the agreed upon consensual norm. Our society has grown, bloated, and overstuffed itself. An experiment in nausea—the Television, the flashing lights, the larger-than-life hair—just look around you!"

Johny was listening intently, and felt a deep thrumming sound somewhere in his head.

Agent 139 raised the knife high above his head. The sound of clattering silverware resounded from the non-smoking section, as knives, forks and spoons dropped to the table. Most of the people in the smoking section seemed disturbingly nonplused. The waitress' mouth dropped wide open, and she took a tentative step backwards.

"Just think about it. Our brains trick us into experiencing continuity from a line consisting of dots, that is to say, the film itself is reality, which is projected onto a screen, which is interpreted by our nervous system. The nervous system sends the message to 'us'—this is a mystery—as a coherent, fluid movement. Hey, if you want to experience some of the way time, and reality for that matter, works without our brain's proper functioning, decoding and decryption, take a large dose of LSD. Order is human. Chaos is divine. I am not implying that LSD imparts a 'higher reality.' Any reality experienced through this flesh-golem here is limited to a singularity, thus ruling out the possibility of it being 'higher' or 'ultimate' in any sense. What I am implying is that the 'normal' operation of our brain is something biologically programmed through evolution, and socially learned. Everything you experience is real... but it is not *reality*! What about my emotions, my secrets, the things most dear to me? Well, you tell me Barbara. Take a nice hard look at how you function, throughout the day. How you respond, how you feel inside as a reaction to the response, why you do the things you do. Start to detect a pattern? Start to feel a little bit like a white rat in a poorly constructed cage? You're nothing but meat, Barbara!" Spittle flecked his lips. His eyes were beacons of hellfire. "You're nothing but meat! Send

$19.95 to my account, which I will provide in a moment, and you can break out of that cage!"

"There's a sucker born every minute," Jesus said, playing with a plastic crucifix he had hanging around his neck on a hemp cord.

The waitress ran over to the phone to call the police. Jesus rose from his chair and stood beside the Agent, who was staring intently at Johny, running his index finger up and down the knife. Now he spoke.

"Backwards swimming monkeys, hairless ape. Up to their eyeballs, I tell you—columns of smoke, columns of smoke, those monkey's, the pesky things, munch-upwards-power-sail-to-'em, too, motherfucker! Running an outboard motor and two, count 'em two, gazelle's with half-back motor-scooter soups."

"Deep under the surface of the soupy chowder lies a gem, guarded by a pesky monkey named Iago. I am not I, he said. Krimpets anyone? They've got jelly centers! Running around Led Zeppelin Hermes Herpes feet, leaden and jumping up and down. St. Ides. Isn't that a dog? (No, that's St. Bernard. The Song of Songs.) Dog star aliens. Keep your eyes out. They'll be on the ten-o'clock news with Tracy Madesac, selling life insurance. Figures, the aliens wear ties, too. Better taste in food, though. Pigs. Now, in other interrelationships, pork rinds for free! Smack them lips, boy—we've got pork rinds. They're crispy, crispy, crispy, and they don't wear leather. Crispier art thou, Freetos; How now, Othello? A morning long, spent amidst the throng of the conservatory, waited with baited breath for my arrival. Waited, Waited, I."

"I have no idea what I'm talking about. I had an idea, but then he told me that this was an equal opportunities joint and split. I had a plan, but it turned out to be an unkempt milkcow. Pull the udder kind of sideways. Beefy-bat-bootch-bandanas all around, folks—it's time for a celebration!"

The Agent caught the glint of silver running from the back of the waitresses' uniform. Recognizing an alien transmitter device when he saw one, he brandished his dagger and let out a howl, lunging at her. Jesus continued to rant all the while:

"I need a club and some cosmic bliss. I'll settle for less smoke columns and deer heads. Less flies and buzzing of Gorbetrov cocktails bursting in the swollen organ of a disgruntled social worker. Freud this, mother fucker! Less brain, more capons! Fuck fork pork rinds, we have capons! Consume Capons! Spare Castrated rooster, mammary glands— er, I mean ma'am? Ketchup down the gullet! Ketchup down the gullet!"

The Agent pinned her to the side of the bar and let out a horrible shriek of ecstatic frenzy.

"Ketchup down the gullet quick before I think, mommy," Jesus continued, not about to stop because of his friend's outburst. "Don't listen to the weird neighbor, children. He thinks too much. Dems strange words coming out of his mouth. Not like I want you to think that we're conforming to anything, mind you, but— Johny, quit yer bitin'!"

The Agent stabbed the waitress again and again in the chest, pinning her to the side of the bar with his other hand. Deep red blood washed all over his arms as he cut off her skin, revealing layers of circuitry and wires. Convinced that the grim job was finished, he got to his feet and motioned at Johny, leading him out the front door. Jesus followed happily behind, waving at the absolutely mute patrons. No one in the store made a move.

Once outside, the Agent put the knife away and walked towards the woods behind the building. More curious now than frightened, Johny followed—at a distance. "What an intelligent being realizes," Agent said, wiping his bloody hands on his pants, "is that this," he waved his hands about him with a sick tone in his voice, "needs to end. The United States of Apathy, I mean. And for change to happen, one must first invert the previous system, and then break that inversion. A 'No' is limited by the same system as a 'Yes,' as it comes out of the same proposition, do you know what I mean?"

Jesus of the Eternal-return nodded his head agreeably, although he was frowning, as if he found something distasteful or out of place.

"Not you. I was talkin' to the would-be Prophet here."

Wearing a blank expression all the while, Johny nodded his head as well.

"Well—the inversion has been made, over the past few decades, and the counter-culture has become the back-bone of the culture, see. So it's time to rock the boat in every way imaginable until the damned thing capsizes. Save the world, burn it down."

"I don't know. Destruction for it's own sake is…what do they call it? Nih… Nihil—"

"Nihilism," the Agent said. "I'm neither pessimistic nor nihilistic. I don't want to destroy, I want to create! To pave the way for genuine human evolution!" He paused and seemed as if he was looking for something. He shrugged and went on. "Read between the lines, man… Do you understand what a metaphor is? I'm talking about ideological warfare. Not bombs, guns. Even economics. That's archaic, brutal... The way of slavery, not freedom. Did you see the wires, Johny?"

"I really don't know what's going on." Johny noticed that Jesus was carrying a smelly, dead fish in his right hand, but he did his best to ignore it. "Well... I... Yeah. I did see them. But I see the antennae all the time. No one else ever sees them."

"When you explore the world, you're exploring your own nervous system—anything believed becomes 'real.'" The Agent put on his sunglasses again. They could all hear sirens wailing.

"How about we talk about this somewhere else?" Johny asked nervously.

Jesus began waving the fish around in the air menacingly. The Agent nodded at him, and said "when a person's world view becomes solid, they can't accept any experience which occurs outside of it. They write it off, and generally forget about it. This works wonderfully well with most cops."

Jesus and the Agent walked calmly towards the solitary police car outside of the store. Johny waited for a minute, and then followed. One of the officers got out of the car and opened his mouth, apparently preparing to say something particularly authoritarian.

Jesus held the fish above his head and cried, "There's a sucker born every minute!"

The cop was unimpressed.

He then paused and gave the officer a very rational look, saying "I plun neposh. Weird needle images, frundmaulein. Avenger-angry-mother-number, loud lavender cries. One hundred and thirty-nine! Oh, the answer! Not unavenged lies Diomedes! Too many candle-retina-burning-cherio-chickens, saran wrap friendships and nodding nonsense. Too many freedlemints for the cockroach, Kafka. Flip-top hat transmuting tricks, lead to gold, lead to gold. For the used and overtired sake of gain, you, loveless Simon and shell backed spinster, would turn me about?! Weird needle images, messenger. Carapace gone rusty, wasted words and rushed dinners, thousand death-chances and sword-rattlers; rattled for State and mindless duty. 'Come alone, and bring Teucros to do the shooting!' Inauthentic people, inauthentic lives."

"Bok, bok, needleknees. Rattle loud, snake-skin-Whitesnake-hard-boot guerrilla in the mist with a cheap whore. Paid much for your fuzzy suit, paid more for your needleknees and curious chickens, self-strangled bodies of artificial pineapple flavor and lemon crunch."

The cop scowled and reached for his handcuffs. Jesus struck a very cop-like posture and waved the fish at him with a stern expression on his face. "He thinks he's the vine, but he's really a leaf!" Jesus said to the Agent.

"Threaten me with your rules of office, rattleback? Rattle it backwards, knocking spinal fluid everywhere in frenzied and incessant cries. Trained muscle response, 'backwards in muscle to discover who I could have been.' Think about tit, unfreed Gottfried, young Percival with a lance and iron lung; trained to do war with transparent nightgowns, self-perverter; trained to stock the shelves twice daily, ready for use inside the breast-work, screaming 'On Trojans! On!' as Apollo, but with sillier hair."

"Lost yourself in the supermarket and cried out for mummy's linen. Mummy was doing cheap tricks in the seafood section, and came back with a bucket of prawns. Daddy was involved in vaginal strangeness with live lobsters, wearing an ancient bronze cod-piece and screaming 'On horses! On! Good men are ready to give way when the offender wants to pay! I am the earth-shaker, my hands are gripping the spear, my heart is beating high, my feet are dancing along, one two, one two! I'm ready to stand alone and gallop the horse to madness!' Equine dollar-bills a George Washington-deep in cocaine. Childhood decisions a Mother Hive Brain deep in decay. And you can quote me on that, sir."

The cop was staring blankly at the limp fish in Jesus' hand.

"Come, Dionysus," the Agent said to Jesus, quickly trotting off towards a cream Nissan Maxima.

The police officer also went to his vehicle and radioed for backup.

⋙◈⋘

I was going to quote, or at least introduce myself, but the mood bummed a cigarette, bounded down the stairs, and stole my car. I suppose I'll tell you anyway. People call me Jay. I am really known as "Handsome" Jim Manitoba, Pugilist extraordinaire. Realizing that you realize as a non-entity that I know that you know that this is an active world, which I still occupy, I feel that I should reply to outsiders using my assumed name of "Jay, Cartesian mystery cook" otherwise I have defeated myself...again. Yes, we all have plenty of crosses here. I lived a life in a toothpick once. Ethics don't work when you're living in a toothpick—there's no "yes" or "no" in a toothpick. Now I work as a cook at Lenny's. The new Aryan race just keeps getting in the way of proper behavior. Barbarians with linen napkins and battle axes and copies of sunny, semi-informational self help books gang-raped me. Broke my nose in the gravel while Jimmy Buffet sang about his broken fucking flip-flop. Afterwards, over drinks, one of the barbarians asked me what I dreamt of. I, of course, was taken aback. They say barbarians don't dream. But I told him... "I dream of tangible nothing," I said.

"So you mean nothing as something, then?" the barbarian replied over the rim of his gin-and-tonic.

"I mean unity, dissolving into non-self," I said, just to be confusing.

He looked as if he was following, but his beeper suddenly came alive, vibrating and playing "Ode to Joy", but in a minor key. "Gotta go," the barbarian gruffed. "I've got to pick my daughter up from squash at eight, and then I've got therapy."

Before I could get a word in, he left. Just as well, I thought, as I sniffled to keep any more blood from winding up in my martini. It was darkening toward translucence, and had picked up a coppery tang. I took a sip, sat back, and sighed. Things aren't what they used to be. I asked the head of the barbarian tribe, an attractive man with an attractive briefcase, for a quarter to drop in the jukebox. He grunted, and gave me forty cents. I swaggered over, apologizing to whoever I bled on, and selected the Jimmy Buffet single. Then I finished my martini...

⇒◆⇐

Inside the Lenny's, all of the patrons were answering the cop's questions so they could fill out their reports. The workers too were assisting as best as they could, except for Jay, the shift cook, who was sitting in the back room, blaring Jimmy Buffet. He stared blankly at the wall, a grease spattered spatula in his limp hands. He had seen the entire incident from behind the window in the door that led to the kitchen. *I am going to die*, he thought. He felt the harsh certainty of the statement, felt the gravity of it in every cell of his organism. *No one gets out alive. You cannot win, and no amount of shrewdness on your part will keep you from passing those gates.* This realization negated time for him, and he suddenly was drawn to ask what his effect on the environment around him was, rather than what he could get from it. *You are a part of your environment and cannot take anything away from it. You simply cheat yourself in the process.* Now he was brought to consider his present condition, and the way he had been living his life. *What the fuck am I doing?* He wondered, staring at the spatula. *$6 an hour? What good does my existence serve?* Who goes home thinking, "that Jay, he makes one hell of a whammyburger"? Suddenly he saw, with absolute clarity, what he must do.

⟺⬩⟸

The general word around the store was that some blonde haired kid had stabbed the waitress, and that he had been talking to himself for some time before he had done it. One of the younger children had seen Jesus walk through the store in a floral print skirt. At the time, she had turned to her mother and claimed that it was "Unkie Ken," referring to her Uncle, who was the spitting image of Christ. The police officer told the girl to save the story for the National Inquirer.

Frederick sat in a corner, his mouth smiling and his eyes crying. With an almost imperceptible sigh, he began wheeling out the door, ranting all the while.

"Long, long hours I spent, waiting for some sort of redemption from that hell; days of walking, running even—from myself. And that which I ran from was a mirror image of what I ran to, but polarized. I certainly had Hope, those long days, evenings, and lives, and it was that which kept me running. Despair, nausea, a gray toad which croaked at every footfall. Fear and desire, one at my back, the other pulling me forward."

"Running for a horizon of possibility. A solution outside of myself. A savior in a transparent nightgown? How much then did I understand the meaning of 'salvation without must come from within?' How much could I appreciate a kind word from a stranger, or the sound and feel of wind and the harsh reality of a dark, overcast day?"

"Now I watch others run to…what?—with my mouth closed and my hands in my pockets. You look everywhere but within yourself! Even when you are looking within yourself, you do it so that you might be seen, inevitably, that you might be saved. Poor soul. There are no solutions in a world of 'maybe,' an existence which has no opposites—has only itself—and has no rectification in the sheer force of the scream 'I AM.' The fear of that harsh reality croaks as that toad, and begins the anti-labor, the anti-birth, of running away from this present, precious moment. Depression is simply the child of fear—fear of living. Maybe, too, even the Hope is but an afterbirth, a placental cord to hang on and climb away to darkness. But—never so with Hope founded on Love. Do you fear your own life so much that you would daily pray for the consummation of walking death? The fear of a blissful life with an end… does the Joy suddenly not taste quite so sweet, then?"

BIRTH PAINS

(AGENT 139'S INTRODUCTION)

At each level of the labyrinth, there is a complex that must be overcome and dissolved so that the next can become apparent. One becomes a victor on one front only to find the lessons they learned there to be their greatest enemy in the next stage of the journey. This is the way of initiation, as we let go of one identity, and then the next.

— Aleonis de Gabrael

The geometric patterns of the flashing lights danced, bursting like fireworks in the negative space between eye and eyelid. He felt his body relaxing, sinking deeper into the cotton sheets on his single bed, the muscles in his upper back, then his legs, feet, even fingers, releasing, one at a time, attention turned inwards on the lights. The deep thrumming of the headset intensified the effect. It also made his cheeks itch.

The patterns were gone. Before him was an enormous, gnarled tree in the middle of a field, well lit by a fierce noon-time sun. The wood was gray, and he knew, though he could not feel it directly, that it was hard and cold to the touch. At the base of this tree, where its roots grew fat and twisted like matted strands of hair, there was a hole in the ground. In this vision, he was bodiless. As he intended to inspect this hole, his intention moved him forward. The tree felt proud but not dangerous. Looking around the field one last time, he stepped into the hole.

Now he was in darkness. All he could see was the light of a single white candle, three or four meters off. The light was cold and sharp, clear in the darkness but casting no light on the rest of the room. Suddenly a young woman stepped into the light. At first all he could see were her round, firm breasts, similarly round belly, and very proud posture, same as the tree. She turned around in a flash of pink skin glittering gold in the light and long, dark wavy hair. Dampness, resistance like a hand

139

passing through water. He caught her eyes behind her hair for a moment, and felt his knees give way.

———⊷◈⊶———

Flashing patterns in the goggles, the humming of the headset. The vision was gone. I was lying in my dorm-room, curled in a ball, with the "brain machine" throbbing and pulsing quietly beside me. I had received this curious little box a month or so before from a tall, angular kid named Nick who lived down the hall. We had been sitting up late in the main lounge, and somehow our conversation had strayed onto the topic of transferring energy, chakras—so called hippie-fruitcake-bullshit. I had of course handed him a copy of my book, being the first to whore out material to everyone and anyone who had a shred of interest in the subject matter. The motivations behind this behavior probably aren't what you assume, but uprooting my motivations and intentions would be an arduous task and I'm just trying to tell you about this strange flashing box lying to my left.

So he says to me that he has been studying Theravada Buddhism, and it really resonates with him. Like many of us, he had experienced some form of existential crisis, maybe he was still going through it, and he needed a place to put his faith and belief so he could get out of bed each morning and feel like there was something to live for after all. I asked him why he preferred Theravada to Mahayana—it's like the difference between joining the army and becoming a Ranger.

When we get to his room, he pulls out a 20 bag of coke and while carefully cutting lines of it on his dresser drawer, he explains that he feels trapped by his ego. And if you're going to do something, you might as well do it right. You won't hear me argue with that. It'd be a rare person who would claim that half-assed is the only way to go. Yet most of us do just that—at best. So much for ideals.

"This is the end of it," he says, finishing his line. "After this, I'm going to the monastery." His voice was even. I felt the reflex to laugh but I could see a sort of frenetic seriousness in his piercing gaze. He wasn't joking. I didn't ask what monastery, or how did he plan to get there, or what will your parents think about it. Nor did I point out the powdery frosting that was still coating his left nostril.

Sure enough an hour later he's walking around the dorm knocking on people's doors, "Hey do you want my television?" "Do you want my Gucci shirts?" I got his brain machine. A week later he was gone, off to "the monastery."

I turned the machine off and looked around my room again, rubbing my eyes. Everything is a mass of audio wires, flakes of ash, well-thumbed books on philosophy, religion, anthropology, and half-empty Tequila bottles. Entropy follows me in eddies, there isn't time or energy to counter it.

Some days I'll spend hours collecting material from the moment I open my eyes, adding those influences to my tabula rasa, with the intent of later stirring it up with ethanol or just the right amount of THC and spewing it back out again in a six or eight hour writing session.

I can see those threads interconnecting everything. Maybe there is something autistic to my obsession, my self-absorption, but I simply don't know any other way. I feel driven. This pressure, sometimes, is unbearable.

It was in Crowley, charlatan that he was, that I first discovered an articulation of a mode of experiencing that I had accidentally stumbled upon in my late teens: mythological thinking. Once the cat was out of the bag I saw it everywhere and took it through Joseph Campbell into the individual mystical traditions themselves. Everything in the microcosm can be related to a corresponding "thing" in the macrocosm, or vice versa. You can't get this from a book you have to apply it to your own experience. The events of the day and even the immediate sensory experiences that comprise it are simply references to internal truths. The reference can be discarded.

I know that I am on the trail of something important, if I can only overcome what I call the gravity of my habits—the complexes that keep us pinned down, closed off, and separate from our experience. Yet I wonder—how is this self-inflicted dissociation different from what I am calling "the gravity of my habits"? Is there any difference? Is this madness or genius?

Wandering the halls at 3:00 a.m. with Jose Cuervo in tow. Time has compressed into fragments of memories. The present disappeared as I slipped into a wider view, a view of all the pieces as interrelationships. I look back on the day that has passed me by, and can't find myself in it.

There comes a knock from downstairs, an echoing voice from down the hallway— I wake up with a desperate craving that keeps me going. I wake up again and again but it is ultimately the same day. That hunger grows even stronger in the early hours of the morning as the pitch black outside my window turns deep electric blue. I can feel the insects buzzing outside my window. My skin itches like I'm covered in scabs. Pink skin underneath. This sensation never finds a home in one particular part of my body. Occasionally it will fixate on my arm, or an organ, but it never sits still long. The craving is itself restless. My attention is a thinly focused beam, red-hot, impossible to pin down.

I go for long walks but my mind still won't stop whirling over and over itself, like a top trying to find equilibrium. The fragments of other people's ideas share equal space in my brain, bounce into each other, cross-pollinate and become my reality.

Fragments bubble to the surface. I feel like I am speaking to everyone through a simulacrum hand-puppet. The attention required to interact with these internal personages makes my external presence just a fleeting shadow. It's the need for a mirror. Without the mirror of others I am unable to gauge relative distances—thinking of "distance" in its emotional qualitative rather than quantitative sense.

I find the time to pump out twenty pages of text a day, and long desperately for someone to find me in it—prowling the hallways, late at night, hoping to catch just a glimpse, find someone that will distract me from this building momentum. As mass increases exponentially with velocity, I feel like I might collapse under my own weight.

This hunger wasn't what I used to experience in terms of desire for sex, or money, or possessions. I was sucked into the undertow beneath those urges, dealing instead with the currents that shaped them.

What I craved was the electrical hum of life itself—I see an image of a surfer, riding along the crest of the wave, in perfect balance with it, suddenly losing balance and realizing that the only way to not get torn apart is to let go and let the fall happen. I'm in that dive into myself, and the further I follow this thread, this obsession with relationships, the more I cut myself off from life in the present. This pushes the craving up a notch. I relax into it, dive forward...

But I need a way that I can understand the ultimate bottom, the underground. What is the basest, most prefiguring drive that gives all the rest their life. What did I find?

That underlying compulsion that kept me whirling, that itch, expressed itself first as sexual polarity. Subversion of the sex drive is the beginning and end of civilization. This is what gets you out of bed in the morning and gets you on to the next job. Not the *idea* of sex, nor even the act itself, but the simple polar magnetism of it. Put bluntly, the yin and the yang of the universe want to fuck each other. And this is what sets life in motion, and what turns you to mulch.

It's universal. The underlying need that keeps you moving from experience to experience, pleasure to pleasure is not at all unlike what drives the junky from fix to fix. If you somehow circumvent this polarity, then you have also circumvented the universe, and taken away your will to live. The junky isn't more addicted to heroin than you are to your identifying desires, you just happen to have a less vicious habit.

The concept is the same: the satisfaction of the urge doesn't happen in the act itself but rather in the conceptualization of it. The perfect moment that we're waiting for never seems to come. There's something that occurs between the day before and the day after that we always miss. All too soon it's the day after, and we have to go out again—again to blink at the wrong moment. Did I miss that moment I've been waiting for?

Taking it down a level of magnitude, more into the particular, we can take a new look at this magnetic pull. Every night I was consumed within visual representations of this—a swirling, brilliantly-colored vortex: every expression of sexual desire from lust to love was expressed to me in vivid detail. And it was also in these dreams that I finally found a nexus of these two poles. Bodies and minds moved together towards one unifying goal, which was the evolution of the race to the point of self recognition in the other. The more we could stoke the fire of life together and direct it towards that goal, the better. Time was running out.

The entire experience was curiously non-corporeal. It wasn't like they show it in movies, and it isn't like Catholics dream of it. There was always a sweetness, as in romance, but no implication of anything except for the interaction in the moment. I did notice that some characters in these dreams would return, but I also felt none of the compulsions I had had in many anxiety dreams I would have, representing the other side of my feelings about the matter, of falling in love and then losing my love, or of jealousy, or of betrayal. It wasn't Crowley who put the thought in my head—it had always seemed strange to me that people do not take their fill of love, when and with whom they please, with the intention of opening up still further, letting go of the need to hold on, which restricts pleasure and chokes the freedom of ones inherent, pure intentionality without the weeds—"should," "don't," "shouldn't," "could have," and the rest. Birth and death is our passage from and to the silence. Why shouldn't we all rejoice now in this manifest chaos that exists, like a star, above the vast desert?

In these rituals, no holding on to form or order was possible—there was no responsibility for us to compromise, or be anything other than that outpouring of pleasure. Societal identities were irrelevant. Maybe, in addition to my obsession with dissolving social standards, I was driven by this on a personal level—having the intensity of love, which I am also quite addicted to, without the possibility of betrayal.

Each morning that I would wake up from these dreams I would try to recall the events of the ceremony, and I would be at a loss. If I say it was a form of communion and maybe you laugh, or think I'm either joking or insane. But that's exactly what it was.

The tension of this as it contrasted the reality of my limited nature has even, at times, driven me to such discomfort that I literally wonder if I can continue existing here, in this body, within these bonds. I can think of no other way for us to break through our barriers then by finding our love, and uniting with it—in fury, in passion, or in tenderness, as per our nature. Not a slow process in pathologically oriented therapy, but a thunderbolt, experienced again and again, until we are broken and reshaped by it and our true fearless nature can make itself known.

Here I am, in a room filled with the pantheon of Western and Eastern Philosophers, most long dead—and I wonder if it was this very conflict of possibility and actuality, this burning potentiality locked in each of us, which was the real cause for Nietzsche's insanity?

This tendency was still very subterranean in me, though I speak of it here in the open. There were many things about myself that I couldn't yet admit. In my conscious life I remained monogamous or celibate, and had little inkling of what was really gnawing at me. I worried constantly about the "other guy." All of my previous relationships had been a struggle with jealousy, borne in an ungrounded or incomplete sense of myself. So long as we remain incapable of complete self-sufficiency, we will have the rug pulled out from under us again and again right when we feel we need it most.

The fact that I constantly found myself unsatisfied seemed symptom enough of an oversight in my present way of doing things. I don't have the answers but I do know a faulty system when I see one. This system I have been operating is not *my* system, it is the system handed to me by my culture.

These dreams started at an early age. I found writing from when I was fourteen already discussing "the Dionysian cult." What I was hitting on here was the basis of a religion that made sense to me. You can even see it etymologically: religion, religio or religare, to bind or to yoke. Yoga, to bind or yoke. It is the binding of the microcosm to the macrocosm. Of subject and object. Or yin and yang. And, unless the sacrament is profaned, what is sex but the binding of self to other? What is it if not the alchemy of polarities? As Joseph Campbell says on page 340 of the *Masks of God IV...*

Oh come off it. See, I'll sit here and think to myself all day like this. I'll give a speech to myself on transcendental meditation and follow it up with Locke. I'm just dying to find someone to connect with in a genuine way, but that look or gesture of genuine compassion hasn't sparked. Our eyes have not met.

I give away too much for those who play games. I'm too ridiculous, too absurd, for those who don't—both too distant and too present to operate within the parameters that most seem to find the norm for social interaction. In the arena of groups, within social boundaries, I can be a guru and a self-parody but never a human being. There's something about my head-trip that won't allow it.

I am now going down into an abyss. My blood has been transubstantiated and feeds the telluric earth beneath me. I cannot say who or what I will be when I have passed through this, but something I read in Nietzsche does come to mind, giving me a hint of what I will do, and what I must endure.

First, he says, one begins as a camel. He has been indoctrinated into a society, and his world is designed in such a way as to contribute to that society and bear its weight. But then, in some, a transformation takes place where the individual becomes a lion, and battles the dragon "Thou Shalt" in the desert. Should he return victorious, he will be transformed into a child, which is like a "wheel rolling out of its own center." It is this descent into the desert, and this battle, that I must prepare myself for. My transformation into Agent 139 is nearly complete.

Interlude II

The Myth of Orpheus

...The chill night air was somehow comforting against his skin, as was the rustling of grass underfoot and everything else that connected him with his environment. He felt incredibly thankful for these connections, only now realizing how long he had gone without them. *But where am I? Who am I?*

This was no philosophical dawdling, since his well being in many ways rested upon the answer. Funny that we can be so self-concerned when we don't even know who we are, he thought, trying to sort through the patchwork of images that comprised his past few days memories. Clocks, a woman in a cage, the terrifying empty house he had once lived in, an abandoned bus, vacant houses, the never ending expanse of desert that only seemed to end when he collapsed in resignation under the coarse sands—back and back this thread lead.

He was passing a small gazebo now, and then a semi-circle of thick bushes. Many yards away, he could see tall trees, many of them oak and birch. They were long slender trees, covered in brilliant leaves like smoldering ashes.

What stood before him now was a thick forest, smelling of early autumn and earth. From deeper within, he could hear the scuffling of animals running about, and occasionally baleful eyes would peer out from the gloom, and then sink deeper in. For many minutes he stood awestruck, maybe even a little frightened.

Overhead the moon finally rent the clouds asunder and poured pale light across the earth again. The leaves on the trees, now bathed in this light, burst to life, no longer a smoldering fire. Now they were the sun at night, the lion in the desert, and this feeling electrified him. Before he knew what he was doing, he padded into the forest, cautious but determined.

There were many paths winding through these woods, and it wasn't long before he felt that he was completely lost. Moonlight still fell to the underbrush beneath the canopy of fire above, but it was as if through a shattered mirror. The outlines of the leaves echoed all through the forest.

The effect on Orpheus was disorienting. The ground began to turn into an incline, as he slowly descended into a valley. Soon he heard water running over rocks, and he turned in that direction. Eventually the forest gave way for a moment, cleaved in two by a river that ran over large weathered stones and cast itself further into the valley.

He made his way through the upturned roots and underbrush to the water, and then started when he heard a voice from beside him.

"Pretty good fishing out here," it said, deep and yet nasal at the same time. The voice reminded him for some reason of Peter Lorre.

Saying nothing, Orpheus spun around. There, silhouetted against the moon, was a man wearing a trench coat with the collar turned up and a beaten up wide-brimmed hat. He clutched a fishing rod somewhat stiffly in his gnarled hands. Orpheus could not see his face.

"Hey," Orpheus said, taking a step back without realizing it. His foot did not find solid ground, however. He sunk to the ankle in mud with a loud slurping sound, and nearly fell face first attempting to right himself.

"I said it's pretty good fishing out here," the man repeated as Orpheus yanked his foot from the ground.

"I used to go fishing with my Grandfather years ago. There's something nice about never knowing what you're going to catch, but over all it's pretty boring," Orpheus said slowly, wiping his foot on the closest dry stone.

The man grunted and then turned towards him. Lit in harsh chiaroscuro from the pale orb above, he looked much like Choronzon, though he was scrawnier and had something goofy where Choronzon was massive and terrifying.

"Who are you?" Orpheus asked, "and where are we?"

"I'll tell you what, boy. Anyone who thinks they know who they are have fallen the farthest from what they are. There is only one time everything falls into place for most, and that's the moment before I come. Read into that as you like...whoah, I've got a bite!" Sure enough, the line went taut, and the rod quivered like butterfly wings. With a sort of grim amusement, the fisherman slowly reeled in his quarry. It seemed he took the most pleasure from letting the fish feel the hook. Three times before he had finished he would let the line go slack, let it think it had escaped, only to snap back twice as hard a moment later, digging the wicked barbs home deeper than before. "The art is letting him think he's going to be able to get away...and then givin' it to him twice as hard." After a few minutes of this, he pulled a fat, wriggling black fish from the dun eddies at his feet. He held it up for Orpheus to see.

"Mmm-mmm," he said, staring the fish in one of its globe-like eyes, "you're going to make good eating tonight. You're not so pretty, all in all, but I won't hold it against you." He absently tossed it, still twitching and wriggling in its death-throes, into an ice-box that sat by his feet amongst the rocks and mud.

"Before you come?" Orpheus asked.

The man knelt down and slowly drove a hook through a juicy worm that he pulled from his pocket. Ignoring Orpheus' alarmed glance, he nodded. "You only come into life one way, unless if you know something I don't, and that thing lures you on your whole life, it calls to you, and eventually..." He cast the line out into the water and looked up at the moon.

Orpheus sat down on dry ground, saying quietly and with a little frustration "I feel like Carlos Castenada."

"Why's that?" the man asked, not looking away from the moon.

"Because I run around from one surreal conversation to the next, trying to make some kind of sense out of things by asking a lot of questions, and all I get are enigmatic leads. You're no Don Juan though."

The man grunted again.

"So what do you do... I mean besides fish?" Orpheus asked a few moments later.

He was still having a silent communion with the moon. "Devour the souls of the damned."

"What?!"

"Just kidding." There was little humor in his voice.

Orpheus let out a sigh and fidgeted for a moment. "Can I wake up now?"

The man finally looked away from the moon and turned to regard Orpheus. His lips were drawn back in a horrid leer, yellowed teeth glinted in the pale light. It seemed that the entire forest fell silent. Rising to his full height, now seemingly dwarfing the entire clearing, he let his presence be known in earnest: "I am the coffin-worm. I am your shadow—I'm surprised you have forgotten already?"

His voice was lower and more menacing than a moment before. "Taking a walk in the forest… Samantha had fallen asleep and you felt 'called,' and in that calling it was as if you recalled an ancient memory and yet also something that is to come. And so you set out into the thick of the woods, as the calling grew louder and more voices joined in. It was misty that night, do you remember? Thick banks of it clung to the trees and rolled through the valleys. And the fog played tricks on your eyes, or so you thought. Diffusion of moonlight in the water vapor, you are quick to interpret your surroundings with untried methods that you read in books. You choose not to trust in the tangibility of the forms that followed you there, but still you answered that call. It was the call of my brethren. I led you deep into the very heart of the forest that night and there I came to you, a black silhouette, a wide-brimmed hat, nothing more. And you made a deal with something, do you remember? Jump ahead about six months. Do you remember the night you were in your house and you heard something coming down the stairs? Do you remember how you blacked out and for the rest of your life couldn't recall what transpired there?"

Orpheus stood stricken. All that he had said was true, in its way. He also remembered leading others to these spots, and returning later, searching for traces and finding none. He remembered a night spent with many friends in a circle. And soon the circle turned into a dance, all running around clockwise and counterclockwise in concentric circles. Then he went down into the woods, again called. Again he led, clapping and then hearing return claps in the woods to guide their way. They moved in pitch blackness in the hottest days of summer, when Sirius rides high in the sky. They came upon a bridge, and the forest was now light around them in a bright green, and the shadows that fell from the trees and the stones, as well as the gurgling stream beneath, were purple and livid, dancing like living things. Each took a pillar of the bridge, and then the chanting began. Soon other voices in the woods joined in, hitting notes lower and higher than most could possibly sing. Their dreams from previous weeks sprang to their minds, and Orpheus—Alexi, he reminded himself—Alexi had in a way sent the message back to himself in the past, giving the first call that lead him on the path in the first place. This kind of thinking boggled his mind, but it was true. All true and all nonsense. "Who are you?" he asked. "Are you me?"

"A riddle you cannot answer. Let me riddle you, young orphan and exile. How long have I been at your side, whispering in your ear? How long since you were called first? And where is your tribe, your lost amber people of the sun? Magus, where are your sheep?"

Tears sprung to his eyes, and Orpheus bowed his head low. "You have bested me without raising a hand, Choronzon. I am, as you say, exiled, orphaned and estrayed. I have, as you imply, been long to pasture. My people, if ever I had a people, are scattered, and my hope fails me."

To his surprise Choronzon also bowed low and looked troubled. He spoke softly but dryly, like the wind through trees in winter, "It has always been thus, and you have always resigned when your victory was nearly at hand. But come Orpheus, you are called again."

"Who calls?" Orpheus asked, standing tall.

"You do. There was a call, to be sure, and you journey not in vain. You let me in that night. I have always been doubt and fear, the fore-runners of failure, but I also keep the balance. I am the lord of time for I am your boundaries. Day and night, life and death, all but two names for the whole I am a part of. I am you as much as time is a part of you, and I am equally dependent. And I am the spiral. In me movement forward and backwards in time is just a lateral jump from one rung to the next, as it is in dream."

Now Orpheus looked up at the moon. A shiver ran up his back and his hands clenched, seemingly of their own accord. As this happened, words sprang to his mind as if from elsewhere, and they rang out clearly upon the river and through the crisp night air. These were not his words, they were someone else's, and they were in a language he did not understand or even recognize. It was thick, staccato, and guttural.

Choronzon nodded. Now he was thinner, less imposing. He sat down again and cast the line far out into the river.

"I came here looking for...a woman," Orpheus said, feeling a little like he was seven or eight, sitting with his grandfather on an extended fishing trip.

"You mean Meredith. You came here looking for Meredith."

"What?"

"You have always been looking for her," The old man turned and regarded him sternly. "The hardest part will be finding her in one form... losing her... and finding her again. For all eternity." He casually began reeling in the line.

He finally finished winding in the line. Now he set to taking off the hook. The action was clinical. "I changed my mind about what I said earlier—the fishing here stinks." He paused a moment. Orpheus looked at him expectantly. He was having a hard time understanding anything that was being said. "Yes, I know you asked a question and I haven't answered it yet. You're always in such a hurry to get to the next chapter. Slow down. If there's anything I've shown you it's how to fish. Where is Meredith? Well, in your dreams of course. And all around you when you're awake, lusty boy."

"I guess you don't have a roadmap," Orpheus said dryly, ignoring his last comment entirely.

"Your dream land is the underworld. Same place. An island, actually. And like a good fisherman I happen to have a boat. Follow me."

As he led Orpheus through winding paths in the thick of the wood, he said "The entrance to this domain lies far down this river, and across a great bay." He gestured with his fishing rod and nearly snagged it in a low hanging tree branch. He continued after grumbling for a moment. "Upon these shores I will leave you. Continue on, but keep your wits about you for there are guardians in the valley. Bypassing these, you will find the entrance, massive and seemingly alive, like the mouth of a whale. A Leviathan. This entrance is girt by two pillars, one white and one black. There you will find this 'girl' you seek."

Chapter 10, Grid 1

The Journey

Those who become enlightened often tell stories of being overwhelmed by a dazzling light or a blaring sound, like a gong, an airplane taking off, or a trash can exploding. Either way, from that point on, their eyes always glow with an inner light.

— Aleonis De Gabrael

The drive to the Radnor train station had an uncomfortable undercurrent. Ken felt nervous about meeting Suzanne, his romantic curiosity mingling with intense anxiety, and he was doing his best to keep his mind occupied with other things. His Maxima blazed down the highway breaking a hundred miles per hour to swing and jazz tunes roaring at a similar pace. Crisp and clear, the blazing sun provided no warmth, but lit the countryside in luminous tones nevertheless.

The station was rather unimpressive, just a dingy concrete building adjoining the parallel tracks. Ken and Alexi mulled about as they talked, Samantha watching in the background and adding an occasional comment.

"Are we planning on scripting tonight?" Ken asked.

"We? Well, I figure that if we have nothing better to do, we may as well... Unless if something else comes up," Alexi said, noncommittally.

Ken lit a cigarette, followed by Alexi, a few seconds later.

"Have you talked to J.B.'s friend, Rob?" Ken asked. "I met him at McDonald's the other night. He's a fascinating guy, full of unharnessed potential."

"I spoke to him online... He'll be at the party, yes?" Alexi peered at the tracks bending round and dwindling into the horizon, watching the train grow from that dot as it approached.

Ken nodded.

A tunnel underneath the tracks provided safe passage from one side to the other, the walls slick with grime and faded spray paint. Out of the corner of his eyes, Alexi saw "MOTHER HIVE BRAIN" painted in bright red letters, and in smaller letters underneath, "In the end, there are no choices." He laughed—of course in the end there are no choices. Is there an end when everything goes around and around?

Ken smiled at Alexi and moved his hand in a sweeping motion from left to right. "My kind of place."

Footsteps echoed throughout the tunnel as Suzanne greeted them. She carried a black portfolio under one arm, her other hand smudged with charcoal. She wore a long gray coat with a hood.

"I'm sorry. I didn't have time to wash up after class," she said, looking over the group. Ken and Alexi stood side-by-side, Samantha behind them. Ken shifted his weight from one foot to the other and back again, saying nothing.

"How about we get out of this tunnel before we continue with the token greetings, shall we?" Alexi headed out into the sunlight, shading his eyes to allow them to compensate.

They hopped into Ken's car and sped out of the station.

Ken looked over at his copilot, his blue eyes twinkling. "I was thinking...we're taught to believe that the real 'out there' is something that cannot be anything other than what it appears to be. We're taught to think of our perception of reality as accidental and insignificant."

Alexi smiled. Ken always had an odd way of breaking the ice. "This conflict between the inner and outer world may reflect itself in the experience we have been calling 'Destiny.'"

The two girls remained silent, Suzanne fiddling with her pencils and Samantha gazing absently out the window.

...she writes in lowercase, in vowels. she doesn't want to break things. she is small. i breathe into my belly. i fill it there. i am breaking. splitting becoming coming. coming. how many people now? how many people know inside?

"When you question, you wind up bringing about the answer, just as the desired end changes the nature of the question asked," Alexi continued.

Ken chuckled, although Alexi wasn't quite sure why.

Jason's house was a one-story rancher, making up in length what it lacked in height. The front garden was filled with withering flowers and lawn figurines. The trappings of Christmas clung to the building, wreaths and flashing light, and glowering lawn gnomes even though it was now well into February.

They ground to a halt in the packed driveway, inches from the road. Ken turned the keys in the ignition, and the purring engine rattled into silence.

"If anyone hits the back of my car, I'm going to hunt them down," he said as he hopped out.

They all headed towards the house, the gravel grinding underfoot. All four were dressed in elaborate costumes. Ken and Alexi looked much the same as usual, their "dayware" as eccentric as custom would allow, with crystals dangling around their necks and sharp, black ink lines accentuating their pale skin. Samantha wore a black dress with leaves of ivy curling up the sides of her neck and face. She was—as always—enigmatic both in appearance and behavior.

Alexi's trench coat rippled in the breeze over his silk pants and shit. He rapped on the screen with his cane, a knobby, oaken staff, capped at both ends in bronze and twisting downwards from his hand like an unnatural growth. Through the window at the top, a face peeped out at them from behind a pair of goggles. It was Jason.

"Hello," he said as he opened the door, "come on in."

Clocks, pans, old instruments, nearly anything that could be hung in one way or another, covered the living room walls.

Numerous clocks ticked and whirred behind a curtain of leaves and branches across the room.

The room was filled with people, some sitting in tall wicker chairs or long, comfortable if worn sofas, others standing in that half-insecure way one does at a party consisting primarily of strangers. Jason quickly introduced them, as they stared, wide-eyed, at the four newcomers. Alexi smiled at Ken and gave a deep bow towards the congregation.

"I'm sure you've already forgotten my name. It really doesn't matter anyway, seeing how often it changes. You may have to remember a new name come tomorrow," he said, glancing towards Ken when he finished his statement.

———————

An hour later, Samantha was lying supine on an enormous soiled bed in the corner of the room, quietly watching the comings and goings of people in the dim and cluttered room. Several forms hunched in the corner across an expanse of half-eaten twinkies, Robotech books, and cigarette ash, shrouded in Mexican blankets and wearing sombreros. Occasionally she could see the outline of a face, illuminated in red, when the hookah making its way around the circle ignited for a moment, and released its cloud of sweet-smelling smoke. She heard only fractured conversation from this group, floating over in clouds along with the hashish. *I have a vagina, but it's not currently open for business ...neither is my non-vagina! ... I was trying to make a bit of bitter social commentary ... Can't follow your marijuana induced train of thought ...Bite of a bit bitter?* Raucous peals of laughter giggle in unison with the sequined sombreros like a flock of tropical birds.

Slouching casually against an overturned bookshelf nearby, Alexi winked at her and returned to playing slow mariachi music on an out of tune, battered classical guitar, nodding languidly for the others to pass the hookah his way.

Her attention disengaged and unfocused for a moment, eyes closed, the voices came as a squawking cacophony. When they opened again, she half expected to find herself in an aviary. A group of women and men in drag writhed in the center of the room on a pile of blankets. Far from being erotic, their movements were grotesque, an intentional mockery of the opium den aesthetic. In the background, a man in a red flannel shirt monitored with a video camera, occasionally saying "gratuitous lesbian scene" in a bland and bored voice.

The man seated beside her slowly rose to his feet. Jason had introduced him earlier as Rob, one of his childhood friends. He had an olive complexion and a baseball cap, pulled low, his eyes constantly darting back forth underneath. He was a watcher, like her.

———————

"I think we should go on a journey," he said. He'd been huddled in the corner for a long time, rocking slowly back and forth. He'd spoken very quietly, but his words silenced everyone, and as all eyes in the room turned towards him, there was a weight and mystery to what he said, a certain sphinx-like gravity.

Ken got up, revealing himself as one of the "sombrero brothers" in the corner, and came over to him.

"A journey?" Alexi asked, his fingers still fretting an E-minor chord on the fretboard.

Rob nodded, a slightly smug smile flashing across his face. The mood of the room had reversed in an instant, the roaring chaos silenced by a whisper, and the cameraman panned towards Rob as the women and transvestites tangled at his feet gathered around him in a circle like children during storytime.

When he didn't continue, Alexi asked if he could explain.

He nodded again. "I talk and I guide you. You relax and explore your mindscapes, listen to the vibrations and pitch of my voice. Every state of mind is a trance state, and I know that as you are listening to me speak, your own mind can determine the most interesting and revealing realities to construct from my words," he said with incredible nonchalance, in just the same way he might have been talking about a loaf of bread, or the weather, or the rubber octopus dangling ominously from the ceiling over Samantha's head. "I'm used to doing this with one person, but I'm not familiar with crowds. I could try it in a little while, in Jason's guest room."

"You'll explain more when we start?" Alexi asked.

"When we start, yes." His voice was deep, and he spoke with a certain no-nonsense matter-of-factness that Alexi found very unusual, so it came as no surprise when he later learned that Rob carried the strong pulse of Native American blood in his veins.

<hr />

Alexi and Samantha headed into the guest room ahead of everyone else. It was painted orange by the amber light of an old lamp sitting on a desk, right beside a small bunk bed. Decrepit curtains flapped idly, draped across half-open windows. There was something about the movement that could only be explained as idle or futile, even though the personification made little sense to Alexi at the moment.

He sat on the bed. Samantha sat down beside him, and looked at his hand, perching bird-like on his knee.

"Hey…," she said breathily.

He smiled at her. "I'm sorry—do I know you?"

Ignoring his comment, she continued, "I've always wondered about the ring you wear. The onyx one—where'd you get it?" Her voice was quiet as usual, almost a whisper in the shadows.

"That?" he asked, pointing.

She nodded.

"Well, if I remember this story correctly, it's my father's. Or it was. He gave it to my mother, for elopement or marriage, I don't know which..." *In the temple of the temple of the temple of the Holy...*

She nodded, listening, saying nothing partially because she knew it wasn't always a good idea to inquire about his father. Alexi's parents had separated under circumstances involving drugs and theft.

"I suppose it doesn't hold much meaning." He looked out the window, thinking. A huge freight truck plowed past, heading towards the nearby food plant, and its blaring headlights filled the room with their luminescence for a brief moment. "Onyx and silver, it has been both a moonless sky and a pregnant moon, what is filled and what fills. Its meaning to me has little to do with its origins... I have been thinking of this a long time now, and I would like to add you to it, as a part of my own marriage to heaven and earth. We've talked about the future many times, and I know how horribly impossible it is to actually plan for something and have it happen, and yet I feel that I, we, have to try. Maybe we try to fool ourselves into meaning, expecting certain things out of our future so that our experience right now can feel like it serves a purpose. But I can't accept that."

With a slight smile, she pulled herself up on the bed and sat Indian style, one arm draped over his back.

"Yes?" she prompted.

"Well, people often like to give material objects to remind them of people, or promises. Is love something that happens to us or something that we choose?" He paused, and then shrugged. "This ring I give to you, not for a temporary purpose, should promises hold true, but for an indefinite one. And should promises be proven liars, then the ring will be proof of the lie as well."

She nodded her head, solemnly.

Sits a woman who is waiting who is waiting for the sun...

"You mean it? When people make promises, I don't take them lightly."

"Yes."

(*i can pretend
      i swallow slowly.*)

Alexi slid the ring onto her finger.

Rob was the last to enter. He slowly trotted in, every step seeming practiced and deliberate, glanced around as slyly as an old coyote, and found his spot up against one of the wall.

"I'm going to need all of your attention for this," he said, slowly. Every syllable was enunciated.

Without saying a word, everyone got comfortable and began to settle in.

"I want you to relax yourselves and listen only to the sound of my voice, nothing but the sound of my voice. You asked me to explain more before we begin, Alexi, and although there is no one right way of describing what a journey is, or how it's done, you may find yourself more at ease, and you're understanding grows, if I tell you that in the younger days, when the earth wasn't quite as old as she is now, when the animals could still remember how to speak and the various tribes that roamed the land regarded the sun, the moon, the stars with awe and wonder, in an age when the gods clad themselves in flesh in much the same manner we do, it is said that then were we taught the art of dreaming. Not the kind of dreaming we usually tend to think of when we hear the word, but the sort of dreaming where our souls become aware of the universal dream and have the freedom to explore and discover that which lies beyond it, to journey beyond the limits we ordinarily place upon ourselves and the world around us. Every journey is different, and although we all may share the same journey, the ways in which our dreams manifest are unique for each of us."

"So I want you all to take a deep breath now, and relax, really relax, listening only to the sound of my voice, and as you hear the sounds between the syllables of the words, allow the feelings and pictures beginning to form in your mind, only, instead of dismissing them as your imagination, to focus on and pull them in closer as you feel each and every muscle, from the top of your head, to the tips of your toes, relaxing, completely. And as they do, you may notice that in the back of your mind there's a dark place, a quiet place, floating through a soft and velvety void where nothing can harm you, where you become the formlessness that exists at the beginning and end of all things, and the spaces in between, pure feeling and sensation."

He paused for a few minutes, allowing them to drift amid the mind-scapes they were weaving.

"And with the passage of time you'll begin to notice how the blackness is ever changing, finding places that are lighter and darker than others, and looking down as you were floating up and right above it before, under your feet now, an endless plain stretches out in all directions towards the horizon, the deepest purple, walking as and where you will, so deep that you'll have to look twice with your eyes within eyes to see it at all, featureless, except for a great door rising perpendicular to the plane before you, growing closer and larger with each step, with every breath, the infinite void of Narcea taking shape in your thoughts as the gates of your soul open up to the place your heart most desires to go, beyond you hear a voice beckoning, summoning you there."

Eyes closed, head nodding, Rob inhaled deeply as he listened to the stillness about the room. The muscles in their cheeks and around their lips relaxed. The group was in the perfect spot for this, chests rising and falling together as they breathed in unison, and he continued, "Now, as you take the first step through and feel the atmosphere, changing in ways you didn't expect, because once inside, that plain that was is now rolling, sloping downwards as your feet follow a path that leads towards the grove of trees you can see in the distance, soft fronds of grass brushing against your soles lightly, the air fresh and moist, so delicious you yearn for the next breath, in, and gulping it down, on the far side of the circle awaits a symbol, a totem of the beast that acts as your guide, protecting and keeping you safe, your relationship to it a thing to explore, growing stronger each day, and when you arrive at the center a place that's familiar appears, a stone bridge and the sounds of drumming, rattling, echoing everywhere though the darkness, illuminated only by the faint glow you can see with your eyes within eyes around the symbol that's here."

While Rob spoke, Alexi felt himself slowing down as the room around him disappeared. In its place he felt the very intense, very immediate sensation of his body. Although his eyes were closed, he was seeing a light, bright and pulsing, inside his body, pulling him in. Vertigo overwhelmed him. The words of Rob's voice spun around, carrying an irresistible power, pitch rising and falling like the distortions of light bending through his eyelashes first close, then far away. The vibration inside his body constant, insistent, he felt himself yielding and merging with it, and the images beginning to form in his mind brought unnatural clarity along with them, each detail as sharp and as vivid as though he'd never closed his eyes at all.

Now, clear as a dream, he found himself standing deep in a small meadow, surrounded by a dark, starlit forest. Crickets sang softly behind him, their voices merging with that of a stream nearby.

"And hear, listen, the rustling sounds of a breeze as it kisses the branches and leaves, shadows of stars, your totem animal singing to you the visions and dreams, glimpsing an age you once knew and thought you'd forgotten, remembering now, the dry desert air stirring sands of time with the chanting of voices, spells woven in overtones of the stories they tell, each note a thread weaving over and back through the Narcean loom, together lives knotted in infinite black, web of the void, felt, smelt, tasting the hot breath on the back of your neck as fires of passion consume, poised on the edge of the pyramid tumbling round the all-seeing eye of your mind reaches out in all directions to gather, collect impressions words form on your senses, connect with the wellspring eternal that's deep inside you, heart beating in rhythm, ba-boom, ba-boom, with the pulse-sing of drums."

After peering into the gloom ahead for many moments and still aware of Rob's voice rolling ever on in the back of his mind, he proceeded forward through the woods cautiously. Soon, the darkness grew so complete that only the crunching of leaves, pebbles, and roots underfoot registered as he made his way down, steadily down to the bottom of this deep valley. He could hear the rumble of breathing somewhere below, the soft, invisible purring of a living shadow.

He would stumble on occasion, his foot snagging on a root or catching on one of the rocks, and finally found his way down to a stone bridge. Inspecting it closely, he saw that it had been constructed from enormous grey slabs of stone, spanning a broad and brackish river winding through the valley and cleaving it in half. The clearing afforded by this open expanse allowed unnatural amounts of light to filter through the canopy forming an unusual twilight, a green and purple haze crystallizing in the air. As Alexi stepped onto the bridge, the air surrounding him felt warmer, and the dizziness returned. The woods fell silent, and seemed to move far away, a distant memory.

Seated on one of the cornerstones and staring into the distance with half-closed eyelids, he could hear Rob's voice speaking to him, so close he felt the warmth of his breath near his ear. Accompanying the words came a rhythmic rattling sound. Alexi closed his eyes, let himself relax into the pulse beat of his heart, the rattling in his ears, and then he found himself...or imagined he found himself, walking alongside the bridge on a path adjacent to the river. At the same time he could still feel the cold cornerstone beneath him. *Which is real, and which is imaginary?*

Too late Alexi, distracted by existential thoughts, realized that the forest had fallen silent, too silent, with only the sound of his footfalls echoing back from the walls of the ravine. He tensed as his heart pounded with adrenaline, senses on alert for whatever danger might be lying ahead, and saw for the first time a pair of yellow eyes trained on him in the distance, following his every move with the casual indifference of a hunter who knows its prey has no avenue of escape.

Alexi was terrified as the haze drifting around the valley like a ghost revealed a gigantic black cat crouched over a log in a beam of pale moonlight, poised to pounce at any moment. The panther regarded him with a bemused and half-disdainful expression on her face, as though she were unsure whether or not that chase would be worth the effort she'd have to spend. This caught Alexi even more off-guard, and as he began to think about it, he found himself rather curious as to what she wanted, figuring that if the panther had wanted to eat him, she'd have done so already.

The sound of shattering glass, like fine crystal striking a linoleum floor, jarred Alexi out of his vision. His eyes darted around the room, but no one else appeared to have heard the sound. They all sat, eyes closed, breathing evenly and in unison, deep in trance. He realized that he couldn't recall where he had just "been," or what he had been doing. Listening again to Rob's voice roll on and on, he let his eyes slowly close...

"And between each vision you see, ideas which rest in the back of your mind come into the foreground as you follow the path, leading forward and down towards the light which spins in the spine of stillness like a thunderbolt, crackling with energy that spreads out through the lattice of places you've been, and are, all now, I know that beyond those gates where the awareness of dreams you've been having expands, there's a space where the spirit of your beast resides and you meet face-to-face your fears with that aura of illumination ever around you, shadows of illusions holding you back fall away, far, far away as the chanting and drums roll across the plain and all that you've learned on this journey remains, sleeping, waiting, anticipating, ready to spring at your beck and call of the forest spirits, howling, growling, the symbol guiding with sureness your step by stepping stones across the creek and under the bridge, the troll pays the toll to travelers crossing over to the other side, hearing tales of passages between distant lands, caravans carrying goods to the sands of time falling grain by grain in an endless parade marching down the streets of the city like a colony of ants speaks words to those who can listen only to the sound of my voice, listening only to the sound of my voice."

Rob took another deep breath and looked around the room as people here and there began to blink their eyes, a few yawning, like waking up from a dream, and he asked, "Where are you?"

"I was in Japan, in Tokyo. There was a graveyard, and I used to go there. I remember once, in the middle of autumn, the leaves were bright, in the trees and on the ground. Everything was so vibrant, the colors were so alive that I've never been able to get the image out of my mind. An old Japanese man walked through the graveyard, peacefully sweeping up the leaves," Suzanne said, her eyes still closed.

"The top of a giant tower. I've set my sights on the very top where a tremendous, overpowering light shines," Alexi said, his eyes also remaining closed. "There's an incalculable geometric process…five sides on the bottom giving way to six at the top, going through the entire spectrum of color until it fades into that brilliant light at the summit. Yet all the same, the entire structure is black, blacker than night can ever be, and I feel absolutely lost looking at it. I entered at the bottom wearing the robes of a Magus and holding a long staff, surprisingly adorned with a cross at its top. Now, after having reached the top, I see myself in that light, and I can't bear it. The robes have been burned from my body by the blinding light. I can't tolerate his brightness, and now I'm falling, falling to the very bottom…" His eyes opened slowly, and he looked out the window, his fingers shaking, hunting for the pack of cigarettes deep in his pockets, with a life of their own.

Creeping shadows, falling darkness, she is waiting for the sun…

Everyone else remained silent, preferring to stay in the place they had found.

"Should we interpret what we saw and draw a contrast?" Alexi asked, still looking out the window at the nearby road.

"No. Only you should interpret it. It's a personal thing…" Rob answered, hesitating, "your energy and mine…they're opposites. When I look in you, I see a darkness, or perhaps it's an emptiness. It grows in you like a hungry soul sickness. You create and you create, but find nothing but yourself in it. It's like you're suffocating on yourself. I too am lost, but upon the other side, lost in Narcea."

"Narcea?" Alexi asked, moving to sit beside him. Rob had mentioned it numerous times, but never fully explained.

"I was riding my bike, many years ago, when something happened. I've thought about it a great deal since, and haven't been able to...well, all I can say is that it was a view of truth. There was this horrible, wrenching noise, something being sheared into a million pieces. I saw everything. No, I can see by the expression on your face that you understand, and yet don't. Maybe I was everything, everyone, everytime for a moment, for all moments. I don't know. I seem to focus on it anymore. All perspectives at once, and now... I can't seem to focus on it anymore... I have these unbearable headaches, almost every day. They don't let me think about it for very long."

"Somehow it makes me think of Harrison Bergeron..." Alexi mused.

"It was Narcea. That is all I can say," Rob said, his eyes eerily distant and vacant.

<hr/>

As Alexi closed the door with a quiet click and turned to look at Samantha, he noticed she had already crawled into bed. He approached, stepping over her clothes strewn about the room. He paused a moment and grinned at her.

Shivering momentarily, he slid under the covers and curled up beside her, unconsciously placing his lips on her neck. Kissing her softly, he left them there a moment before rolling her over. She greeted him with a smirk, which vanished as their eyes met. In its place she wore a mixture of adoration, affection, and...a little fear. Closing his hand around hers and bringing it to his mouth, he noticed that the smell of her skin was so familiar now.

She looked up at him expectantly, her mouth small and partially opened, and he felt himself pulled towards her. Her eyes fluttered closed, dancing rapidly behind thin eyelids. As their lips met, he felt a pulse in her hand, still held tenderly in his, and then he realized that what he was feeling was not the pulsing of blood through her veins, but the throbbing of her energy.

They began moving together gently at first, waiting for that pulse to spread. His hands running down down her back lightly, he could feel the thrumming intensify with each breath they took together. And now she was arching her back, thighs and belly taut, her mouth gasping open.

Although he grew increasingly aroused, this intense throbbing pressure he felt remained fixated at the base of his spine. With no physical reaction, this energy sublimated elsewhere, his groin incredibly cold. She laid still and peered up at him.

"Am I doing something wrong?" She asked.

The roaring in his ears was all he could hear. His eyes were darting from side to side, his body rigid.

"Alexi?"

With inhuman alacrity, he spring up from beside her and scampered to the far end of the bed. From the corner of the room he regarded her through the cold, unblinking eyes of some predatory animal. He began to rock to and fro and chuckled to himself.

"A…Alexi?" she mumbled, very frightened now.

"Not anymore," he replied in a low, only half-human growl.

"This isn't funny! You fucking stop that right now!"

"No, not anymore," he repeated. "We need to go back into the woods. Now. I can feel *them* calling, we need to go. We need to go now. They need me. They need to give me something."

Crouching forward on his haunches, back arched sharply, he whipped around. His breath came in long pants.

"What are these things? What do they want with me?" he asked, gruffly.

"What are you talking about?" She backed up against the far wall, pressing her knees against her chest.

He shot through the air, faster than she could move, faster than she could blink, and was right up against her, eyes wide and pupils dilated, his hand an inch from her throat. Then he blinked, and looked around the room as if with new eyes.

Samantha was shaking, tears glittering on her cheeks.

"I… I'm sorry. It was *him*, don't you understand…or should I say it. My *third*." His contorted hands rent the blanket under them as every muscle in his body tensed and relaxed spasmodically.

She shook her head. "You can't keep doing this Alexi. You need help."

He pulled the blinds closed and collapsed in a heap beside her. "The light burns my eyes," he said, after a moment. "No one can help me. I need a shaman, not a psychologist. I need to find someone in this barren culture that knows how to...how to deal with these things...how to master them. You just don't understand."

"You can't keep putting me through this. You have to stop."

"I know," Alexi said, his eyes already closed.

⊷⊶

About a week later, Alexi received a phone call. "Hello?" he asked, trying to rouse himself from his nap.

"Hello, this is Renee. Did you hear?" the grave voice asked on the other end of the line.

"Hear what, Renee?"

"Jason broke up with me. Just cut me off. And he did it because of the changes...you have made to his personality."

"I changed...? Wait. I never made anyone do anything. Whatever Jason decides may be influenced by my presence, but I don't make other people's decisions for them. I know you're hurting, but there's no reason to point blame."

"No, I'm quite certain. I see what you're doing, leading the group, and maybe you don't see it yourself. Well, I'm not the only one who feels this way, although I may be the one who feels it most strongly. Thanks Alexi."

"Renee, I—"

<click>

Alexi hung up the phone and rolled onto his back.

"And so it begins..."

INTERLUDE III

THE MYTH OF ORPHEUS

He approached the valley with a feeling of trepidation, ringed by cracked and broken statues, all of them mirrors of the same female image carved of rose and ivory marble. She stood tall and forlorn, a stern guardian of an ancient and forgotten shrine, pointing towards the horizon. A feeling of unease crept up his back. It was as though she had always been standing there, always pointing on, leading him towards a rendez-vous he couldn't possibly predict. Still, although he couldn't yet see it, he knew the entrance lay ahead. It wasn't just because of his trust in the old man's word—he could feel its presence.

Stopping to look up at the statues, he saw them breathing ever so slowly as if she were encased in the rock, frozen in time but still aware. Waiting. And as he stood there staring up at her, a song began in his head. At first it had a distant quality, as if passing through miles of air and hundreds of years. The song seemed to emanate from these statues, and this ghostly voice which echoed across the hill tops and over the water was like those faces: eerie, cold, and yet full of hope...and so, so familiar...

In the temple of the temple of the temple of the Holy
sits a woman who is waiting who is waiting for the sun
in the temple of the temple in the temple of the Holy
creeping shadows falling darkness she is waiting for the sun.

For the people of the people by the people making people
in the temple of the temple of the temple of the Holy
She is weeping for the people of the people
making people in the temple of the temple in the temple of the sun.

No one's listening are you listening? I'm not listening
no one's listening in the temple of the temple in the temple
of the Holy to her crying she is crying I am crying in the
temple in the temple of the temple of the temple of the sun.

Hearing voices crying voices wailing voices all in chorus
of the temple and the temple and the temple of the Holy
falling deeper ever deeper even deeper than the Holy
in the temple of the temple in the temple of the sun.

Grass crunched thickly underfoot. The warm haze in the valley was
thick, but as he pressed on over the slippery, barnacle covered rocks the
air grew cold. (His breath was ice but it was also the middle of summer.)

As he traversed further inland, now on solid earth and granite, he realized that he was phasing out between this landscape and somewhere else.
The ground was solid, now sloping down into a valley…

*My view blurs at the edges. The smell of vegetation poking through
the last, melting snow of winter. Damp earth. The ice brings fertility.*

*There's a deep pulse that reverberates all around me, a bass thrum-
ming sound, so deep that you feel it in your chest more than hear it. The
air is humid, yet I can see the cold of my breath in the air, the pale
reflection of yesterday.*

*I'm still conscious. For the first time now I think over all that has
happened to me, and I know for the first time that I was dead, that there
was never any turning back, that right now I am doing as I must do and
as I have always done, there is no effort, there is no ego, all is as it
should be, as it always has been, as the earth swallowed me, as I made
love, as the water passed above my head, my lungs aching, as I was
frightened and hid from the predators, as I turned to Ken when I did, as
we played the roles we did because he needed someone to confide in and
I needed to be confided in, as the fire burned away my skin and the
remaining ashes were dispersed in the four directions, light and paper-
thin like hummingbird feathers… Yet after it all, there is something
remaining. And it is not regret.*

*Now I walk through the heart of this forest in autumn. I'm thinking:
I've got to really push for something…the smell of fresh earth, the feeling, that fleeting feeling that always comes along with it like the onset of
vertigo when you realize you're falling in love, and there's no turning*

back now... I always think for a moment, amidst a flash of memories—was that me? and that sensation too? and the reaction? My head and heart swimming with the recollections, I'm thinking about sitting in a restaurant, someone beside me, gun fire, confusion, explosions.

Back and back in the valley, I think how I had come a long way and thought "learning, really learning," and yet underneath that, too, I feel an uncertainty, like the difference between how I'm walking and how I feel, and I ask "am I, really?" The voice, deep and insane, rolling on and on, "learning and learning, you are really pushing on and soon, so soon your genius will explode out, your genius will explode out it's only a matter of taking something you really believe and something you want to believe and switching them learning really learning" I have nothing left to say, my skin is sun burnt and raw, there is no cause worth fighting for, the desert sand washed over me, I am drowning, suffocating, burning, and now I am back where I began:

Learning really learning the insane voice continues on steadily, slowly, with the terrible ferocity and gravity of a freight train. Still, I feel a certain fondness for this train, even for the engineer. The insanity is in his eyes, the kind of plastic, neon-glowing Prozac grin I imagine Arnold Schwarzenegger would have, standing there so straight-backed, his immense teeth shining in fluorescent lights. "Learning, really learning," he would say in a deep Baritone, and I can hear trees creaking when his arms and legs move, giant sinews stretching under leather-tanned skin. He would lean down over me and—his hands are so much larger than mine, I feel like a child, and still he's saying "learning, really learning," and the smile just keeps growing, the picture growing brighter, "learning, really learning," he says, I'm four years old and he's towering over me, and now his grin is a grimace, his handshake a convulsion. I can hear Beethoven screaming his last in the 9th Symphony and there's the same kind of overload, you just have to put your hands to your ears, look life in the eyes one last time, and scream: enough!...

There's that thrumming sound still, growing deeper, flashing lights in the forest with every pulse, every pulse sending a shiver down my spine. My chest is on fire. With every breath I know I'm falling deeper into sleep, and it is with this knowledge that I cross the threshold, enter the tunnel, and the last remnant of consciousness drops away like the final, fleeting image of a dream upon awakening.

He had finally reached the bottom of the valley.
All around him stood metallic buildings

these buildings were the source of the thrumming noise.

He looked into the sky where the ripe, full moon hung low,
dripping silver in long strands like spider webs,
the silent shadow
to this wanderer
of
winding paths.

Now he could hear it—feel it—in every bone of his body, pulsing, tingling, colliding. The moon, the trees, the buildings, all singing together, all of the songs the same, all of the voices, tempos, and articulations different. But still it was that one familiar song, echoing…the song you feel when you look her in the eyes and remember how it's going to be, so familiar and yet so achingly other.

Scale, he realized, was not the same here as in the waking-world, the square-world. Dead now, dreaming now, but the story continues, unfolding in an endless spiral, constantly casting off and taking on forms.

Here, where there are more dimensions, seeing is not so much a matter of simple first, second, or third person perception. Aware of himself as a he, the third person singular awareness of self, first person without ego. Being without I?

The buildings laughed. They communicated with each other in pulses, with the dance and music of their existence, and he moved closer to investigate. He was at once walking down a street lined with cylindrical, self-illuminated disks. The birds-eye view approached this space-craft, glowing long and true in the predawn sky.

⇒◦⇐

There are faceless people in other frames of time, moving quickly but in jumps—

Sometimes he feels them pass through him, and in those places he feels a particularly strong resonant buzz or hum. *The resonance pattern is the interaction of two or more sine-waves,* he thought, *I really must learn more about fourier transforms.* In the waking world, people feel his passage but don't know what they're feeling.

⇒◦⇐

An aspect at a higher frequency, the last remnants of the square-world, shoots an image of a beaming Arnold, his echoing voice drifting across the distance, "learning, really learning..." but the reaction is a belly laugh. He feels the laugh run up into his throat like bile, burning acid aftertaste. At the same time, there is the feeling of a heavy object in his hand. A silver, new .357 is solid in his left hand, a physical anchor point for the experience.

Now he is totally on that street, surrounded by buildings, heading towards the middle of the circle with small but determined steps. His strides are strong and quick, he looks from side to side slyly, eyes dilating, pulse raising, muscles tensing. The gun is heavy and comforting. Internal monologue overpowering, traveling back to the visions of the city, of the spacecraft of our past and future.

thousands of eyes
thousands of where's
thousands of how's and who's and what's?
I thought
of them at first as aliens—
thousands of people
thousands of worries
time to sleep.
I mean,
we the square,
caught in the web of time and space,
live by its mandates so long as we believe,
really believe
in the weaver
    that the sun will rise tomorrow,
molder of chaos
       that there is such a thing as "gravity,"
  creator and creation of our "logic"
           we have faith in God
           dreamer and dreaming of our cities
           Vishnu asleep in the cosmic ocean
           because we have faith in grammar.

Along with this monologue ran images, shifting framerate faster and slower, in a jittery, too-blue instructional montage. Over the city of metal, I can see a tremendous ebony spider, shiny like polished onyx, with long, slender legs, weaving its web over and over, dancing where each of its legs touch a strand, a thin silver strand, almost invisible to the eye, that supports the matrix of all that can and will be. She moves from one junction of the grid to the next, enters those places, those times as well. These aliens are spiders with thousands of eyes, each of those eyes a person in a particular time, a particular place. Unknowingly, we are all one of them.

The weaver crawls along her web freely, and we, the eyes, wonder where last weeks paycheck went.

The weaver spins on...

———————

A sliver of robinegg blue light cut through the swaying curtain, thin and transparent like gauze. *Awake, I'm awake. What a dream...* Cold night air, his throat is sore. Eyes focus and follow the light, like a thin pointer, from the dusty windowpane to a silhouetted form in the corner of this room.

As he became aware of a faint bubbling sound, like molten metal churning slowly, his eyes locked with *hers*. Pale eyes, glowing the color of the moon, regarded him coldly. As he lay on his side, the thick down covers of the bed pulled to his neck, he watched in horror as a young woman slowly, deliberately pulled a long thin silver strand, hand over hand, from between her quivering lips. It pooled in her opalescent lap. He heard a rustling, like a snake slithering through dry leaves, her hands working like a spider, weaving the filament into great webs. Struggling to move he realized he was trapped in it. His eyes widened as he realized that what she was weaving were his thoughts, tying them together in thick braids. The covers were made entirely of solidified, sticky, silver liquid... *Trapped!*

...White cinderblocks and a small, constricting room. The lattice-work of the grout is like the weaver's webs. Dense rock. Underground. He had looked at an intersection, where one strand crossed another, the space ship had launched into the pastfuture, and now: a square room. Square, the law of four...the apriority of space and time...and 4x4 window panes in my sight now. 16. A hiss of steam like a dragon erupting into the air, wreathed in flame. One plus six. 7. She must be here, some-where. But where was *here*?

Eyes, come on now. The lights are harsh and blinding. Suddenly he realizes that there's a tall, slender black man in a white lab coat speaking to him, hobbling about the room slowly. Club-footed? Bald head waxed to a shine, he sees his knobby reflection distort in its surface, like the faucet of an old, dirty tub. The blood rushes to his face, a cold splash of water from that faucet—how long has he been daydreaming? He'd better pay attention. He remembers, foggily, going to a mental hospital, remembers the collapse of something, a structure volcanically erupting, all meaningless to him now, loves, meaningless to him now...

He'd better pay attention, he realizes—the man's speech is very slow, grating like gravel rubbing together, and there was a quality to it that he recognized. It reminded him strangely of Choronzon's inflections.

The doctor talks in that trance-like way, and even thinking about what he's saying makes me go into a deep state of trance. I can see a stethoscope hanging on his neck and I stare at it dully. (The solid sensation of the gun was still in his hand, he realized warmly. He realized he was talking with the doctor, he had been for some time.)

The feeling was like nitrous oxide, coming out of the stupor in a flash of light, false lucidity. Here's this man in front of you, clear and real as day. And he's speaking:

"...Alexi? Tell me more about Dawn."

He wasn't going to be fooled. "I don't like how the Secret Chiefs are bending people into the same reality frame. Why aren't most people aware of their infinite incarnations? How many of us know about the Secret Chiefs? How many of us are Secret Chiefs and don't even know it?"

The doctor nodded calmly. The stethoscope gleamed maliciously in the light. "The note A is 440 Hz. Is this inherent to the nature of the note A? Of course not. Some English orchestra's tuned to 445 Hz for a number of years." He chuckled for a moment heartily. Too "heartily." Orpheus had no idea what he was talking about, or what this had to do with his questions. "We need to agree on a pitch to play a symphony, my friend. You have to understand this. These places that you've been telling me about, the man in the spiral, Aleonis De Gabrael, the spiders, the Secret Chiefs, the tunnel—don't you see why you need to be locked up here?" The doctor's voice bounced, vibrated, bent and distorted like an enormous rubber band.

"You think I'm crazy," he said indignantly.

"Heavens no," the doctor said, laughing, "they're crazy though. A sane person like you will get tangled in the webs. You have to learn, son, how to walk before you can fly."

Orpheus looked at him straight in the eyes, and said in an even tone "you're not here."

"Play along," the doctor said. "You're half right. But after going up upon the mountain, one must return."

"So it's okay that you're not here?"

"Doesn't mean we can't have a conversation, does it?"

"No, I suppose not. I'll tell you what I'm thinking. I'm thinking in relation to time now, and how the demarcation of time into a linear progression rather than an experiential one is absurd. My experience of time is in spirals. Rungs relating to each other. You can feel a tugging from each event if you look for it, and see it spreading into the future like ripples on the surface of a pond. Corresponding future and past events 'ring' like glasses do in harmonic sympathy to certain pitches. Our entire lives are previously conceived from this standpoint—but we still have free will in the moment. ...I'm just not satisfied that I'm confined in this concrete room when I already know the rules of the game at any level. I know I'm dreaming. I know about the spiral. Why am I still encased in flesh? Why am I still floored when something trivial doesn't go my way? I am the whole, what is this trivial fragment?"

He's taking me into a deeper state of trance with him, I think, but I don't feel any problem with this on a subconscious level.

"...I feel uncomfortable speaking of 'conscious' and 'subconscious' as if there's some kind of clear distinction. One moment I'm asleep with one kind of awareness, the next I'm dreaming awake in another. One moment there is a 'he,' then I'm a 'me.' I can't tell when I'm talking and when I'm thinking to myself. There is no inside and no outside. I'm awake when I'm asleep, and sleeping when I'm awake. Days or months disappear without recollection and then re-emerge years later, *more* real then than the first time around..."

"You are Alexi. You committed yourself to the hospital claiming that you had come in contact with immortal intelligences that play an intrinsic role in the unfolding of your life. You claim that all of this is true yet you still came here, of all places. I am also told that you were recently dumped by your girlfriend, and that—"

Orpheus looked at him with bloodshot eyes. "Oh come off it. Who are you? Don't play this game with me."

There's a tension in our conversation now, but it's all on the surface. The tip of the iceberg. I can feel the water underneath, and it is immeasurably deep and ice cold. Underneath, I'm soaking it up like a sponge.

I see hundreds of crows with great iridescent feathers flap from his open mouth, the beating of their wings like clapping, worn hands. With a steely voice the aged crows relate to me their wisdom. I receive their message in translation, garbled by my obsessive need to rationalize and make orderly the pristine chaos of the universe. *Belief and emotional connotation are what anchor an experience, and time is merely the progression of memory.* This is how I understand their message. Not so much things learned as things remembered, I remember. So familiar. But still when I punch a wall, the hand bruises. The wall stands firm.

A nurse comes in that I recognize, although at this point she doesn't look the same. She looks like the girl in the statues. It's funny how you already know what kind of future impact you're going to have on a person when you meet them. It's like an echo. "It's funny how we met," they say, but they don't mean it. They knew all along. They willed it that way, even if they weren't conscious of it. And they can unwill it, too. She doesn't recognize me, but I kiss her and let her know that sometime in the future script, we'll be very close. She seems confused but secretly flattered. We're still cast into roles by other people here, still confined by the boxes and cinder blocks of high schools, homework and recesses on various levels. Soon we will be cast into our own roles. I can feel a warmth spreading through my body when I remember our future together.

Soon she will be trapped.
        Soon I will be sitting with Ken,
                and he will have a vision.
        Soon I will meet Gabrael.
                Soon I will be dead.

Then I turn to regard the doctor again. His posture asks me to be all business. I don't remember what happens immediately after this, but pretty soon I have the Secret Chief—I know now the doctor is also a Secret Chief, thanks to a remembered memory, from the future or the past... I can't recall, and somebody named "Gabrael"—up against a wall with my gun pointed at him. There's no anger in the action, although the weight of the gun still feels comforting. I know I'll never shoot it. I'll never have to. I have the force of my will here. This is my magickal wand, the totem of my will. But the Chief is calm. I think he understands my ploy, the sly old wolf. His eyes are like glacier ice. It burns when you look at them. Yes, he is wolf clan, enemy of crow.

It is very clear to me now why I have a problem with his clan's intentions in the reality war. Of course I can't tell him this, and I certainly can't tell him that I have allied with panther. He would kill me for sure.

This is what I'm thinking but it is not what I am saying. I'm explaining how easy it is to break out of programmed responses in times that our nervous system interprets as life-threatening danger. These are times of imprinting, not all that unlike the first sexual encounter. I am explaining all of this to him, but I'm the one being tested. I feel frustration that most behavior is purely on the level of reaction, that the webs are binding and no one sees the freedom of *becoming*. I'm suddenly in twenty places at once, on all levels, some of them feel very deep under water, seeing movies of people behaving mechanically, fight or flight, do I look big or little? will to power in the most rudimentary sense, subverted sexuality and the revenge of the repressed, the doldrums and cages that spring up with every opportunity in thought and in action to keep us from really seeing eye to eye. Seeing past the mirror, under the appearance. It is very clear to me here that lying "under" the visual phenomenon is a being on all levels, apprehending all possible states—

※

...No time for this, though—he's sitting in a hospital trying to explain the basic premises of quantum physics, western esoteric Qabbalah, and relativity to a board of doctors. A futile attempt at explaining his condition.

He paused. The doctors were staring at him blankly with the heads of mighty beasts.

"There are birds pecking out my eyes! birds bad!..." he screamed suddenly.

No reaction.

"BIRDS! MY EYES! AHHHH!"

All of the doctors have heads like animals. Great and hairy, slender and covered in slick scales, their stares are ominous and thoroughly disorienting. They're all the tribal chieftains of a particular belief, the tribal belief pacts of nations, religions, icons and symbols. He recognizes the rat, crow, cat and bear lords before the scene fades.

He's standing in a dirty subway train in New York city. The squealing of the wheels is deafening, the feel of tense metal, slick with oil, screaming. You can feel how hollowed out everyone is just from the dirt on the trains, the gray, muted blue and faded yellow tiles; like standing in line all day, watching television shows selling products you're indifferent to, living with people you're indifferent to, feeling emotions that you're indifferent to. He looks up and sees buses moving on the street above through concrete and the sewage system. Every area has a consciousness all its own. This is how it speaks to you:

His attention is drawn back to the train, the tiles flying by, the hypnotic, lulling rock of the cabin. A man leaning to the side, drool slowly collecting on his lower lip, regarding him with glassy eyes.

Looking out one of the streaked windows, one of *them* is crawling on the outside of the train, crawling on hands and feet that connect to the smooth metal surface like a spider. No one else appears to notice. His movement is bizarre and unnatural to me, and I feel that he's mocking me with each precise movement. It's the jerky and yet careful way he moves that makes him invisible to these indifferent people in the train, like he only moves when they aren't looking. His head rocks from side to side in an alien way, and I imagine him telling me: "why can't you do this? Look, I can do this! This is how you do it! This is how you live in and out of space and time simultaneously!" Now I have a clear look at him. He has bright blue skin, reflective like shiny plastic and an elongated face.

Orpheus remembers in a flash being in a bedroom and seeing a face like this raising as if in a mist from the wall. His eyes sockets are empty, his two eyes slowly orbiting around his limbs, looking one way and then the next.

I notice him by looking between the cracks, in the silences, the hollow spaces. There are kids on the train that begin to notice him, (maybe, I think, "it" is more appropriate. They are beyond gender.) He continues his grotesque dance—there's a sudden feeling of revulsion and horror, and then he melts and steps into a passing train headed the opposite direction.

───◆───

Orpheus awoke, lying face down in wet grass. His long hair flowed around him, and he now wore a loose fitting silk shirt, gray wool pants, and a leather vest. Affixed to the fine tooled leather was a silver brooch embossed with the sign of Cancer, the crab.

With a moan he rolled onto his back, and then leaned back on his elbow. Surrounded by twisting brambles, each clothed in thorns like knives, there was an immense yawning hole in the ground ahead of him. Great gusts of damp air issued from it in a constant rhythm, and he could hear that thrumming bass sound, deep in the earth.

He walked to the edge cautiously and saw to his relief that a massive stair spun around into its depths, clinging to the wall. The ledge was narrow, and there was no railing, but it still looked an easier route than jumping. He began the long descent.

━━━◆◆◆━━━

Again, I'm bathed in fluorescent, humming in my bones. Where am I? This is the part where I look around, and going outside, forget who I am. Rows of herbs in labeled bottles above an old stove with gas burners, yellow walls... I think they're yellow. The closer I look the more unsure I am what color they are. The more I pry into this sensation, the more the room pulses around me, fading to black and then returning. Did I take acid? Am I a forgotten trip?

Two eyes are regarding me now, bringing me out of a final dip into darkness. She is wearing a dress, again I cannot discern its color. Is it blue? Green? She gestures with her hands while she is talking—she has been speaking to me, her voice low and plain—for some reason those thin hands strike as two doves, with their fingers curled outwards like fragile feathers. Her lips are thin and yet full—I am watching them move, so slowly. So slowly and silently. Her hair is a deep red, of that I'm sure.

The fingers move sinuous now, like snakes. I can feel my weight compressing in the padded chair beneath me, the sensation of my breathing, and now I am really here. Alright, what is she saying, now that I am here, now that I can pay attention—

"...If there were only that day, I wonder if I would love it as I love you now. If I would collect moments in my mind, gather them in my arms, and hold them up to the light to illuminate another angle. Like the angles of your face, my love. How strange to think of every second like I think of the dilation and contraction of your pupils as you look at me, and a moment later look away. Would the day stretch so we could all live the same amount of the time and our lives shrink so that it was only a day, a moment, a breath and it was gone, that first breath and hold, that last and let go, the seconds overlapping, lapping at your toes as you wade through taste touch dip inside your fingers curled in the air so slowly, so slowly, as into the hands of the young or the old?…"

Now I am seeing long reptiles, plumed with brightly colored feathers, unblinking eyes—

"It was on Tuesday and it will be on Sunday and if you close your eyes you can still hear it humming …still alive, still alive, still alive, still alive… and even if you beg for just a moment longer than we have, we never get it. So it might as well be Tuesday. It's the same the way it's the same if we're fat or your thin or there was time or there wasn't. We all loved and we all didn't and we begged begged begged and we always lost gloriously."

A burst of pleasure runs through me, unbearable ache. There is a yanking, rending, of my insides and the room around me. I am reaching out to her, I so desperately want to stay here… To get close enough to allow her to become first person and myself third, let myself go to let her in… I can't even remember what she was saying, now.

The sensation of thick downy covers brings me awake. Blankets almost as thick as pillows. Samantha is curled beside me. I nudge her. She groans a little, her breath grows uneven just for a moment, then she returns to a low steady pace. I nudge her again and she wakes up. I try to describe what just happened, thinking that maybe I'll recall the details in the retelling. I'm holding the images behind my eyes but the words won't come. How can I describe the valley? The depth of my interaction with the doctor? My feeling of love for that woman?

As I'm speaking I notice that the wall behind her is rippling like a curtain in the wind. Suddenly I feel terrified at what might lie behind that curtain, and I turn towards her. She can tell I'm frightened, but doesn't seem to understand why. She asks me if I'm having another "one of my episodes." Everything is rippling now, almost a whirlpool—and I am clutching her, clutching through her flesh to her bones. Everything turns upside down, inside out. I watch her face melt. Then blackness.

But I am still here. I am still *awake.*

The sensation of thick downy covers brings me awake. *Fuck. Not again.* I open one eye, quickly close it. Samantha is beside me, just as she was. Is she really there? I poke her quickly, though of course in my first awakening she had felt quite solid, quite real. As had the chair under me in the kitchen, when I was with the woman. This time she opens one eye, stares at me dully.

"Mmm. Mmm?" The other eye half opens. After much effort, it drifts closed again.

"Are you...here?" God, I feel stupid. She was there before, too. Then she melted. I'd have felt even more ridiculous asking her if she planned on melting again, and if she did, she should at least have the decency to warn me. Forget it, I'll never know the ground is solid again. I'll just have to learn to live with it.

Chapter 11, Grid 2

PG. (Pig Without an "I")

Everything is bullshit. I'm just concerned with the bullshit that works.
— Jesus

Highlighted in blistering red neon hung the crucified baby Jesus, framed in gilded mahogany, with an inscription reading "DEATH TO ALL FISH." Vague, ethereal music wafted into the hallway like smoke, emphasizing the feeling of alienation Pig felt. Looking down the other side of the hallway, she saw the highly reflective doors of an elevator. On the panel to the left of the door, instead of buttons, was a plaque which read "IS YOU A WOMAN?"

Pig turned and stared hard at the crucified baby Jesus. Its tiny head slowly melted into that of a hawk, screaming silent vengeance. Pig unconsciously took a step towards the elevator, taken aback by the sudden transformation. The face reverted back to its former state and frowned. She felt sick to her stomach as the scream continued to increase in volume, silently. *I am encrypted from your deep roots, a multiplicity of truth and falsehood. An undertow of indecent deceit, though innocent by all accounts. Oh you—falsehood! I am the silhouette against the amber dawn, oval, wide-hipped and proud. I possess the tactile sensations of vinyl and the memory of wood.*

Now walking quickly towards the elevator, Pig saw two men get in before her. She thought she recognized them, although she wasn't sure. The doors slammed shut, and then a minute later, they stepped off and disappeared. Before the mammoth doors could close again, she stepped on. The lights immediately went off, clothing her in a blanket of darkness, and she had the distinct feeling of falling, falling down forever. Fucked in every orifice. Overcome with vertigo, she collapsed to the floor, feeling pummeled, beaten, and crippled. Words formed in her head: *This pig feels like she should be feeling. But this pig can't allow herself to feel, because when she does, she feels very sad and shits a lot. And it's useless, rambling shit, just like this. And it would take another pig to bother with this pig's shit.* Something was strangling her. A sharp pain, and even deeper darkness, as her throat constricted and her eyes slammed shut. And then she was drowned in what she somehow knew was sperm as the words "the Holy Ghost" echoed loudly in her head.

⬤◆⬤

Pig woke up, bathed in cold sweat, on her bed. Her thick down comforter was wrapped around her legs, and it took her a few moments to untangle herself. It was still dark out—she had only been asleep for a few hours. Uttering a feeble groan, she rolled over and picked up the phone, dialing a few numbers.

"Hey..." she breathed, fumbling around the side of the bed for some cigarettes.

There was a long pause. Silence on both ends.

"I know I didn't show. I had, uh—other things to attend to." She nodded her head and then laughed quietly. "No, it doesn't have anything to do with a Hispanic guy named Juan—and no, I haven't been abducted by aliens. I've just been busy. Out with old friends... Well, some things just can't be expressed that easily in words or with actions or anything. It sometimes seems... I don't know, so hard to—yeah, that's it. It reminds me of the lyrics to a song which has continually been running through my head ever since we began to hang out and...and the frustration I have experienced in attempting to say, show, tell, or in some way reveal to you how I feel—"

She paused as the person on the other end spoke.

"Yeah, we'll talk about it later... I'll see you soon." She hung up the phone and prepared to call the other guy. *The things I get myself into,* she thought with mixed regret and excitement.

...Silly girls, they gag on the advertisement, they gag but they don't throw up, too embarrassed to complete an action their bodies have deemed necessary. Silly girls (I am shaking my head) they are so silly. They have flowers they kiss the rosebuds and snarl at the sunflowers. They don't even have thorns, they say, relishing the prick, the response of the blood, rushing happily towards the hole, the oxygen, the light. The

blood cells die, they abort themselves, and are forgotten as the girls go
to pick more roses...

━━━◆◆◆◆━━━

Agent 139 hung up the phone and tried to go back to sleep.
!
HOW
can I be certain? I close my eyes and try to forget. Try not to remember (And, there is no ownership of flesh.) How many times a day do I
have to go through this? She said...no good. Shut up and move the pillow. Crick in the neck. Slender neck, pale skin. Howdohowdohowdo: I
stop this and try to remember her smiling. Tension builds to a breaking
point. Fists clenched. Backs off right before the tears come.
DO
Howdohowdohowdo: I know? there is nothing certain. "Maybe" is
always the answer, no better than random chance. Prefer to be lied to.
"It's all going to be okay." There is an uncertainty in every movement.
You can never be certain what impulse lies underneath an action. Everything she says: Do you mean that? Then I turn on myself: Do I say this to
be heard? Ethics is just a means of protecting yourself. Insecurity always
gives rise to conscience. Aginbite of inwit. It bites on both sides. Roll
over, my back is sore.
I
can still see her face. (No, that isn't her at all.) Why did the mystics
always turn to prostitutes? Shut up. You set yourself up for failure with
this. (It's just random coincidence that you always chose the rotten one.)
Peer Gynt. What was it again? had too much attention from mommy,
only child, always looking for princess.
(No, that isn't her at all.)
K(NO)W
beneath. Above. She can keep the candle lit back home.
(No, that isn't her at all.) I'm dedicated. Her, Briar Thorn. It begins
with him on top. Turn over. Just go to sleep. An onion, was it? Keep
peeling the layers. No center, just masks. An ontological crisis clothed in
this? It's all about
K(NOW)
-ing
That you cannot. Do I let her stay home and go gallivanting as
revenge? Impenetrable. No, I can't. Sincere, and I don't know what to

do. As an Agent, as an executive, I can hide behind the mask, become the part. Idealizing again. Does this cycle repeat

For*ever*

?

<hr/>

The cream Nissan smoothly edged into a parking spot alongside a tall metal fence. The sounds of industrial music could be heard from a nearby nightclub. Agent 139 got out of the car and motioned to Johny, who tentatively nodded and followed his lead. Even this deep in the city, the crisp smell of autumn, the cloying scent of rotting leaves and something else, something indeterminable, was in the steely air. The Bank was a hunched, sprawling structure, a crooked form backlit in the style of a 1930's horror movie, replete with stone teeth and steel bars for eyes. The Nosferatu aesthetic was alive and well here.

Jesus looked at Agent 139 incredulously. "The club over there?"

The Agent slipped on his sunglasses. "It's called the Bank. If we're going to find any of the members of this elusive little organization, well. This'd be the place to start, I'd say."

"Mother Hive Brain?" Johny asked.

"No. Order of the Hidden Path."

"Oh," Johny said, now twice as confused as before.

<hr/>

The tall, vaulted ceilings in the room gave the impression of a cathedral. The walls were aged stone, streaked by thin white lines—apparently water damage, adorned with ancient, tattered paintings. A thick, cast-iron chandelier hung from the ceiling on a chain, casting a ring of shadowy light from the tiers of white candles affixed to its edges. There were sofas along each wall, most of them inhabited by gaunt, skeletal people dressed in black. Everything in the room felt slightly damp, more like a crypt than a cathedral.

"Really? I'm only on Paxil and Zoloft. Yeah—they said it was manic depression. Well, whatever, I've always known I was fucked up." The girl who was speaking was wearing a tight fitting purple velvet dress. Her skin seemed as white and thin as egg shells.

Another fragmentary conversation caught the Agent's attention from across the room. "Before they put me in, I cut myself with a razor, see? ...I know, I did it the wrong way. I was young, right? So..."

"That's no good. You have to cut it the long way...look." A boy sat forward and pulled his shirt up to reveal numerous scars and lacerations along his right arm, including the name "KURT COBAIN" cut in deep—and probably permanently—with a pocket knife.

Agent 139 wisely decided to head downstairs.

The bathrooms were made of corrugated metal, the air thick from sweaty bodies. As crowded as the room was, strangely, all of the bathroom stalls were unoccupied.

A cluster of young men and women hovered about the sink, speaking rapidly. Johny quickly brushed by a very tall, skinny black man with short dreadlocks and a fishnet shirt. He moved closer to the sink as he saw one of them bend over and snort a line of something yellow.

"Hey kid," he said, absently wiping his nose and sniffling. "Want some Dexedrine?"

Johny declined and was about to head to one of the stalls when a piece of paper on the floor caught his attention. Another typed message.

Gentlemen;

It is in great optimism that I write to you. Attached is a portrait of my left wrist as it is today, the source of unspeakable grief in my life.

It was manipulated to its current state by a salvage operation performed in October 95 by Dr. Hozan of the Temple Sports Medicine Center; an attempt to rectify a malunion resulting from a closed set of a break in late 91 when I was involved in a sport that has since been outlawed in 48 states. The frustration resulting from this handicap has waxed consistently since then, not to mention my frustration, considering that I was an incredibly talented in the writing.

And I now feel that it presents an unacceptable hindrance to my quality of life, as well as the myriad of other things that I enjoy doing with my wrists and joints. You can't imagine how much it has damaged my income. I lie awake at night, staring at my wrist. I cry out to Allah: "WHY?! WHY HAVE YOU DONE THIS TO ME?!" Doctors repeatedly advise me to submit to the joint's mediocre performance, and that complete rectification is an impossibility; but I assure you, sirs, my body says otherwise! Please know that I refuse to compromise, that I love my wrist, and that i have not a doubt that my body will be delivered again to it's natural state.

Let me tell you my secret: I watch bees all day. I cover my wrist in honey and I pray to the bees as I watch them. This has given me many ideas about how to return it to its natural state.

Being as how I have been able to devote an inordinate amount of consideration to this particular injury since I lost my job, I am sure that correction lies essentially in first the removal of the screws from the body, and then a severing of the radius at the point of original malunion.

I recommended this to my doctor, but he told me I was crazy, that I wasn't a doctor and that I'd hurt myself very much. But he is wrong! He is wrong, this is MY WRIST AND I CAN DO WITH IT AS I DAMNED WELL PLEASE! The distal portion, the hand, must then be simply reintroduced to its natural alignment with the arm, restoring the subtle but crucial bow of the radius. Good casting (perhaps in supination) should allow for osteogenesis in the radius, and the wrist now has the potential to achieve full functionality, rather than stagnate and decay as it does now. This is a simple case of the physician healing and nature making well, the latter, in this case, being anxious to do her job.

Please know, sirs, that I do not by any means consider myself a medical doctor, and should one of you ultimately accept my case, this procedure is of course subject to your professional refinement—but I do, however, exist in a communion with my body that is wholly unfathomable to any other individual on the face of this wretched planet. Because of this if you do not reply I will be forced to attempt the surgery myself. I track migratory birds in my sleep. I just can't explain. I understand that this is a rather unorthodox procedure, and it would be easy to follow the trend of your colleagues and choose to err on the side of caution, but I ask only to enter into dialogue at this point with a physician who sympathizes and feels competent of healing me. If you see no potential in my proposal, please simply e-mail and make that known and I will not contest you; however I will not be convinced.

Let it be known: this is the will of my God, and no one shall contest him. If you do, on the other hand, foresee any possibility of restoring this unnatural thing to the state of its partner, I thank you and look forward to seeing you.

very hopefully and sincerely yours:
Pedraic N. Ravavullovic
Vice president of CAR
And co-founder of the PAAC foundation
Beekeeper of the MHBS.

As he stood, leaning against the stall and reading this, he heard a voice behind him call his name. He could also hear Robert Smith crooning through the speakers upstairs, and it made him shudder involuntarily. Somewhat on edge due to the unusual surroundings, he spun about. A man in a long gray trench coat regarded him with amusement from behind his wire-brimmed glasses. His long hair was swept back stylishly.

"You're Johny," he said. It was a statement, not a question.

Not knowing what to say, Johny said nothing.

"My name is Alexi," he paused, waiting to judge Johny's reaction.

Johny looked at him blankly and fidgeted a little.

"Oh. You haven't heard of us. I just wanted to let you and your friends know that you're getting in over your head."

"How do you—"

"How do I know who you are? I've got contacts." Johny noticed that under the fluorescent lighting, his skin was white. Not a touch of color anywhere. Must be one of those LARPing people that were gaming here tonight. "But if you are certain you want to involve yourself, I have a little bit of information. There's an apartment...here, I'll write it down for you." Alexi pulled out a notepad, scrawled something with a long, glistening black pen, and handed it to him quickly. "Show this to your friends as well, and tell them it's Gabrael's apartment in this area. I have a feeling they'll be interested, since they've accidentally been pulled this far in already." He took a step back, as if he was about to leave, and then changed his mind. "One more thing, okay? Get off the alien lead. It's all wrong. Mother Hive Brain is a joke. A sham. I don't know what nutcase came up with it, but it certainly wasn't one of us. Good night, Johny."

<hr />

Leaning over the long, polished bar in the main room of the club, Jesus motioned to the bartender, a heavy-set man with a series of scars running down the right side of his face.

"What happened?" Jesus asked politely.

"Eh?" the man grunted, his attention apparently elsewhere.

Maybe he has A.D.D. like everyone else, Jesus thought. "The scar?"

"Accident," he said, still looking at the dance floor. "So, you drinkin or what?"

"A bloody Mary," he said, trying to avoid looking at the throng of people walking around the dance floor. The women, in particular.

"You got I.D.?" the bartender asked, reaching beneath the bar for a glass.

"Uh, no. A virgin bloody Mary." *Fucking barbarians.*

———◆◆◇————

Alexi had a note-book and pen in front of him. It had been two long weeks since he'd started working on this book with Gabrael. He would occasionally look up into Gabrael's very clear, pale eyes, ask a question, and then continue with his note taking. Two weeks of living at his apartment and working on the Project, day and night. And two weeks of the most mind-bending conversation he had ever experienced.

"So are you saying here that the, uh...thought-reality is every bit as 'real' as the, well. Real-reality?"

Gabrael smiled quickly, and then turned to watch the rain slipping down the tall windows along the far wall, throwing globules of light into the air.

"This is really the heart of the matter, Alexi. There is a distinction that you will find in all modern philosophy, however generally speaking in the past the implications of this distinction were colored strongly by attachment to a Christian worldview. Indeed, the human soul recoils in many ways from these repercussions, as they leave us no certain ground... I have often felt, quite deeply, that it leaves us with no certainty at all, except for what we experience right here, right now, in this present moment. Once the moment has passed us by, you store it in memory, anchoring it to a word, or a sense...and the next time you see this present moment, you will experience it not as it *is*, but rather as you choose to see it. But... I beg your pardon Alexi," he looked around the room, briefly removed from his reverie, "I am giving you the conclusions. I should instead start with my premises. This distinction I mentioned to you is being for consciousness, and being in itself. Being, here, now... Being for consciousness is your subjective experience, your 'take' on this present moment, that we are experiencing here together. Being in itself, however, is not experiential. This is a premise we make... and quite rightly...based on the fact that the sun has risen ten million times before, in our consciousness, and so we propose that it is incredibly likely that it will rise again. We put faith in the idea that there is some reality behind the experiences we have. Contrary to Wittgenstein's assertion that the world is fact, it is these ideas which have the most tenuous existence if experience is our pole-star. It is nevertheless also a requirement, or perhaps a result of, scientific thinking. Now another point…which you should remind me to return to…is that most of the Traditions we will speak of emphasize one of these *over* the other in one way or another. For instance Christianity places emphases on the objective world, and it is out there, on the other side you might say, that we will find our redemption. Thus we are forever estranged from ourselves… From our meaning *in here*."

Alexi nodded. "And this is the… ideological basis of our culture."

"Yes. This absence is a product of ontological uncertainty that arises from how we relate to the world, thinking of ourselves as things born into an alien environment, rather than beings born out of it and nurtured by it. This schism shows itself in our religious and cultural beliefs, but its roots reach into our psychology, even our biology. Many have looked out in the world for God, when they should have turned around and looked into themselves. If we find the heart of our own mystery, then we find the heart of the universal mystery as well. As something other than me, nature becomes something that must be subverted. In America, the body is an enemy that must be starved and beaten into a mold. Yet paradoxically obesity is most prevalent here… Now in some, this absence and ontological uncertainty reaches such a level that they begin questioning not only the established order but also the ground of their own being. You see this happening in your little group, and I see it happening all over the country. More and more people drop out of the adcult daily."

"Okay…" Alexi said, digesting what had just been said to him, "how do you relate this back to what you were saying earlier about the apparent world and the world as idea?"

"Well, when we experience something, we are focused not on its ultimate nature, on its nature as idea, but simply how it is known to us through our modes of apprehension. Our concern lies in how this relation effects us. In other words, we are subjectively concerned, yes?" Gabrael tilted his head as he always seemed to when asking semi-rhetorical questions.

"Well… yeah. It's a given with direct experience. But even if I am abstractly reasoning with a problem, like say how to build something or what to make of test results, the only motive for doing that reasoning is its ultimate effect on me." Alexi paused. "I had assumed this kind of thinking would push you into solipsism but you're talking about concern, not existence…"

"Yes. So to conclude that thought... In asking 'what is my relationship to the divine,' or even 'what is my relationship to the world,' one is essentially asking 'what is my own nature?' An experience is ipso facto an experience of ones nature – as other. There is no actual separation between self and world, nor is there a separation between being for consciousness and being in itself..."

Alexi's brow furrowed. "But wait..."

"Thought makes distinctions. That is its function. By talking about something, by categorizing it, we are changing its nature. Any relation always changes the participants. Being in itself and Being for consciousness are both themselves just thoughts or abstractions, and what they refer to is a singularity which we have to think of as a duality. That is to say, for instance, that the universe expresses itself—in totality—within my body. My body is a mirror of this world around me, and the world around me is then in return just a symbol of our bodies, or our minds...or this present moment... But here we have this problem of memory, which I related to you earlier. So long as this present moment is not an eternal one, we live more in the fragmented associations of our memories than in this lightning flash-here, now. This is how the symbol of the shards comes in. Every thing is devoid of selfness-in-itself. The Hindus have an interesting meditation on this idea which they call the Net of Indra. Imagine a net, stretching in every direction, with a highly reflective, clear gem at each nexus-point... Each gem exists, you might say, as a reflection of all of those around it... Its very being is given identity in its relation, through whatever mode, with those that it relates to, in the way it relates to them. Thus I say, as you read in the last chapter, 'existence is purely a relation of surfaces, only subject to evaluation within the very specific context that gave rise to all related phenomena...' And so on. Didn't you ask a question about this passage?"

———•◆•———

"Acid?" Johny asked, making sure he had heard right. Two disembodied voices floated over his shoulder. "Nice dress...Want to fuck?" Johny ignored them.

"Yeah, that's right. Five apiece." The man looked around, running his hands through his thinning hair nervously. Somewhat old to be in a nightclub, Johny thought. He looked more like a collage professor than anything else. Well, except for the clown suit. His eyes were unusually luminous, though. *Sure, why not.*

"Some for my friends, too?"

When Jesus received his change, he noticed that George Washington's eyes were X'ed out with a thin black marker. Curiously, he turned it over and saw that 139(13) was written under the Illuminatus triangle. Before he could continue his investigation of this rather bizarre artifact, his attention was grabbed by a girl wearing tight-fitting velvet that left all of her long legs in plain view. Glistening lips, subtle swan-like curve as the neck turns into the back. She walked by, eyeing him with a sultry, bored look. It was a look of total indifference, of trained apathy. He could picture her standing in front of a mirror for days—weeks—practicing that look. It was still impossible for him to deny the familiar sting he felt in his chest; at first, an irrational and almost overpowering hunger, followed by a torrent of guilt and self-loathing. *I don't deserve that. I don't want that. I can't have that. She's worthless. I'm worthless. Fuck me you whore.* In a flash, he was sucked into a rapid-fire succession of sexual, even misogynistic, day dreams. They were too fast for daydreams, really. More like a series of motion slides. At first, he was fucking her from behind, pulling her long sweaty hair with one hand and using the other to keep his balance, screaming "fat bitch!" and then, a moment later, he was the one on the bottom, and she was the one taunting him, her voice shrill and hoarse. A moment later, though, he was masturbating fiercely while driving and eating a cheese stromboli...and realized that his genitals had been replaced with his mother's face, slick with pizza grease. Horrified, he came, yelping like a puppy that had just been kicked. Thrilling guilt continued to mount as the visions intensified. Growing brighter and more intense now, they involved various religious figures. It was only when a most auspicious Buddha and lust-crazed Virgin Mary were gang-banging Lao Tzu, (Mary was using a strap-on that looked disturbingly like a cross, inset with LVX at the base and NOX at the tip), that Jesus was finally able to get control of himself and clear his mind of such thoughts. The comforting form of his lipstick, deep at the bottom of his pocket, re-assured him.

Through columns of smoke two simian looking men usher into the adjacent room. Everything is developing a phosphorescent sheen. People's voices and bodies are coalescing into a single mass, an enormous gibbering organism. We are seated cross-legged on red satin pillows. The walls are black. Purple smoke. Lights dim and the thousand-voices grudgingly die away. *There is a tickling from the base to top of my spine, and my legs feel like rubber. I have to consciously keep my jaw from clenching. Deep breathing, focusing my attention on my tailbone, allowing that attention to build there—most of the unpleasant symptoms subside. Music has started, chanting— I turn around just in time to see the silhouette of a naked woman. More dance out from behind the smoke, into stark, intense lighting. The phosphorescent sheen is now a wave of colors and fractal patterns that coats the forms of the bodies in front of me. Suddenly I am incredibly aware of the sound of breathing in the room—the music is barely audible over this cacophony of fat belly breaths, open mouthed pants, and nasal hyperventilation. Why is the air a liquid?*

I'm not sure how much time has passed but now I'm staring at an entirely gold, cherubic naked girl. (It looks a lot like Her. Could it be? What is she doing up on a trapeze?) The breathing, the fat gnomish old man sitting beside me that keeps poking me in the ribs with his paradoxically bony knees, the thick smoke that smells like soap, the incense—the whole scene comes to a grinding halt. Where have I seen you before? My attention is totally pulled, and though I can't be sure, I don't think it is just because she is naked, painted gold, and wearing a wig. This isn't a dance club—this is a pagan ritual!

———◆———

No, *no, this is not your head. This is my head.*

She reluctantly agrees. That wasn't what he was asking, but it was what she heard, what she knew. It was, then, what he was asking. She sat alone in a corner of the club; Agent didn't know she was around. But their trips were intertwining. She lit a single white candle on a stand beside her. And it was her dream all over again—a chance to break out of the pattern?

Oh my God! In my next incarnation, she will be my wife. Both of them would have to die, be reborn—

"Sure God's rockin', but does he have lips?"

He couldn't place that voice. Does he mean that a God that doesn't speak to his followers is worthless? *She couldn't speak. Looked around anxiously at the throng around her. Felt small, frightened.*

"They'll have to get jobs and get married and fuck once a week and have 2.3 children and a dog that wags its tail altogether too much and a mortgage and...no, it's much better if I continue to live this lie. I don't do it for myself, you see. I do it for the good of humanity. I am a warrior upon the battlefield of eternity. I am mighty and I have legs like tree trunks. I am full of shit," he said, defending her current opinions and behaviors. In her mind, he maintains some dignity. Everything she did was a flight, an escape. Because they are incapable of sweating, Pigs like to wallow in mud.

Nothing. She wonders where he went. She is trying to remember how to feel. To feel for real, to be for real. When she was little she learned she could impress the big people if she did a little dance.

"The bees!" Johny screamed. "They do a dance..."

She grew up and made herself out of porcelain, a warrior girl trained to do battle in transparent nightgowns. In her mind, the intentions were all pure. But wait, there's more: The fish lie! Death to the fishes! And there's the elevator, down the hall.

Meanwhile, a commercial was blasting out of the television, always running in the background: IF YOU EXPERIENCE VAGINAL DRYNESS, TRY THIS! IT S LIKE YOUR NATURAL VAGINAL MOISTURE! IT HAS NATURAL ALOE AND ITS SAFE TO USE EVERY DAY. At the same time Agent was thinking

more more *more* more *more* more *more* more...

"AHHHHHHHH! Yeah, I feel better now." It was three years ago, and he was in his dorm room, blowing an eight-ball of coke with some friends. Equine dollar-bills a George Washington-deep in cocaine. Childhood decisions a Mother Hive Brain deep in decay. The flashbackwards was too fast; before he could get the dollar bill to the paper, he was four and thinking to himself: I'll beg my mummy and tell her she's big and sweet and it's my birthday and I'm pretty. I lost myself in the supermarket and cried out for mummy's linen. Mummy was doing cheap tricks in the seafood section, and came back with a bucket of prawns.

The dragon laughed at him: "Lavender stockings! Lavender stockings!"

"Little girl!" the duck added helpfully.

Agent 139 had always been the little girl.

She hasn't breathed since she was two. The constriction in her throat is unbearable sometimes. Tonight she tries. They won't have that kind of power over her anymore.

It takes me a few minutes to realize that I am casting a line of bright green energy straight out at her heart. What the hell am I doing? Next thing I know, it's running both ways. Certainly, she isn't aware of it—but I'll be damned if this isn't happening on its own. I see a spider web of these interlocking beams, running in both directions. Then, just as suddenly, it stops. There is incense burning, desperately competing with the soap smelling smoke machines. A woman behind me coughs loudly and I can feel the breath and flecks of spittle on the back of my neck.

Stop face shifting! Mummy? She will not fly. Shut up, will you! You feel it in your chest, that pulling tugging. Call it whatever you want. It's real. She will put it there where the breath cannot go where the air cannot carry it through her break it up she is afraid to absorb it she is afraid if she keeps it she will break she will become it will become her (she will become Her.)

"My love," Agent mouthed mournfully. Alexi sat in the mental hospital, surrounded by unforgiving white walls. "I miss her…"

Two men dressed all in black, their gender only apparent because of their broad shoulders, beckon to me slowly from the center of the room. A blue circle of light vaguely reveals glints of bodies, writhing impossibly slowly to Arabian music, all thick and syrupy. The men approach, seemingly gliding across the floor. I felt stricken, still gazing up at the nude gold girl, dangling from the trapeze above me.

The men usher me into the center of the room, into the halo of light. The women gyrated all around now, forming a complete circle. It is time.

DEAR GOD, WHAT IS THAT THING?!

A few months ago. There were half empty bottles of alcohol. A woman—barely a woman—was sitting across from him. It didn't look like she was wearing anything, but it was all so blurry anyway… *I know I shouldn't*, he thought, *but…but I noticed that as the light got fainter and fainter she got hotter and hotter.* We pay our debts sometimes. And we get the abuse we think we deserve. Look: she's running around in a circle, screaming "Look at me! Look at me, mommy!" Johny's bee trip.

A letter to the department of insecurity: If you see Atlas, tell him he can have his stinking rock back. I fear that if this condition lasts too long, I will abandon all of this mess I have created in favor of the Real world, and a Real job, and a Real marriage. Not good. I don't want to quit this early in the game, but things seem grim. I just want to remember what it feels like to breathe.

"...I feel as if I'm slipping into a dream within a dream..." The music continued to play. Multicolored lights dancing off of the black lacquered floor, swimming around the dancers. Everyone dancing, watching others watch them. I'm pretty, see? Look at how pretty I am. Sewer screw me like an animal, bitch.

Atlast shrugged?

"You'll never be free." Who said that? Who heard?

The department of insecurity sends a reply a few days later: What I once thought was a golden cage has turned out to be steel after all. Just a cheap electroplate. I scratched through to the core. Control of my life has passed out of my hands.

She goes to a place she knows it is best not to explore. Peel back the skin. Flashes of hallucinations from before she had the word for them. She didn't realize that it was real. She had hoped it wasn't.

When she was little she had a distended belly / beer gut / she was a chunky girl / briefly anorexic hollow belly never fit. Thinbelly hollow-spot. Nihil fit.

"Never be free, unless...unless..."

Epistemological wonder. Give me your benediction. Apostle. Enforced with the biggest guns. A pistol. What's under that dress?

Three of the women approach from the edge of the circle, their skin glittering silver in the light, paralyzing me with their hungry, emerald eyes. My hands were bound behind my back with what felt like silk rope.

Everything became a blur. There was hysterical laughter, bright pastel trails hanging in the air like confetti. One of them produced a wine bottle, another held a clear glass aloft. Red liquid rushed into its container, and the three of them exclaimed "Evohe!" simultaneously. All three holding the glass, they pulled my head back by my hair and poured it slowly into my waiting mouth. Incredibly flavorful, dry wine burned as it went down. I was left with an aftertaste of flowers and earth. Trickles of it ran down my chest, tickling me.

They gestured for me to lie on the floor. It was cool and incredibly smooth. One of them lit a candle and placed it carefully above my groin. I could feel the warmth spreading through its glass container. The sensation was pleasant but almost too intense to handle. And not because it was hot. Another leaned down and cupped my head in her hands, pouring another giant gout of wine. Much of washed over my facial hair, and dribbled down to my chest. Now completed with the first candle, another was placed on my stomach. Again wine was poured.

Another candle was lit and placed over my heart. I could feel a throbbing sensation clearly now, flowing upwards from the candle at my groin, through my stomach, and into my heart, growing with each and every breath. One of them picked up the candle on my heart and began dribbling hot wax in a perfect circle, while the other two chanted something that I could not make out. The sensation came as bursts of light. It snapped me into the moment, completely awake.

She put the candle back down on my heart and lit another, placing it under my chin. "Don't move," she whispered firmly into my ear, "or you will get burned." Then we locked gazes. The shark-like intensity that I found there frightened me. "What are you most afraid of?" she asked.

I opened my mouth to reply but she put her finger to her lips. "Sssh."

A blindfold, also black, was slowly secured over my face. Hot, wet mouths moved along my chest, up the back of my neck, meeting my mouth, half open. ...A low moan, close to my ear, and then what felt like a nipple, entering my mouth. My mind went blank. I felt something inside me reel for that momentary lapse of linear time... I couldn't place it, and then I made a decision. The process was too quick to catch but I felt a change. It was time.

Then I heard a voice full of mischievous laughter, softly in my ear, "See, now you are the virgin sacrifice." I felt her breath along the back of my neck for a fraction of a second, and then felt cold all over. Somehow in all of this I had become naked. Was I still in the nightclub? What was happening? I struggled to remove the bonds, but could not. A sudden detachment overcame me, followed by a type of elation I had never before experienced.

(who would ever think the sun's core was rotten
inside the
velvet
flamepromise
in the temple of the temple of the temple of the Holy

/seems bursting at the seams the light bursts through/
She drags on her cigarette. She can see him across the room.
/too red/
.)
ARE YOU LISTENING?!
they are plucked blindly from the earth
no one's listening are you listening? I'm not listening in the

they paint her face and her words
color them gold
/she hides her dignity underneath/
(i can pretend
/they paint her face/
(i can pretend
/she smiles ( ) swallows slowly/
(i can pretend?
/remembering his arms vast embrace/
shedivesdeeper
(it is warm inside)
...and so She was There. (Was where? Who was She?)
wordsrodsdoors
She opens the doors and steps into the well-lit outdoors. Into the light of the
sun. It is golden. She smiles /is beautiful/ smiles and walks towards something in
the distance. She opens her eyes and remembers. Hot sun, she remembers
/feeling/ beautiful she remembers /being/ beautiful. She smiles. She closes her
eyes /she closes the doors/ so no one can get in, and walks toward the subway.
The sun is hot. herback(breaksopen)thelight(breaksthrough) breaks through
(THELIGHT

Too late.
Tonight she will fly
Sweet dreams of falling
She decides, she jumps!
She does not drown.

FIN.

The play is over, and I am again clothed. I shuffle out, still in a daze,
thinking about that girl, nonchalantly nodding my head at the proper
times when Jesus makes a comment. Once you have developed a rhythm
with someone it is often hard to actually listen to what they have to say.
The point-counter-point focuses around when it will again be your turn to
speak. You latch on to a word or a gesture which makes you think about

something else, and like this the two of you can move from tangent to tangent to tangent for hours without ever having scratched each other's surface.

Chapter 12, Grid 2

The Cartesian Mystery Cook

The waiters of the best eating-houses mock the whole
world; they estimate every client at his proper value.
This I know certainly, because they always treat me with
profound respect. Thus they have flattered
me into praising them thus publicly.
Yet it is true; and they have this insight because
they serve, and because they can have no personal
interest in the affairs of those whom they serve.
An absolute monarch would be absolutely wise and good.
But no man is strong enough to have no interest.
Therefore, the best king would be Pure Chance.
It is Pure Chance that rules the Universe; therefore,
and only therefore, life is good.

— Aleister Crowley

Death rides the N and the R.
Here I was, standing in the subway station headed to a friend's house,
(from Atlantic to Union Square), musing about the letters Nun and Resh,
and I turn to my side, and there he is. Black as night. Tall guy, wearing
this long shroud. Or was it a cloak? I don't know. At any rate, he turns to
me. And now here's the crazy thing: the lights are real bright in this sta-
tion, but I still can't see his face. It's just pitch black in there. Then I see
that he's carrying this huge scythe. You know, the kind they use to plow
fields?
So he kind of nods at me. Says "do you have the time?" in this real
deep, slow voice. Have the time? Fuck, I don't know where I am half the
time. What, death doesn't carry around a time piece?
Then he waves his scythe, maybe to get my attention, and I think: does
death want a shot at the Pugilist Extraordinaire? I'd take that son-of-a-

bitch in a heartbeat. Well, that's when my train pulls up and my story ends...

———◆◆◆———

"Another Cod dinner," the new waitress said to Jay, Cartesian mystery cook. He was staring off into space, lost in thought. She pulled her hair back into a ponytail. "And I think he wants it cooked this time, hmm?"

Least my story was over, damned bitch.

"D'ya think?" the Cartesian mystery cook answered sarcastically, reaching into the industrial sized bag of Cod patties with gloved hands. "D'ya think it's really fish, I wonder—"

"Hey, if the bag says it's Cod, it's Cod." She walked out to the main room and returned to her indentured servitude. Jay shrugged and, after finishing the meal, headed into the bathroom to post a piece of paper that he had carefully folded in his backpack. *You always believed what they wanted you to believe.*

> I don't believe I shall knock about much longer, whether at sea or at shore, more and more sick every day in body and brain. I am at Devon which I shall be leaving because of the constant storms, the rains, and the humidity. I am at the end of my strength and I haven't slept in four months. "Silly Rabbit, Trix are for kids," can only be construed as a call to class warfare. Also, do not e-mail Saddam Hussein at Hussein@Iraq.com, we believe it to be a false address. In addition to all of this, I am made of tomatoes and olives working in concert to form the perfect personal government based on torture, death, and the inherent right of vegetables like myself. Support the graft in your hometown.
>
> A public service announcement paid for by the mothers of the Cuban revolution.
>
> — "Gorgeous" Larry Snodgrass, et al.

Jay Roberts had been working as a cook at Lenny's for over two years, and by most people's reckoning, it had gotten to his head just a little. He was the last employee working who had witnessed Barbara's brutal slaying, some weeks back. It wasn't that he couldn't still cook up any of the "traditional" Lenny's faire. It wasn't that he was stupid; he was probably the most intelligent worker in the building. This might have been part of his problem: being a cook allowed him plenty of time to think. All things considered, his co-workers knew to keep their distance and just nod their head like they understood. So, when he stepped out of the kitchen, holding a frozen fish stick over his head triumphantly, no one was particularly surprised. Even when he proclaimed "GOD—COD—GOD—CŎD! Permutations of the divine name!" they took it in stride, although the manager asked him to return to his station, and one of the waitresses had to calm down an elderly man in a yarmulke who was becoming confused and lead him back to his seat. However, when Jay threw the rock-solid cod stick at the manager, shrieking "you don't pay me enough to buy into this lie you call reality! I quit!" they were rather taken aback.

———◆◆◆———

The Mystery Cook rubbed his blurry eyes. They seemed shrunken and yet somehow altogether too large for his face. He was convinced that they would retract, iguana-like, into the inner recesses of his skull. Three days without sleep, two days without food, just pounding on his old typewriter. He ripped a page out of the unforgiving machine and slapped White-Out on his most recent error. "God damn," he cursed. The exhaustion was almost overwhelming. Almost. With an amazing amount of will, he reminded himself that he had to elucidate his vision—it was time the people knew the truth. *Fuck it, who am I fooling. One lie deserves another. At least Mother Hive Brain is funny. Not that stolid Order of the Hidden Path horse-shit.*

With the unstoppable, unrelenting melodious pounding of Beethoven in the background like some never-ending tantric orgasm, he completed the document and posted the first draft on the message board.

Sometimes Jay considered his work an even mixture of the theological writings of the East and philosophical writings of the West. (Though not always.) He was horribly frustrated at his lack of success with the publishers, as well as their apparent inability to realize the evolutionary nature of his creations.

> In the following essays we will be investigating the usefulness of mythology for the sake of creating a ritual that is based on your own life and life-goals. The first section of the book deals with theory, to introduce you to a variety of potential beliefs and familiarize you with a history of mythology, mysticism, and magick. A great deal of earth will be turned up, but I do not intend on digging especially deep into any one particular topic. That you may do at your own leisure and through your own thinking.

What you learn from this book, and any and all of the other information present to you in this lifetime is only relevant when it is interpreted by yourself as an individual and then brought back to the world as living mythology. We transmit this living mythology to each other through our art, and through the ways we choose to live our lives. If I could have any one message from this book conveyed to artists, it would be that. Legends and heroes always lag a generation or two behind the present. You're living it right now.

To live our myth we need to come to terms with our history as an individual. What it means to be at this place and this time, and how it has made you who you are. This can be found in our family trees and personal psychological makeup but it is also present in the history of our culture. Watching people interact within different cultural paradigms from the perspective of a foreigner can be a first step in learning about your own cultural complex.

The world that we live in is the direct result of our ideas and understanding of the universe. However, in many ways, while we advance exponentially in technological capability, our biological technology, in other words our maturity as a race, is still two or three thousand years in the past. This is because many of us live in maps that were original, ground-breaking ideas…in 500 B.C. Our current technology is ecologically and spiritually stupid, in that it was not built with the bigger picture in mind, nor was the motivating factor in most of our technological breakthroughs anything other than the urge to destroy or multiply.

The basic premises of our world today, and realities we each live in are a direct product of certain archaic behaviors and beliefs that are erroneous and incongruous with the universe as we currently know it. So-called "Western" knowledge has been built up upon itself without critical analysis of the history of our axioms. This mentality in a capitalistic world climate engenders a short-sightedness towards the repercussions of our actions that leaves the public mind malnourished and culturally impoverished. A history of dates and facts is somewhat irrelevant; all axioms and preconceptions must be evaluated from the vantage point of the task at hand. The value of historic knowledge lies in an analysis of the evolution of ideas, rather than in the necessary validity of "facts."

Advanced breakthroughs in science, philosophy, and the arts have all come about through critical analysis of the corpus of available knowledge in addition to individual, creative thought. Creativity thrives in an environment of nurturing conflict. Though this may seem at first an oxymoronic statement, it is clear that the life-blood of artistic and philosophical advancement lies in struggle: each new "great" school of art or philosophy comes about as a reaction to the previous, now ossified and static system. Many of these breakthroughs come as a result of critically analyzing these axioms, as we see with Galileo. The story of Buckminster Fuller's life is a wonderful parable about the absurdity of our modern practices when compared with where we *could* be, technologically, spiritually, and ethically speaking. In this day and age there is no reason for starvation except for greed and ignorance. These problems are unresolved not because they cannot be, but because they cannot be within our current global structure. Familial structure breaks down around 150 members. Interest focuses again entirely on individual interests. Tribes that grow beyond this point must schism as a point of progress or the schism will merely occur as cultural schizophrenia. The binding glue of compassion turns to competition. Greed and competition are biological imperatives for primates, however so is cooperation and nurturing. We can choose which impulses to act on.

Our current corporate, mass-media culture owes itself, in part, to an ideology that poses itself *against* nature and the natural order. In the religion of Zoroaster, Judaism, Manichaeism, Christianity, and to a lesser extent within the works of many of the Greek philosophers you find this ideology present, and while most people today are unaware of Zarathustra, all of us live in a world fashioned from these models. A world where the human dimension is held in tension against nature, where the purpose of the human animal is seen as bringing light to the world, changing a dark, wild world into a world of light through conscious intention is also—as we can see in the history of Western thought from 500 B.C. to the present age—inevitably a world governed by the laws of rationality, with all of its blind spots. The world we exist in *experientially* was formed by Newton, by Descartes, and so on. When we deal with maps and models we will really bring more light to this matter.

Study of the theory provided here, followed by the practice of the ritual itself, will invariably provide initiations to your nature in accord with these myths. However the way this initiation unfolds will be unique in each and every one of you, as we are all inventing new mythologies, most of which will likely remain untold and die with us.

The method that will be used to bring about this change is simple enough in theory, it is in the practice and application that you will find your trials and rewards. Because we create maps of our environment that are not the same as the environment, we may analyze our maps— our history, as I said—our symbol systems, and, through this, continually deepen our experience of our self. I would like to eventually express to you that symbols, religious symbols in particular, are literary devices which when used properly refer to the human psychology with precision that is nearly mathematical, so long as you can decipher the reference. Through unraveling the reality that the symbols points at, and invoking it into the present as it applies to your Will, one may not only understand religious symbols but also live through them. And this, not fanatical belief or even faith, is what religion is.

—————◆◆————

At the same time, at the night club, Johny was speaking rapidly, tripping over his words in terrified excitement. "You can't control the machinations of life... People have been spending all of their time to understand not to adore, they wanted to control. And...and... Where did they learn everything from? I mean, for most of our history, people have learned from, what you said, uh—shamans. Shamans and religious leaders. Then political leaders. But...but where do they learn about life now? The media. And where does all that information come from? Was there A.D.D. before the label was made? Manic depression? I mean, did the disorder exist as a thing, as a real thing? I read somewhere that seventeen million people have been prescribed Prozac in America. And that's just...that's just one anti-depressant out of many. Has twenty-five percent of the human population always been depressed? Or were they just human, then? No labels, no hard-core this and gothic that... Uh, but I guess they had tribes. To identify themselves with something so they could be someone, be someone in another persons eyes... So they could see themselves mirrored. But you can't see yourself then. You don't see yourself when you become something else so as to see what it is you are. You...you mess the whole thing that up. The, uh...process. So you always wind up prostituting yourself for the sake of other people, so as to exist together under a name and a label. That's what it is, isn't it?"

"Paid much for your fuzzy suit, paid more for your needleknees and curious chickens, self-strangled bodies of artificial pineapple flavor and lemon crunch," Jesus said as if it were self-evident, nodding. Jesus realized the drugs were really kicking in now, as he had the distinct and now familiar feeling of being sucked into the maw of some huge, moist, monstrous beast. "My God!" he screamed suddenly, "It's here! The Leviathan is here!" He could feel the air leaping into and out of its lungs, a low rasping sound with a little bit of a rattle at the end of each breath. The whole room had the goddamned death rattle. It was like the dream, where he was inside that monster's looped digestive system, right before the Jesus trip had really started. He started looking around for his Windows 95 interfaceable gun. *The Leviathan is Amoco,* he realized with sudden certainty, his eyes narrowing.

"Jesus!"

Jesus' eyes lit up, looking as if he was about to say something. In actuality, Johny's outburst made him lose his revelatory train of thought. *The Leviathan...and Amoco?* The Agent shot him a look that shut him up before he even spoke.

"Jesus," Johny repeated, "I don't know who the hell I am! Am I myself, or am I that reflection? But what's reflecting? ...I'll die without ever having known what I am. Die, and it'll have been lost for their sake, because I wasn't ever allowed to be myself."

The Agent looked mildly concerned. As a result of this, more than ten thousand miles away, a rooster crowed. A perfect example of Jungian synchronicity at work. "I understand. Be careful, now."

"How? How can you speak about yourself?" Johny almost screamed, his voice hoarse.

"No, I really do. A while back I realized that identity was a...well...a mutually created object. Before I lost her and gave my identity for the cause," he said, a tinge of regret in his voice. "But I realized that you can't ever lose anything, since there's no singular you in the equation. Everyone you have ever loved lives on in your inner world. Death? Without it, there wouldn't be life. You have to open your eyes to the big picture, see that we're all the part of the same massive organism learning what it is to be alive, and what it is to experience itself. An absolutely single thing can't possibly perceive itself—it can't even exist! I..." he looked over at Jesus and his voice trailed off for a moment. "You remember, I'm sure... I felt like everything I had ever wanted suddenly showed itself to me as a tablet of values that had been *sold* to me. It's not God's wrath, the vengeful pentagon in the sky, that is to blame. It is simply equilibrium, which we sometimes call 'Karma.' Karma 'tests,' but not consciously. Shake your fist at it, but it doesn't change anything. There is no higher power listening. This is *it*. If I let go of this quarter here," he said, showing Johny the shiny coin, "it will fall. And that's the most painful thing of all—that this 'I' must die, that it is powerless, that it is nothing. It isn't even I...do you see? Just continue unearthing those deep roots, 'cause the leaves have always been dead. But your redemption, your birth, is also contained within this death... We're just too damned attached to them to let them fall without sorrow."

"So what you're saying is that there is another mythological reality behind this one, and that we may ascend to that plane—to meet with God, if you will?" Alexi was asking, sipping port from a crystal glass. Beethoven's Piano Concerto number five was playing in the background.

Gabrael put his hand to his chin and though for a moment. "That's getting there, but it isn't there. Being-in-itself is just an idea, and that collapses the whole dialectic. What one means, generally, so long as 'one' hasn't been consumed by doctrine and or stupidity, by 'meeting God' is Union with the Absolute. 'The absolute' basically means 'any absolute,' since there can only be One absolute, otherwise it isn't fucking absolute." He smiled, and motioned for Alexi to hand him a cigarette. "'I' and 'you' can unite and become 'we' or even 'us,' but these are just stepping-stones on the path. When 'I' and 'you' become nothing—the Qabbalists call non-dimensional nothingness Ein Sof, and confuse the whole matter. Now, see, the trick is that they were that nothing all along, but... Anyways, what was I saying? Oh, yes. Uhm, no subject, no object, and no not-subject or not-object, then 'you're' there, although at that point there isn't any point in talking about 'you' or even 'not-you.' ...Our essence outside of individual consciousness has always been the same, although it isn't quite an 'always' since it is effectively out of the field of time, the illusions of having a nervous system such as this."

Alexi chuckled. "If I understand what you're saying...there's no point in talking about it."

An amused sparkle never left Gabrael's eye. "None what-so-ever," he said firmly. "Would you like another drink?"

———◆———

"No!" Johny screamed, taking a step back. "You're all wrong. All of this is all wrong. It's all programming." His eyes widened suddenly as his body went rigid, held tightly for a minute in the clutches of some deep realization. "You're one of their Agents, aren't you? One of the aliens, communication through the device...one of the...them. God! No I am not one of you. No I am not something for you to shape and mold am not a robot or a creature cerebral cortex which is without thought feeling time-space continuos—Stalin said comrade, not a friend an equal un-abashed in the light not one of them—he knew something was going down no way of knowing efficiently knowing on the inside like a...like a...but he's having a thing with what's-her-name. I am not like anyone else! I am different! I have no patience for your time for your numbers for your promotional premonitions. I woke up to your straight lines Cartesian geometry two-dimensional planes and...six references...six reference points to the dot not three, how could they think it was three? Ninety three miles away is the thing, one hundred and eleven is half the story half a union half a blot, an annihilation...the trinity! The hermit! The nail! My fist! Sweet Jesus..."

The Agent ignored his blatant Qabbalistic references—certainly random connections caused by the chain reaction of neurotransmitters, that out-of-control, unstoppable train resulting from the acid. "You're in this mindset... It's like everything happens fast these days. Death is antecedent to life, and yet it follows so quickly on its heels, that you can't even tell the difference. Eat big meals, boy, because the cycles just come faster and faster, and there isn't any release. It shrivels and drops off before it was born. You hope and it hurts you, fear and it paralyzes you, live—and it kills you. Right?"

"Uh oh," Jesus said, pursing his full lips as Johny continued to rant. "I've got Godot in my pants! Godot in my...my...pants! Beckett means something in the reversal. Something has changed something this day danger came changed wicked this way comes. You can see the nothing that has happened maybe a Wagner routine with hats playing a game of abuse let's make it up... Lookit—the Pathfinder bees discover Nectar and go back to the Hive. There the Pathfinder dances, to explain to the other bees exactly where the Nectar is. Don't you get it? He does a figure eight on the honeycomb...the direction of honey in relation to the position of the sun. He speedily explains how far it is. The wings strike 250 cycles per second...two, five, zero...eight! And it's in the key of B, naturally..."

Jesus looked over at the Agent. Two plus five plus zero most certainly does not equal eight. "J? You don't think we got the wrong kid, do you? Doesn't seem much like a Prophet to me."

"What?" the Agent asked. "The telephone listing we used said J. Roberts. In Devon. I'm sure of it. Hey, Johny. Your last name is Roberts, right?"

"Yes no all the same hey, tell me though, is it true? One of them? Remote controls, y'know? Cars?"

"Uh oh," Jesus said again, feeling very foolish.

"Jay's last name is Roberts."

"He doesn't live in Devon though," the Agent said tersely.

"He moved. And he works at the Devon Lenny's as a cook."

"Fuck. Well, I'm sure the 'prophet-priest' isn't him. I love the boy, but he isn't wrapped too tight. One of who, Johny?"

Johny took a deep, Herculean breath and almost fell over. "I knew for so long that Lenny's was a communicator device. Oh, I know. It seems silly at first. But I was sitting, sitting in Lenny's. I mean, and it came to me: the pictures on the menu, you know? They're made of plastic. They aren't real food. The food they serve you—it isn't real food either. They're just convincing you into their reality. A bee does a little dance when it gets back to the hive to tell the other workers where the pollen is. But, with us, it isn't pollen, it's money. THE BEES DO A DANCE!" He started gyrating his groin lewdly. "This realization, it didn't hit me like a thought, you know? It hit me like a voice, telling me the truth. I knew that I'd tapped into the hive mind directly. And you know what the voice told me? It said all communications are transmitted through the mass media, all thoughts are sent from the queen bee to the workers so they can do her bidding. You fools, you pathetic fools! All money is based on nothing. All money is without value. All of reality is based on money. All of reality is without value. I know that human brains are more complex than bee brains...but... Everything it is, it isn't. I thought it was all crazy thinking, but after everything I've heard from you guys, and everything I've seen in the past few weeks... I know now. With...with... certainty."

"We're losing him," the Agent said softly to Jesus. "Believe nothing, Johny. You cannot, you must not, forget that. Ever."

"He bought what was sold," Jesus said under his breath. "Only a follower can truly hate a follower."

"No." Johny said. He was rocking back and forth slowly now, swaying in time to an internal symphony. "No. Wrong, wrong... I have to go!" he said fiercely, turning and breaking into a run. The crowd of undulating bodies on the dance floor swallowed him whole. Just like the monster in my dream, Jesus thought.

Looking at my own warped and knobby image in the faucet of the bathtub, I realize that I am not only "Handsome" Jim Manitoba, Pugilist Extraordinaire. I am also Hephaestus, club foot. I am proud of my deformity, my dissimilitude, my difference defines, clarifies... Every room of the house is a metaphor of a place inside myself. Or does the place inside myself mirror how the house is made? Another toke, relax a little more into the murky, steaming water. There is nothing real in my living room, nothing aesthetic in my bedroom, yet in the small, confined space of my bathroom, I may be free, I may be Hephaestus without shame, without lie or facade. My chaotic self-energy is formed by the feminine hands of my environment, and I am not angry at what it has made me. The language of my inner dialogue forms my house, I am a product of it, a servant of the Mother Bee, my home, my society, free to be as I am, Hephaestus, Club Foot—a bivalent builder of forms, molded by those forms I make—lame, erect, and proud!

The Agent was talking on the phone now, his voice hushed, almost ♦ whisper. "Where were you last night?" It seemed that he was trying to hide the layer of ice in his voice. He paused, tapping his finger idly on the receiver.

"Well, the frustration, which I am sure you are well acquainted, is now interfering with my ability to re-express. But this, too, I see as a sort of test, from the outside-in or inside-out—both in fact, and I know that, if our determination is as strong as our feeling warrants, little short of death really has any right to interfere. Even that raises a certain question mark, on both ends. I'm assuming that your absence doesn't have anything to do with a Hispanic guy named Juan?" he forced a quick chuckle and then paused again.

"I should like to simply encapsulate my entire soul and hand it to you to swallow, right? But, souls, being boundless, don't compact, but only specify and lose meaning. I do know—in the manner which anything is known, that is to say 'known, but shakily,' that the boundlessness of the joy, offset by the abysmal fear of the loss of my individuality, equilibrates the journey. This is boat knowledge, in its manner of being creaky and bound to spring leaks. My innermost nature was, for a while, worn on my sleeve as an act, and as such it became cheap. So it hid and became a subterranean being. Maybe a wise captain with enough scars to know when to stay below deck, for the storm to plummet, touch water, and pass away. Still, there is no real self understanding without a self outside, a true mirror with which to judge the innermost character. And that, I see in you. The treacherous abyss yawns beneath it, screaming regret and warning, and yet, with boundless infinity, represented by Hope, in the sails, the boat continues undaunted." Suddenly, his voice grated harshly. "And yet, you ask me to throw Hope even onto what appears to be a sinking ship?! 'We'll talk about this later.' I have never been known for my patience, and yet, most predictably, I show sudden virtue only when I am in the position to be wronged. I'll continue on this sinking ship for the sake of my Hope only when it is unwarranted, it seems. I'm sure I'll be seeing you soon... Goodbye. Mm hm." He was surprised to note that when he looked down at his hand, upon hanging up the phone, his onyx ring was no longer there. A moment later, he found it lying on the floor. In two pieces.

<hr>

Jesus had been swallowed. Was he not also Jonah, he wondered, and all mythological figures? Were they not all references to his innermost being? He thought about how his ancestors were reptiles, that he was in fact descended from every form of life that had ever existed on this planet, and that we all share the same code. The air was downright humid. Turning around, he saw two elderly men, holding a conversation.

"Is that a cat?" Schrodinger asked, motioning towards a breast that presently belonged to a dancing girl nearby.

"No, it's your mother," Freud argued.

"But my mother isn't green," Schrodinger reasoned.

"Then it must be your mother," Freud concluded.

And then, in another corner, seated upon cushions that looked disturbingly like toadstools, mottled gray and speckled with bright, almost phosphorescent colors, sat a young girl, and a deep green and purple caterpillar. The insect was seated upright beside the girl, and was inspecting her most curiously with its two eye-stalks.

"Well, perhaps you haven't found it so yet," the girl was saying, "but when you have to turn into a chrysalis—you will someday, you know—and then after that into a butterfly, I should think you'll feel a little queer, don't you?" Her voice had a melodious, bell-like quality to it. Jesus could hear Bach in that voice.

"Not a bit," said the caterpillar, his voice more of a deep baritone.

"Well, perhaps your feelings may be different. All I know is, it would feel very queer to me."

"You!" snorted the caterpillar contemptuously. "Who are you?"

The drugs were definitely working.

<hr>

At the same time, elsewhere in the club, the Agent had wandered from the hard black floor, speckled in glistening globules of sweat and god knows what else, into someone else's thoughts. At least, this is the impression he had, because he could neither feel his body nor see his surroundings. It wasn't that everything had faded to black—far from it. Rather, his mind was focused on these thoughts, these transmissions he was receiving, and had no time or attention for such decadent illusions as sight or touch. The external roar of the crowd, even the music, seemed as present as a refrigerator hum. This internal transmission—there was no other way for him to think of it—was quite real, inasmuch as anything was real. That is to say, he experienced it vividly, possibly more vividly than the flashing neon of bookstores and video arcades that most considered real. But his thoughts weren't really on this boorish, philosophical train hurtling through the bleak landscape of Platonic dialectics and the nature of reality. No, what the Agent found most enthralling at this very moment was the giant rodent, hiding somewhere under a bed, like some minotaur deep in the inner labyrinths of his mind. The beehive buzzing of his memory.

Agent walked into this bedroom, his room when he was a child, to find that a conversation had already begun without him. The impatience of empty rooms is unmatched in this corner of the galaxy. Hiding amongst clumps of rabbit-like dust balls was this gerbil, it's little pink nose twitching at an impossible rhythm. Behind the rodent was the stuffed dragon that he had lost as a child. Agent was somehow under the bed he had slept in when he was seven years old, and his dead gerbil was getting ready to talk to him. Finally, the gerbil spoke: *I was pretty sure I knew what I was talking about when I talked to my gerbil, although it's so hard to tell sometimes because he's dead; claws still, neck stretched slightly upwards—rigid, in my hands. He's a nice guy, really. He just isn't very responsive. Then again, they say that it's better to be able to listen than speak, and he listens real well, only talking to me through recordings using crystalline technology recorders left from Atlantis and passed down through generations in the Masonic brotherhood and encoded using mathematical constants found within the structure of the Great Pyramids of Giza, the Cydonia Pyramids on Mars and the Qabbalistic tree of life.* The gerbil paused and cleared its throat rather loudly. *Now I am living between the lines, hiding in the cracks, hiding in ( )'s... Once you've been processed and beaten down, they can shove you in the ground and wash their hands of the deed.* The gerbil paused again, it's nose still twitching at that impossible rate. Agent noticed that a monocle was dangling over one of his coal black, beady eyes. It adjusted it with a furry left paw, hemming and hawing, clearing it's throat, (there was a report that sounded like a horribly bent, wet French horn), and otherwise making a great deal of the fact that he had forgotten his point. *Yes, now I have it... And the yo-yo encrypts us more then a thousand spider's webs I'm sinking into and yet all of you keep smiling Jell-O smiles and hot dog grins. Underneath there had better be the blackness of time and water stains that would make the Mississippi bow in shame or else you haven't lived like I have. And I envy you.*

So it came to pass that the Agent and Jesus decided to travel to the apartment of this Aleonis de Gabrael. With an increasingly bitter wind hard upon their backs, they headed around the back of the club.

As they rounded the bend and headed for the car, there came a rattling from a nearby dumpster. A form, hunched much like the building, stole along the shadows; he attempted to move stealthily, as a stray cat might, hunting for food in the refuse, except he made a great deal of noise, kicking soda cans and rustling papers bags under foot. A most ineffective thief in the night.

He seemed absolutely unaware of the sound, continuing to sneak towards them, convinced he was the most skilled burglar to have ever set foot within Philadelphia. Although the shadows were deep and concealed most of his features, they could still make out a worn leather eye-patch on his left eye, fastened with a thin cord wrapped over the back of his oblong head. His clothes were shabby, yet they seemed to have been regal once, a navy or marine officers uniform perhaps, even a rattling sabre affixed to the crooked belt upon his waist. The Agent was growing anxious, thinking it quite possible they had accidentally wandered into one of Nathaniel Hawthorne's novels, and what a terrible time they'd have getting out of the predicament. "Avast!" the hunched form called, finally officially giving his presence away to the pair, standing transfixed in the half-light of the baleful moon, hanging directly overhead, their hands twitching nervously, eyes bugged out and pupils dilated to their fullest extent. The Agent's heart sank—this was more likely to turn into a Moby Dick re-run.

"Avast, I say," he called again, a hand held out in greeting or warning, (they couldn't tell which), stepping forward again. His footsteps sounded like gunshots on the concrete. Now they could clearly make out his features. An undeniable fishy smell seemed to emanate from him as a fog, his teeth were misshapen, striated in muddy shades of yellow and green.

His one good eye, bloodshot and glassy, seemed to grow larger as he regarded them.

"For 139 resounding chimes I have hunted the great white whale, verily it leads me ever on," he began. The Agent began to fear his worst suspicions confirmed. An awkward and uncalled for Melville metaphor at work—who had bothered to write them into this nonsensical novel? But he continued: "and yea, I now find myself charged to warn thee, thou Judas with a most shabby Jesus beside. Deep under the deck of thy vessel thou lurk, subterranean worm," he was looking at the Agent now, "thinking 'thou hast betrayed me, a million upon a million times hast I been betrayed, and now I may hide from life, from my emotions, from my being, from my love.' Thy love and thy quest are thy life, thou zombie walking in a half-life... Never again shall I recount this to thee, so take this as a true lesson and write it in thine innermost chamber, the tablet of thy heart. This worn man before you, with hands like parchment and face like raw-hide, is thy future." Ahab motioned towards himself.

"O, list. Take heed, phantom who puts the highest in the lowest and the lowest in the highest, setting the world upon its head as Hegel before thee: from the sleep of day and the dreams of night, this man, but a shadow of his Self, a phantom in his imagination climbed upon the Universal height, and bearing fire as Prometheus, set himself into the reflected light of those four nines and from the dream of waking awoke. He stood on 42nd street, wandering around as if he were lost, holding his head in his dirty hands, never looking up. Hunting for thine opposite, an eternal feminine that thou mayest write thine own image upon, that thou might deify thyself in, the sin of every theologian is committed: thy divine subjectivity is objectified in that other. Thy nature becomes as nothing, thy purpose grows ever more empty and corrupt while thy seek thine marble goddess. O fool! O monotheistic tramp! Transfiguring the overpowering need to be loved into a will to meaning, need to lead, need to intellectualize, mummify, and categorize—thou hast become a priest, and no philosopher. Waiting on 42nd street, with thy breath hanging limp in the air, deep down knowing thyself lifeless and cold, waiting and waiting for thine lost love. Pitiful wretch. Thy search for love, and all that thou mayest love in life, is thy grave. The serpent of truth is the coffin worm. My poor, single-minded friend: do you love in hope of gain? Still you must pass on. Do you starve for the sake of a feast? Pass on. There are riches at my core and I must be hollowed—thus cries the lover. Only when you do not starve, do not carve deep valleys 'for her sake,' may you escape your self, in essence, escape your telos, your eternal return—the quest, the conquest, and finally de-thronement by the wandering, errant knight. You are still hollow that ask to be filled, even in abstinence, even by carving. You are wholly corporeal and earthly that ask for a spirit: even more is this the case with one who claims his every movement is spiritual. You who follow the play the closest, with eagle eyes and an open heart—is it not because you desire to be in it the most? And is it not you that stands outside? In every action lies an opposite, just as the drive to look up, to hope, is driven by the fear of looking down, of falling. Do you sacrifice in hope of gain? Still you must pass on." And with that said, he turned upon his heel and left.

———◆———

Agent 139 ran his hands through the stubble of his hair, flecks of water spraying in every direction. They were in the cabin of Jesus' car. Their only sense of connection to the outside world came from the low purr of the motor. Scenes flew by at impossible speeds, illuminated for a brief moment, passing again into non-existence.

"Make a left here, right?" Jesus asked. The engine hum dropped by a minor third. He caught the shift and laughed. "I'm just getting the image of some twentieth century composer driving drunk and trying to explain how he doesn't need a tachometer to shift as long as he can hear the intervals."

Agent 139 checked the scribbled directions he received from Johny in the halo of a passing streetlight. "Yeah, I think this is it."

Jesus glided into the turn. "This is what I get with a philosopher as my copilot. You *think* it's the right turn?"

Agent 139 was nonplused. "It might not be. Have you ever read Wittgenstein's On Certainty?"

Jesus was scanning for house numbers. Cookie-cutter apartments floated past, their bricks warped by the constant flow of water across the windshield.

Eyes passively gazing at the passing buildings; Agent 139 asked, "Hey Jesus, did you know that your car is a white tiger named Ranesh?"

"No I didn't... Where did you get that from?"

"Ranesh has become my spirit guide. He told me," he said cryptically, patting the windshield.

"What are we going to say when we finally meet him?" he asked, a few moments later.

Jesus spotted the number and found a parking spot. "I have no idea. I kind of hope he does all the talking. You still tripping?"

Agent 139 stopped, looked up at the stars. "It would appear so."

A moment later they were standing in a cloud of moths and mosquitoes on what they assumed was Gabrael's porch. It looked the same as the other apartments, the only identifying markers the rusted 111 hanging over the door and a beat up copy of *Wired* on the ground by the door.

Hesitantly, Agent 139 raised his hand up to the knocker and felt the cold metal between his fingers. The moths swarming about his head left long trails of white wings which danced in descending spirals around him. He knocked against the door once, then twice again in quick succession.

They waited an anxious minute, stuffing hands into their pockets and rocking back and forth on their heels, and just as they turned around, preparing to leave, the door creaked open behind them.

A calm voice asked, "Can I help you?"

They turned in unison to meet a tall man of medium build and nondescript features. The faint scent of baked yams wafted through the doorway as his scrutinizing blue eyes moved up and down, in perfect counterpoint to the tinkling of a harpsichord inside.

Agent 139 bit his lip and asked, "Why are we here?"

The man smiled with raised eyebrows, pausing just long enough before he answered that Agent 139 felt a little uncomfortable. "That's a good one," he said, raising his hand to his chin, "but you're going to have to leave."

"I believe we're part of the same brotherhood," Agent 139 said, "I feel I was brought here for a reason, I just don't know why."

The man shrugged and asked, "What are your names?"

They replied without hesitation.

"So you've come here to find out why you are here. Interesting," he mused. "Well, would you care to join me for dinner? I have yams and a turkey that's just about done. I'm not sure I can answer your question, but at least I can give you a good meal."

They both looked at each other. Jesus shrugged, looked back at the man, and asked, "You *are* Gabrael, right?"

He nodded and went back inside with an absent gesture for them to follow.

They were greeted by the pleasant smell of food simmering in the kitchen, mixed with an aroma that was exotic and hard to identify, something between the cloying spice of an ashram and the lion house musk at the Zoo. Agent 139's mind swam as it attempted to sort through the conflicting messages it was receiving. The flickering candlelight illuminated Zen calligraphy, Hindu Yantras painted in deep blues and vermilion, Escher prints adorning the walls of the living room. The antique mahogany bookshelves were piled high with books, and the lacquered chestnut floor glistened, drawing his eyes towards the far end of the room. The open door of the kitchen cast a steady incandescent beam upon a wrought iron cage standing tall as a man. Why did this ring a bell? He spied a russet flurry of fur near the bottom and a pair of beady little eyes peering out. Glancing back, he noticed that Jesus was examining the bookshelves and Gabrael was nowhere to be found. Agent 139 inched closer to the cage, combat boots rapping on the floor, and came face to face with a tiny chattering monkey whose bushy tail curled around one of the long bars behind it.

Jesus ran his finger down the spine of one of the black bound books, pulled it loose, and started reading at random:

As detailed in the first essay, plunging into this water is generally a reference to the subconscious, or more explicitly, to the order of life which informs our conscious sensibilities. It suddenly appears to one, as they are making this plunge, that they are Jonah in the whale: this power is primordial and to the initiate appears terrible. Generally speaking an encounter with it leads to an at least temporary plunge into the abyss. Or in modern terminology, a schizophrenic crackup. In terms of the models already discussed, this may be a right hand or left hand process, however it is at its culminating moment always a motion on the part of the individual: a vertical re-organization of models rather than a vertical exploration of pre-existing forms. While the initiation may be into a Gnostic cult or larger societal role, the experience, and the solutions to the problem that it poses, must arise from ones inner life.

Now this crack needn't be confused with the medical condition of schizophrenia. It is situational, and may in fact be a necessary life experience for any would-be shaman or artist—the two are in function nearly the same—and so long as the individual is given the tools to deal with the experience, or invents them himself, he will return the world whole, and what is more, aware of his true depth potentialities. If he remains in that plunge and never comes up for air, he will be lost in the realm of the subconscious.

From here we can already see the relationship of the fish symbol. It is within the abyssal darkness of the water that the fish swim. The fish is a Mercurial symbol. Mercury, or Hermes, is in this respect the figure who brings souls to the knowledge of their immortal character as well as their guide through the underworld. The Caduceus of Hermes, a symbol that has since been taken over by the Western medical establishment, is a glyph for this and can be considered his "tool," much as the thrysius is Dionysus'. The snake here is a glyph of the intransience within transience. It is also not accidental that this figure it arranged in a double helix. The full import of the fish symbol to these myths will be explored later through the Orpheus, Jesus and Parcival myths, but keep the connection to Mercury in mind as we proceed.

The key to this "immortal life" lies in two realizations. The first is an identification, not of thought but of experiential consciousness, with the image of Osiris. The microcosm is identified with the macrocosm. This is the son redeeming the father, and the internal meaning of the son being his own father. If there is this identification, then we see a mythic conception of genetic transmission, which must be considered alongside the ark symbol already described. This message can be considered metaphorically as the evolution of ideas as well, as each generation comes to exist as a reaction to the one before it; we must avenge our father's death but also his very way of existence. It is certainly no small secret to historians or lovers of Hegel that the history of ideas is a sine-wave progression from thesis to antithesis, generally swaying in accord with the passage from one generation to the next. From this realization comes a change in behavior. The entire universe becomes impersonal.

The second realization is the reverse identification of the macrocosm and the microcosm, of the Dionysian God image within each of our individual lives. This brings one to be an agent of evolution, riding the crest of a wave as it moves forward, breaks, and is continued on. From this realization within life, we can move forward and perform our Wills as individuals, free from guilt or regret, nevertheless operating as the fingers of an unseen hand. This is the first boon of initiation.

Various mystery cults have existed, from the time of the Osiris myth until the present day, which claim to perform initiations which, in a series of steps, bring one to this identification. Whether or not these societies have ever successfully performed such initiations is a matter best left to the experience of those who have sought them out.

Jesus paused a moment, and looked up. *We're really in the lion's mouth here, aren't we?* Agent 139 was still on the far side of the room, inspecting the cage. He turned his attention back to the book.

All societies have inevitably created at least one secret society, so the names and specific functions of these Orders are vast. Some of the most famous are the Knights Templar, the Assassins, various Sufi cults, countless Gnostic and Hermetic organizations, the Castrators, the Cult of the Black Mother, the Rosicrucians, the Bavarian Illuminati, OTO, the Golden Dawn, A∴A∴, Freemasons—the list goes on and on. Each of these cults generally has any number of sects operating at any given time, oftentimes enmeshed in squabbling with the others over who has direct lineage from the "original" order.

In Orpheus' decent into the underworld, there is a reaction to the eternal realization or gnosis these schools or cults intend on presenting: here we see the futile efforts of the individual will and ego to cling, out of turn, to a particular time or impression. This interpretation is strengthened by the fact the Orpheus becomes the figurehead of the initiate within many of these cults. The Orphic egg also becomes an important figure, representing the potentiality in spirit of the initiate which may be released through an alchemical process (the initiations.)

While each of these may have different intents than the Gnostic/Orphic cults we're discussing, they all have certain qualities in common. In fact, these organizations differ only in intent and the symbols used in their initiations to create a somatic link to the brainwashing techniques taking place. We can see certain techniques being used across the board to brainwash people; and these are the techniques that have been used by religions and cultures, which invariably develop side by side, and by our modern corollary, media.

A biological imprint is created based on that society's understanding of nature that has direct and far-reaching implications on the individual's activity and behavior within the world. The basic nature of these techniques and the structure of the society is generally static, perhaps because the human psychology is similar, insofar as our biological apparatus of consciousness is similar.

Those two reflective orbs regarded Agent 139 for a very long moment, finally the Agent chuckled to himself and smiled.

Seeing bared teeth, the monkey gave an ear-piercing shriek and sprang towards him. The door to the cage flew open, hinges groaning, and Agent 139 was bowled backwards onto the floor with a grunt. Frenzied, he tried to claw the thing off, but it held on, its iron grip relentless while needle-sharp teeth worked their way along his neck and hunted for a vein.

A series of clicks and chirps came from above him and the monkey leapt towards the ceiling in a flash. Gabrael's silhouette loomed overhead, his face tilted sideways and wearing an unreadable expression. "I see you've met Suke, got him all riled up. Come down here, Suke." He chirped several times more and the monkey dropped back down from the rafters, landing on Gabrael's shoulder and clambering around to find a comfortable seat. "Suke means sweet, in Japanese. Back in your cage now, there you go."

Jesus clucked to himself and looked down at 139, still lying wide-eyed on the floor. "Never bare your teeth at a monkey, man."

Suddenly Agent 139 remembered where he'd seen the cage before, or imagined he'd seen it. *Wait, no, was it just a fleeting dream? Jesus bringing that cage to his room, a form wrapped in burlap dangling inside?*

Gabrael nodded. "Incredibly similar, genetically speaking. Still, some of our social mores differ dramatically. Dinner is served."

The two of them followed him into the kitchen, where he'd already served the meal around a wooden table. The black and white tiles of the floor melted, smaller, then larger in Agent 139's vision, and he stood at the entrance-way, transfixed. *Yin-Yang, broken into trigrams, hexagrams...the I-Ching! Now it makes sense!*

"I'm sorry about my friend," Jesus said, sitting down and taking in a deep breath of the steam that rose from the yams on his plate, "he's still tripping his balls off, I think."

Gabrael smiled and said, "Of course, of course." The wicker chair creaked as he leaned back. "Ahhh. Have you noticed it's been raining for three days straight? Of course you have, of course you have."

Jesus nodded. Agent 139 still stood in the doorway, staring down at the tiles. He looked up, squinting, and asked, "Do you think that means something?" *Three...three. And rain. The flood? Yes, here we go: the flood and the ark myth. Genetic transmission. The 42 days of the flood is AMA, the mother, still dark. The 42 judges of Amenti, the 42-fold name of the creative God. The black mother, the forces of creation in silence.*

Gabrael popped some turkey in his mouth, chewed while deliberating on the question, swallowed, and shook his head. "No, I just thought it was interesting."

Agent 139 pulled himself back from his reverie and took his seat at the table. "This is some damn fine turkey, if I do say so myself. It seems so simple, more wholesome than any I've...," he trailed off, looking at the salt shakers. *One black, one white. The pillars in my dream, the passage into the underworld.* His eyes remaining on Gabrael, he took the shakers and slowly moved them to either side of his plate.

"You like my salt and pepper shakers?" Gabrael asked.

The Agent continued to stare at him. "I do, very much." With a wink at Jesus, Gabrael said, "They *are* very good shakers, you know."

Jesus let out a snort and almost shot masticated yam through his nose.

The Agent turned his attention away from Gabrael, back to his plate, and they continue eating in silence for a few more minutes.

Then Gabrael sat forward and said, "Those above me in the Order would frown on me for saying this, but I'll tell you this much—the real order that doles out initiation, that creates the kind of synchronicities that brought you here and will carry you on to the next step of your mission, is the Universe itself." He leaned back. "Sorry about the mess, by the way. Would you like some sangria?"

They both accepted, and as Gabrael was filling a goblet for Jesus, Agent 139 picked up his and held it up to the light, examining the room through its crimson-colored lens.

"A toast," Gabrael proclaimed, "to Love, Light, and Liberty."

They clinked their glasses together, a high-pitched note that faded over an eternity of moments, very much, the Agent fancied, like the ringing of a bell.

Gabrael got up and lit a pair of candles, putting them on the table before walking across the room to switch off the lights. "Incandescent lights get to me, sometimes," he explained.

He picked up a knife and carved off another slice of turkey for each of them, the flesh peeling away like butter. "The tryptophanes in turkey tend to make you sleepy, you know. Of course, most people find it can be very relaxing, going down into that state. A few try to shake it off, worrying about this and that and what will happen to them while they try to resist in vain, but there's no need to get *really* tired. It's just pretend drowsiness, so I'd like to suggest you can notice how your breathing is already beginning to slow down, and simply relax." Gabrael picked up his wineglass and finished it off. "What did you find so interesting about my salt and pepper shakers, by the way?"

Agent 139 shook his head. "I can't say, really. It has something to do with a dream I had. I keep seeing things that tip me off to that, but when I try to bring light to it and piece it all together, they resist."

"I understand," Gabrael said, his eyes glittering in the candlelight. "You need to feel, rather than think. Dreams seldom make sense out of their element. Instead of trying to bring them up to you and figure them out, you need to go down to them, deal with them on their own plane."

Agent 139 nodded and shook some salt on his yams.

Gabrael turned towards Jesus, who was sitting cross-legged in his chair, his long white robes splayed open and revealing most of his chest. "Care for some more wine?"

Jesus tilted his head forward, a slow smile creasing his lips. "He who drinks of my lips shall be me, and I shall be him," he said, cupping both hands around the bulb and lifting his goblet to accept the libations. The ruby liquid gurgled as it rushed from the bottle and splashed against the glass. Jesus nodded again when it was three-quarters full, and then looked down into at his reflection mirrored on the burgundy surface. Everything around him brightened for a moment as he drank deeply from his grail, various objects on the table catching his attention, crystalline and fixed, standing still in stark contrast to the fascinating interplay of motion on his companion's faces.

Agent 139 was still transfixed, staring down at his yams and watching the tiny grains of salt melt into them. He didn't respond to the question.

"It's good, right? I believe with those dreams you'll find that when you drink a little more and allow the wine to mellow your thoughts, the mysteries they conceal will become clear to you," Gabrael said. "So, really, what brings you here?" As he was reaching across the table to refill Agent 139's glass, his elbow brushed against his own and tipped it over the edge. Jesus watched it tumble end over end as it fell, landing with a high-pitched crack and a slight bounce, followed by a raining patter of shards as it struck the tiles a second time and shattered.

The sudden sound startled Agent 139 so much that he almost fell off his chair. Blinking and looking around the room as if for the first time, he said, "They're the same, aren't they? ...The contents of my conscious and subconscious, I mean."

Gabrael, beginning to sweep the shards into a pile, paused and looked up. "I couldn't tell you," he said. "Our experience, from a literary perspective, certainly is a palimpsest."

CHAPTER 13, GRID 1

THE DOWNWARD SPIRAL

Life changing events are burglars. They steal into your house, turn everything upside down, and it's only in looking back and realizing the change that the thief, for better or worse, is realized for what he really is.
— Aleonis De Gabrael

Alexi was standing nervously at the base of the staircase in his apartment. He had been in his room, reading and preparing for sleep, when he felt a presence—*that* presence—from upstairs. When it was followed a moment later by the sounds of footsteps, slowly creaking from one floorboard to the next, he was forced to put down his book and inspect.

So now he stood, absolutely terrified, looking up into the shadows of the foyer and dark hallways beyond. Suddenly, he felt like a small child, hiding from that ever-present monster under the bed. Trying to write it off as a product of his overactive imagination, he slowly ascended the steps, the hair on the back of his neck prickling and adrenaline coursing through his veins. In fact, he could feel the blood pounding through every single capillary, pounding with a horrible, monotonous and steady rhythm. He felt he would find something, something absolutely unimaginably bizarre and terrifying at the top of those steps. The impression was so strong that he was resigned to a long and painful death by the time he reached the top. He reminded himself of the dangers of believing in absurd possibilities too easily. Occam's Razor—demons, or pressure changes?

His sheepishness was intensified two-fold when he found absolutely nothing. His senses continued to tell him that he was being watched, but he found nothing, no bloody corpses, no Cthonic squid-like creatures from Beyond. Pounding down the staircase now, he brought his mind back to the state it had been in, preparing for another round with the monstrously engaging hunchback of Denmark, Kierkegaard.

Chuckling at himself, he lay down and grabbed the book. At that very moment, he heard footsteps, now slowly descending the staircase. Each step was deliberate, unusually loud, as if a great weight was slowly rolling down the steps towards him. Alexi froze. Every muscle in his body went rigid. An icy chill shot up his spine, and directly into his cerebral cortex. The footsteps had stopped now. He could see that his door was locked, which did provide some degree of comfort. His mind was somewhat prone to paranoia; he had spent many hours of his childhood planning every single action he would take when that dark intruder would break into the house. It was only a matter of time before that intruder snuck in and turned everything upside down. All of those memories came back to him in a flash. He groped around under his bed, finding a knife that he kept there. And he waited.

As he waited, time slowed down. Listening to his breathing like enormous bellows, he suddenly felt alive. Awake. All of those passing moments, lost between the cracks between one memory and the next, became a cohesive whole. Singular. Then, in the middle of his terror, he found himself laughing. When he was young, maybe seven or eight, he could remember lying in bed holding his stuffed dragon. Terrible insomnia kept him up at night, the air would turn sparkling green and purple, a lattice work like spider webs on the wall, and he would sneak about his room with a marker, tracing them with a sharpie.

The two beaded eyes of his dragon stared at him. With a chill that froze him in place, froze him into awakening, those two eyes turned to regard him and he heard a voice in his mind say "I am going to have to leave you now." The next morning his mother chastised him for drawing all over the walls again. He endured it, silently, not able to explain, his dragon tucked safely under his arm. And when the bus came, and he passed the big 13, he realized with sudden panic that the dragon was no longer there. He had left.

The bronzed doorknob was rattling now, shaking back and forth rapidly. Alexi leapt to his feet...darkness. Complete, absolute darkness. There was a sensation of timelessness, of floating... Suddenly, he was in his room again. He heard a rattling sound, and the doorknob was unscrewed. His mother stood there, frantic. Apparently she had been trying to get in for more than ten minutes. Looking over at his clock, Alexi saw that it was two hours later than when he had gone upstairs to investigate the noise. He felt a breeze against the back of his neck. His window, which had been closed and locked, was now thrown wide open, letting in the frigid winter air. He could find no explanation for the loss of time, or for the open window, then, and, what is more, he never did find out what happened that night.

◀▬▶◆◀▬▶

Alexi lay in bed, wheezing and coughing. Crumpled tissues were scattered about his room.

He dialed up Ken's number. His mother answered and told him that Ken was out with his friend Jay. Alexi hung up the phone quickly and closed his eyes. A feeling of panic was setting in. He could identify it, could pick apart every single isolated psychological phenomena, but it did no good. The desperation and irrational anger just continued to build. He experienced his emotions from the outside, and was incapable of interacting with them on their own level.

He dialed Samantha's number a minute later. It rang a number of times before he got an answer.

"Hey..." she said, out of breath. He figured she had run up the stairs to get the phone.

"I'm not doing so well," Alexi said. It was all he could do to keep from pouring out an endless stream of complaints. Not that he hadn't been more and more prone to do just that lately. Still, he could watch this degeneration with complete passivity, from up on his mountain. It seemed that there was an ever-widening gap between his body and the center of his consciousness. The machine is getting annoyed. "When I wake up... I generally throw up... The headaches have been getting so bad that I can't think. Throbbing, every day, for almost a month now. Can't do anything. I'm starting to worry...that it's not a virus... Every second I think of you, and feel something terrible growing in the pit of my stomach." He paused, took a deep breath. "What've you been up to?"

"Nothing much." She hesitated. "I've been hanging around Jay and Ken a lot."

"Right...Jay." He felt a sudden flush of heat on his cheeks and neck. "Do you want to come over? I really shouldn't go out, but I could use the company."

"I don't know," she said, after an even longer pause. "I just don't see how I can help you. You need it more and more these days, like you can't exist on your own or something."

Tears almost burst into his eyes. Partially because she was dead right, and partially, Alexi knew, because she was dead wrong. It wasn't as simple as that. "I'm losing my faith, Sam. I really am." He couldn't keep his overwhelming feelings of hopelessness, desperation, or frustration from entering his usually carefully monitored voice.

"Your faith?" she asked.

"Yes. How is it that our tribe can become 'fair weather' so suddenly? That people can be so fickle as this, that when I'm doing well, they ask for my help, and I give it freely, and then when I need support..." his voice trailed off. Something clicked in his mind, a sudden realization that explained at least part of the situation. "Virtue is," he said, a certain rhetorical tone in his voice, "the most misunderstood and rare quality these days."

"Well, I usually can get a ride over, but not tonight—tomorrow. I have plans tonight. I'll bring some food, and we can just spend some time together," Samantha said, ignoring his last comment completely.

"I just got this feeling...call it an intuition," Alexi said.

"What about?"

"You and Jay."

"Don't be ridiculous. We're just good friends, and you know it. I just enjoy hanging out with him is all," she said. Alexi listened very closely to the quality of her voice. She may believe what she's saying, but I certainly don't, he concluded. Unexplainably, his feeling of despair suddenly turned almost into a light joy, as if the strain had become so much that his consciousness just gave up and disconnected from the body altogether. There was a certain fear underneath the experience, though. He could tell that it was a bad sign. Suddenly the despair returned. "Right, right...just my paranoia. Just do me a favor and be honest."

"Just get better so you can come out of the house again, O.K.?"

Alexi's face suddenly burnt red hot with desperation. All of the emotions which he generally kept locked, chained, and barred came forth in a series of staccato, agonizing notes of fury. "Do you have any idea how I feel? I've spent months helping you and everyone else in the group. I've been strong. And now it's a time when I'm not strong, when I'm both sick physically and mentally... Who's got a shoulder for me, now?" He knew he was being horribly self-indulgent, but the feelings were so true, so dead on target, that he couldn't ignore them any longer.

"You'll get better. That's all."

"Will I? My body will, of course. But the knowledge, that I can be left alone like that, in a second. It does serve me right for being an idealist."

"What?" she was becoming angry as well.

"I had a little bit of hope left, you know, for the goodness of human-ity. The will to power conquers all, you know…" Samantha could have wiped the sarcasm off the phone on her end. "I don't see anything of goodness. Opportunism, yes. I'm through with it. You won't find any-thing of goodness in me either. I fold. Another fifty dollars to the cynics. Goodbye, Samantha."

"Whatever," she said impatiently. His posturing was just too much. <click>

The bright lights on the ceiling of the Carriage house reflected yellow-orange across the bare wood floors. Everyone was seated, some on the sofas, others on high stools next to the kitchen island. Alexi was sprawled out on a sofa, gazing blankly at the lights on the ceiling, mutter-ing to himself.

"You O.K., man?" Ken asked from across the room. There was an unusual uncomfortably in the air, even more oppressive than the common billowing cigarette smoke.

No one's listening are you listening? I'm not listening no one's listen-ing in the temple of the temple in the temple…

Alexi turned a flashlight on and off a number of times before answer-ing. "In all honesty, no. However, I can't tell you what's on my mind, because of present company, and you'll probably write it off as my imag-ination anyway, and—" Ken opened his mouth to say something. "Eh, don't even bother, Ken. I know you're going to say that you'll hear me out, but in this instance, I can't see any resolution coming from talking about it. Fate will run its course. I already tried to talk to some people about it, and it is, quite apparently, all the delusion spawned of a sick and demented nervous system." Alexi pointed the flashlight suddenly at Samantha, who looked in the opposite direction.

Ken seemed annoyed. "Whatever," he said, turning his back on Alexi. "You think that the issues of the group are central to you, and that you started things. You're wrong."

Alexi glared over at him. "Is that so? Who introduced everything? Who was the workhorse and theorist? Tell me if I'm wrong, please prove me wrong. How is it that we have hundreds…thousands…hanging on our every word online now? Where do you think this came from? You have the intelligence, I'll never doubt that, but your apathy keeps you from doing much of anything. We're all supposed to be fucking family, man?

What is this? Maybe someone else will actualize what we had the vision to at least dream of. But not us. Everyone sees everyone else pulling away and falling apart, and we're all too fucking timid to so much as acknowledge it, let alone try to fix it. Maybe we can write if off as a process of growing older. 'It happens to everyone.' Don't you think that it is our own actions that result in our future? Or do you think we can sit around and just wait for our 'promised land' to come? And this is how it ends..." Alexi said.

"Whatever," Ken said again, walking away. "I need to go home. I'll catch you all around."

Samantha walked over to Alexi's side, sitting awkwardly on the end of the sofa.

"Yes?" he asked.

"I'm going out to the field, to watch the stars, maybe sleep," she said. Then, almost as an afterthought, she added, "I think Jay's coming along."

"Oh, you think?"

"You can come along," she added after a moment.

"What an honor. I can tell by your eyes that you don't want me to."

"My eyes?"

"Tell me one thing, alright? What are your intentions? If you would just bring this out in the open..."

She looked at him for a second, thinking. Then she bent over, her mouth an inch from his ear. "I don't know, maybe. Maybe you're right. I don't know."

His eyes rolled back, almost into his head. "Get out of here then." She hesitated. "Go!" he screamed.

<hr>

An hour after Jay and Samantha had left, no one could find Alexi. Don headed up the stairs, to go to the bathroom.

<hr>

Inside the bathroom, Alexi stared at himself in the mirror. Minutes passed slowly, but all that changed was the dilation of his pupils. This was his worst nightmare. What was more distressing was the peculiar familiarity of it. How many times would this story repeat itself? Shattered possibilities, broken plans, and wasted work. Yet he could feel that the real cause of the fracture lay far beneath these desperate grasps at rational cohesion. How many faces can you wear before you forget your own? The role had been a game based on an ideal that did not exist in reality. Formulated and preconceived. *Samantha had merely been playing the role she had been given. We all had.* It was not a familiar face that returned his questioning stare.

"This is the biggest joke I've been part of. A cosmic joke," he said, watching his lips moving in the mirror, amazed at how much they felt like rubber. Certainly not a part of him at all. The sudden thought of cutting them off flashed through his mind. It wasn't his lips that he wanted to cut off though. He wanted to cut her out of him, cut away his past with her, amputate it like a limb. Bleed her out of him. Yet, like his consciousness, she didn't exist in one part. She wasn't his foot or his arm. And neither was he. To kill her, he would have to kill him.

There was the sound of dripping water. He looked down at the floor to see drops of blood splattering scarlet across the white tiles. His nose was bleeding.

Cursing his luck, he grabbed some tissues and sat down, tilting his head back to slow the flow of blood. The red stain quickly consumed the tissues until they too were just giant blood clots in his hands. Still the flow didn't relent.

"When it rains, it pours..." he said, still performing for someone in the mirror. The tissue against his face made it rather hard to speak.

A humming sound issued from the floor itself. He looked around, suddenly frantic. The humming grew louder, until it was a deafening roar that blotted out even the sound of his own thoughts. He got to his feet shakily and staggered over to the mirror again, the blood continuing to pour from his nose.

There was something about the room that seemed wholly synthetic, like he had been taken out of the real bathroom and placed in an imitation. He looked out the window and heard the howling of the wind, the barking of one of the mastiffs in the driveway sharply attacking and then fading away. Something was certainly not right. It was all brittle, fake, and far away. He could feel harsh gazes burning into his neck—the synthetic bathroom was a display. He was on display.

His entire face was now covered in blood. The walls were screaming. He had to grip the sink for balance. And something was flowing from the back of his mind, like a serpent uncoiling up the length of his spine into his brain.

As his nervous system began to fly apart, the voices continued to raise in volume and tempo. Twisting and intertwining, hundreds of streams of thought, running in those now-familiar fractals in every dimension. He felt as if he could reach forward and backwards in time with this current of thought, he could feel the crushing momentum of it dragging him in its wake. It seemed that they would reach a crescendo, and yet they just continued to build, expanding in sheer ferocity and making progressively less sense.

Every movement of personality, lie within a lie, and gut wrenching emotion is disemboweled before it even arrives. It's like you see a shadow, an after effect, of what really happens, of what is really me. I am you. You are my result.

...My own wake. I am coming into the moment.

———◆◆————

Alexi was sweating profusely and shaking. He clutched the sink, his knuckles going white. "Me?" he asked hoarsely. *Who has been watching me through the mirror?!*

I couldn't stop looking, unblinking, unflinching, at myself looking at an image of myself looking at myself... I stop that chain in language— although it continues forever. Somewhere, disengaged in time, who can say that there is not an infinite chain of self-identified images of myself looking at images that it perceives as itself? Why does it determine, a-rationally, a-systematically, that this pale image is itself?

A pause, a sudden fracture of time. He was detached, lecturing to himself about himself, while the blood continued to well from his nose. *This is what I had been determined to answer. It burned my mind from the moment I woke up to the second I fell asleep. I was studying every book I could get my hands on that regarded psychology, identity, philo-sophical and religious texts that deal specifically with perception and credibility—phenomenology and epistemology because the need to answer this question had become more important than anything else... More than eating, more than breathing. I desperately sought to under-stand what it meant that I was aware of myself, that I could ask questions, that I existed and surely would die. To most people this was material for a classroom. To me it was the very point in existing—to figure out the puzzle.*

This is what set me on the path that leads to this point, that simple, simple question. Who or what am I? How am I aware of my body as other? Why am I aware of the world as other when my wisdom tells me I cannot be different from that which birthed me?

Mysteriously these questions were linked to what had happened with Samantha. They were linked to his friendship with Ken, the image of a spiral, the sound of a clock ticking, and these two figures—Meredith and Gabrael. A sacrificial flower. The cage. He couldn't sew the pieces together with logic, though he could distinctly feel the invisible thread that ran from one to the next. Notes everywhere, on computers, scraps of paper, recording everything because all of it is a part of the big picture, formed through chaos but as orchestrated as a symphony. There was a pattern there, a bigger picture. Alexi had always planned on disproving God, not finding IT by accident. *This thing with Samantha is just the trigger for what has been building in your subconscious for months, even years. This is the initiation you have been asking for.*

Then, calm. He could see a vaguely man-shaped form, standing in the corner of the bathroom. More the impression of a form than an actual form. So familiar. This form had been at his side for many years now, whispering secrets in his ear. Through the window he could see the moon, like pewter. He could sense that this being wanted to make a deal. It was time. Nothing to gain, nothing to lose. *He would be their emissary.*

There was an audible popping noise—the top of his spine suddenly felt like jelly—and this entire story unfolded itself before Alexi's eyes in the course of seconds.

CHAPTER 14, GRID 1

ANTI-CLIMAX

There was a razor, lying on the sink. A straight, sharp, perfect edge. Alexi blinked the tears and sweat from his eyes, as he prepared to cut himself open. He didn't want to do it, but felt he had no choice. His anchor to this world had been cut. The story had to end this way. It always had to, he realized. He had known all along.

A moment later the door opened and Don peered in.

"Well dear," he said. "For God's sake. Put that thing down, it won't do you any good. You can't get out that easy. You read the script right, but you mistook the symbol for sign. A metaphor is subtle, a razor is not."

Alexi looked over at Don, and smiled serenely. Such genuine peace in contrast to the scene around him. *I choose to stay.* The razor fell to the sink with a dead clang, a noise that also echoed and then died away unnaturally quickly. Suzanne came up the stairs as well and stood behind him.

"How about you clean yourself up, and we'll go for a walk. I'm new to this whole scene, and so you can't expect me to understand any of these so-unusual social dynamics. However, like most people, I'm a most biased ear, and if you're lucky, you might just bias me in your direction." Don smiled sweetly at Alexi.

"All...all right. Give me a second. The nosebleed seems almost gone," he said, pulling the mangled tissue away, gingerly touching his nose. "Yes, it's done." Don waited, his face completely serene. He just stood there, smiling ever-so-slightly, his eyes glittering intelligently. Suzanne looked anxious.

They headed out across the field, but didn't find Samantha or Jay. Alexi led them down into the valley, right up to the factory, retracing steps he had grown so familiar with. He walked this path now habitually, automatically, without any clear motivation. On the way, Don and Alexi talked.

"...You're often mentioning 'the Group.' Could you explain to me what that is, or was?" Don asked.

"*Was*...most definitely. Should I say even...could have been. I mentioned Gabrael a few moments earlier...he gave me the blueprints, although I didn't realize it at the time. I put them into action. Simply its just a return to a basic tribal structure. Family by choice, rather than by chance... Each member dedicated to their own evolution...and to helping the others find that end for themselves... Each individual dedicated foremost to the unearthing and honing of their unique nature. For them. For the group. Our tribe. Not at all what this society offers...or doesn't. A group that can trust one another—" Alexi noticed a look of confusion on Don's face, and so he stopped.

"Trust? You expect human beings to do that without infantile strife? One-up-man-ship? Petty drama? A person is smart. People are stupid." Don said, curiosity in his voice. *That's why we have to keep up this silly Mother Hive Brain game, he thought.* Then, *I'm pretty sure this "group" is a test run. I wonder what the real show is going to be. And who will be the players.*

"We've all failed. Every single one of us. I have found the source and definition of loneliness, and it is this: none of us can ever experience life as anyone other than ourselves, and with that limitation, we are completely bound to react to others as objects. The desperate urge to unite is also the urge to annihilate, and although it is acted out in sex, it is a mockery, a farce motivated by the hope of being someone else. The sacrament is profaned. It all amounts to the same thing. I want, I dream of being anyone or anything but myself, I run from myself and hide in my vices, hide in my virtues, and know myself least of all when the play is through. I hate none of them. I am incapable of hating them; even my pretense of hatred is really just a movement, a deception, of my love. But I hate this entrapment, this cage." He viciously motioned to himself. "I am like a moth pulled to the flame that it is charged to trespass, which beats and bloodies itself knocking against the thick pane of glass barring its entry. I may knock and knock until the very flesh falls from my bones, and I'll be not one step from where I started, having chased my own shadow in circles across the sun, that burning inferno which I necessarily must enter." Don was having a hard time keeping from chuckling to himself. *Je-sus... Who was this guy's script writer? Maybe he could hook me up with an eight-ball or two?* At the same time, in a way, he could relate. "...The sun where my self is burned away as it unites with its opposite. And here, that which showed me the way in the first place has turned her back upon me. The world that I entered with her became me. It was my pole-star. What can I do to aright this? Fight?!" his monologue was reaching a fever pitch. He had lost himself in the speech, but when he looked up, he found a look of understanding in Don's eyes, although there was something hard there too.

Alexi continued. "Oh, yes. I 'fought.' I fought so hard that I lost sight of what I was fighting for, and possibly, although I can barely dare to admit it to myself, I was blinded in the sun. Text-book Hubris. Maybe I am not so much betrayed as betrayer, as I drove away her affections in my feverish, blind and stupid charge for our future, a future only imagined, dreamed of, and then frightened off. ...How could I talk to them about the plans that I had without it short-circuiting? It was only myself, my dreams, and my hopes that I loved, and in that, I have betrayed them all. Here it has become a fight against 'society,' when we are the real enemies and the real barriers against our safe passage. One layer of mask is cut away merely to reveal another, as every 'perfect idea,' every utopian dream of ours becomes little more than a cage, revealing nothing other than the very nature of our most base desires and fears." He paused a moment, re-oriented, and then leaped forward again, suddenly on a new tangent. "This novel I have committed myself to, I fear, is a tragedy, and I am too immersed in it to write myself any ending but that which is expected: all tragedies end in death. And yet, paradoxically, with the knowledge that this is merely a novel, there is nothing to lose and nothing to gain. None of us contain anything but words and the paper they are written on, and it is those words which allow us to define our rising and falling action, our enemies, and even the character that we are to play. There is no escape from the forces of equilibrium, the silent and deadly gravity which forces you to live your past over and over again. This is the irony, we don't write our characters on a blank slate. Don, I feel that you speak my language, and that's why I'm telling you this. I don't see any reason to believe in 'truth,' nor any blemish or flaw in a world without certainty, yet I must say that all I have said to you tonight is a lie that lies closest to my heart, and whether it proves itself foolish or false, I still call it 'true.'"

They continued on towards the factory.

"What's the deal with Jay?" Don asked.

"How do you mean?"

"I mean, first, why is everyone gravitating towards him more now? He seems like a nice guy, but not... I can't find the words for it. His strong sense of humor seems to undermine the possibility of anyone really seeing anything serious in him." Don was getting more amusement out of what he was saying than Alexi realized. *Humor's one of the only things that keeps you intact.* "I don't know," he continued, "That could, of course, be more to his detriment than betterment. You might actually have a lot to learn from one another, though I know that isn't what you want to hear right now. Have you talked to him about this? Or simply passed judgments? ...I'm also talking out of my ass, since I really don't know him."

Alexi paused. "The irony here is that I don't think Jay knows about any of this. If I try to explain it all now, he'll just think I'm crazy."

Don stopped and looked at him. "There's no such thing as 'insanity' or 'madness.' Anyone who listens to such nonsense is possibly the only true kind of lunatic, a Yes-man that's all ears, and no brain; the kind who believes anything, what is worse, who buys what is sold to them... Anyone who is truly crazy, in my book, wouldn't be able to understand the dialectic of crazy and not-crazy. Listen, I've worked for the pharmaceutical companies, they have a vested belief in making you believe that if you have a chemical imbalance you need them to be 'cured' of your current issues and personality. Indefinitely. Imagine diagnosing personality only in terms of its negative aspects. Does this strike you as a strategy designed for health? The only way to deal with a problem is to fucking deal with it. Get inside what positive motivation, what intention, makes you behave in the way you are...and how you could maybe satisfy that need in a healthier or at least more agreeable manner. America wants quick, easy and painless; being a real person is slow, difficult and very messy. Alexi, you have to take responsibility for your own life and makeup, look at what needs to be done and do it."

Alexi nodded, but seemed not to hear. "I have a question for you, Don. How do you manage to appear so happy about everything? I can tell it isn't a lack of intelligence—you can't hide that, so ignorance isn't your trick."

"I don't have a trick," Don said, "I live day to day, deal with it the best I can. Oftentimes I go to sleep lonely and unfulfilled. But I make the best of it, and don't call the game a loss because I lost a single round.

Every breath is a birth and a death." He smiled and nodded his head very agreeably.

"That's what I was afraid of. You know...they all think I'm crazy," Alexi said, softly. "And none of them seem to really be listening to a word I say, any longer. Yes, it's over. Let's find Samantha and Jay."

Don and Suzanne shrugged at each other and followed Alexi up the hill to the field.

———

They found them, lying next to each other on a blanket, talking under the clear night sky. The bitter cold seemed to make the stars that much more precise, like tiny holes in a blanket, just feet over their heads. When Alexi saw the pair in the distance, he motioned for Don and Suzanne to stay behind. Without a sound, he strode right up to the side of the blanket.

"Hello," he said, rather loudly. "I fear I may be interrupting?"

Jay looked up. Samantha spun around.

"Uh, hey man," Jay said. Then he looked closer and saw the bags under Alexi's wild eyes, the blood stains on his shirt... "You don't look so good. What's up?"

Alexi looked at him hollowly, but didn't say a word. He pointed at Samantha a moment later.

"Samantha, I need to speak with you. Please."

She glared at him, and turned to Jay. "I'll be back, O.K.?"

———

The two of them walked back to the carriage house in silence. Once inside, they strode upstairs and went into the guest room, next to the bathroom. Alexi sat on the bed.

"Can you do something for me? At least do this, to ease the pain on me," Alexi said.

"What's that?" Her voice was cold and forced, as if she was holding in any feelings she was having.

"If you do want to leave me, go back on your word, and be with him, at least tell the others. At least admit it to me and more importantly, yourself. I can see how they're all looking at me, Sam. They're convinced that I'm making this up. It all sounds so infantile, and intellectually I suppose it is, but emotions don't really demand intellectual validation. They just are. I can't rationalize this emotion into non-existence any more."

She looked at him. "I am interested in Jay."

"Then tell them! End it now! I can't just passively watch you do this. Take a stand, make an action!" He pounded his fist on the bed.

"I can't."

"What?! Why not?" His eyes bugged out of his head. It seemed likely that they would leap out at any moment.

"I just said I'm interested. Look, we're going to be okay, alright? I promise," Samantha said.

"You promise? What good are promises?" Alexi's eyes were rimmed with tears. He looked away.

"Hey, look at me." She moved his face to look at her, a little more emotion in her voice than before. "These things happen."

"Yeah, they do. But I need to know—what do you want? What do you want to do about it? You tell me one thing and then reverse it a second later."

Her eyes went cold again. "Well, whatever."

Alexi screamed absolute nonsense, pounding his fist on the floor again and again. Blood began pouring from his nose, and he collapsed into a heap on the bed. The stain continued to grow larger and larger.

"Shit... I'm going to get my mother, okay? Don't move. She'll know what to do." Lying limp now, Alexi didn't think that movement of any kind was in his near future. Suddenly finding comedy in the whole situation, he chuckled to himself and looked out the window. The deep, velvety black of night was giving way to the unreal, neon hues of early morning.

"It's a shame you can't 'go get your mother' about everything." He still couldn't shake the feeling that he was an actor on a stage. Only through observation, he realized, did anything hold any meaning. The man alone in a room may as well not exist. As usual, his thoughts continued unabated, even during times of such extreme emotional duress. This too he suddenly found perversely funny, although his laughter turned to a gag when a stream of blood poured down his throat. He fell back to the bed and lay still.

Dawn and Samantha entered the room shortly thereafter.

"Alexi..." Dawn said, kindly, non-judgmentally. She helped him roll over. "Alexi," she said, this time slightly more firmly, looking right into his eyes. They were like two dull marbles, soulless balls of jelly.

"Well," she said, looking at Samantha, "he's breathing fine, maybe even hyperventilating a bit. It looks more like emotional shock than anything else. Do you know what happened?"

Samantha shrugged.

Dawn produced some rags and held them over his nose. It was many long minutes before the bleeding stopped.

"Let's all go downstairs, alright? I want to get you something to drink," Dawn said.

She went ahead.

"What did you say to her?" Alexi asked Samantha.

"Nothing...well, that you got a bad bloody nose."

"Ah. I'll change that, then." Alexi said. "I need someone to know, or I'm going to explode."

"Don't..." Samantha pleaded.

"Please. It pains me to see that you value losing face over the truth. Although," he added, mock-thoughtfully, "perhaps I will agree some-day."

⚊⚊◈⚊⚊

Once downstairs, the three of them sat on a sofa.

Alexi turned towards Dawn.

"I think I should tell you what happened..."

She nodded, looking intently at him over a mug of hot chocolate.

Alexi quickly paraphrased the situation with an absolutely calm and controlled voice, and then, towards the end, suddenly exploded and fiercely slammed his fist into the wall. Although Samantha seemed frightened, Dawn didn't even flinch. In fact she seemed to have expected it somehow.

"This one," Alexi said, pointing at Samantha, "has backed down on every promise she has ever made me. Everything is unraveling."

Samantha sat in silence, fuming. On the inside, however, she was completely conflicted. She hadn't intended any of this to happen, and had no idea what to do.

"You could do something that you almost never do: let it out," Dawn said.

"There's so much held in— I'm like a walking, pressurized tank walking about in a circus of the grotesque and absurd."

Dawn decided not to mention that he had horribly mixed his metaphors.

Over the next week, Samantha continued to persuade me, trying to convince both of us, I think, that things between us weren't really "all that bad." Well, she nearly had me convinced by the time we decided to go to Virginia beach during spring vacation.

I had caught a fever of 103 two days before, and was still very sick when we headed onto the road in Jay's Volkswagen van. Truthfully, I didn't want to go, but I couldn't trust Samantha and Jay going together. I knew, deep down, that it was ridiculous, having such a lack of trust in any relationship and expecting it to work. Despite my rationalizations, I had to go.

I remember little of the ride down, just the uneasy swaying of the vehicle and the horribly piercing sound of their laughter. The delirium was a thick cloud that enveloped me in the back, lying wrapped in a blanket, shivering on a wooden plank. Less than one hour on the road, I realized that I never should have come. They danced about and listened to music. Occasionally they turned to talk to me, their voices all seemed slowed down and distorted. It seemed that they were taunting me with their nonsense intentionally, laughing at my inability to do or say anything. I felt absolutely forgotten and useless.

We rented a hotel to stay for the night. When I went to the bathroom to wash my face, I found a washcloth that read **"THE ABYSS HAS COME: prepare to meet your maker!"** *in bold, black print. It made absolutely no sense to me, so I decided not to wash my face. I slept that night next to Samantha. However, she insisted on rolling as far away from me as possible on the double bed. I tried to sleep, but could not. I must have spent an hour or more in that bed, looking over at her familiar face. I felt as if I was looking back at this time, this time right now, from some distant point in the future, remembering what she looked like, reminiscing. Her face had been permanently engraved upon my memory, it may as well have been my own face. Eventually, I was granted the purgatory of sleep.*

All of this agony was setting me up for the events of the next day, although I couldn't have known it then. We set off to the shore, and Samantha was right on Jay's heels the entire way. I tried to explain it to him. He thought I was crazy. I tried to beg her to tell him. She held firm to her silence. I went so far as to try to scare her into it. But both of us knew that I couldn't do a thing, my validity slowly whittled away to nothing over the past month. It wasn't jealousy that consumed me though, but the fact that my quickly erected self-identity, dependent on her, made it impossible for me to function properly within that identity. It was no longer home. I was no longer home. Even things, once so famil-iar, were all strangers to me now.

I went back to the van to be alone, although I couldn't be, constantly haunted by flashes of memory, the sound of voices—some her voice, some Ken's, some that I could not place. Of course I wanted her to come back and find me, I wanted her to apologize for how she had made me feel and to talk to me about how we could work things out. But I knew she wouldn't. The audience had departed.

Yet, I was being watched by everything and everyone. Where they gone? Where they everywhere? I hid under blankets to try to avoid being watched, but even that was just a part of the play and somewhere, deep down in my impassive recesses, I knew it. It was for my own amusement but the game wasn't amusing any longer, I just didn't know how to stop.

It was time to practice what I had been preaching and transcend myself. I had been right, that night in the carriage house—transcendence meant death, to make room for new life—and that's also where I had gone wrong, by concretizing the realization. It was strictly metaphorical, like the death and rebirth of the Christ. This was suicide, but there would be new life to takes its place. I had to live through this, my greatest fear, and come out the other side – finally alive, but also alone.

Calmly, I walked to the beach, listened to the waves beat slowly and calmly away at the tightly packed sand, and let the life I had lived wash away, devoured hungrily by that eternal tide. When it had taken it all, I turned and walked away. I didn't know where I was going or why. I just walked.

The next thing I knew, I was wading through deep, sharp grass in marshlands, surrounded by a chain link fence five or six feet tall. Without even a second thought, I leapt over it, and looking back now, I have absolutely no idea how.

My memory beyond this point is very hazy, but I will remember what I can. The sky was a deep shade of orange, I remember that. And birds, huge water birds, flew by—calling out. Out in the marsh, I spotted a kingfisher, its head ducking under the tide for food. The birds, they were calling my name. But it was no longer my name. I was to die.

I took my shoes off, ceremonially like I was entering a house in ancient Japan, and continued barefoot through the warm muck, reveling in the feeling of soft, wet mud under my bare feet. There was no litter or glass, which meant that it was probably a wild life reserve. I briefly wondered what it would be like to not breathe. Not the suffocating. I realized that though I knew intellectually I would die, and that dead people don't breathe, it never struck me immediately in my body that there would ever come a time when I stopped breathing. I couldn't remember not breathing, but it was possible to feel that empty space, before my coming into being, and imagine it stretching out infinitely into the future in front of me, into the past behind me, and suddenly this growing horizon was not a before or an after. I saw my life as a self-contained bubble, a secret never to be known, all of our lives and trials: secret, silent.

The sun was beginning to set, and the crickets were singing. So I sat down and listened to them. Tears were streaming down my face, but I couldn't remember why. It was like sitting in a theatre after a movie you particularly enjoyed has ended. Everyone else long ago filed out the back, but you still sit expectantly waiting for all the actors to come back and do it all again.

Unexpected thoughts entered my mind at this point. Amidst this confusion I found myself thinking back to the woods that I had explored with Ken and my other friends, and I thought about something Dawn had mentioned to me in passing: that they were selling those lands, those sacred lands, to help send Samantha to college. I imagined it torn apart, leveled, sterilized. They would become a housing community, yet another identical outcropping of the alienating suburbs that were blighting the country. ...The night in the carriage house, staring in the mirror, They came to me. Now it was clear, if only for a moment, what exactly I had agreed to. The woods somehow knew what was coming...though it seemed crazy, for a moment I understood that there was a struggle on, here, now, this very moment, for the future of the planet. But it was waged here in the present between the future, and the past. Sides are being drawn. Those who hear this, and feel the call, will make themselves known. Then the lucidity was gone. Briny taste of tears in my mouth.

In a while, I couldn't remember who I was at all.

When my self-awareness returned, I wasn't myself any longer. It was like returning to your home after a war, a burnt out shell of what had been. Love had passed through hate and become absolute, ineffable indifference. This was my second real initiation, the first of course being birth, though whether it was to be a success or failure remained to be seen. What returned to take my place was something hardened, more powerful and resistant to the secret gravity of life. I had begun the process of attaching to perception itself, existing as a passive, steely lens that, in doing nothing but watch and wait, is nothing. And to this very day, although I can remember those distant memories of being someone wholly different, someone who could reach out, touch something and feel it in that adolescent way that makes even the most mundane aspects of life a convulsive, overwhelming undertow, I remember them as someone else's memories. As I write this now, with mixed feelings of fond remembrance and deep sorrow and regret, I close the final page of this story, this life, and must continue on without looking back. Because this is not the end of the story. This story has been a prologue. The story that is to come will be lived, in all of our lives from this point.

When I returned home, I checked myself into a mental hospital. And it was when I was there that I received a message in the mail from Aleonis De Gabrael.

Alexi:

Solitude is the cost of our free will. This distance, this fresh air, is what gives us our self reflection, but it also risks cutting us off the real flavor and meaning of life... which as you know is a mutual experience, a shared now. I know this is little consolation, when you realize with dreadful finality what you must sacrifice to break out of the habitual patterns that define and cage you.

Further, this isn't a singular test. You will be tried by these same forms time and again. You will be forced to give up your closest companions, and all of your ideals, so that you can find still deeper truths. Not all such truths are pretty, or pleasant.

The only solace I can provide is that to us, other people really are archetypal—they are Gods and Goddesses—and those you have loved and lost will return to you time and again with new faces, and new lessons to teach you. From this vantage point, our lives are a process of synthesizing the same energies again and again in new guises. Each time you are given the chance to make new choices. Maybe you can find a way out of your own labyrinth, into a new story.

This is what it means to be one of our Order: not to claim mastery, but to strive for it, no matter how larval your present state; not to parrot another's wisdom, but to find your own, hidden in your darkest grottos.

I say I am inviting you in, but this is a mere formality. If you are a member, then you have always been a member.

I know you will have a lot of time to think while you sit in the hospital. What I would like you to consider carefully is this: everything you have faced, and all the pain you have endured started and ended with you. You created your own tests. What a difficult thing it is to lose what you hold most dear, and at the same time say: I willed it thus. What joy and strength can be found in this... but also, what unspeakable sadness. Embrace it all, frater.

Aleonis
0=11

CHAPTER 15, GRID 2

THE LABYRINTH

Never console yourself into believing that the terror has passed, for it looms as large and evil today as it did in the despicable era of Bedlam. But I must relate the horrors as I recall them, in the hope that some force for mankind might be moved to relieve forever the unfortunate creatures who are still imprisoned in the back wards of decaying institutions.
— Frances Farmer

The moon hung in the sky, invisible. She sent her borrowed sunlight off into space, perhaps jealous of her big blue sister.

On earth, right here, right now, there is perfect velvet darkness. The compound is quiet. Royersford is sleeping. To take advantage of this darkness, Jesus hides his dark car behind a nearby factory, kills the motor, and slips out into the warm air.

Just uphill is the road that encircles the target for the evening— Pennhurst State Hospital. From previous experience, he knows a rent-a-cop will be along in a wheezing Cavalier, about every 20 minutes. He crouches in a conveniently located bush and checks his gear while marveling at the quality of the evening. Stars shone through the canopy, and the hill that holds the complex is awash in the night smell of a thousand unseen blossoms. He is five minutes away from a decaying industrial town, but all that is hidden from his perch.

No longer right here, right now. Here operated under different rules. *Here* was a deserted asylum, being slowly eaten by the encroaching forest, vines replacing windows, morning glory augmenting the brick facades of what appeared to be a college campus. *Here* was timeless.

Interrupting his musings, the aging Chevy passed, windows rolled down and some Styx love ballad blasting from the tinny speakers. The fortyish man behind the wheel didn't slow, didn't even look around. Jesus waited a polite moment, then crossed the cracked pavement. Dead

242

reetlamps flanked the overgrown paths, some tilting crazily like runken soldiers. Rusted iron railings drove straight lines through napeless shrubbery, and as Jesus crept along them, he could hear, in a ear-perfect circle around him, the rodents, the insects, the creeping ings fleeing at his bow and in his wake. The wave-front of the present ad passed, failing to take this quiet place along with it. His carefully eddened flashlight didn't cast enough light for anyone but a nocturnal othead or a cat burglar.

Jesus smiled to himself at the thought— *Been both of those, I suppose.*

He drew closer to the center of the campus. From his vantage point, e could see 15 patient buildings poking up through the scrubby growth nat sprung up everywhere there had been a lawn. All were three and four ory brick structures, linked by elevated concrete paths. On the far side as a veteran's hospital, still operating. Security patrolled that area more ntensely, so close approach to most of the buildings was impossible. A uilding between them looked suspiciously like the steam plants found n most college campuses. Memories from a drunken weekend under- eath a friend's college campus surfaced, oriented, and sank in. Steam ipes were prone to leaks, valves needed to be accessed, and so the engi- eers built access tunnels, to every building in the complex. *Bingo,* he nought. *Tunnels—all I've got to do is find the steam feeds in the base- ents!*

A huge brick L, almost centered in the paths, seemed a likely entry oint. The crook of the L would provide him some cover should the ounds of his entering attract attention. Around the eaves, Jesus saw usted black and white signs displaying the letter "C".

Building C had seen better days. The slate roof was shedding, and everal wounds showed frame along the peak. Windows showed broken ehind their bars as paint flaked from their sills and fell to the ill melling soil. In the darkened elbow of the L, Jesus found a loose win- ow, slipped his crowbar under the sill, and carefully levered. Lead dust uffed in a neat line, and soon Jesus was pulling himself up through the ortal, careful not to cut his palms on the dirty glass shards, savoring the mell of rust, mold, rotting paper and damp menace, as well as just the nost thrilling hint of forbidden asbestos.

He had to resist the urge to light a cigarette at the very thought, and huckled quietly to himself.

Jesus entered an office just across from the entranceway. Polished narble slabs decorated the walls. He couldn't estimate their value.

Desks, chairs, and telephones crowded the halls, as if the employees and patients had half-partied, half-rioted away their last days. Filing cabinets lay on their sides, dented and spilling their contents on the floor. As Jesus picked his way around them, he noticed, with some trepidation, a mattress on the floor with a recent copy of *Newsweek* sitting beside the dirty pillow. The date was less than two weeks ago, the cover story an expose of cult membership among New York City cab drivers. Jesus smiled, shook his head, and pressed on around the bend and into the long side of the building. He walked as softly as he could, yet still his footsteps bounced and echoed off the empty halls, coming back to him in differing rhythms.

Paint hung from the ceiling in foot long strips, dangling there like some cheeky demon's version of crepe paper ribbons. More of their brethren littered the floor, breaking slowly down into the dust that coated every dry surface. Ahead was a bigger office, and the concentration of filing cabinets increased here. Patient files formed a surface like white autumn leaves on the tile floors, abandoned just as readily as the patients themselves were when the asylums started to shut down. Jesus picked one up and read:

```
John Doe (AKA Jesus, et al.)

Current Diagnosis DSMIV:

Axis I:     Schizoaffective Disorder (Bipolar Type)
            Depersonalization Disorder
            Gender Identity Disorder NOS (Partial Remission)
            Dysthymia NOS

Axis II:    Antisocial Personality Disorder
            Schizotypal Personality Disorder

Axis III:   No physical conditions noted as of this time

Axis IV:    Difficulties with Interpersonal Relationships,
            Disturbances in Primary Support Group (Death of
            parent), Disturbances in Primary Support Group
            (Discord with remaining parent), Disturbances in
            Secondary Support Group (related to Difficulties with
            Interpersonal Relationships), Job Dissatisfaction
```

Case Study:

[Prepared by Dr. Harold Fein, M.D., Ph.D., in consultation with Dr. Bernard Spitzer, M.D., Ph.D.]

Patient is a six foot, five-and-one-half inch tall Caucasian male presenting with unstable affect and posture. His appearance appears consciously crafted to communicate a disdain for proper dress and hygiene, though I note that his fingernails, hair, and areas of exposed skin are scrupulously clean. He is wearing the robe of his hospital gown open and appears to have deliberately torn his pants at the left knee. Hair is unbound and worn long. Jesus, the only name to which the patient consistently responds, demonstrates severe Schizoaffective Disorder which may, in time, degenerate into Schizophrenia (Catatonic Type), in addition to severe depressive episodes, depersonalizing ideations, delusions of reference and grandeur, and features of Gender Identity Disorder which may at this time be considered in partial remission.

Jesus was involuntarily committed to this facility following his arrest in connection to a riot which completely destroyed a Lenny's Restaurant in Devon, PA as well causing severe property damage to surrounding businesses. Jesus himself claims numerous fatalities resulted from the riot as well, though none were noted in the accompanying police report. Law enforcement authorities indicate that he was potentially acting either on orders from or in the name of a terrorist organization known as the "MHBS". Jesus has not been forthcoming on this topic. He was remanded to our custody after tearing a stigmata pattern into his flesh with his teeth in a police detention cell following his arrest.

⟫◆⟪

Thoughts came on too fast for Jesus to grasp them.

I was never committed. To any *facility. Could I be losing it then? I feel fine. I feel...*

Images spin and collide. *Kris's hair haloing around her head, looking down into Jesus's eyes from above as they lie coupled. Jesus means to tell her he loves her, but holds back. Kris's hands run up the curves of pig's back as they sit facing each other, the little grin in pig's eyes gloating, "I posses what you thought was yours." They kiss, but pig's eyes stay on Jesus as he lets his drink fall from numb fingers.*

A spider, its green metal lair disturbed, crawls up Jesus's pant-leg and finds a place to plant the fangs...

Pig, seen through a veil of jealous tears and anger, years before... Jesus looks over at his doughy, pouting girlfriend, then over at pig grinding 139 under an upturned sofa, and finally down at his exquisitely manicured hands laying in his skirted lap. Thinking about the shoulders he'll never touch, and more, thinking about the same shoulders that will never be his. He deserves her body. Suddenly he feels the shame he felt the first time his mother caught him dressed up.

"Does this mean you like boys?"

<hr/>

Agent 139 was riding a camel in Egypt when the screeching woke him.

He adapted over his committal to the tortured circadian rhythms of his neighbors. Those not under sedation whimpered, hissed, screamed, lectured, barked denials at their dreamscapes until Wake Up at nine o'clock. At first he was an avid listener to these nocturnal improvs. He hung on One-Eyed Steven's raspy punctuation to Al's post-traumatic stress. He wrote reviews lambasting the one-upmanship of the psychotics, huzzahs to the delicate percussion of the catatonics upstairs. He bit his nails and stared out the window.

Eventually, boredom triumphed and he slept like a baby.

But tonight's shrieking was a whoopee cushion in *Turandot*. He kept his breathing sleepy and even and cracked his eyes, scanning for a source.

The screech came from his window glass, behind the mesh that held him in. A small circle of glass *cracked!* and was pulled out into the night.

Agent 139 rose slowly and walked over to the grill, a mounting sense of disbelief upon him. Standing on his toes and placing an eye across from the hole did no good, as he found himself looking into a mirror. A shiny, human eye peered back at him, widening with dawning confusion, darting as his own darted.

"What the fuck," someone breathed from the other side. "139, that better be you."

"Nope," Agent 139 grinned. "You're breaking into a hall of mirrors."

A chuckle drifted through the glass, darkly, and he was ordered to stand back. The glass wobbled as it was cranked out of its frame on suction cups and lowered to the ground. "There. Didn't want you to get cut up if that didn't work."

Agent 139 giggled. "Wouldn't that be the least of your worries?"

The shadow began to smear a thick, vitriolic paste on the metal grid between them. "Nope. This part scares me a bit, though." It withdrew a squirt bulb from its vest and began dripping it onto the mass, which bubbled and spat and smelled like a portal to Elemental Pigshit. A bubble popped and hit Agent 139 on the bare arm. He bit through his lip choking the scream.

"Imagine my joy," the figure said, lowering the grating to the ground next to the glass, "when I did this hanging from the roof." It extended a hand through the window and boosted Agent 139 to freedom.

His first free breaths since the explosion were laced with boiling acid, the crickets were silent, and it was cold and overcast. And god damn was it good.

Until Agent 506 handed him the rope.

"Um."

"What? I can't get him out of there alone. He's too god damned big. Oh, and he's a fucking vegetable. What the *fuck* is he doing in a coma?" 139 heard the faint constriction of tears building in his voice. "Was it the drugs? Did they—"

"It wasn't them." He placed his bleeding arm on his friend's thin shoulder. Agent 506 shook with grief and rage.

"They fucking fried him. They killed him."

"He escaped. He can be Meredith all the time now. Our freeing him here might cage him forever."

"What?"

"Can we talk while we run?"

⊰•◦❖◦•⊱

"Well," Jesus giggled, "It means what you think it means! I'm trying to model an entirely impossible situation in my poor upturned wreck of a mind! God our Father, why art thou drinking? Delusions of grandeur! Such a thing for those doctors to say about your reborn martyr son!"

He pocketed the file for later examination, blushing, and headed towards a nearby stairwell, switching on his carefully reddened light. The air coming from the stairwell was cooler, wetter, somehow more rotten than the already thick atmosphere of the building. Graffiti covered the walls here, in magic marker, nail polish, mustard, betadine—whatever was handy to those souls who walked these halls before. Scrawled in red chalk on a support beam was the phrase, "Abandon hope all ye who enter here," with an arrow pointing down the narrow, dank hallway. A few empty offices flanked the hall, but Jesus had his eyes on the hall's far end. He knew there was a doorway there, he could see it in fact, yet he saw it as an absence. Windows were few down here, and his flashlight didn't provide much illumination, but whatever lonely photons made it down to the end of this corridor were swallowed up by the doorway. As Jesus inched toward it, he noted with some satisfaction that insulated pipes ran down toward the dark doorway.

My tunnels await!

There wasn't much of a room behind the doorway's outline. The space opened up into a concrete closet, 6 feet on a side. Cracks riddled the surfaces, and cobwebs shared the ceiling with a bare, broken bulb dangling on its cord. One of the walls held a barred set of institutional double doors, the other a cast iron door that looked to Jesus like the door on his Uncle's wood stove. It was roughly two feet by three, and several inches thick, stamped with the name Morven Foundry, Chicago, IL. Jesus turned the stainless handle and eased the heavy door back, showering his high boots with flakes of rust and dried mud. Something unpleasant coiled in his stomach as he felt the cold air roll past him, heavy with moisture. He crouched obscenely, and taking care not to bump his head or dirty his hair overmuch, waddled in.

The tunnel itself was a simple box, smooth, regular, and seamed every few feet. Jesus shivered in the damp air, his light playing out only a few feet in front of him. Every so often the squared tube turned 45 degrees, branching off at these angled junctions into the darkness beyond. Jesus stopped, not quite sure why he did so. Something nagged him at the corner of his vision. His eyes searched the corridor, found a green blob roughly the size of his hand nearby, and focused. A translucent green spider hung inches in front of him, its inner workings laid bare, backlit by his flashlight. While he was no arachnologist, he did know enough to believe that spiders were supposed to be symmetrical. The legs on the left side of this specimen were longer than those on the right, and seemed to have too many joints. As it feebly waved its forelegs in Jesus's direction, a wave of nausea swept over him. *It's lived its entire broken life*

own here—what's the point? Jesus panicked and fled, not noticing at all
1at he had been a girl since he'd passed through the light-eating door-
/ay that had long since vanished from his memory.

Brushing the last of the spider webs out of her hair, Jesus surveyed her
urroundings. The small concrete box tunnels had disgorged her in a
exus of sorts. Pipes and corridors ran in every direction. This room was
t least 30 feet tall, and she could barely make out the stars though the
1etal grate that served as a ceiling. Valves and hideously tangled
lumbing clung to the walls, while smaller pipes led out from this knot
1rough a number of openings—from the size of a normal door to spaces
1at could barely accommodate a prone human. The tunnel she had origi-
ally come from opened high above the floor, too far to reach back up to,
o she followed the largest path out of the junction room—an arched
rick tunnel with a few inches of slimy water in the bottom.

This was a truly unpleasant passage. Mud sucked at Jesus's boots as
he made her way around the damp strings of moss that hung from the
eiling. Here and there, bricks had fallen from the loose and crumbling
1ortar, leaving holes in the arch. Gnarled roots had grown through some
f these holes, white sickly things that looked as if they deserved to be
own here. Jesus shivered as she picked her path carefully—there could
e deep holes concealed underneath the oily black slime she trudged
1rough. Every so often the archway spun off corrugated iron side tun-
els, but Jesus didn't think her shoulders would fit.

"Besides," she said to herself, "if I were to get stuck in there, I'd have
o back out the whole way."

She shuddered at the idea of being trapped down here, screaming her-
elf hoarse while the world carried on above. Jesus briefly wondered if
1e security guards even knew these tunnels existed. *Guys like that took
1eir paychecks and went home to beer and television, never wondering
1hy anyone would want to see Pennhurst from underneath.*

What a place it was, though! The brick archway began to widen, and
espite her dim light, Jesus thought she might have seen a glimmer of
1candescence up ahead. Up until now the moss had been tolerable, but
1 this end of the archway entire sheets of the stuff hung all the way to
1e floor. As she began to round the heaviest of the moss, Jesus noticed
1at the archway did indeed end in a lit room here. Eager to be in a
omewhat familiar environment, she dashed toward the light a trifle too
uickly, slipped on the bottom of a mossy curtain, and wound up nursing

a hurt tailbone in the black sludge. Cursing her impatience, she stoop up carefully, wiping her slimy hands on the front of her jeans.

This was a room worth the sludge, at least for an intrepid underground explorer. A bare but working light bulb hung from the ceiling, illuminating the damp concrete walls and two sets of institutional green double doors. Jesus stepped in, slowly. She saw a desk showing signs of recent use—a coffee ring stained the blotter, and a half empty pack of cigarettes sat next to a full ashtray. Shelves lined the walls and were filled with strange and frightening paraphernalia. Jesus saw wicked looking leather restraints, headgear, stainless steel trays, and things she just plain could not identify. Hidden in the far end of the shelves, Jesus found a rusty metal box, with vacuum tubes peeking out through a decaying grate. "Somatics Thymatron® System IV", read the front panel, in green paint on a white background. Clustered around the product name were various dials, gauges, and jacks. She bent down to examine it more closely, and as soon as she saw the word "electrodes", she dropped it in revulsion, realizing it was an electroshock device.

The sound of the heavy metal box impacting the concrete floor rung and reverberated through the tunnels and came back to her in echoes. Fearing discovery, she tried the first set of double doors, only to find them barred tight. On her way to the second set of doors, Jesus passed the desk and froze, staring. There was a girl looking back at him from the window over the desk. Window? Mirror, she corrected, and suddenly Jesus felt it click into place. She looked down at the swell of her small breasts distorting the logo on the black Primus t-shirt she had been wearing all evening, then back at the mirror, tingling with excitement.

There was a smudge of greenish mud on one cheek. Her hair was plastered across her forehead, but as Jesus looked into her shining blue eyes, he recognized them as his own. He was seeing his face, undistorted by the Y chromosome and years of testosterone. Presently, it was too much to bear, and a tear rolled down her cheek, but she could not look away.

I knew it I knew it I knew it! Only dreaming. Tell yourself you're only dreaming!

A fist pounded against the locked door, shocking Jesus away from her recognition. As she turned to run, she heard keys jingling, then the sound of a lock beginning to turn. Time slowed down, forming knots in her stomach.

This is your *dream. Make the intruder go away. Make him disappear.*

Jesus gathered her will and concentrated, imagining the intruder vanishing. Keys still turned in the lock, and she thought she could hear the muted scratching the rest of the keychain made as it swung against the rust-blistered door. Doubt intervened, and broke her concentration as soon as it had begun. *The world does what it pleases whether or not I sleep, it seems.* Quickly, she made her escape through the second set of doors and down the stairs behind them.

"So much for lucidity," she sighed.

Steam hissed ahead, leaking from one of the insulated pipes running off into the concrete-lined gloom. Jesus crept forward carefully on the crunchy floor... *Crunchy?* She swept the beam of her red light down to shine on the floor. Little white sticks littered the floor, and round balls. Rolling one of the balls over with the toe of her boot, she was suddenly looking into tiny, empty eye sockets. *Rat bones? Jesus.* She smiled to herself at the internal pun, then pushed on. *Something was dreadfully wrong here for the floor to be this strewn with rodent remains.* The corridor, filled with fog from the leaking pipes, presently sloped downward, and the floor became less crispy as the rat remnants gave way to black, slimy water.

Above her head, safe in its darkness, the Leviathan waited. Minute hairs on its wet surface vibrated to the disturbance Jesus caused in the air. As much as it could, it anticipated her arrival. Glands emptied into its looped digestive system, disgorging their numbing poisons. While it did take its nourishment from the flesh of its prey, the Leviathan savored the terror of its victims more than the life they provided. Anesthetized, the prey could be kept alive, while other enzymes broke down and digested the still-living tissues. It always saved the eyes for last—that way its subtle psychic meal of the victims last moments could be viewed through their own eyes. If it had a human mouth, it would have grinned like a fool at the very thought. Pseudopods rippled from the surface of its bloated sac of a body, and began to search through the darkness for the prey that would prove far more entertaining than the sickly rats it was used to...

The stagnant water deepened as Jesus waded further. Something up ahead drew her, and despite the slippery bottom, she all but *charged* ahead. Through the fog, she thought she could see movement. As she passed the break in the pipe, she was almost sure of it. There was a dim light source, perhaps a hundred feet down the hallway, where it opened into a room. By now, the water was up to her knees and leaking into her boots. Slime was starting to cake up on the front of her jeans. In the room ahead, something gently splashed to the surface.

"Hello?" she whispered.

Jesus was surprised how loud her whisper seemed down here. It came back to her in reverberations from all directions, and she felt the unmistakable tickle on the back of her neck that came with being watched.

A breath of warm, moist air from behind startled her and she spun around, changing her grip on the flashlight. Holding it like a nightstick, she swung blindly though the air. Nothing. Adrenaline began its ancient task and her heart began to hammer. Ripples grew in the water in front of her. Something was swimming back towards the rat-room. Jesus spun again and ran towards the lighted room, where she had first sighted movement. Heedless of the splashing muck, she sprinted through the slime. Sounds began to come from everywhere. Breathing. Splashing. Unpleasant squishing and crunching. Something hit the water behind her, and as she turned to look, pain exploded in her shin. Her feet slipped out from underneath her and Jesus fell headlong into the muck, dropping the flashlight as she tripped.

Water slopped in waves against its tentacles, and the Leviathan now knew it prey was in trouble. Her pheromones tasted panicked, and even at this range it reveled in her terrified thoughts. It wriggled a couple of pseudopods behind Jesus, thrashing the water. The prey will run from the commotion, it thought, like they always do. Enzymes flooded its branching body, and it readied itself. The wait would not be so long, now.

Sputtering, Jesus rose to the surface. *Eyes, eyes, come on now.* She struggled to regain her bearings. Moss and ooze covered her completely now, and burned her slightly where it touched bare skin. Her eyes watered, and a corrupt smell hung in her nostrils. Terrified, she immediately began to run, losing her footing again when something disturbed the water behind her. She rose to her feet again, and more carefully began to flee. The breathing sounds were now clearly in front of her, but that was of secondary concern to her as the splashing and slithering behind grew closer. She could see the outline of the room now. Machinery poked out of the slime, and stairs rose along the far wall to a not quite closed door. Beyond the door was light, and it was to the light that Jesus ran. Before she took two steps, a great fleshy bag dropped from the ceiling and Jesus screamed. Something opened in it, and finally she knew what was breathing.

The smell of rot that had been background until now hit her squarely in the face as the Leviathan growled. Tentacles thrashed and crawled across one another and as Jesus turned around looking for escape, she realized she had been flanked. Pseudopods hung from the ceiling, stretched across the walls, and writhed beneath the ooze. Something coiled around her ankle, drawing tight, then pulled her into the air. Then darkness, constriction.

———◆———

Agent 506 sipped casually on a latté as he punched in some numbers on a pay phone somewhere in King of Prussia.

"Pennhurst State Hospital, how may I direct your call?"

"I was wondering if you could help me. I'm an intern over at *Psychiatric Annals*... Are you familiar with the publication?"

"I'm sorry, I can't say I am."

"It's pretty dry, doctor's-only stuff. Anyway, one of your doctors has sent us an incredible article on the treatment of catatonics—groundbreaking material—and I need to get his permission to print it."

"I can connect you to their office. Who do you need to speak to?"

"That's the problem. This guy could totally get famous with work of this caliber, and he didn't sign it!"

"Really?"

"Yeah, can you believe it? I hear Einstein couldn't make toast, go figure. Who treats the catatonics at your facility?"

"Doctors Fein and Spitzer, mainly. They handle all our tough ones."

"Sounds like they're the guys."

"I can connect you to Doctor Fein's office."

"Wait! One more thing."

"What can I do for you?"

"I'm sorry to drop all this on your lap, but my boss is already fuming and I don't want him to take it out on me, you know what I mean?"

"Yeah, I hear you."

"This doctor, he mentioned one of your patients by name."

"Uh-oh."

"Yeah, serious HIPPA problems. Who's your compliance officer? I don't want to get Dr. Fein in hot water, I just need to check this so *I* don't get fired."

"That would be Mrs. Marsh, but she's not in today. She's been out sick a few days."

"It's going around, I guess. Who else handles patient record requests?"

"I suppose Hank over in Personnel. His office is right next to hers."

"Thank you, you've been very helpful."

There is time to take in a deep breath and toss the now empty latté in the trash. *Next victim...*

⟡

"Personnel, this is Hank."

"I'm Frank Vincent with the State Board of Medical Ethics. I think we have a problem, Hank." A mischievous grin spread across Agent 506's face. He made sure to keep it coming through in his tone.

"What's going on, Mr. Vincent?"

"The family of one of your patients, a Mr. Joyce-Vivian, has filed a petition with our organization to investigate your facility for violation of the HIPPA act. They're waving patient data at us that they say were inappropriately distributed by your clerk at Records. He mentioned several distinct items which could bring your facility out of compliance if not addressed immediately. I don't need to remind you that we are talking about some serious fines, here, Hank."

"No, sir. Um, I'm not the compliance officer, really. I'm not able to comment—"

"I'm tired of being stonewalled, Hank. I've been waiting for Marsh to get the ball rolling for days now, and you're out of time. Do you think the admin over there likes you enough to swallow a forty-thousand dollar judgment because you decided to pass the buck on this?"

"No, sir."

"I'm trying to save you a lot of grief. This is probably a bullshit charge, pardon my language. Help me out now and I can close this file before the courts and the papers get involved."

"Our compliance officer is out sick."

"Look, I know this isn't your job, pal. I'm trying to stop a very crazy, very loud family from slapping you with a forty-thousand dollar HIPPA fine, plus civil lawsuits, plus bad press... We're looking at a nightmare, Hank. Marsh could have stopped this days ago, but she's not answering her phone."

"She's out sick."

"It's going around, I guess. The thing is, I have a meeting with the family's lawyer in less than an hour, and if I can't show him that these charges are bullshit—again, pardon my language—your boss is sunk, the facility is bankrupt, and your name goes on the report."

"Why me?"

"It's nothing personal, Hank. But my boss wants me to settle this matter. I think he's old golfing buddies with somebody on your board, or something. Either way, it's my job we're looking at, too."

"Okay, okay. What can I do?"

"Fax me a copy of Ian Joyce-Vivian's patient records. If I can just look em over and see right away that there's nothing at issue here, it all goes away."

"Okay, I'll fax it out to you right away. What's the number?"

—————◆·◆————

"Mailboxes Etc., Brian speaking."

"Hey, Brian. I have a bit of a problem I think you can help me with."

"What's up?"

"Some records for a patient from my office are being faxed to your store by mistake... It's supposed to go to the Mailboxes Etc. in Audobon."

"Audobon?"

"It's all the way across the state, I know. When it comes in, could you fax it back to the Audobon store?"

"Sure, I guess."

"One other thing. These are sensitive documents, and we can't just leave em lying around."

"I'll shred 'em as soon as they're sent off."

"Thanks, Brian. You sure saved my bacon."

"No problem, man. Have a good one."

—————◆·◆————

"Personnel, this is Hank."

"Hank, it's Frank again. I have good news."

"Yeah?"

"You saved the day, Hank. Looking over these records, none of the supposedly leaked information is accurate."

"So it's over with?"

"Problem solved, yeah. Thanks for your cooperation, Hank."

"I'm just glad it turned out to be nothing."

"Yup. Have a good one."

—◆—

"Fourth Ward."

"Hey, I'm over in Two. I have a phone call holding for Mr. Joyce-Vivian. I think it's some kind of lawyer."

"Has it been approved?"

"The guy says he spoke to Mrs. Marsh and she okay'd it."

"Heh. Ian's in one of his vegetable moods."

"I've been trying to tell him that, yeah. But he keeps insisting on speaking to him, saying there's no restriction on his file that prevents it, threatening to sue. It's crazy."

"Yup."

"Can I transfer him to you? I ain't got time for this, with all the shit over that guy getting out last night."

"Sure."

—◆—

"Pennhurst State Hospital, how may I direct your call?"

"Fourth Ward, please."

"One moment."

—◆—

"Fourth Ward."

"Hi. My name is Anthony Pierce, I'm representing Microsoft. I was told you could put me in touch with Mr. Joyce-Vivian?"

"I could, sir, but Ian is non-verbal. Wouldn't do you any good, see."

"What do you mean, non-verbal? This guy owns three patents for advanced database pathfinding heuristics and two for flinching."

"Flinching?"

"Programming term. I could go into it, but it's terribly complicated and completely besides the point. The man's a genius, and we're gonna make him rich. Or sue him. It depends on what he has to say about it."

"Um, he's a charity case, sir. Ward of the hospital."

"So we sue the hospital. Funny how these things work, isn't it? Can I get your name, please."

"Why?"

"I need to know who refused to let me speak to the man, for the paperwork on the lawsuit."

"Hey, I didn't say you couldn't speak to him, I said he probably wouldn't speak to you."

"Probably wouldn't? You admit that he does talk, then."

"Sometimes."

"So put me on with him."

"How?"

"Hold the phone up to his damn ear or something. I don't care how you do it, just do it."

"I can't do that."

"So we're back to you getting sued Listen, okay, you know your patients best, I understand that. And you're right, put me on the line with him and he'll most likely just sit there. But it's his problem if he doesn't talk, not yours. You wouldn't be at all at fault."

"I need permission from his doctor."

"Doctors Fein and Spitzer have already green-lighted this, after checking with Mrs. Marsh to see if the legal end was fine."

"Maybe I should check with them first."

"Jesus christ. Do you have any idea what I'm dealing with, here? Mr. Gates has been waiting on this for three days while those people made up their minds. You know how rich people are, he doesn't want to wait anymore. If he has to crack that hospital open and suck out every penny, he's gonna do it so that I get my phone call. Well, after he fires me he will."

"Shit, I don't know."

"Think about it. On one side, we got Microsoft suing the hospital, suing you, and firing me. One the other, we got you holding the phone up to a vegetable's ear for a minute, after which I hang up and it's all off your lap. Which way do you want this to go?"

"All right, all right. I'll do it. You're wasting your time, though."

"Mr. Gates is paying me very well to waste my time. Thanks for your cooperation, sir."

———◦———

"Dude, it's me. 506. Talk to me, man. I had to go through hell to get you on the line."

Silence. Jesus breathes, and the sighs are scrambled and shot down the wire at light speed without losing their lethargy.

"I tried to get you out last night, you were out. Cold. Drugged or something. Look, I busted my ass getting this call in, can you fucking answer me?"

Nothing.

"Great. Look, I've done it. I've found you a surgeon that won't ask questions. There's this lady up in Boston, she can do the whole thing. Hormones. The surgery. I can get you out of Jesus, Meredith."

"Mere-dith?"

"Oh, thank God. Yes, yes. I've got it covered. I can get you out of there, I can get you out of…" Rustling papers… "I can get you out of the cell. I can set you free."

"You can really get me…"

"Shit, don't say anything, the dumb bastard with the phone thinks I'm from Microsoft and we're talking about a patenting issue."

"What?"

"Long story."

"Okay. So you're a lawyer."

"Yup. Working for the Man himself. Tell the guy what you like, or hell, don't tell him anything. You're catatonic, right?"

Jesus giggled. "Yeah, I am that."

"I'll be there tonight. At your window. Fucking Peter Pan, gonna take you away."

"And you'll handle everything?"

"All you gotta do is wake up."

That evening, Meredith sat up in her bed and rubbed her eyes. There was a dream behind them, a nightmare. She was in some cell, someone had put her there by mistake. Mistaken identity? The dream was already unraveling. She was a saint of some sort, maybe Christ Himself. There were some explosions, and this Kafka thing with a hospital…

"Nevermore," said a voice from the window, and she laughed softly to herself.

12/17/02 17:49:31 The Journal of Dr. Fein, M.D., Ph.D.

I find myself resistant to morning. Waking before the alarm, I hide next to my wife and play dead. Slow breaths, deep. Eyes closed. Relax the facial muscles, don't clench, you're asleep. I wonder what I will do when the alarm rings. Call out today? I could, I could just stay right here. I could choose sleep. But then tomorrow? The day after?

Dream images from the night before assemble behind my eyes, awareness attempts to impose reason on neural static. The new patient is in them. A Santa hat. Lake George, NY. I've never been there; the name is all I have. A homeless man wrapping a triple-A map around a brown bottle. Seven minutes to decide.

Decide what? A Santa Hat?

Almost time, now. My wife, she is blessed with an incredible sense of time. She begins to stir, knowing that in seven minutes—six—my alarm will go off and wake her. For a moment I entertain myself with the notion we are both lying awake, lying to each other that her languorous nesting and my diligent relaxation are a game.

The thought makes me reach for the alarm, but I stop. Any disruption in routine would just go to show, (wouldn't it?), that the new patient was getting under my skin. I rigidly feign sleep until it buzzes me awake.

Shower, dress. Match tie, because appearance is important. Kiss wife, still maybe—sleeping. Coffee, bagel, long for a cigarette and congratulate self on quitting. Think about fixing the door (creaks) and drive away.

Routine. Structure. My life is together. I am the one in control.

Here is the life I have chosen for myself: I arrive at the hospital every morning at seven. I am not expected until eight, but I use the time to digest the reports from the evening staff and have a cup of coffee in my office. Pink, blue, yellow pages, I match checked boxes and phrases of jargon with known faces and emotions. "Unusual or excessive emotional reaction" dryly encapsulates bloody shrieks and hoarse-voiced prayers for death. "Weapons prevention violation" neatly condenses hours spent patiently honing a length of table leg, visualizing my face slit to ribbons.

Today I feel dysphoric. Sleep disturbances, lightly
depressed mood. Negative ideations and a sense of
removal, of biological mechanization. Perhaps the
first creeping of depersonalization. This new patient—
he has a gift for lessening the self.

Today I am specifically sorting for references to
him. I am not allowing myself to notice that I am not
allowing myself to notice this. Such behavior would
indicate an unhealthy fixation. The reports indicate
that he has quickly gained rapport with the other
patients on the ward. They shuffle into a loose circle
to hear him rant, whether his glazed eyes focus on
them or not. I imagine their thin hospital robes
transformed into vestments, then forget I have done
so. They become agitated when staff acts to redirect
them, protect them. Shared Psychotic Disorder is
interesting. It is unstable, contagious, like a virus.

The carrier, the new patient, is calm. Scrawls
delusion case studies of such incidents into his
robes. I believe he plots.

I open my desk, pop out a sample of Wellbutrin, and
drink it down. Wellbutrin is indicated. Clearly.

———————————

He plots disorder. Plans it. I think he understands it.

Lately I have not felt entirely present. Another world is opening up
beneath me. I shouldn't think of this.

Twenty minutes have changed since the clock on my desk showed
eight o'clock. The first patient arrives soon. Coffee cup is removed to a
drawer in the desk (the cup is a weapon), pens removed save the one I
keep to write with. My desk is cleared save for paper and a few rubber
squeeze-objects, there to offer something softer and more amenable than
my own flesh to vent rage upon. I pull out the patients manila file and
open it on my desk. I rearrange my features to be pleasantly interested
and engaging.

The desk is a metal barrier. It is too heavy to move easily, and long
enough to provide me with something to run around until orderlies can
restrain an agitated patient.

The first one is yet another John Doe, though he has been using "Ian
Joyce-Vivian" in recent evaluations. Caucasian male, height six feet,
five-and-one-half inches tall, age unknown but estimated to be late-

twenties. Expected to present with a depressive affect, possibly catatonic throughout our session. Guiltily, I love the catatonics. I gaze, and sit with them in silence. Sometimes I use them as a blank-affected analyst and babble for the few minutes we have together each week. This frees me for a time, yet leaves a thin patina of shame.

I flip through his file without reading any of it. My brow is furrowed, posture enrapt. I present deeply in thought, concerned, silently strong. I wait for Mr. Joyce Vivian.

Another minute and a knock. He shuffles in, braced by orderlies, and sits.

He matches type, initially.

Joyce-Vivian slumps immobile across the desk. His hair is straggling, long, it's unbelievably long because he attacks anyone who comes near it. His robe is worn open, his clothing wrinkled and stained. Staff insists he stains them deliberately, smearing little impressionist doodles with ketchup and crayon and occasionally blood. None have ever seen it happen.

I make my face still and welcoming. I smile with a cautious degree of warmth, enough to seem friendly but not intrusively so. "Good morning, Ian. I've been looking forward to meeting you." He slumps regally, sternly lose and uncaring. What would bring me that detached, rigid pose of comfort?

"You haven't been with us very long," I continue after a polite interval. "My name is Dr. Fein. I will be your psychiatrist while you are staying with us, here."

Joyce-Vivian shows no response. The orderlies make he's-all-yours gestures and depart. Grateful, I take my coffee out of the drawer and proceed to ignore him. It is still warm.

I catch my reflection in its opaque, glossy surface.

"What you're looking at is the cessation of falsehood," he says, and I spit coffee all over his file.

"Entropic, yes." Joyce-Vivian nods slowly. Only his head has moved. *Heh. Bastard spat his coffee.*

Regaining control I smile precisely. He caught me by surprise again. Shallow, existential problems melt to the demands of skill. I may be sick, but I'm a damn fine psychiatrist.

"Thank you, Ian."

"Don't thank me yet. Stillness here is a denial of patterning. ...Of the lukewarm order of coffee in your mouth. Jumping straight onto the desk to start. Flesh, you see? I chose to ignore Ian-Joyce Vivian. He is not me." Pause. He shifts, glacially. Affective cues are subtle, languorous as tectonic plates. But present. When he shifts ever minutely to attention I speak.

"Who were you when you were admitted?"

"Jesus," he sighs. This is noted, I wait. Ping the Gender Identity Disorder? Yes. "But even then, you were someone else, weren't you, Jesus."

"Meredith." With the name, Ian perks up. He is now a perky catatonic. Don't laugh. *Started doing low doses of estrogen internally—a constant, low-grade E buzz—was gonna go through with the whole thing...saw three random meteors tonight...one was pretty bright for a random bit of space junk.*

"Thank you. Are you still Jesus?"

Ian snaps to his feet. I saw it coming and remain warmly patient.

Him again, him of the cage. He came again. Locked her away entirely. You see, it's really a question of solipsism. Copernicus rolls both ways in a dusty little pocket of a grave. Locked away, or spread apart? I burrow into my flesh and reproduce.

<hr />

"We'll show you a trick if you can learn it, Doctor. You don't have to play along. You don't have to be Doctor Fein, or Meredith, or even a primate. Just choose." He stiffens slowly. Affect drains from his eyes, face, he is still. "You gotta get out more, Doc." Then he is still as stone.

I record our brief exchange in my notes, lean back, and stare at his forgotten body. Jesus has left the building.

Eventually the orderlies take him away. I don't notice until minutes have passed. I am staring at where his eyes used to be.

Her time is up, for now. He slides open the cell. She offers no resistance as he cuffs her and leads down a dark hallway to a cell, also sealed from all light. He hears some soft, muted screams, and his grin widens. He thinks he has won. Back in the cell, she cries herself to sleep...

Static. Unchanging, day after day. Just sitting, waiting for the sun to rise in my cell, and never seeing it come. She sits on the cold concrete, crying now. Softly. Because she knows that there is no more. The story is told and the actors have all departed. So she sits, curled into a ball, fighting against the cold and the damp and the dark and the depression.

She waits, hoping, asking, begging the Fates to be kind and cut another piece of string. And it can be done, but she doesn't know how to go about it. And the Spiral rotates slowly but steadily, sucking away minutes until all that is left of her is a memory in one persons mind. Only one. But for now, she waits for the sun to set and the lights behind her eyes to slowly fade, barely daring to hope that her counterpart will arrive. Her perception of time grinds down to an empty black void, softly echoing "could have" and "would have."

My coffee is cold.

It is cold, and it is nine o'clock. I have experienced lost time.

There is a knock. "Come in."

"You smell better," grinning, it's my next patient. His orderlies step in like cops, survey the room and nod in unison. He grins wider and they depart. The door is shut with quiet respect.

"Caught me napping, I'm afraid. Have a seat."

The notations across his robes are complete. Sprawling cabalistic geometries, dates, sketches of faces and ANSI patterns. He is scrubbed pink as a prom queen, stern as a magi. Damned if I don't buy into it, just for a moment.

I am centered. The moment passes.

I glance at the notes on my desk, notes that I wrote a number of weeks back when he was brought in with Jesus. John Doe presents as a six foot, four inch Caucasian male, heavily tattooed, and in excellent physical condition. He suffers from a range of depersonalizing ideations and delusions of reference, persecution, and grandeur, as well as inexplicable somatic complaints which cannot be linked to physiological causes. Agent 139 also presents numerous features of Antisocial Personality Disorder (flagrant disregard for societal mores, manipulative behaviors, amoral conduct), though it is difficult to isolate this diagnosis as being independent from his Depersonalization or Schizotypal features...

"What box are you going to try to squeeze me into today, doctor?" he asked.

I carefully avoided his question. "You have taken great pains with your appearance today," I say slowly.

"Indeed!" He sobers, wryly tugs his robes like a starship captain. "My 'cabalistic geometries' are complete today, Doctor Harold Fein."

I look up from my notes again. "Agent 139?"

"To name a thing is to have a word for it."

"What are you planning?" It's out before I think it. "No, that was inappropriate, I apologize."

"Apology ignored. Still wanna know?" The grin is back and Agent 139 nods expectantly. I reflexively warm my affect.

"The primate bares its teeth when offered knowledge. Interesting, Doctor. Indicative."

"Who are you, really, right now?" I asked.

"A shard, Doctor. On, off, broken, whole, fine, Fein—I'll give it to you either/or." Wow, he's in form today. "Break your cup next time. You're a shard. A shattered wine glass. The cup is implicit in the mess you've made, being just a shard. Our experience occurs in self-contained wholes, time creates this illusion of fragmentation. I, right now, am a shard."

"How have the medications been treating you?"

"My hands shake."

"It is too soon for TD. Do you know where you are, right now?"

Agent 139 sighs tragically and slumps. "In a hospital, in your office, Agent 139." *Indolence. Eight of cups.*

"And do you know who I am?"

"You are still who you were before I came in."

I pluck a green pig squeeze-object from the desk and pinch. "Yes, but you know the drill. Who am I?"

"You're Dr. Harold Fein."

"Good. What's today's date, do you remember?"

"No."

"No problem, I'll just ask your staff when they get back. Your hands have stopped shaking."

Agent 139 smiles quietly at an intersection of whirls on his left pant leg. "What did you do this morning?"

I recall sitting at breakfast, reading the essays Agent 139 has been preparing for me, leaving on my desk after each session.

"I was out."

"You're starting to question the nature of your experience." Agent 139 straightens his back, taking on an authoritarian air.

"What are you referring to?" I find myself slouching back into my chair slightly.

"Why do I have to spell this out for you? Didn't they learn you any philosophy in school, Doc? The tension between what you perceive of the world and what we assume to be the world is existence. Existence doesn't lie with the subject or the object, but as a result of a relation between them. It is the simultaneous correspondence of two things, the thing seen and the thing seeing, which neither proves nor disproves their actual existence separate from each other. If you get sucked up into a vacuum, doctor, and don't come back, existing in discontinuity within yourself, *then* you're a fucking nut. Johny? He's the one who bombed the fucking building. I'm really getting tired of these meds, the bad music, the dusty rank air. Do you have asbestos in the ceiling? I feel like I'm choking in here. I'm tired of the catatonics always choosing the movies during movie hour, and I desperately need a shot of tequila. Or a cigarette."

The ticking of my clock. I'm staring blankly at him, transfixed by something I can't explain.

"You know," he suddenly says, "the loss of reality-testing is considered a symptom of psychosis. In most cases, where this removal isn't by choice, this classification is wholly valid. But we can learn to control it, to slip into trances and experiences those states of altered consciousness ourselves, to open our eyes and dream together. You can bring it into your consciousness right now. We call those who have returned from this journey…well, mostly intact…shamans. I'm a shaman in training, not a psychotic. Sometimes the distinction is hard…if control is lost the shaman descends into self-obsession, personality fragmentation, and finally incurable psychosis." I continue to stare into his eyes, feel myself nod slowly.

"What you're offering me isn't a means of controlling what I'm experiencing so I'm going to resist you every step of the way. But if you can *wake up* and work through this problem with me, maybe the two of us can find our way out of the labyrinth."

It's the last thing I remember for a while.

———◆———

I spent two hours trying to conjure money from an ATM before choosing the right PIN. Occasionally I give the audience at home a quick wave. Even cameras have a grainy universe which demands respect.

It seems I can transfer myself between different "selves." I'm not exactly sure what this means yet. Focusing on the selection of desired probably outcomes, using whatever methods present themselves to weigh the odds in my favor. I have noted that the simple execution of will provides the tipping point. I present myself with a numerical code device—a combination lock or keypad, a rubic's cube. And I try to watch myself select the right answer.

Results have been mixed, yet exhilarating. I may be able to exploit this principle without losing ego integrity. (Dying, alone and quite mad.)

———◆◆———

There are occasional discontinuities, like this one. Reaching for the keypad, I find myself seated in a banquet hall across an expanse of esoteric crockery and scarlet cloth from a child with a bowl haircut in a choirboy uniform. He is perched on a shifting mountain of paperwork. I can hear what sounds like a steam locomotive in the background.

"More to drink, Doctor?"

"Pardon me, " I begin calmly. "I'm getting used to this, but what were we talking about?"

"Your glass."

"Yes." There is the shrill sound of an old locomotive whistle in the background.

"You really don't want to allow considerations of sanity to prevent your ascension to godhood, do you, Doctor?" he asks solicitously. My glass bubbles and fills with coca-cola. "This could be a very important development. Imagine the freedom granted in being able to live all of your lives to the fullest, instead of threading a hallucinatory back road past them."

"But without integration, what's the point?" I gulp awkwardly and continue. "A tide of masks. I don't get to share any of these experiences under one identity, they never happened to me."

One thing is very different. No one wants to just talk about the weather, anymore. It's always cosmology, or psychology—usually a disturbing mysticism blending the two. There is certainly a scientific model for this. My training is almost entirely inappropriate to offer one.

"Grant me, for the sake of conversation, that this I of yours is a sensory construct."

I can't take much more of this empty empiricism.

"Granted for the moment. The string beans are excellent, by the way." Deep breaths. Polite.

"Thank you, Doctor."

"Harold."

"Fine. Harold."

The boy chases a thoughtful mouthful of potatoes with Coke before continuing. "From there, it's easy. If the mechanism of perception were to change drastically, don't you think you would find its construct similarly warped? Would not the form it takes be entirely foreign?"

"Sure, maybe. I would really like to talk about something else, please."

"No!" He pounds the table ineffectually with a babyfat fist. The steam engine sound in the background ceases abruptly, and he continues in hushed tones, as if he is trying to contain great anger. "You have to decide, Doctor. Do you think there are no dangers in this new world of yours? You have to choose, now. Now."

It's night. Thick fog. I'm in a car. Back seat. I think it's Jesus driving. Light of the panels illuminate his vestments in red.

"There's someone else in the car," a form next to me says immediately. His tone is matter-of-fact, as though my appearance were the solution to a tedious math problem. I squint through the smoke and can just make out a wiry, sharp-faced youth squatting on the seat cushion.

"You know who it is?" Jesus asks from up front. The third occupant is clearly unmoved.

"Nah." He turns towards me casually. "Who are you? What are you doing in our car?"

"I am Doctor Harold Fine. I'm a psychiatrist."

"506. I'd shake, but I'm holding a gun on you." And Jesus kills the lights and the engine and we glide to a stop.

It's very quiet for awhile.

"New plan, " Jesus notes. "First, we figure out who the teleporting weirdo is, then we blow up the place."

506 grunts and turns back to me. "Why don't you start us off."

The bullets, the bullets. Bullets in a box, thousands in a factory, and some are duds. Choose the duds. Decide he's loaded duds. "I am non-local, I think. Becoming. I keep opening my eyes on all these people, places, these people. Everyone wants to talk about physics, I think."

"Fuck physics. Let's talk place."

"Why am I here? I don't know, really. It started this morning..." Jesus is rummaging around for something in the front seat as I answer. Worrying about what he may be pulling on me, I lose my place.

"What's today's date?"

James Curcio

"6th October, 1999."

He grunts. "Add thinking you're from the future to the list. It's 97. April." He shifts, and I hatefully feel myself wince. Duds.

"Two years ain't bad," the other passenger comments, and Jesus nods. "Do you know where you are?"

"Sadly, no."

"Sadly. Non-local, huh. I suppose I can't just ask you to go away, then."

"I can try."

Jesus turns around, revealing what he had been looking for. "Honey roasted peanuts?"

<hr>

Suddenly it is five-thirty and so distractingly hungry. Doctor Harold Fein is hungry, swaying on a corner amid flowing and anonymous foot traffic. People are looking at him, his rumpled suit and coffee stains. People are looking at him, swaying and still on a corner with the people marching around him. They flick cutting glances and chip his contours into consensual reality.

I am hungry.

A newspaper kiosk provides a break in the crowd and I take inventory leaning up against its flyer-bombed back. Smells like New York. No city in the world smells quite like New York. No wallet, no keys, nor identification. No money or phone.

Starving, my stomach is eating my spine starving, I am made of sore glass starving. And no sign of the euphoric possibility I emerged from, the sensation of... multiplicity. Omnipresence, of a limited sort. Multipresence? A whole new vocabulary will be required if I turn out not to be psychotic.

"...so, then he turns to his uncle, right, and he says, 'That's Grandpa's ashes!'"

Guffaws from the kiosk. "Three dollars even."

"Here. That joke was fucking terrible."

"Up yours, and have a good one."

Starving. The matter of my sudden collapse into a single identity pales. And needing food, after what I've done, that seems petty. Focus. My body needs food. I have no money, no clear idea of where I am. I have the following: a pen, a formerly nice suit, a notebook, a paper clip.

And of course, the ability to expand over multiple quantum states and select one of my choosing to inhabit from moment to moment.

I try to simply reach into my pocket and find a twenty dollar bill, without success. I repeat the experiment with my jacket pockets and the sidewalk around me. No dice.

"Hey, whatever it is you looked here already. I don't do handouts," barks the news vendor. "Get lost, okay?"

Ah. I looked there already. Exactly. I thank him, then reach into the garbage can and find an ATM card streaked with overripe banana.

———————

My affect is one of settled concentration. I am the one in control of this life. Everything in my manner, voice, my surface thoughts all scream, this man *knows*. He is integrated, wise, with a sturdy grasp on the here-and-now. He takes care of his suits, short of obsession. He is practical, short of boring. Low-carb dinners, exercise on the weekends. Here is Sane Man, Modern Man. I understand everything now, he tells himself. I'm on the shoulders of rational giants. His shoulders are broad with it, back straight with it, his breath is slow and even with it. He knows. He knows who he is, where he is, when he is, and why. He knows when yesterday was, when tomorrow will be. Things fall down, the center holds. Mere sanity is loosed upon the world.

This feeling lasts until I open my mouth to speak the truth. And I gag. Iron bars wrap my waist and squeeze, and I jackknife vomit in a steep, sour arc. I think I'm on the grimed street of an alley, outside my box, vomiting. I think the fire escapes are leaning down to push me over.

Worse, I know I'll be here before. I'll have been here tomorrow.

Anything, anything, anything but this.

———————

"Wouldn't you feel less incurably mad after a nice, long nap?"

I taste vomit. That happened before. I'm at the table, the boy is there. He is saying something, I want to say something back. Smile and make a joke and bear down on my gorge. But all the words have turned to grease and are coating my tongue black.

"Go to sleep, Doctor. Rock-a-bye, Harold, on the wave front..." The boy leans over the table and opens his mouth. Wide. Stretch marks form at the hinges of his jaw before the skin tears with a running wet zzziiiipppp! and he is growing, looming over the table, rows of sharp

baby teeth sprouting from his palate with muted pops. He leans with
babyfat raptor claws on the table and tilts it up, the crockery sliding into
his maw with cracks and crashes.

"You're not real!" I shriek. "None of this is real!"

"Then hop in," he smiles.

I feel myself screaming.

⬛◆⬛

"Oh shit, oh shit, are you okay, is he okay?"

Pavement on my cheek.

"He just ran out in front of me, there was no time-"

"Give him room, people!"

"Somebody call somebody. Call—somebody, somebody!"

I don't need to feel my ribs to know they are broken. I remember an
old joke: Doctor, Doctor, everything I touch hurts! And the Doctor says,
that's cause you shattered your fingers!

Laughter. Wait for the crest to abate before the next line, or they'll be
too afraid of missing something to laugh. Wait for it, then:

I realized something the other day, folks, and it totally baked my
noodle. I realized—and here's the really, really funny part—I've spent
the last four years of my life living in a box, believing I was a psychiatrist! I know, I know. Trippy, isn't it? Now I've been hit by a truck in one
universe, being eaten by a giant toddler in another, I'm homeless and I'm
consorting with known terrorists and I'm dying, all at once!

What an eternal now this has been.

"I'm a doctor, let me through!"

Hey. I'm a doctor.

⬛◆⬛

"I am Doctor Harold Fein. I'm a psychiatrist."

"506. I'd shake, but I'm holding a gun on you." And Jesus kills the
lights and the engine and we drift to a stop.

It's very quiet for awhile.

⬛◆⬛

"In a few years," I begin slowly, "your friends will be involuntarily
committed to a psychiatric hospital under my care. " Jesus stiffens and
turns to regard the man in the front passenger seat with flat, startled eyes.

"It is there that my sessions with Agent 139 will trigger a process leading to the cessation of my existence as a linear intelligence."

"Is that so."

"As I can determine."

"Huh." My interrogator shakes his head, slowly. "Okay, you're a fucking lunatic. I say we throw him back."

"Let him speak," Agent 139 says from the front. He giggles suddenly as he slips on a leather glove.

"Three minutes," Agent 506 prompts, settling into his seat.

Jesus is munching raptly on honey roasted peanuts like he's watching a ball game.

"First, I should probably say that you'll never end up killing anyone. You've thought about it for a long time, calculated all the death blows Gray's Anatomy could teach you, worked the problems of corpse disposal front and back until you dreamt lye and hacksaws. But you'll never kill anyone, and I already know you won't kill me tonight. Right?"

Agent 506 tilts his head to the side. Then, "maybe."

"I could be wrong. You might not be the you I'm thinking about. Or my telling you that could bring about the realignments that turn you. I don't think I'm wrong. I've taken the precaution of loading your handgun with defective bullets, just in case." *Did I do that, this time?*

"What were you saying about the hospital?" Jesus asks.

"You and 139 are patients of mine, for a time. I either become enlightened or go insane, or I've been insane, but I end up leaving the hospital. I have no memories of your treatment past that point." I sigh. "But something happened, and I'm losing it. For a while, I could pick and choose who I was, and they all were recognizably me. Some details varied, but we shared memory. Everything up until I met your friend, there, matched. Cohered."

"And now?"

"Now I keep finding myself in different places, talking to people about what's happening to me. Well, mostly they tell me about it, or try to kill me. And I think I was hit by a truck." A sob forms and I swallow it. "Nothing makes sense anymore. Giant babies try to eat me. You threaten to shoot me. For a moment I thought I was living in a box and hallucinating, all of it."

The three of them are silent for a moment, shifting uncomfortably as I struggle to compose myself. "I just want to go home. I just want to go home and go to bed."

"Okay, I've got it," Agent 506 chuckles suddenly. "I know how to get you home. But first I need some information."

The two in the front swivel to face us as I reply. "Anything."

"If I give you a pen, can you draw a map of the hospital grounds, with their rooms marked? I will also need to know everything you can tell me about their security measures. Daily routines. That kind of thing."

"Yes, of course. How are you going to get me home?"

"I'm not, Doc. You are. Now get writing." He hands me a pad and a stubby pencil, and I bend to work in the dim light.

———⋙◆⋘———

I replace the pig and straighten my tie. The coffee is abysmal, so I leave it there on the desk, in the precise center. And I walk away. Glide, positively glide away. Nurses look down to re-inspect charts, orderlies glance at the caged clock on the wall. I am invisible. I pass Jesus on my way to the elevator, lying catatonic in dreams of Meredith, and slip away.

I am wearing a sweatshirt, a rumpled sweatshirt. And jeans. Boots. I am waiting in the bushes for the gate to open.

I am returning to my office. I stand and stare at the centered cup in befuddled interest, then pick it up and drink it. The coffee is abysmal.

The gate attendant waves in a man driving a Durango, and I am away. The next patient enters my office, flanked by orderlies.

I choose them all and sail off, a fleet of shards.

———⋙◆⋘———

The jeering crowds pass them by. They rock back and forth and hold each other close, waiting for the curtain to draw. As they close, their clear blue eyes gaze upwards, and the disabilities of physicality are no more, the separation of male from female, and indeed of all the passions from existence, are lost in the light beyond darkness...

APPENDIX

THE MOTHER HIVE BRAIN DOCUMENTS

Case Studies:

CASE I: John Doe (AKA Jesus, et al)

Current Diagnosis DSMIV:

Axis I: Schizoaffective Disorder (Bipolar Type)
             Depersonalization Disorder
             Gender Identity Disorder NOS (Partial
               Remission)
             Dysthymia NOS

Axis II: Antisocial Personality Disorder
             Schizotypal Personality Disorder

Axis III: No physical conditions noted as of this time

Axis IV: Difficulties with Interpersonal Relationships,
             Disturbances in Primary Support Group (Death of
             parent), Disturbances in Primary Support Group
             (Discord with remaining parent), Disturbances
             in Secondary Support Group (related to
             Difficulties with Interpersonal Relationships),
             Job Dissatisfaction

Case Study:

[Prepared by Dr. Harold Fein, M.D., Ph.D., in
consultation with Dr. Bernard Spitzer, M.D., Ph.D.]

Patient is a six foot, five-and-one-half inch tall Caucasian male presenting with unstable affect and posture. His appearance appears consciously crafted to communicate a disdain for proper dress and hygiene, though I note that his fingernails, hair, and areas of exposed skin are scrupulously clean. He is wearing the robe of his hospital gown open and appears to have deliberately torn his pants at the left knee. Hair is unbound and worn long. Jesus, the only name to which the patient consistently responds, demonstrates severe Schizoaffective Disorder which may, in time, degenerate into Schizophrenia (Catatonic Type), in addition to severe depressive episodes, depersonalizing ideations, delusions of reference and grandeur, and features of Gender Identity Disorder which may at this time be considered in partial remission.

Owing to his criminal history and amoral conduct, he is also considered an excellent candidate for Antisocial Personality disorder. Staff is advised to maintain heightened awareness of Jesus' feet and hands as he is prone to violent emergence from apparent catatonia.

Jesus was involuntarily committed to this facility following his arrest in connection to a riot which completely destroyed a Lenny's Restaurant in Devon, PA as well causing severe property damage to surrounding businesses. Jesus himself claims numerous fatalities resulted from the riot as well, though none were noted in the accompanying police report. Law enforcement authorities indicate that he was potentially acting either on orders from or in the name of a terrorist organization known as the "MHBS". Jesus has not been forthcoming on this topic. He was remanded to our custody after tearing a stigmata pattern into his flesh with his teeth in a police detention cell following his arrest.

It should be noted that "Jesus" is identified as such in both hospital and police record as such owing to the complete lack of identification at time of arrest. He has identified himself as Jesus consistently throughout his contact with the legal and mental health systems, and no positive matches have been made tying him to a name or social security number within the United States.

Early in the course of his treatment he "confessed" to a series of several names, claiming each time to be "miraculously cured" of his delusional identity. While no supporting evidence has been found connecting him to any of these stated identities, a partial list of them is provided here: Alex Crowley, Richard Bandler, Ken Schaeffer, James Gideon, Peter Kent, Jack Kolojdecik, Stuart Mills, Richard Nairn, Brett Henderson, Greg Herrmann, William Kerslake, Robert Perley, Jack Upham, Andrew Heaton, Christopher Heady, Hugh Howard, Nikolas Colvin, Adam Lynch, and Ian Joyce-Vivian. On each occasion Jesus was able to persuade several patients to refer to him by his "true name" exclusively, and many continue well past the exposure of that given identity as a fraud. One patient refers to him as "Meredith", a name which to date has not appeared in any other context and may be part of that patient's own delusional system.

Jesus claims that he is, in fact, all of these identities, though "never all at once." He continues to hint that one of them "could very well be the actual me" and encompass "all of my earthly splendorous malodorous me's and thee's." When pressed for more information, Jesus has at time indicated that "if you see me here, it's probably not the real me. I'd hate this place."

With this in mind, the only features of Jesus' background which remain consistent across assumed identities are regarding family history and feelings of learned social isolation. One of his parents (gender changes) apparently died at a critical phase in his adolescent development, leaving him in the care of the other with whom he experienced marked discord. He apparently experience a period of strongly fluctuating gender identity during this time which may be ongoing. (In some versions Jesus states he has undergone sexual reassignment surgery in the recent past. There is no physical evidence to support this).

Recently Jesus' condition has deteriorated markedly. He has begun lapsing into periods of catatonia of increasing duration, after which his affect and mannerisms are markedly feminine. Pending his next Mental Status examination it is under consideration to update his diagnosis to reflect this, upgrading his condition from Schizoaffective Disorder: Bipolar Type to Schizophrenia: Catatonic Type, while retaining his diagnosis of Schizotypal Personality Disorder.

In the interim, staff is to avoid Jesus during periods of catatonia.

Jesus still exhibits manic phase behaviors on occasion, during which he is to be considered extremely dangerous. While incidents do not usually occur involving harm to others, he is highly unpredictable during these events and could very well prove a threat to health and safety. Many staff report Jesus to be pleasant and engaging, but caution is none the less strongly indicated at all times.

Prognosis in this case is poor. It is thought likely that Jesus' periods of catatonic withdrawal will continue their gradual increase into a steadily vegetative state. At that time a treatment team will be assembled to consider surgical alternatives to treatment.

CASE II: John Doe (AKA Agent 139)

Current Diagnosis DSMIV:

Axis I: Schizoaffective Disorder (Bipolar Type)
            Depersonalization Disorder
            Cyclothymic Disorder NOS

Axis II: Antisocial Personality Disorder
            Schizotypal Personality Disorder
            Rule Out Histrionic Personality Disorder

Axis III: No physical conditions noted as of this time

Axis IV: Difficulties with Acculturation, Disturbances
            in Primary Support Group (abruptly ended
            romantic relationship), Moderate Difficulties
            in Interpersonal Relationships

Axis V: GAF 58, moderate disturbances in social,
            vocational, and relationship functioning

Case Study:

[Prepared by Dr. Harold Fein, M.D., Ph.D., in consultation with Dr. Bernard Spitzer, M.D., Ph.D.]

Agent 139 presents as a six foot, four inch
Caucasian male, heavily tattooed, and in excellent
physical condition. His affect is inappropriate to
context or topic of conversation, ranging from flat to
marked hilarity without apparent external reference.
He suffers from a range of depersonalizing
ideations and delusions of reference, persecution, and
grandeur, as well as inexplicable somatic complaints
which cannot be linked to physiological causes. Agent
139 also presents numerous features of Antisocial
Personality Disorder (flagrant disregard for societal
mores, manipulative behaviors, amoral conduct), though
it is difficult to isolate this diagnosis as being
independent from his Depersonalization or Schizotypal
features. Individuals expecting prolonged contact with
Agent 139 should maintain heightened awareness at all
times, as he is both dangerous and highly intelligent
(Stanford-Binet 174 at last evaluation). One staff
early in the course of his treatment began to exhibit
symptoms of Shared Psychotic Disorder and had to be
committed to a separate facility (see personnel
records for Barb, J.F.S.)
Agent 139 was admitted to this facility following
involuntary committal. He was judged dangerous to self
and others on the basis of his incitement of a riot in
Devon, PA and in a conspiracy with Johny Smith and
"Jesus", also held in custody at this ward, which
resulted in the destruction of a Lenny's restaurant
and numerous nearby businesses. While law enforcement
officials wished to detain him indefinitely in order
to further investigate his background for clues as to
his actual identity and possible connection to a
nihilistic terrorist organization known as "MHBS", it
was judged upon psychiatric evaluation that he could
only be safely maintained in the context of long-term

committal to a high security psychiatric facility. At the request of law enforcement he is to be allowed no contact with the outside world.

While his only confirmed contact with law enforcement prior to committal stems from the Devon riot, he himself has confessed to a checkered career of extortion, fraud, conspiring with known terrorists, drug trafficking, unlicensed psychotherapy, unlawful sexual acts, vagrancy, and being the agent of a hostile foreign power. It should be noted that much of this alleged criminal history can be explained as the products of a delusional, highly disordered mind.

Further, it should be underscored that Agent 139 is to be closely monitored in his contacts with other patients due to his desire to disrupt treatment protocols. He has triggered Shared Psychotic Disorder in several patients and one staff member to date, assaulted one psychiatrist with apparent intent to kill, and gains satisfaction from causing major disturbances in crowds. He is never to be out of eyesight. He is not allowed to have anything which could be used as a tool or a weapon. Writing implements are restricted to crayons only.

Agent 139's delusional system is remarkably complicated and internally consistent. He maintains that the hospital and everyone in it are real, yet "meaninglessly so, like pennies against Swiss billions." Apparently it is his belief that we are all aspects of a single "author" personality, akin to a God-figure, condensed into "single threads of character" with their own associated "reality grids" in a narrative construct prepared by God for inexplicable purposes. He claims to simultaneously exist as three patients in this facility and numerous other individuals still at large. Dr. Spitzer and I are, on the other hand, simply "caricatures of primate-scientists groping greasily at the Totality," so foreign and inimical to Agent 139/the Author that we were, in the end, subcontracted to another Author for final preparation. None of these delusions are susceptible to reality-testing as Agent 139 is alternatively too logical or too disordered for this approach to analysis.

It is unknown at this time what caused Agent 139's initial disintegration, though it should be noted that he himself claims full responsibility for his "becoming as a non-local multifold awareness." Drug abuse is suspected.

Prognosis in this case is guarded. Agent 139's ideations and delusions have continued unaffected by medication or conventional therapy. His reactions to medication are often unpredictable. Surgical interventions are being investigated as of this writing. It is possible that Agent 139 will have to remain institutionalized for the remainder of his life to insure the safety and stability of the community.

Mother Hive Brain Document 11:
(reproduced with permission of Frater Gazebo)

"It is our express belief that though there is not an active conspiracy against the public, (via the FBI, CIA, Aliens or otherwise...) there is a far more dangerous secret, silent enemy—stupidity and ignorance. Stupidity and ignorance is an illness that has killed more than cancer, heart disease, Castro, and crack cocaine combined." — MHB Mission statement III.

Interview with Agent 139:

Luke: Just because you're paranoid doesn't mean they're not after you. I think uncovering conspiracies is actually a very good motive, if only because these "conspiracies" must be draining valuable resources if they do exist. I don't want the government, the Illuminati, and extraterrestrial beings taking a piece of my pay check just so they can rule the world...

Agent 139: How about $83 billion to continue operations in Iraq? (laughs) Well, of course. I certainly believe a great deal of information is kept from "us," however, I find it impossible to believe that any one person or organization has the capacity to deal with all of the information that flies by every day. ...At the same time, stories that would have seemed like leftist paranoid fiction ten years ago are now the bread and butter of the evening news.

L: "Mother Hive Brain Syndicate" itself sounds like some sort of conspiracy name. What exactly does MHBS want humanity to be in the end? A happy-shiny place, a chaotic crazy place, a bubbly Nirvana place?

A: I don't know if the annihilation of Nirvana is exactly bubbly… Well, to be honest, the only thing I think the people who are drawn to MHB have in common is a certain stubborn individualism, creativity, a distaste for stagnation, and the status quo… I really like the idea of people developing their own familial, tribal units…and whether or not I like it, it's a phenomenon that's *happening* and which, I think, has some authoritarian figures a little concerned. These units can piggy-back the larger society. Wait? Did someone say cult? Not in the way that most cults have been handled. Okay we're calling these "communities." Okay? Communities. It's a lot more PC than Cult.

L: (laughs) No Waco for you, huh?

A: No Kool Aide either… Seriously though, obviously our philosophy is almost diametrically opposed to theirs… and most other Christian cults. And our modus operandi is in no way violent… which of course doesn't mean that someday the feds might get concerned and decide to firebomb us and say we were housing cocaine, missile launchers, and 12 year old Thai prostitutes. This is about freedom and not slavery… to a person, or an ideal. And I won't deny that having fun is a big priority. What's the point if there aren't any dancing girls and live music? (Laughs) Cults don't know how to have fun these days. If a cult doesn't have a hot tub and live music, then they're doing something wrong… Anyway presently we're scattered all over the US at the moment, with a few here and there in Europe, Russia, and China… there's a fairly large group working the media angle in NY, and another group working in Arizona… if you're curious check out the website.

L: Is stopping cultural pre-programming a goal? If so, which kinds are "good" and which "bad"?

A: We're just trying to become more aware of ourselves and those around us. That's really all there is to it… Not stopping cultural pre-programming, you can be sure of that. Not only is that impossible, it'd be an absolute catastrophe. I think the French Romantics were idiots. The "sin" is that people aren't taught to know that they can change, that beliefs are not reality. I just want people to know what the possibilities are. I'm not coming from an enlightened position and asking people to be like me, I'm just saying that I'm struggling towards my own potentialities, and hopefully other people out there would like to do the same. What they do with it is up to them. Of course, my opinions are not necessarily those of the Syndicate. I can't speak for other people... You know I should also mention, "we" are known by many names in addition to MHB. TGW, ZZ, OHP, EMN, Babalon—we gotta keep the game interesting, y'know what I'm sayin'? It's interesting because these organizations all arose concurrently... and definitely there has been overlap in terms of founding members and so on... but it wasn't designed this way, we just all found that we were trying to reach similar goals through different means. And maybe at times there's has been competition, especially between the organizations more business oriented than the disorganizations like ZZ and MHB... but this life thing is all just a game anyway, right?

L: What does a mission entail? Learning something new to spread knowledge? Pranks?

A: You can get involved with magick, or you could go around leaving dead fish on people's doorsteps with "MOTHER HIVE BRAIN WANTS YOU!" written on notes crammed in their mouths... I've heard some talk of rituals for the sake of spreading the MHB conspiracy. You'd have to talk to someone else about that, though. This is a disorganization. Meaning there is no official leader though some people serve certain functions... and who is "in" and "out" is based simply on who can hang. Who is on the frequency to get the message, and to propagate it. It's kind of "anything goes." So if you "join," you can always feel free to give people missions without anyone else's knowledge. A Mission could be a music project aimed at altering consciousness in any number of ways, a gathering, dressing up as Ghandi and raiding a supermarket, an orgy, teaching free yoga classes to people who could benefit from it. It could be spreading dead fish to the doorsteps of all your neighbors with cryptic messages stuffed in their mouths. It is a bunch of people giving each other ideas about how they can have fun, prophet, and shake things up enough that we can start being divine humans again. Order is human. Chaos is divine. This is actually backbone of our guerrilla tactics, as no one takes responsibility for our actions but ourselves—but we all give each other ludicrous ideas. You're acting on our behalf if you say you are, if you have digested our intention, though there isn't actually an "us"...

L: You speak a lot about "evolution," and "consciousness frequency..." How do you plan to measure it?

A: Everything you think about is a meditation, and you could say that the very form of your consciousness follows what you put your attention to. So Chi is really just focused attention, and it is attention, or awareness, that brings about results of whatever kind, rather than some nebulous energy or vril force. But energy is a good metaphor.

But about this in relation to the Syndicate... The Mother Hive Brain syndicate was originally planned as a sort of secret society without the "I've got a secret and I ain't tellin' nobody nothing—GIVE ME MONEY ASSHOLE!" bullshit that infects so many other orders. At the same time our goal isn't as expansive as the A∴A∴. And it's a great deal more fun, all things told. (Unless if you like balancing saucersfull of water on your head.) I was told recently by a reliable source that in many O.T.O. camps the money goes, at least in part, to champagne toasts to Nuit, so maybe there's more to that than I had thought. No one in their right mind can argue with sex magick and champagne. Though I'm not sure how I'd feel about buggering Aleister Crowley in a bathhouse for the XI° "secret"...

As for how we plan on measuring consciousness frequency, well that's also tricky. But it is also an incredibly valid question, possibly the best question one could ask if they actually take this seriously. If we were an organization like A∴A∴, "method of science aim of religion," we would have a ruler. Tests. Grades. Proper initiations.

Truth is, I think life provides these things through its natural processes. You don't need a secret guru to hang his laurels on you, fart three times in your direction, and proclaim you free from the sorrows of the world. You know when you're on and off the beam. Why add an MHB "official" name for it? If anything, I chose the title Mother Hive Brain for much the same reason that Crowley kept the term "Holy Guardian Angel." For Christ's sake, don't get stuck on the symbol or the system! If an initiation is successful, you know it because your whole psychology is changed in reference to the particular initiation. Some initiations take time to manifest on various planes. In an adventurous way of thinking, all life is just one long serious of initiations, guiding you in for the death initiation, which I think is not only necessitated by the process but also foundational to it. I'm not going to tell you where you stand. I can't.

What I'd like to see as a reaction to these "pranks," and the whole consciousness expansion thing I talk about, is that many people are so hardened or lost that they don't know where their heart is. The mention of this idea, put to them rationally, would produce a scoff. These are the Babbitt characters that actually buy into the machine and keep the horrid thing running. Back to work, sir. But when someone sees the seams at the corner of their self-produced illusion, questions begin to arise. Energy is contagious. A group of Agents working together can do anything. I have helped organize this for that reason. Maybe you see this and something clicks in your head.

L: What are you measuring the evolution against, who/what does the MHBS consider to be the primordial man from which to evolve from?

A: First off, I obviously refer to the personal evolution of an individual over—since you must use that word—his or her self. In Hindu terminology, this is the turning about the of the shakti. If we buy into the good/evil premise—I don't, by the way—we have an equal amount of each within ourselves. Now I think this premise is dangerous because of the power that can be wielded for the sake of the "good." But it is useful allegorically because there are potentials within all of us that are ignored.

I believe very strongly that each of us has a particular place, or "course," that we are a very specific person, and that "destiny" is both spiral shaped and is a natural result of our nature. We live a life complementary to the energy that is "you," even though maybe you didn't know who you were in the first place. ...Who knows?

Most of us are not aware of our place, we stagnate, grow frustrated, and take those frustrations out on others and ourselves in various ways. Re-living old patterns again and again, the person we present now being just an echo of a person long ago and we live in a circle rather than a spiral. This life is the animal life, and the only positive result or evolution that can come from it is the birth of progeny and the hope that they will awake to the spiritual life that the previous generation was ignorant of. I'd say it's common for people to have a certain feeling about childhood, or at best, adolescence, where there was something very different about the quality of experience at that time. You'll notice the main characters in *Join My Cult!* are all rather young. I'm not advocating people regressing into melodramatic teenagers, but I do think that, if tempered by experience, it is in that intense, emotional center that we might find ourselves again.

I think that what is lost is a connection to ones self, but it is never severed, so long as you're still drawing breath. Maybe some of us are on that same path again. Some of us never left it. There's no doubt here. You just know.

So in one sense evolution is just a process of following that path, following the footsteps to ones center and finding what really matters.

As it is written: "YE SHALL KNOW ME BY MY SMELL. YEA, BY MY SMELL."

FROM ROBERT ANTON WILSON

COSMIC TRIGGER I
Final Secret of the Illuminati

The book that made it all happen! Explores Sirius, Synchronicities, and Secret Societies. Wilson has been called "One of the leading thinkers of the Modern Age."

"A 21st Century Renaissance Man. ...funny, optimistic and wise..."
—*The Denver Post*

ISBN 1-56184-003-3

COSMIC TRIGGER II
Down to Earth

In this, the second book of the *Cosmic Trigger* trilogy, Wilson explores the incredible Illuminati-based synchronicities that have taken place since his groundbreaking masterpiece was first published.

Second Revised Edition!

"Hilarious... multi-dimensional... a laugh a paragraph."   —*The Los Angeles Times*

ISBN 1-56184-011-4

COSMIC TRIGGER III
My Life After Death

Wilson's observations about the premature announcement of his death, plus religious fanatics, secret societies, quantum physics, black magic, pompous scientists, Orson Welles, Madonna and the Vagina of Nuit.

"A SUPER-GENIUS... He has written everything I was afraid to write."
—Dr. John Lilly, psychologist

ISBN 1-56184-112-9

FROM TIMOTHY LEARY, Pʜ.D.

NEUROPOLITIQUE

A New Vision of Neuropolitics
With Robert Anton Wilson &
George Koopman

The first version of *Neuropolitics* was written between 1973-1976 when Dr. Leary was in prison. Several chapters were composed during solitary confinement. Leary explores the role of the dissident/ philosopher and offers a multitude of brilliant observations on our past, present and, especially, our future. One of his best. Updated and rewritten for the 90's.

ISBN 1-56184-012-2

INFO-PSYCHOLOGY

A Revision of Exo-Psychology

"The Info-Worlds our species will discover, create, explore and inhabit in the immediate future will not be reached from launch pads alone, but also through our personal computer screens."

Dr. Leary explores the *real* issues of our time: Space Migration, Intelligence Increase and Life Extension in this "Manual On The Use Of The Human Nervous System According To The Instructions Of The Manufacturers".

ISBN 1-56184-105-6

FROM PHIL HINE

CONDENSED CHAOS
An Introduction to Chaos Magic
by Phil Hine
Foreword by Peter J. Carroll

"… the most concise statement … of the logic of modern magic. Magic, in the light of modern physics, quantum theory and probability theory is now approaching science. We hope that a result of this will be a synthesis so that science will become more magical and magic more scientific."
— William S. Burroughs, author of *Naked Lunch*

"… a tour de force."— Ian Read, Editor, *Chaos International*

ISBN 1-56184-117-X

PRIME CHAOS
Adventures in Chaos Magic
by Phil Hine

An overview of the fastest-growing school of modern occultism: Chaos Magic. Simple, effective techniques for becoming proficient in practical magic, including ritual magic, sorcery, invocation, possession and evocation. *Prime Chaos* also explores some of the lighter—and darker—aspects of modern occultism, and presents new ideas for developing magical techniques.

"I wish I'd written this book!"
— Peter J. Carroll, author of *Liber Kaos* and *Psybermagick*

ISBN 1-56184-137-4